Deadly Deterrent

JOHN HENRICKSON

Suite 300 - 990 Fort St
Victoria, BC, V8V 3K2
Canada

www.friesenpress.com

First Edition — 2016

Front cover photo: by Dana Bergh,
Front cover body model: Skylar Price,
Back cover photo and front cover concept by my wife Elaine Bergh.

ISBN
978-1-4602-9542-7 (Hardcover)
978-1-4602-9543-4 (Paperback)
978-1-4602-9544-1 (eBook)

1. FICTION, CRIME

Distributed to the trade by The Ingram Book Company

This book is dedicated to the following:

My wife and partner Elaine Bergh, whose assistance has been immeasurable in so many ways, from: editing, grammar correction, word flow and readability. Her support and guidance has been of huge benefit to me and I am so very much appreciate it.

My son Matthew and stepson Tyson, both of whom I am so proud.

To my parents, may they rest in peace.

CHAPTER

1

DUSTIN FORD PRIED open the back door of Elwood Hooper's house with a twelve inch flat screwdriver. His heart pounded and his palms sweated. He slowly pushed the wooden door open. It creaked. Ford froze. A putrid smell wafted through the small door opening and he gagged. He held his breath while he got the small flashlight from his pocket and turned it on. Ford pulled a .22 Caliber pistol from his jacket and flicked off the safety.

With his left foot, he pushed the door open further, flashlight and gun at the ready. Ford swept the light from left to right, looking out for obstacles. Seeing none, he continued down the short hallway toward what he guessed was the kitchen. The ticking clock and his rapid breathing were all Ford could hear as he went from the kitchen to the living room. His pulse raced with anticipation and fear of being caught or killed.

He felt electric.

Ford swept the light around the living room. Satisfied, he turned and began to inch his way along the hallway, to the bedroom.

Halfway down the hall, Hooper's phone rang. Ford panicked. His breathing stopped, and his heart rate doubled. He didn't know what to do. He wanted to run.

Ford began to step backwards toward the living room. At the junction to the kitchen, he figured he would be home free. He took three more steps backward when suddenly he felt cold steel being rammed against his skull…too late.

"Freeze asshole, unless you want to die," Hooper barked. He grabbed Ford and shoved him hard against the fridge. "Drop it!" Hooper shoved the weapon harder into Ford's head for emphasis.

Ford complied and dropped the small handgun on the floor.

"Kick it back." Hooper ordered, as he stepped back and turned on the light. He waited…nothing. Hooper cocked his weapon, "Now asshole! I won't ask again."

Ford searched with his foot to find the weapon. Hooper grinned as the weapon slid across the floor. He laughed.

"You weren't going to kill me with that puny pop gun, were you?" He laughed again. "*This* is a gun!" He boasted, ramming the Beretta into Ford's head again. "This is what serious people use when they want to kill someone. Get it?" He spun Ford around and ripped off his balaclava, exposing him to the world. "Why me…butt-plug? Why try to kill old Hooper?" He ran his hand through his graying hair, and instinctively he sucked in his ever expanding beer belly. Hooper didn't think he looked bad for fifty-seven years old.

Ford's head hung low, eyes glued to the floor, afraid to make eye contact for fear it would get him killed.

"How old are you kid?" Hooper demanded, "Come on, don't make me wait. Old Hooper doesn't like waiting. Come on boy." He stomped his foot, "Now!"

"Seventeen!"

"Seventeen? Hell kid, I've got tee shirts older than you.

What's your name? And why me? Who sent you?" He walked up to the kid and stood face to face. "Who fucking sent you to kill me?"

"The Numbers Gang. It's my initiation." Ford said.

"What the hell is the Numbers Gang? And you haven't told me your name yet, kid?" Hooper sprayed spit as he spoke. He backed away and carefully picked up the pistol.

Ford wiped his face. "Felix Seven ordered it. He told me to do it."

"I say again, what's your name?" Hooper cuffed Ford across the side of the head. Ford fell sideways to one knee.

"Ow! That hurt! What did you do that for?" Ford yelled.

"Tell me your goddamn name, so I'll know who I'm killing," Hooper said, with a grin on his face.

"Dustin Ford."

"And what, pray tell, is a *Numbers Gang,* and who the Sam Hell is Felix Seven? And what kinda name is that?"

"That's what they call themselves," Ford answered.

"Bullshit," Hooper yelled.

"No sir. They're called the Numbers Gang because each member has a number given to him, and they pick their first names, like Felix Seven."

Hooper shook his head.

"So, what should I do with you, Dustin Ford? Kill you quickly, one shot to the head, bam? Or…perhaps a gut shot here, bam, a couple shots in the chest there, bam, bam? Until you die a slow painful death? Then again, I know a guy with a woodchipper. Hum! What would you prefer?" Hooper laughed fiendishly. "Better yet, I can phone the cops, and then your life goes down the crapper."

Ford shuddered. "Can't you just let me go? After all,

you're still alive. No harm, no foul?" He offered hopefully.

"Sit down and shut up. I'm thinking. Say another word, and you're dead." Hooper leaned against the kitchen counter. "Shit, I need a drink." He ushered Ford into the living room and plunked his ass on the footstool. "Don't move a muscle, got it?"

Ford nodded and watched as Hooper walked into the kitchen and brought a glass and half bottle of scotch back into the living room and sat down. Hooper poured himself a stiff drink and took a swig then set the glass down on the milk cartoon coffee table. He picked up the .22 Caliber gun.

"You know, Dustin Ford, that this is a women's gun? It's commonly known as a 'Saturday night special.' Why, you ask? Because it holds only two shots." Hooper tipped the gun back and opened the breach.

"Well I'll be damned…that Numbers Gang dude didn't even put bullets in this thing! Didn't you check it before you broke into my house, you dumb shit?" Hooper tossed his head back and laughed. "Boy you're dumber than a sack of broken hammer handles. I can see why you'd want to join a gang, 'cause you're too stupid to work for a living."

Ford mustered his courage, "You ain't so smart either. Hell you're a snitch, just so you can keep your sorry ass from going back to jail."

"Shut your mouth kid, you don't know shit." Hooper yelled.

Ford tried to get up. Hooper fired two shots it the floor in front of him. Ford fainted.

CHAPTER

2

OSCAR NINETEEN FLASHED a wide gold-toothed grin at Chevy Three, the secretary of the Numbers Gang, pointing at the pile of cash on the table. Oscar was proud of their latest score, a truckload of cell phones that they had boosted the night before. He figured it netted the gang roughly fifty grand, which would add nicely to their bulging stock pile of cash from their drug business. Oscar looked at his watch and wondered when Felix Seven would call him about the hit on the informant. He hated when they gave out this kind of assignment to prospective members; some succeeded, but most failed. He hoped the kid would succeed, as this informant needed to be dead. He hadn't liked Dustin Ford when Felix had introduced him a few weeks ago; there was something about the kid that he didn't trust; he was too eager.

The Numbers Gang had come into existence five years ago as an offshoot of the Big Valley Boys. The gang splintered due to the Big Valley Boys being older and somewhat reluctant to use violence to achieve their goals. Oscar, Chevy, Sky, and Throb all left to form the Numbers Gang. They decreed they could pick their own first names and then choose a number for the last name, that way it would be virtually impossible for the police to know who they were if they were under surveillance.

Oscar had chosen the number nineteen, as this was his lucky number and he had used it on school sports uniforms and on his personalized license plates. Oscar Nineteen was twenty-four years old. He had been in two gangs since he was thirteen years old.

Oscar's smart phone came to life with his favourite rap song Death Maiden as his ring tone.

"Nineteen," was all he said, after pressing the talk button. He listened intently then slammed the device down on the arm of the sofa. "Goddamn it! The fish didn't do it." Oscar shouted to everyone and no one. "That was Seven, Ford hasn't called him and Seven said it's been nearly an hour since he broke into Hooper's house. Felix figures the kid's been caught. Should we send in the cleanup crew? Or cut our losses?"

Chevy Three looked up over the cash on the table and adjusted his glasses. "You didn't trust the little puke anyhow, so ditch his ass. What's another dead fish?" He said coldly.

"You're a bad mother, you know that? A bad ass mother-fucker, that's you," He said pointing at Chevy. "Okay, I'll call Seven" He pressed Seven's speed dial number. It rang three times. "Yo, bust your ass outta there. The fish is cold." He said, then he severed the connection.

Down the street from Hooper's house, Seven sat slouched in the front seat of his Cadillac Escalade. He rolled his eyes after Nineteen had ended the call. "Shit." He said aloud. "Shit, Shit, and Shit." Seven slammed the steering wheel then sat up. He turned the key and the big motor came to life. Shooting a quick glance in his side rear view mirror, he pulled away from the curb. As he drove past Hooper's house, he caught a glimpse of light through the drawn curtains. "Sorry kid, you're on your own," he said and continued down the street, not looking back.

Felix Seven arrived back at the gang's lair shortly after midnight; he'd taken the long way back. Parking the large vehicle away from prying eyes, Felix walked slowly up the curved walkway of the monster house they called home. The raspberry farm was a good cover for their operations. He was sure the cops knew, but wasn't sure how much they knew. He pressed his security code into the panel and walked in. Loud music greeted his ears, and the living room was busy as usual. Scantily clad young girls seemed to be everywhere. Seven made his way upstairs, which was off limits to all guests and hangers-on and reserved for full-fledged gang members. Entering the office, he saw Three and Nineteen sitting around the table with a pile of cash on it.

"You guys still haven't boxed up the green. Lazy asses." He said, laughing while sitting down next to Nineteen. They bumped knuckles, signifying all was okay.

Three rocked his chair back and placed his hand behind his head, "So, do we throw an open contract out on Hooper if the fish has failed?" He flashed a grin to the two others, "I really want that motherfucker dead. Because of him, Twenty-One is doing a nickel. Goddamn rat-bastard informers, they should all die."

Nineteen and Seven looked at each other and shrugged. "Whatever," Nineteen said coldly. "Cap his ass. Makes no never mind to me. How 'bout you, Seven?"

Felix Seven looked at Nineteen then at Three, "I'm good. Waste his ass if the kid has been screwed over."

"Okay we wait until we know the snitch is still alive and then we contract," Three said, righting his chair.

CHAPTER

3

DETECTIVE MICKEY O'DELL was sitting at his desk in the bullpen reading the sports page when his phone rang.

"Yah, O'Dell here," he said gruffly, then paused while he shifted the phone to his other ear. "Not so fast. I'm writing this down." Again he paused. "Are you nuts? We can't meet. You know why asshole, so put it through the regular channels and we'll look at it." O'Dell slammed the phone down on the cradle and turned to his partner, Detective Shelley Weeks. "Do you believe these scum-bag informants? Demanding that we meet whenever they call…Shit, what does he think we are; a goddamn concierge program or something?"

"Whose informant was it?" She said, without looking up from the entertainment page. Detective Shelley Weeks was forty years old, and had been a policewoman for twelve years and a detective for six. She knew the importance of informants and keeping them safe.

O'Dell folded up his newspaper and swung his chair to face Weeks, "It's one of mine. You remember Hooper, that sleazy jackass that ratted out the gang-banger a little while ago? Oh shit, what was his name?"

"Oh, you mean Trevor Coles?" She said from behind the newspaper.

"Yah, that's the bastard. Anyway, Hooper said he's got one of their prospects in his house. He said something about a hit and wanted to know if we'd come and pick him up." He spun back to his desk. "Can you believe that crap?"

That got Weeks' attention. "Geez, Mick…maybe we should pick him up. Even though he's a low life scum sucker, if someone's trying to hit him, we should at least investigate it, don't you think?"

O'Dell spun back around to face his partner, "I really don't give a rat's ass if Hooper is dead or alive. He thinks that because he flipped this Coles dude, we owe him. Not bloody likely. If you want to go pick up the prospect and do all the paper work, knock yourself out. Me? I'm staying right here." Mickey O'Dell was sixty-two years old and had been a cop for thirty-five years. He made detective twenty years ago and he was old school through and through.

Weeks stood and grabbed her gun. "That's what I like about you, O'Dell; your sense of duty is outstanding." She put on her jacket, "What's his number?" She watched as O'Dell leafed through his notebook, and then slammed it shut.

"Okay, Okay, damn it. We'll go." O'Dell threw on his windbreaker. "Lead on, oh loyal crusader for the imbeciles of the world." He caught her finger gesture as she turned away from him. He smiled.

The ride over to Hooper's place on Surrey's west side was quiet. O'Dell wasn't in a talkative mood and Weeks was just happy she had back up, even if it was O'Dell. As partners go, O'Dell would not be anyone's first choice, but Weeks had learned to cope with his arrogance over the past three years. She knew that he was rough around the edges, wasn't politically correct and had a mean streak a mile wide. Weeks had heard after they were partnered up that O'Dell had been run out of the OPP (Ontario Provincial Police) for excessive force complaints and other violations, but she couldn't verify any of it. The drive took them about twenty-five minutes, and O'Dell parked the unmarked car across the street from Hooper's dilapidated old house. At twelve-thirty in the morning, there wasn't much traffic, so both of them headed straight across the street, guns drawn, just in case.

O'Dell used the barrel of his gun to knock on the door. "Hooper, it's me, open up." Then, O'Dell stepped back and to the side, Weeks did the same, gun at the ready.

"Whose there?" Hooper said from behind the door.

"It's me, asshole. You called." O'Dell said shaking his head. "Fucking idiot." He whispered to Weeks.

"I heard that, O'Dell. Come on in."

O'Dell turned the doorknob and pushed the door with his foot. The door swung open.

Weeks saw Hooper sitting on his sofa and a kid lying on the floor, trussed up like a pig at a barbeque.

"I like what you've done to the place," O'Dell said, as he stepped over some trash.

"Up yours, asshole." Hooper replied, standing up. "I see you brought your tart with you."

"Shut up, asshole," Weeks barked at him. She trained her pistol on Hooper's forehead. "Just give me a reason, and we can all go home early."

O'Dell stood over the body on the floor. "Okay, everybody, just chill. No need to go off half-cocked," he said, looking at Hooper then at Weeks. "Is this the prospect?" O'Dell said as he kicked him lightly with his foot.

"Yah, that's the little bastard." Hooper kicked Ford hard in the stomach. "You believe this moron came in here with an unloaded weapon? Said his gang made him do it. Can you believe this shit?"

Weeks looked down at the young kid. "What's his name?"

"Says his name is Dustin Ford, but I couldn't find any ID on him."

"Where's his weapon?" O'Dell said, squatting down next to the body.

"On the coffee table behind you."

"Why are his pants all wet? Did he piss himself?"

Hooper's face lit up. "Yeah! Not only that, but he fainted when I fired two rounds at his feet. Damndest thing I've ever seen. Thought that only happened in the movies."

"Why did you fire two shots at his feet? Is your aim that bad Hooper? You getting old?" O'Dell said, with a snicker.

"Stow it, O'Dell, just doing my civic duty. You know, upstanding citizen stuff."

Weeks surveyed the home of the informant; it was run down, to say the least. The furniture looked like it was all from Goodwill and smelled like it had gone a long time between cleanings. She guessed that Hooper wasn't the 'Suzie homemaker' type.

"Where did the perp break in?" She asked as she shone her flashlight around the dimly lit room.

Hooper looked surprised. "You know, I never did check that out. I heard noise when I was in the kitchen and came out and here he was all dressed in black and looking bad."

Weeks watched while O'Dell pulled back the drapes to see if any windows were open. He found none.

"I'll check the back door," she said. "Maybe he got in here

before you came home, or have you been home all night?" She knew what the answer would be before Hooper even opened his mouth.

"I got home around eleven or so." Hooper answered as he followed Weeks into the kitchen.

She held up her hand, "No need for you to follow me. You stay here with O'Dell." She glared at him as she watched him stop dead in his tracks and do an immediate about face.

"Yess'm" was all he said.

Weeks gave a shudder at the very thought of him being close to her. *I feel like I need a shower*. She shone the flashlight around the back door and noticed that it had been jimmied and took out her digital camera to record the evidence. Weeks slowly opened the back door and stepped onto the concrete pad. Perhaps the kid had left the implement lying nearby.

She grinned. Just off the path was a twelve inch flat screwdriver. She recorded that image as well, then pulled out a plastic bag from her inside jacket pocket and with gloved hand placed the screwdriver inside. Weeks returned to the living room and found the young kid conscious and sitting against the wall.

"Found the break-in tool. He pried open the back door with this," She said, holding up the screwdriver in the plastic bag. "My guess his finger prints will be all over it." Weeks squatted down beside the kid. "You realize you're in big trouble? Break and Enter, assault with a weapon, carrying a concealed weapon…should I go on? You're looking at some serious jail time here, unless you give us something to wipe the slate clean…"

The kid looked at her. "My name is Dustin Ford. That's all

you get until I see my lawyer."

O'Dell snapped. "You little piss ant. You're in no position to bargain. And besides, who said we're taking you back to the lockup? Hell, we could leave you here with Hooper. I understand he's good at getting rid of problems. So, you little prick, I'd suggest you answer all our questions, if you know what's good for you." O'Dell waited as his words sunk in and the sweat formed on the kid's brow. "What say, Hoop? You up for some hunting in the park?"

Hooper reached for his Glock on the coffee table. "Why, Mr. Policeman, it would be my pleasure to rid the world of this little scumbag. I'm sure his gang buddies have forgotten all about him already, being he's such a failure. What self-respecting gang would have him?" Then he laughed.

Weeks couldn't believe what she was hearing. "Uh guys, there's this little thing called 'breaking the law.' Cops aren't supposed to do that, remember? As for you, Hooper, aiding and abetting is a felony, regardless of who started this. Guys, he's a kid, for Christ's sake."

Ford looked up at the three of them. "Can I go to the washroom please?" he asked sheepishly. He began to squirm. "Look, man, I've really gotta go. Unless you want another mess to clean up?"

O'Dell shrugged his shoulders. "It's up to you, Hooper. Can the kid go take a leak?"

Hooper sighed, "Come on, you little angel, get up." He reached down to grab his arm to hoist him off the floor. He untied him, and together they walked to the bathroom. Hooper opened the door and pushed Ford inside. "Make it quick."

Then, he returned to the living room, where O'Dell and

Weeks were writing in their notebooks. "You cops are all alike," he said. "Details, details, details."

Without looking up Weeks replied, "That's why we have such a high conviction rate. Want to add to our total?"

O'Dell looked over at Hooper. "What are you doing here? Get back to the kid. Shit, do I have to do everything around here?" O'Dell wheeled past the stunned Hooper and, without hesitation, kicked in the bathroom door, gun drawn. "Shit. Goddamn it Hooper, get in here," he yelled.

Hooper and Weeks darted to the bathroom. Weeks expecting to see the kid had cut his wrists, or done something else as stupid. She saw O'Dell standing in the middle of the bathroom.

"Is anything missing here?" O'Dell said as he holstered his pistol. "Where's the fucking kid, Hooper? The little shit for brains opened the goddamn window and crawled out. Don't just stand there Weeks. Get outside; see if he's still around. Go with her Hooper, this is your goddamn fault. Goddamn it to hell anyway."

Hooper and Weeks each took a door and exited the small house. Weeks took the front, and Hooper the back.

Weeks darted out onto the sidewalk and looked first left then right. It was too dark to see anything. O'Dell stood on the front porch.

"Let me guess, he's in the wind?" he said, disgusted. "Come on, partner. No point in us hanging around this dump any longer. Next time, Hooper…" He didn't finish his rant, choosing instead to grab his keys and get into the car. Weeks did the same. O'Dell wheeled the police car down the street. He kept his eyes peeled for anything that moved. Weeks was doing the same thing. They turned sharply and sped down the street. Nothing. No sight of anyone fleeing on foot. They stopped in the next intersection and looked both ways. Again nothing.

O'Dell slapped the steering wheel, "Shit. Looks like the little piss ant has vanished."

Neither one spoke of the matter all the way back to the station. As far as the Metro Police Department was concerned, they had just gone for coffee.

CHAPTER

4

THE SUN WAS just starting to rise and Felix Seven was crawling into bed when his cell phone rang. He checked call display.

"Yo, Ford. Where the hell have you been, man? I've been waiting for you to call for six goddamn hours. You'd better have a good goddamn excuse motherfucker?" Seven cradled his cell phone against his shoulder as he walked around the bedroom, listening to Ford's reason for being late. "You mean you didn't check your gun before you left the crib? You dumb ass, you should be dead for being so dumb. So, did Hooper beat on ya?" Seven sat down on his bed. "You got wheels?"

He looked at this Rolex. "Stay put. I'll have one of the guys come pick you up." Then he pressed 'off' and threw his cell on the nightstand. It woke his girlfriend up. "Go back to sleep," he ordered.

Seven walked into the living room and kicked a sleeping Thirty-Three, "Wake up." He said. Thirty-Three didn't respond, so Seven kicked him harder, this time getting a rise out of him. "Wake up dog." Seven watched as Thirty-Three wiped his eyes.

"What's going on man?" he said, still mostly asleep.

"You gotta go and pick up the kid. He's in Surrey at a diner on One-Sixtieth and Ninety-Sixth. Bring his dumb white ass here and don't let the motha-fucka leave."

Ford sat in the smoking section, and had smoked several cigarettes and drank multiple cups of coffee waiting for his ride. He surveyed the patrons of Gilles Dinner. Most of the early morning customers were people on their way to work. Two individuals sitting in a booth near the back attracted Ford's attention. He was positive they were gang affiliated, but to which gang he didn't know. One of them was an Indo-Canadian, and the other was Asian. Ford knew enough about gangs to know not to draw their attention.

Nearly an hour passed before he saw the blinged out Chevrolet Yukon pull into the parking lot. He knew it was his ride, as he'd seen it at Seven's many times. He liked Carlos Thirty-Three. He liked his style and he wasn't much older than Ford. Ford watched as Carlos made his way up the sidewalk to the diner, and out of the corner of his eye, he saw the two men in the corner fix their gaze on Carlos as well. Ford began to panic. He knew this wasn't right.

He should warn Thirty-Three, but he couldn't move. Before he could compose himself, Thirty-Three entered the diner and immediately the two gang members stood and drew their weapons. The diner exploded with gun fire, all aimed at Thirty-Three, who didn't have time to react to the onslaught. Both gang members continued to fire as they walked quickly towards the fallen Carlos. Casually, the two men approached Carlos and stood over the body. Each pointed their weapons at his head and squeezed off a round for good measure, then stashed their guns in their clothing and ran out of the diner.

Outside, they darted across the street and hopped into a tricked-out grey Honda Civic and sped away. Ford was horrified at what he had just seen and silently thanked his lucky stars that he hadn't greeted Carlos, or he'd be dead as well. Without drawing attention to himself, he slipped out the back of the diner and disappeared down the street.

Ford walked for blocks trying to determine how best to tell Seven that Thirty-Three had been gunned down. He knew that Seven would be pissed off and would want to know who the two gang bangers were, what they looked like, and what they were driving. He also knew that Seven would want revenge.

The rain was coming down sideways as Ford continued on down the street, he desperately wanted to get somewhere dry and warm so he could sleep and try to forget this past night.

As he walked, three police cars went screaming by, lights and sirens going full bore followed closely by an ambulance and fire truck. He pulled his hoodie down so his face was almost covered as he bent forward into the cutting rain.

Ford walked for nearly an hour, the clock in the bank window said it was eight forty-five. He spotted a pancake house up ahead and made his way to it. Inside the lobby, he grabbed the pay phone and reached out to his buddy Alex Thomson, a fellow foster brother. The phone rang several times before a sleep deprived teenager picked up. "This better be really important or I'm going to be really pissed. Who is this?"

"Hey buddy it's me, Dustin. I'm jammed up and need a ride, like now." Ford said. People walking by looked at him snobbishly.

Thomson rolled out of bed "What do you mean jammed

up?"

Ford stared down an elderly man who was gawking at him, "I can't say over the phone, just get your ass down to Papa Mike's pancake house on One Hundred and Fourth and Eighty-Eighth. I'll tell you all about it."

Thomson was pulling on his pants, "I'll be there in about fifteen minutes, so sit tight." Then pressed end on his cell.

Ford found a booth near the back of the pancake house and ordered a carafe of coffee and a stack of pancakes. He was surprised at how hungry he was. He lit up a smoke and watched as the smoke curled towards the roof vent. Ford was looking out the window and didn't see the three employees converge on his booth.

"Excuse me, sir," the young lady said. "There's no smoking in this restaurant. You'll have to put it out."

Ford looked at her in disbelief. "What do you mean I can't smoke in here? Since when?"

"Since the company chose not to allow it. So extinguish your cigarette please."

Ford looked at her name tag. "Okay, Sadie, I'm not looking for trouble." He took one last drag then plunged the half burnt cigarette into the glass of ice water, then smiled. "How's that? Everyone happy now?" He exhaled into their faces, his smile widened.

Shaking her head, Sadie and the other two employees returned to their duties.

Ford devoured the plate of pancakes with abandon. As he was finishing the last morsel, he spotted Alex making his way through the maze of booths toward him.

"Man you look like shit. Rough night or what?" Alex said as he slid into the seat across from Ford.

Ford clenched his fist and bumped knuckles with Thomson, "Both. Rough night *and* an 'or what'. Coffee?" he asked, as he lifted the carafe to pour.

Alex looked around the restaurant. "Sure man, need something to wake me up. Last night was a blast, you should have been there. Remember Dean, the geeky little freak from Spiller's industrial arts class? Well the little nerd has designed some kind of computer game that he just sold to some gaming company for mega bucks. Ran into him and his group at The Cavern last night. He's not a bad guy once you get past the bad breath and dorky looks. At least, he's pretty liberal with spending his loot. What the hell happened to you? You look like you've been dragged through a ringer." Thomson picked up the cup of coffee and took a drink.

Ford leaned back in the seat, "Man, you wouldn't believe me even if I told you."

"Try me." Thomson replied.

For the next fifteen minutes, Ford related the experiences of the night before, and he could see from Thomson's facial expressions that he was amused.

Thomson sat there, listening to the tale that Ford was spinning. "Are you bull shitting me, man? Dustin, I thought you had more sense than that. Fuck, getting involved with a gang? Are you fuckin' nuts? And you never thought to check the gun before you broke into the guy's house?" He shook his head. "Man you are fuckin' lucky that you're not dead. Christ man how stupid can you get?"

Ford bristled at Thomson's scolding, "I like how they operate. Nobody messes with them, and I like that. Besides you get all the dope and broads that you can handle."

"Yeah, but at what cost? Look what happened to…what's his name." Thomson said coldly.

"His name was Carlos Thirty-Three, and he was a friend." Ford said firmly.

"Well Carlos Thirty-Three is dead, so how fuckin' great is that?" Thomson swallowed the rest of his coffee, "Let's get the hell out of here. You need to get your shit together or you'll be dead. Buddy, I'm here for you, but not if this gang thing is going to be your new life. I don't want any of that shit coming back to haunt me, are we clear?"

Ford nodded his head in agreement. "Okay, let's book it," he said, standing up.

CHAPTER

5

FORD STOOD IN line at the YVR departure gate for United Airlines Flight 882 bound for Los Angeles. He had lost his swagger since the death of his friend, and now he had the unpleasant task of telling Carlos's uncle. Now that Carlos was dead, he needed to explain to his uncle, a member of the dreaded Crypts out of East Los Angeles, how Carlos Thirty-Three died. Ford remembered Carlos saying how ruthless his uncle was. Julio Sanchez's father founded the Crypts back in the late sixties, and Carlos would have been the third generation to run the gang, had he not bolted to Canada to avoid a murder trial.

The trip down to Los Angeles took one and a half hours. Coach was packed with sun seekers and wanna-be movie stars. Ford detested both and couldn't wait to deplane into the warm sunshine. He had never been to Los Angeles. In fact, he hadn't been anywhere. His foster parents could never afford to travel, and vacations were usually camp grounds around British Columbia and Alberta. It had been one of his primary reasons for running away and adopting the gang lifestyle. At least, in Ford's mind, there was some excitement in that.

Ford's fake ID showed he was twenty-two years old

which enabled him to secure a rental car in California. The map quest search for Compton, a suburb of LA, gave him the necessary information to plug into the GPS unit for directions. The 2009 Crimson red Camero convertible was well suited for southern California and Ford immediately put the top down and cranked up the tunes. He needed to make a stop at Quick & Clean Laundry to inquire about a gun for protection. He'd also heard Carlos talk about the place as being the gun distribution centre for the Crypts, so he figured it was a way to try and find Julio Sanchez without driving over all of Los Angeles.

The drive to East Compton on Transit Way took Ford nearly ninety minutes and it wasn't even rush hour. The navigation system made finding the outlet easy, and Ford parked the rental near the far end of the Atlantic Mini Mall parking lot on Atlantic Ave. The Quick & Clean Laundry façade was nondescript, with only a small sign hanging in the window proclaiming its existence. Ford walked casually towards the front door, his eyes checking out the group of Latino men standing around a Chevy Impala low-rider. He avoided eye contact as he pushed open the dirty glass door. Ford removed his sunglasses and his eyes adjusted to the considerable light difference. He surveyed his surroundings.

There were various outdated pictures of movie stars on the walls, a few plastic stacking chairs, a coffee table piled high with an assortment of magazines. The counter was covered in posters from community events in East Compton; one was dated 1997. The cash register was older than he was, and the top of the counter was glass with an assortment of papers stuck under it.

He pressed the silver bell sitting at the end of the counter and waited. It seemed like an eternity with nobody coming out from behind the curtain covering the doorway, so Ford rang the bell again.

"Hold on, I'm coming," A gruff voice shouted from the back. Ford began to sweat, both out of fear and from the heat. Moments later, an elderly man with long gray hair and a grizzled beard parted the curtain.

"What do you want?"

It wasn't the greeting Ford expected.

"Hi, my name's Dustin Ford." He paused. "I just got in from Vancouver, and I'd like to see Julio Sanchez. I'm a friend of his nephew. It's really important that I talk to him."

The old man looked at him with dark steely eyes, his lined faced not giving away any tells. "Sorry, kid, nobody here by that name."

Ford stared at the man behind the counter. He could understand his reluctance to tell him the truth. "Please tell Mr. Sanchez that I'm in town and have information about his nephew's death. I'm staying in a motel just down the road a ways. I think it's called the Desert Oasis or something like that."

The old man started to come around the counter, "Are you deaf, kid? There's nobody here by that name, so fuck off." He placed his hand behind his back. Ford saw the gesture and immediately turned to leave, but two large men sporting bandanas blocked his exit.

"May I please get through?" Ford pleaded, fearing a beating.

The large man on his left looked at the old man. "Anything we can do?"

The old man smiled. "The little white boy is looking for

someone named Sanchez. I've told him twice there's nobody here by that name and now he expects me to get a message to him. If he doesn't fucking exist, how am I suppose to do that, hey amigo? Show him the door."

The second large man grabbed Ford by the shoulder and shoved him towards the glass door; it was obvious he wasn't going to open it first. Ford's face slammed into the glass, which propelled the door open and Ford could feel himself falling to the sidewalk. He looked up and saw that the group of men he'd seen when entering had surrounded him. He was going to die, or at least get a good shit-kicking. He prepared himself for the onslaught. Ford pushed himself up on his hands, waiting for a kick to come, but none did.

Sensing a break, Ford slowly rose and stood erect amid the group of men. All eyes stared at him, with nobody speaking a word. Ford figured he had nothing to lose, so he took a few steps toward the edge of the circle. A short, beefy looking man with long straight black hair stepped in front of him and smiled. Ford could see there was menace in his eyes and was expecting the worst. The short man looked up at Ford and said, "Boo," then began to laugh with the other men. The circle parted slightly and Ford hastily left, not looking back at the group of men all laughing at him. *Fucking assholes,* he thought.

Ford got in his car and shot a quick glance back at the men. They'd moved back to the low-rider. *They gotta be Crypts,* he thought, as he piloted the rental back onto Atlantic Avenue. A few blocks away on Atlantic, he saw the motel he'd seen earlier and quickly entered the driveway; he was close with the name—it was called the Desert Palms Motor Inn, but that all seemed moot now that Sanchez wasn't there. Ford wondered if the old man *was* Sanchez, especially with the guards out front.

Fifteen minutes later, Ford was checked into the motel and was lying on the bed watching a snowy television program. Ford looked at his watch; it was almost four hours since he'd had breakfast, and he was hungry. He peered out the window, saw a Sammy's across the road, and figured it was as good as any other place, so he threw on his jacket and grabbed his key.

Ford dodged the traffic jaywalking the busy Atlantic Avenue and soon found himself in a nearly deserted restaurant. He ordered the daily special, Salisbury steak, and waited. He'd picked up a copy of the Compton Review and was leafing through it. He was absorbed in a story about a local businessman who had refused to pay protection money to an Asian Triad gang, so they torched his clothing store.

A large fist slammed the booth table and Ford jumped, dropping the paper. In front of him were two of the men from the laundry; he hadn't noticed them come in and sit down. He was terrified.

"What's your story, kid?" the heavy-set man covered in tats demanded.

Ford was shaking; he didn't want any trouble, so he just stared at the man.

"What is your fucking story, kid? Tell me now, or you're dead. You a cop? A narc? What?"

Ford mustered his courage and slowly picked up his coffee cup and took a small drink, "As I told the elderly gentleman at the laundry, I'm a friend of Mr. Sanchez's nephew up in Vancouver, Canada. Something has happened to him, and I need to tell Mr. Sanchez what happened."

The other tattooed man spoke, "What's this nephew's name?"

Ford still avoided eye contact. "Carlos Thirty-Three."

The first man laughed. "What kinda fuckin' name is Carlos Thirty-Three?"

"He's a member of the Numbers Gang. They all have numbers for last names," Ford said matter-of-factly.

The second man laughed, "You think we're loco, homes? How do you know Sanchez?" He glared at Ford who was visibly shaken, "You ain't seeing Mr. Sanchez until we're satisfied so you'd better start talking motherfucker or you're a dead man?"

Ford's heart rate ramped up so he inhaled deeply and summoned his courage as they talked, "Carlos told me about his uncle and that his grandfather was a co-founder of the Crypts and how he had to flee the US to avoid a murder charge. He also told me his real name, Ildefonso Sanchez." Out of habit, he lit up a smoke and exhaled to the side, careful not to blow smoke in their faces.

The first man raised his arm and snapped his fingers and pointed to the table. The waitress, seeing this, hustled over with the coffee pot, poured each of them a coffee and left as quickly as she came. "My name is Jesus, and this here is Gomez. We work for Mr. Sanchez, and it's our job to screen all those who want to talk with him. So, what is it you want to talk to him about?"

Ford again summoned his courage, took a drag on his smoke and a sip of his coffee, "I want to tell Mr. Sanchez that I was there when his nephew was killed, and I have the image of the two motherfuckers who shot him burned into my brain. If I ever see those bastards, they're dead, but

I've never killed anyone and don't know if I have what it takes. But for Carlos's sake, I want to learn how so I can get the bastards."

Jesus looked at Gomez and grinned, "Homes here wants to become a killer. If Julio welcomes the kid to discuss his nephew, maybe we can hook the kid up with Alverez. There's nobody better than him. Chico's been icing Bluds and others for nearly ten years and he ain't been caught, so if anyone can teach a white boy how to do it, Chico can."

Gomez shrugged his shoulders, "Hell, he taught me how to do it. But he'll have to lose his whiteness, or he'll be dead within the week. Hey, I know. You should visit my cousin Ellemelda. She has a tanning studio in Bakersfield, and she's not bad looking either." Both men stood up and looked down at Ford who was casually sipping his coffee.

"Are you coming kid?" Jesus said coldly. "What, you need an invitation to change your life?"

Ford was caught off guard, "Now? We're going to see Mr. Sanchez right now?"

Gomez looked at Jesus. "Kid, meet Mr. Jesus Julio Sanchez."

CHAPTER

6

DUSTIN FORD REAPPEARED in Vancouver near the end of March 2010; eighteen months after Carlos Thirty-Three had been shot. Ford had grown substantively while he was away; he'd matured rapidly, grown into his large frame and lost about twenty pounds of fat. When he looked in the mirror, he saw a lean, mean killing machine. He had taken Thomson's warning to heart and did not call his buddy when he got back into town.

Ford had spent the last eighteen months in the Los Angeles area, where he acquired the skills of a cold-blooded killer. In thirteen of those months, Ford had notched fourteen kills on his belt, something that he wore with pride. He didn't mind the financial benefits either.

He had returned to Vancouver tanned, relaxed and quite well-off for someone his age. He sported several elaborate tattoos that he loved to show off whenever the opportunity presented itself. He had also learned to not draw attention to himself while out in public, so he drove a stock 2007 Pontiac Grand Prix that he'd bought at the Surrey Auto Auction. The first thing he did was have some of the windows tinted. Every vehicle that Chico drove had blacked out windows.

Dustin Ford had come back to settle some scores from

his previous encounters with the gang world. Foremost on his list of to-dos was Hooper. He wanted to kill that son-of-a-bitch more than anyone else on the planet. Well, maybe not. The two cowards that killed his friend Carlos Thirty-Three were up there as well. He had burned their faces into his mind and knew that if he saw either of them, he would execute them just like they had his friend.

It had taken Ford only two days to track down Elwood Hooper, who was still the slime-ball he remembered. He had heard that Hooper had survived two separate attempts on his life while he was away. Ford had also found the two cops who had humiliated him in Hooper's house that night. They too would be dealt with. One of the lessons he had learned from the Crypts was that respect was all important. The two cops had disrespected him, so they would have to atone for their mistakes. *All in due time,* he thought.

Ford followed Hooper for nearly three days learning his habits and tendencies, something he had learned from Chico Alverez. The outcome of the game was already predetermined. It was the when and where that Ford was now figuring out. He wanted Hooper to die a slow and painful death knowing exactly who killed him and why.

Hooper got into his yellow 1995 Volvo station wagon, pulled into traffic on King George Highway and headed east toward the Newton area. Ford followed a few cars back. Hooper was talking on his cell phone the entire time he was driving, nearly having three accidents along the busy corridor. He turned off King George on Seventy-Second Street and headed south toward Delta. A few blocks down, Hooper pulled an abrupt left turn and sped down the quiet side street, shooting a quick glance in his rearview mirror. *Cagey bastard. Run, you chicken shit,* Ford thought as the tires protested making the corner. He tromped on the accelerator and rocketed down the street. He slowed as he approached the next intersection and eyed the cross street to his left. *Ah ha, there you are you son-of-a-bitch, not so smart after all, are you?* Hooper's Volvo passed through the distant intersection. Ford continued down the adjacent street. *Where are you going?* He sped up and hung a hard left at the next intersection, followed by a more relaxed left at the next one. His eyes strained to find the yellow Volvo, but nothing. Ford's heart rate accelerated as he slowly drove down the street, his eyes darting left and right to see where Hooper had pulled off. The next block over he, caught a glimpse of the tail end of a yellow station wagon nosed into a carport. "Gotcha, asshole," he said, then immediately pulled over and parked about four houses down. He settled in for the wait.

From his vantage point, Ford saw Hooper peek his head out from behind the curtains in the living room. Ford guessed Hooper was checking to see if anyone was out there or afraid somebody might be. The life of an informant usually was short lived and ended in a violent death, at least that's what Alverez had told him when he did his third kill for the Crypts.

Ford waited for nearly three hours. His bladder was screaming for relief when Hooper finally emerged with a young girl. *Why you dirty dog, she's young enough to be your daughter*. He watched as they both got into Hooper's Volvo and moments later backed onto the street. Ford started his car, popped it into drive, and waited.

Hooper sped away down the street heading for Seventy-Second Street. Ford waited until there was about a block separation then followed. Ford wondered if Hooper and the girl was an item, or was he merely picking her up and giving her a ride. This would make a difference should Ford decide to hit Hooper right away. He didn't want any collateral damage.

The two vehicles played hide and seek for the better part of an hour with Hooper finally stopping at a gigantic house off 176th Street and 88th Avenue. It looked more like a small motel than a single family dwelling. Ford extracted his binoculars from the glove box and focused in on the house. He counted at least seven vehicles parked in the tree lined circular drive way, and Hooper's made eight. His old Volvo seemed remarkably out of place among the tricked out Hummers, Escalades and Yukon's that made up the contingent of vehicles. Ford had seen similar abodes in Los Angeles and this reeked of gang activity. He panned his binoculars up and down the street to see if anyone else was watching and quickly spotted a white Dodge van parked about a half a block away. *But who was inside, police, another gang, or maybe another hitter?*

Ford settled in after relieving himself in a pop bottle. This could be a long evening. As the sun set and darkness descended on the Lower Mainland, Ford switched over to his night vision goggles and his world became an eerie green colour.

In the following hour and twenty minutes, three more tricked out vehicles arrived and then left shortly afterwards. The white van was still on scene. Ford reached into his back pack and pulled out an infra red scope, and adjusted the focus on the van. It was another trick he had learned from Alverez; it made determining enemy numbers a cinch. Ford played the scope along the van, he saw a lot of red against the cool background colour, so guessed there were at least two or three in the van. Ford noticed a black sedan pull onto 88th Avenue and douse the lights as it came to a stop. He grinned. *Was a police raid about to happen*? He wondered if the two cops that humiliated him would be there.

Reaching inside his backpack again, he pulled out a silencer, then pulled his 9mm Glock from its case under the front driver's seat and absentmindedly screwed the silencer onto the barrel. His attention perked up when he saw a black unmarked van fly into the driveway. Doors exploded open and men in black outfits carrying assault weapons poured out. He dropped the gun and picked up the night scope. Another van came to an abrupt stop across the driveway entrance, while another stopped just off its rear bumper. More police poured from both vans. He couldn't see what was happening at the rear of the house but assumed it was much the same. He was sure that a fire-fight would soon erupt, especially with the large number of participants on both sides of the equation. He rubbed his hands together excitedly.

Ford ducked down in the seat as an unmarked police car pulled into the street about a hundred feet ahead of him. *Shit* he thought, while quickly stashing the scopes and making sure the gun was back under the seat. He peeked up, but didn't see any cops. Slowly, he rose in the seat and surveyed the area. He noticed black silhouetted figures moving towards the driveway. Ford was tempted to get out of the vehicle for a better look, but the roar of an overhead helicopter squelched that idea. He rolled the passenger side window down to hear what was going on. Ford could hear wild shouting coming from the cops. He grabbed his night scope again and trained it on the front door. Several flashes nearly blinded him as gunfire erupted from the building.

He quickly scanned the structure and noticed gunfire from almost every window facing the front; it was an all out assault on the cops. He began to laugh as the cops began to return fire from behind whatever cover they could find. Sparks flew off the vehicles as bullets ricocheted here and there from shots fired from the house. Ford focused on the second story windows. He could see figures dart from behind cover, fire then dart back. Bullets fired by the cops hit the house and left a heat trail. Ford shook his head in approval; whoever had built the house had hardened it against light weapons fire, likely steel plating. He saw tear gas canisters being fire into the windows and the plume of gas bursting into the air. Ford was glad he wasn't on the receiving end of the assault.

The battle raged on for nearly an hour without any indication of who was winning or who was losing. Three cops had been shot and had been hustled away in ambulances. All traffic on both streets was blocked and police reinforcements were arriving constantly. Ford had lost count of how many cops were on scene.

"Sweet Jesus, would you look at that fuckin' thing?" Ford shouted as an armored bulldozer plowed its way through the many vehicles parked in the driveway. *They're going to breach the building. This must be some serious shit.*

Ford desperately wanted to get closer but knew the cops wouldn't allow anyone near the action; in fact he was surprised that they hadn't come and told him to get lost. As the action heated up, Ford gripped the steering wheel even tighter. With his night scope trained on the dozer, he watched as it easily pushed expensive vehicles into each other and ultimately out of the way. He reveled in the mayhem he was seeing. There was nothing standing in its pathway to the front door. Bullets bounced off the armor plating, and he could see cops lining up behind it for protection.

Within minutes, the dozer was directly in front of the large arched doorway, poised to drive through it. The operator lifted the blade and throttled up. With the speed of a turtle, the large, cumbersome machine crawled up the six steps and pushed in the wall, door included. Soon, there was a gaping hole where the heavy oak door had stood. The dozer swung its blade sideways, gashing open the wall, then the operator spun the dozer sideways and drove down the length of the wall toward the large glass picture window. The carnage to the building was extreme. Cops following as the dozer poured into the breached building, gun flashes nearly blinding Ford's eyes in the night scope. Ford knew this wasn't going to end well for those in the building, and he hoped that Elwood Hooper didn't get killed. He wanted that pleasure for himself.

CHAPTER

7

THE FOLLOWING AFTERNOON, Ford woke up in the motel room he'd rented on the King George Highway. The police incident, as the radio called it, had ended around five-thirty a.m., and Ford had seen several of the house's occupants being taken away in handcuffs after they surrendered. He hadn't spotted Hooper in the bunch.

Was he dead? Did he escape? Or was he hiding inside the building? Ford didn't know; he'd have to pick up his trail again. At two-thirty, Ford showered, shaved, and readied himself for what the day might bring then left his room. He drove towards the Guilford area of Surrey knowing he needed to eat something. As he passed 96th Avenue, he spotted a local diner and nosed his car into the parking lot. The neon sign on the post flashed "All Day Breakfast," and Ford knew that was what he wanted.

As he settled into the booth, the waitress handed him a menu and left a carafe of coffee. His mind flashed back to when Carlos was killed; the setting was eerily similar. Ford surveyed the occupants and determined that nobody posed any threat to him, so he focused on the menu contents. The waitress arrived, took his order, and disappeared with military precision. He liked that, no idle chit-chat, like many in her profession seemed to do for no good reason. A year ago, he would not have minded chatting up a waitress primarily to see if he could get into her pants, usually without success, but now he was a different person with different goals and objectives. Now he liked his solitude. It suited his style.

A short while later, his breakfast arrived. Steak, eggs, hash browns and toast. He dove into it. From the corner of his eye, he glimpsed a lowered Honda Civic with two occupants. He did a double take. *Nah, it can't be them,* he thought. Then he took another look, more of a stare than a look.

Ford stood and threw fifteen dollars on the table, then rushed out of the eatery. He bolted across the parking lot and hopped into his car. He momentarily fumbled with the keys, but quickly got the engine to fire up and into drive. Ford smoked the tires as the car rocketed out of the parking spot and into traffic. He cut across three lanes of traffic on King George Highway to get in behind the Civic that was somewhere up ahead of him…at least, he hoped it was.

Ford weaved his way through the midday rush hour traffic to the dismay of many startled motorists who were very liberal with the use of their middle fingers. About eight blocks down King George, just before the transit station, he caught a glimpse of the Civic. Ford slowed down and began to tail six car lengths behind. The two in the Civic did not notice him. Ford lit up a cigarette and inhaled deeply allowing the smoke to reach the very bottom of his lungs. It felt good, even though he knew he should quit. Ford noticed a sign that read, *White Rock – 8 km*. At least he knew where they were headed.

The grey Civic turned off King George at 24th Street and proceeded northward past a car dealership before driving up to a bar. Ford slowed down to a crawl, not caring about the cars behind him, and pulled into a spot as far away from the pub as he could get while still being able to see the two targets.

He waited until they got out of their vehicle and walked into the pub without a care in the world. Ford grabbed his weapon and tucked it into the back of his pants, under his jacket, and proceeded towards the pub. He slowed his pace in case they came back out again and stood window shopping at a travel agency a couple of doors down. He looked around and didn't see anything suspicious. Checking that his weapon was in place, he walked the short distance to the pub and swung the door open. The noise from inside slammed him in the face and he was met with an onrush of foreign smells.

A shapely young girl wearing way too much perfume passed by him and smiled. He paid her no mind. Letting his eyes adjust to the lower light, he soon found his two targets sitting with their back to the wall at the west end of the pub. Ford found the washroom and made his way inside. Inside the closest cubical, Ford pulled out his gun and fixed the silencer to the barrel and tucked it back into the back of his pants. Alverez had taught him to always remove the silencer when not in use, as the penalty for being caught with a silenced gun was greater than if it was just a gun.

Back at the bar, Ford ordered a draft beer and paid with an American five dollar bill. The barkeep was making change, and Ford waved it away and made his way towards the west side of the pub. He sat at an empty table, spitting distance from the two targets. He scrutinized every feature on their faces. It was another lesson Alverez had taught him. *Make sure of your targets before you start blasting.* Ford's mind relived the horror of when Carlos was shot; his mind slowed down as he recalled what the pair of shooters looked like. One was Indo-Canadian, the other Asian; one had a slightly crooked nose with narrow set eyes, an elongated face, long black hair, and stood nearly six feet. The other was stockier with a more rounded face with heavy, bushy black eyebrows, eyes set farther apart, and he stood about five-eight.

Ford looked at the two of them, seated within gunshot of him, and matched up what he remembered to what he was seeing. There was no doubt these were the bastards. Ford wanted to light up a cigarette, but knew it would draw unwanted attention. Instead, he signaled for another beer and waited. He looked at his watch, and then at the sign announcing the next show, knowing that when the stripper came out the house lights would be dimmed.

His beer came and he again paid with a five dollar bill and wouldn't accept any change, as the announcer said, "Okay, ladies and gentlemen. For your viewing pleasure, the Red Velvet Lounge is pleased to present Miss Judy Jingles, live from Las Vegas. Come on people, put your hands together and give her a big Red Velvet welcome." The music system kicked in, blaring out more noise than music, as a scantily clad woman emerged from behind the red velvet curtain onto centre stage. Instantly, those sitting away from the stage made their way to the nearest empty seat. Ford's two targets remained seated against the wall. Ford smiled.

The stripper began her prance around the stage, whetting the appetites of all those watching. Ford sensed this was his chance, as all eyes were on the stripper. He undid his jacket and stood up, placing one hand on his weapon. He noticed the two men were watching the action on the stage, so he edged his way toward them with one hand on his gun.

Ford calmly sat down across from the two men, who were shocked at his audacity; they didn't see the gun. Smiling, Ford fired off four rounds in rapid succession from under the table, directly into their chests, two in each one. He glanced around, nobody was looking at them. He lifted the gun from under the table and fired one single shot into each man's head, then watched as they slumped backwards against the seat. Ford quickly stashed the gun in his pants, took a photograph, turned and casually walked away, waving at the stripper as he passed the stage.

CHAPTER

8

FORD WAS PLEASED with his handy work as he watched the local news on Channel 9. His killings were the lead story. The pretty blonde anchor read, "The killing is the latest in the escalating gang war that is plaguing the Lower Mainland. Police sources say they have no leads at the moment and are withholding the names of the two individuals who were gunned down at the Red Velvet Lounge, a known gang hangout. Both men were known to police and are believed to be members of the International Brotherhood, a gang based out of the Fraser Valley." Ford started to laugh at the reporter. *If people only knew how much gang activity there was, they would move,* he thought.

Ford took a pull on his Corona; he'd always known it was a gang that hit Carlos but he wasn't sure which one. He knew from his brief dealings with the Numbers Gang that they were at war with five other gangs for control of the drug trade in the valley. The International Brotherhood was one of the more powerful gangs in Western Canada, with tentacles stretching as far south as Columbia. He was sure that his act of revenge would not go unpunished, but it wasn't his problem.

Looking out the window of his motel room, he stared

blankly at the chamber maid across the courtyard and wondered what it would be like to go through life without any fear of being killed. In some ways, he envied her.

Ford's next mission was to find Hooper again. He prayed he was still alive. Ford grabbed his coat and keys then left his humble abode for the nearest internet café, where he could search the various newspapers and television stations online to see if the police had released any information.

An hour later, he'd found what he was looking for on the RCMP web site, which detailed a large portion of the events. He snickered as he read the article, which painted an entirely different picture than what he had seen at the "incident", as the police called it. The account listed that three members of the Ja'Nall family were killed in a drug-related take down. Ford put two and two together and deduced that Hooper was not a member of the Ja'Nall family, so he must be alive. But where?

His first place to look was Hooper's house, so he paid his computer user fee and hopped into his car and headed for the small pig sty Hooper had called home. It was dark when Ford eased his car into a parking spot down the street from the small house. The windows were black, so he guessed Hooper wasn't home. He waited.

Three hours later, a large four door sedan pulled into the driveway and three figures emerged from its cavernous interior. Ford smiled as he watched the three walk up the sidewalk, two men and one woman. He recognized Hooper, and as luck would have it, O'Dell, and his partner Weeks. He momentarily thought about busting in, guns blazing, and knocking off all three in one fell-swoop, but the teachings of Alverez jumped to the forefront of his mind. *Choose your execution spot carefully ensuring you can complete your hit without any harm to yourself.* Taking on three at once wasn't a wise thing to do. Two maybe? But not three. So he settled back in and waited.

At ten after eleven, two figures emerged from the house and stood on the porch that was lit by what seemed like a twenty-five watt light bulb. He could see that it was O'Dell and Weeks for sure, and they were arguing about something. His money would be on Weeks, from what he remembered about her in their first encounter. Ford watched as Weeks poked O'Dell in the chest, giving him royal hell; Ford couldn't stop grinning.

"You go girl," he said.

The row went on for over five minutes before they both walked back to their vehicle. Ford sensed an opportunity to finish off Hooper. He would wait until they left then he'd knock on the door. Hooper, being the stupid fuck that he was, would think it was O'Dell and Weeks back at his door, so presumably he'd open it up without checking.

He watched the sedan back out of the driveway and head off down the street. Ford quickly started his car and waited for them to disappear. When they turned the corner, he dropped his car into drive and pulled into Hooper's driveway. He hopped out, leaving the car running and the lights on as he darted up to the door.

Ford pulled out his weapon and quickly attached the silencer and used the barrel to knock on the door. He heard a voice inside.

"I'm coming. What did you boneheads forget this time?"

Ford felt his heart rate quadruple as he heard Hooper undoing the chain. His breathing increased. He felt the usual knot in his stomach begin as he released the safety off the gun. Ford began taking deep breaths as he noticed the door opening and light from inside escaped through the small slit that was widening. He booted the door fully open, taking Hooper by surprise.

Ford heard him gasp as the door swung wildly out of his hands. He saw his eyes widen when he saw that it wasn't O'Dell or Weeks. He didn't see the gun in Ford's hand "Remember me, asshole?" Ford fired three shots in rapid succession into his chest.

He had a pained look in his eyes. "Who the fuck are you?"he asked.

Ford watched him fall to the floor, dead. Ford took a picture and quickly closed the door, then casually walked back to his car.

When he was a block away, he called 9-1-1 and reported that he'd heard two or three gunshots and seen two people leave the house then quickly drive away. Ford hung up and continued to drive back to his motel. The kill was very satisfying.

CHAPTER

9

"O'DELL, WEEKS, GET into my office, now!" Duty Sergeant Webber Lamp hollered from behind his desk, loud enough to be heard at street level. The bellowing caught both of them by surprise and they looked at each other as they stood. Both shrugged their shoulders and shook their heads.

"Sit down," Lamp commanded bluntly.

"What's up, Sarg?" O'Dell said, sitting down.

Lamp stood over his desk, his upper torso resting on his bear-like paws. "Where were you two last tonight?"

O'Dell looked at Weeks, then back to the sergeant. "You know, the usual. Pumping our snitches for info…that sort of thing. Why?"

"I need to know exactly where you were, and at what times, and I need to know it now. So don't jack me around with your double talk."

Weeks began to speak, but O'Dell abruptly cut her off. "You want to see our log book? Will that suffice?" He said, getting up to go get it.

Weeks instantly became irate, "I don't appreciate being cut off O'Dell, I'm a big girl; I can look after myself." She turned back to Lamp. "We were at Hooper's house last night. We had a meeting with him about some low level drug dealers, and we left just before eleven."

Lamp held up his hand, "Sit down O'Dell, you aren't going anywhere until I get to the bottom of this. Hear me?"

O'Dell sat down, looked at Weeks then at Lamp, "Yah, we were at Hooper's place. So what? What's the big deal here, Sarg?" O'Dell said.

Lamp threw his arms up in the air which in turned raised his ire, "The big deal here is that nine-one-one got a call about your guy. Seems he's been shot dead and the caller ID'd two suspects, a male and a female driving a dark four door sedan. Does this remind you of anyone?"

Weeks sat upright in the chair, her attention fully on what Lamp had said, "He's dead? Trust me Sarg, we didn't shoot him, god knows there were times I wanted to, but he was alive when we left him." She looked at O'Dell then at Lamp, "What time did the call to nine-one-one come in?"

Lamp paced furiously behind his desk, periodically looking out at the peering faces of other detectives in the bullpen area, who were accustomed to seeing him on a rant. "I was told the call came in just before midnight last night. Lamp returned to his chair, "So, let me get this straight, you were both there near eleven last night, he's still alive. Then at midnight we get a call he's been shot by a man and a woman driving a dark sedan."

O'Dell stood up. "When we left his place, he was alive." He too began to pace behind his chair. "Why would we kill one of our more valuable snitches? That makes absolutely no sense whatsoever. We didn't shoot Hooper."

"Well somebody did, so get your butt's outta my chairs and go over there and see if you can figure out who would want to finger you guys."

Weeks and O'Dell grabbed their things and wasted no time leaving the bullpen. No one spoke a word to them as they left. Once inside the elevator, Weeks asked O'Dell, "What was that all about? Who knew we were there? And who would kill him. Was the killer waiting there for us to leave?"

They got in their car and O'Dell was backing up as Weeks buckled her seat belt. "Beats the hell out of me." He said popping the car into drive.

He squealed the tires as they left the station, and headed back to Newton, where Hooper's house was located. The trip there was done using lights and sirens. O'Dell and Weeks rounded the corner and were met by a sea of flashing red and blue light; it reminded Weeks of a Christmas parade. O'Dell found a spot to park the car and both he and Weeks quickly exited the vehicle and made their way under the yellow police tape. They walked up the short driveway to the door, which was wide open. Inside, two forensic technicians were gathering what little evidence there was. They looked at O'Dell and Weeks as they stepped over the body. "Hey, where's your booties?" one of the technicians shouted. He reached into his kit and tossed two pairs of white shoe covers. "Put these on before you go any further."

Weeks immediately complied; while O'Dell leisurely walked over to the sofa and sat down to put his on, much to the annoyance of the technician. O'Dell smiled. Weeks looked at her partner and thought *'what a pompous asshole'*.

"So, what have you got Preston?" O'Dell said leaning back on the sofa. He'd worked several other crime scenes with Preston Majors, a lab geek who had progressed through the ranks to field investigator.

Preston looked up at O'Dell. "Three taps right in the chest.

All within inches of each other, which suggests close range and by someone who knew how to use a gun. My guess this was a targeted hit."

O'Dell got off the sofa and stood over the body, "There you have it, case closed Weeks. We have an unknown hitman to look for. Let's go."

Weeks kneeled down to get a better look at the gun shots. "What type of weapon was used?"

"We won't know until we get him back to autopsy, but, judging from the entry holes, I'd say medium caliber hollow points." He stuck his finger into the top hole. "The reason I know this is because, A, I went to school and B, because of the cavity inside the wound." He extracted his bloodied finger and held it up for Weeks to see, then winked at her. Weeks stood and looked around the room. "Door looks intact. So this wasn't a robbery gone wrong? And the body being this close to the door suggests that he either opened it for his killer or it wasn't locked. My guess is he opened the door. Did you find any shell casings, Preston?"

Weeks stepped outside and stood on the small porch where she and O'Dell had argued the night before. She could hear O'Dell and the technician talking so she began to look around. "Got one, two, three shell casings out here," she shouted to O'Dell. "Looks like nine millimeter, but I can't be sure."

O'Dell stuck his head out the door and Weeks pointed to the three casings, "So it looks like our shooter came to the door." Weeks said.

O'Dell looked at the casings, then to the doorway, "I wonder if the shooter knocked on the door, waited for Hooper to open it?"

Weeks studied the door, "There's a foot print about waist high on the door, so my guess is that after Hooper opened it, the shooter kicked it in and began firing. The dumb bastard wouldn't have suspected a thing." Weeks bent down and with her pen she picked up the shell casings and put them into a plastic envelope. She stood and turned to O'Dell, "Why don't you go and talk to the neighbors to see who called in the Nine-One-One and if anyone saw or heard anything."

Weeks turned to Majors, "Can you get an imprint off the door? It's likely the shoe print from the shooter." She watched as O'Dell sauntered off the property onto the side-walk and to the neighbouring house. *How he remained a cop was beyond her*.

Weeks stepped outside and walked to the middle of the short driveway. She looked at the two neighbouring houses, trying to determine who made the 9-1-1 call. She saw that the hedge would have limited their view of the driveway, so it must have been somebody across the street. Weeks could see people peering through their curtains at all the activity on their street.

Fifteen minutes later, Weeks and O'Dell were back together, leaning on the hood of their cruiser. "The first house there isn't anyone home, and the second house woke up after the first police car arrived so they didn't see or hear anything," O'Dell said matter of factly.

Weeks pulled out her notepad, "My gut is telling me that whoever was the shooter was likely sitting around here waiting for us to leave. And the shooter likely used a silencer. Nine mils are loud, so somebody would have heard firecrackers going off if it wasn't silenced."

O'Dell looked at Weeks, "Sounds about right, nine mils are loud suckers so somebody would have heard something especially at that time of night."

Weeks looked towards the house as the Medical Examiners removed the body encased in a black body bag. "So let me see if I've got this straight. An unknown person waits for us to leave, goes up to the door, knocks, the door is opened, kicks it in and shoots, then leaves…Do you think this unknown person also called Nine-One-One?" She went to the driver's door and reached in, grabbing the radio mic. "Dispatch, this is Weeks. Can you put me through to Nine-One-One dispatch, please?" She paused, waiting for dispatch to answer.

"Weeks, this is dispatch. I'm connecting you now." The line went silent. Several moments passed.

"Nine-One-One operations supervisor," a voice answered.

Weeks sat down in the driver's seat, "Oh, hi. This is Detective Weeks. We're on scene at a murder, at three-seven-eight-seven, Seventy-Fifth Avenue. The call would have been before midnight. Does your system give a number for the caller?" There was silence.

"Sorry, Weeks, looks like it was from a cell phone. The number looks to be one of those disposable phones. I'll send the number along."

Weeks looked at the M.E.'s van, "Okay, thanks," She said, and cradled the mic. "The caller used a burner phone, so I might be right. Maybe the killer called Nine-One-One, but why? Why risk being caught, unless you knew your number was untraceable?"

O'Dell was leaning against the open door. "Because… because the killer knows us? I'll bet the son-of-a-bitch was sitting here watching us like you said."

Weeks stood up, "What do you mean, the killer knows us? What makes you think that?" She moved to lean against the front fender, "Maybe it had nothing to do with us whatsoever. Hooper was an informant, it's more likely that he pissed somebody off and they wanted him dead, after all they only tried two times before. Our being there may just be coincidental?" She looked at Hooper's house, "We leave, and boom. You think Hooper thought it was us returning? Would he open the door to a stranger?" She scratched her head.

O'Dell leaned on the hood with both hands, "I don't know. You're right, it could just be coincidental, either way we have a dead snitch and from the looks of things, we've got squat to go on."

Near the end of the block, the green light of the night scope gave Ford a ringside seat to the activity around Hooper's house. He saw Weeks and O'Dell discussing something, likely his handy work. He smiled and started his car, backed around the corner, and drove off pointing his finger at them. "Pow."

CHAPTER

10

EIGHT DAYS LATER, Ford was still tailing O'Dell and Weeks. He'd learned their habits, where they lived, who they associated with after work, and where they ate their meals when away from home. His note book was full of useful information on the pair. O'Dell frequented a bar in the Whalley Ring area after work called the Foxy Kitten. It was a 'B' circuit peeler bar, and judging from the reception he got, he'd been going there for some time.

Two nights ago, Ford had sat only four seats away from O'Dell, who had looked right at him and did not recognize him. Ford had sat outside O'Dell's condo three nights in a row. He knew where he parked. He knew where he ate breakfast, both in the morning and at night. He knew from where he'd take a shot if he decided to kill him there. Same place each time, no deviation in his life.

Ford had determined that the best place to get O'Dell was right at the police station, when he got into his Honda to drive home.

Detective Weeks' daily routine involved going to a gym on the Surrey-Delta border; there she would meet up with two other women, one Asian, the other Indo-Canadian. After their work out, the three would go further down Scott Road to a place called Java Jones. Weeks lived in an upscale townhouse complex in the Guildford area which had underground parking and lots of trees. As he watched her, he'd felt pangs of uncertainty about killing her, and wasn't exactly sure if he would or not. She had been the only one that displayed any sense of kindness or humanity on that horrible night almost two years ago. Ford would decide her fate later, so for now, he was concentrating on O'Dell. He knew O'Dell had to die because of the humiliation he'd caused him. Ford remembered something that Alverez had told him. *If you're going to off somebody, do it for the right reasons.*

Ford followed O'Dell as he left for work in his Black Honda Ridgeline, he had determined the when and the where of O'Dell's impending death, but first he would need to make a stop to pick up some essentials. Ford mused about how arrogant O'Dell was, as he never checked at any time if anyone was following him. He figured he could tailgate him all over town, and O'Dell would never know he was there. *His arrogance will be his ultimate downfall,* Ford thought. He quit tailing O'Dell at the intersection of Ninety-Sixth and Scott Road. O'Dell headed east and Ford headed west.

Ford took his time shopping for his items on Columbia Street in New Westminster. There were several shops that specialized in what he needed, so he chose his items carefully, as it was absolutely necessary that everything fit. When he was satisfied he had everything he needed, he travelled back across the bridge to his motel on the King George Highway.

He slept for over three hours, waking up at four-thirty in the afternoon. Ford quickly showered, shaved, and partially dressed for his part in the up-coming ruse. Satisfied that he was the best he could be, he left the room and headed for the Metro Police substation and his meeting with O'Dell.

Ford looked at his watch. It was five twenty as he pulled his car into a parking spot a block away from the police station. From his vantage point, he could see O'Dell's Ridgeline parked in its usual spot in front of the tall cedar tree. Ford guessed that his seniority allowed him the privilege of the same spot each day.

He looked at the police hat in the box on the front seat. It had taken him awhile, but he'd found a replica of a Metro policeman's hat in a pawnshop off Columbia Street. The shirt was a movie prop he'd found in a secondhand store, which from all accounts would pass perfectly as a cop's uniform shirt. His aviator sunglasses were his own, and completed the disguise to a tee. Now all he had to do was to wait until O'Dell came out of the station for his trip to the Foxy Kitten. *If you want to stay alive, never get stuck in a routine that someone can confirm. Always keep them guessing, keep it fresh and different each and every day. You'll live longer that way, kid.*

Ford waited for another two hours until O'Dell finally came out of the station. Ford quickly threw on the shirt and hastily buttoned it up, then he clipped on the standard issue blue tie, and, finally, as he stepped out of the car, he placed the policeman's cap on his slicked back hair. As he walked, he put on his sunglasses with his left and took off the safety on his gun with his right.

Ford quickened his pace as he began the short walk to where O'Dell's Honda was parked. O'Dell was just opening the driver's door as Ford rounded the rear of the vehicle.

O'Dell nodded his head to the young officer and got

behind the wheel.

Ford was at the passenger door and peered in through the glass motioned O'Dell to unlock the door.

O'Dell hit the unlock button on the driver's door trim panel and he watched the young officer slide into the seat.

Ford, realizing his chance, reached over with his left and quickly covered O'Dell's mouth, while he pulled his gun out with his right and rammed it into O'Dell's rib cage and squeezed off three shots in rapid succession. It was over in a matter of seconds. He was dead.

Ford, with hanky in hand, pulled a half mickey of whiskey from his back pocket, placed it between O'Dell's legs, and leaned his head against the door glass. The scene was complete. He quickly took a photograph. He used the hanky to open the door while he holstered his weapon, got out, closed the door, and casually walked back the way he'd come. Ford was smugly happy with himself.

CHAPTER

11

THE METRO POLICE station was electric with the news that O'Dell had been gunned down in their parking lot. The reporter on CKQX radio said this was the first police officer to be assassinated in over twenty-five years. Weeks turned off the small radio at her desk, finding it hard to believe that her partner had been killed just after they said their good-nights. She was sure that it was payback for something that O'Dell had done, but what she couldn't figure out, as her ex-partner was not into sharing much information about what he did.

Detective Sergeant Webber Lamp looked at Weeks through his office window. A disturbing thought ran through his mind. *Was O'Dell's death a random event, or is someone else next?* He got up from behind his desk and walked into the bullpen.

"Okay, everybody, listen up. Right now, the only case you're working on is O'Dell's. Find the son-of-a-bitch that did this and find him fast. Assuming it's a guy. From what I know of O'Dell's private life, it could just as easily have been a pissed off woman." Lamp gazed around at all the officers looking to him for guidance, and support. "We cannot take this lightly. The death of one of our own in our own back yard is totally unacceptable. So work your contacts, work any leads, no matter how trivial they may seem. Talk to anyone who has a story. IHIT is coming on board in a support roll so we'll have access to whatever intel they have." His eyes searched the room. "Yes, Rockwell?"

Martin Rockwell was a twenty-year veteran of Toronto police homicide, and he had done five more on Vancouver Metro PD SWAT before transferring to Main Street Metro. Lamp was glad to have his expertise. "Has anyone viewed the video surveillance of the parking lot? Any clue to the perp's identity yet?"

Lamp sat against the nearest desk, "Glad you brought that up. The surveillance shows a uniformed officer getting into O'Dell's vehicle just after seven twenty-five. As yet, we haven't been able to identify the officer, if it even was an officer. If it turns out this was an imposter, then we have a targeted hit on our hands, and that presents a whole new level of concern for the brass upstairs." Lamp was surprised at how many hands shot up. "Okay, Rosewood, what's on that warped mind of yours?" He said, and several officers snickered. Everyone in the department knew about Rosewood's antics at the last barbecue, and how embarrassed the chief had been.

"O'Dell was into some kinky shit after work, just ask anyone down at the Foxy Kitten. I saw him one night get up on stage, and if it wasn't for the bouncers…"

Lamp cut him off. "Is there a question in there somewhere?" The room erupted in laughter.

"My question, Sarg, is this. If O'Dell was targeted, is there any reason to believe someone else will be targeted? I mean, is this a cop killer thing, or a case of…revenge?"

Lamp walked across the room to the coffee machine. "I think it's too early to speculate whether this is something other than just a homicide. Don't anyone jump to conclusions or let your imaginations run wild. We'll let the evidence tell us where this will go." Lamp looked around the room and saw that Dhaliwal still had her hand up. "What's on your mind Rita?"

"Sarg, the pipeline is alleging that O'Dell was drunk. Any truth to that? And if he was, is that something we should consider in this investigation?"

Lamp put up his hands, "Okay let's put a lid on any speculation. The M.E. is still doing the autopsy and they'll check his blood for both drugs and alcohol, so as I said earlier, let's not jump to any conclusions. And to answer the last part of your question, it doesn't matter whether he was drunk or not. Some son-of-a-bitch shot and killed him." He paused to let that sink in. "And that, people is our sole task, find the bastard who did this. Got it?"

Lamp walked towards his office, the reflection in the glass showed him everyone was still sitting. He spun around. "What, do you guys need a special invitation to get off your asses? Come on people let's get a move on, now!" Opening his door, Lamp saw that Weeks was getting up. "Weeks," he said, "Inside." She just nodded and slowly made her way to Lamp's office.

Lamp lowered his 6'4" frame into his worn high back manager's chair and rocked backward. "You were pretty quiet out there. Anything you want to tell me?" He put his hands behind his head.

Weeks shifted in her chair remembering the last time she and O'Dell were in this office. She tucked her hair behind her left ear and massaged her neck. “Never lost a partner before. I’m not sure how I should be feeling right now. I know I want to get the bastard more than anyone else does, but I’m wondering if I can be objective in my work.” She lowered her head and wiped a tear away from her eye and took a deep breath.

“Have you seen the department shrink yet? You want me to get you a session? Who knows, maybe it’ll put things into prospective and help you with those…feelings.” She shook her head. “Tell me what I can do to help, then. This will take time, Shelley. Trust me; I’ve lost a partner, and it’s not easy.” He paused, “I found that throwing myself into my work helped me a lot. You can try that if you want, or I can put you on leave. Your call.”

Weeks looked up, her eyes were wet and her nose was running. “Just a little space would be nice right now, Sarg. Just a little space.” She looked at Lamp. He’d been in her corner ever since she transferred into this department. She remembered coming here after she’d passed her detective’s exam, green as grass and naive. He had sort of taken her under his wing, protecting her from the sharks that were her peers and spoon-fed her assignments to build her confidence. She remembered the day three years ago when he’d asked her for a favour…become O’Dell’s new partner. There were countless times she had wanted to tell Lamp to separate the two of them, but she had worked through the problems with O’Dell and finally had forged a reasonable working relationship with him, even though there had been times she would have liked to have put a bullet in him.

“Okay Weeks, I can live with that. You want some space, you’ve got it. But, and I mean this, if I hear anything or sense anything about you going off the rails to get at somebody… well then, you'll have to deal with me. Are we clear?"

Weeks nodded agreement and got up, wiped her eyes with the backs of her hands, straightened her shoulders, and walked out of Lamp's office, head held high.

CHAPTER

12

Ford exited the Purple Sky nightclub at closing time. The Granville Mall was full of party patrons making their way home in varying states of intoxication. At three-thirty in the morning he was surprised to see so many Metro police patrolling the area. As he walked towards the parkade, he spotted Felix Seven coming out of the Great Ape Escape nightclub, so he quickly turned away. He wasn't ready to renew acquaintances with the Numbers Gang just yet.

Ford watched Seven out of the corner of his eye as he made his way to a waiting Escalade parked off Nelson Street. He immediately recognized that Seven had a new lady on his arm, and couldn't help but wonder what happened to Venda. He'd liked her. From where Ford was standing, it seemed to him that Felix had gained a lot of weight in the past year, unlike him. He wondered if they would even recognize him if he showed up at their sanctuary?

Ford walked towards Nelson Street, making sure that he wasn't too obvious. As he followed a group of college student's way too drunk to walk, let alone drive, all hell broke loose. A black Chevy Blazer squealed around the corner, music blaring from open windows. He saw that Seven also heard the aggressively driven vehicle, so Ford ducked into a doorway so he wouldn't be noticed. Ford watched Seven react to possible danger as he moved to the inside of the sidewalk, leaving his lady friend on the outside. Ford chuckled. *You bloody coward.* As the vehicle approached, Ford spotted people in the rear seat and immediately knew this was trouble. All at once, the loud thunder claps of automatic gunfire erupted from the Blazer, sending bullets flying. Glass windows shattered from the onslaught of metal travelling at hundreds of feet a second sending icicle shaped shards in every direction. Ford heard screams of pain and watched as innocent bystanders took the brunt of the attack. Then the vehicle sped off down the Granville Mall to Helmcken Street and took a left so hard it rode up on two wheels.

People were screaming and yelling for someone to call 9-1-1. Several of the police foot patrol ran to the scene, guns drawn ready for action, shouting instructions on their radios.

Ford made his way through the gathering crowds of onlookers and craned his neck to see if he could spot Felix Seven. He couldn't, but guessed his cowardly move to the inside of the sidewalk had saved his ass. In that instant Ford sensed that his services might be made available to not only the Numbers Gang, but also the International Brotherhood. He smiled all the way back to his car.

CHAPTER

13

WEEKS DROVE HOME from the station in a virtual fog, as if she was on auto-pilot or having an out of body experience. Her thoughts kept returning to the fact that O'Dell had been murdered in the police parking lot. She had never lost a partner before and she didn't know how she should feel. Weeks knew she felt sadness and empathy for his family, but to what extent? Should she cry? Be pissed off? Angry? She didn't know? In some of her thoughts she felt guilty, but she couldn't understand why she should.

The rain pounded down on her windshield but she didn't pay it any attention, in fact she hadn't even turned on her windshield wipers. When Weeks arrived at her Guildford townhouse, she couldn't even remember what streets she had taken or why she was soaking wet. She soon realized that her side window was down. Weeks knew she needed to regroup, and she had to do it fast, if she was going to be of any help in tracking down O'Dell's killer.

Weeks hurriedly entered her refuge and locked the doors then leaned against the solid wood door and slowly slid down to sit on the floor. She began to cry. Several minutes passed before she stood and made her way to the kitchen where she poured herself a glass of Sumac Ridge Merlot.

Standing beside her kitchen island, she downed the entire six ounce glass and poured another one. This one she let breathe and made her way to change into something more comfortable. Her favourite relaxation attire was sweat pants and a baggy tee shirt. She wished she could wear them to work, but knew that Lamp would go ballistic.

Shelley Weeks picked up her replenished glass of wine and moved into the living room, where she plopped into her recliner and leaned back in the darkness. She groped around for her remote control to turn on her stereo. Finding it under some papers, she clicked on the power button and music filled the darkness. She lowered the volume and closed her eyes, allowing the music of Edith Piaf to wash over her from head to toe. Her mind began to unwind and de-stress, and before long, Weeks felt a little better. She recalled circumstances and events that she and O'Dell had shared, and willed her mind to replay each and every one so she would remember the man not the badge.

An hour later Weeks was becoming sleepy and was a little tipsy, when out of the blue her mind flashed on an incident that had happened almost two years ago. Weeks struggled with the details, everything was blurry. She forced her mind to recall the details of a visit to one of O'Dell's informants, a guy named Hooper. The same Hooper that was just killed a few days ago, now O'Dell? She sat bolt upright in her recliner. Was it related to O'Dell's death or was it her imagination? Weeks was puzzled as to why she remembered something from so long ago. Then she realized a cop and his informant were dead within a week of each other. Could it just be a coincidence? Weeks crawled out of the recliner and found her notepad; she would write down her thoughts and get some sleep. Weeks looked at the clock on the wall, it was eleven-thirty. The thought of calling Lamp entered her mind.

"Shit, I can't call Sarg at this hour, he will be pissed." She muttered to herself.

"Think Shelley," she said aloud, "What would you tell him? You remembered something from nearly two years ago. He'd laugh, then chew me a new one." She ruffled her hair with both hands then looked around her living room.

Weeks shook her head; the memory of the event faded and she became frustrated. Standing she turned off the stereo and headed for bed.

Sleep didn't come as she expected; her mind wouldn't shut off. It kept replaying snippets of interactions with O'Dell. She tossed and turned. Every so often her mind would return to the Hooper memory again. And again it would be blurry, almost as if it hadn't happened. She rolled over and looked at her alarm clock. It was two a.m. already. Weeks stared at the ceiling; the same thought appeared again only this time a little clearer. She propped herself up on her elbows, "Notebooks," she said aloud, "my bloody notebooks." She sat up. "Damn it, they're all at the station."

Rubbing sleep from her eyes, Weeks threw on her sweats and a tee shirt and trotted off to the kitchen where she began to brew a cup of coffee, extra strong. While it was brewing she washed her face and brushed her teeth. She returned to her kitchen, poured her Kona coffee into her favourite travel mug, grabbed her keys and left her townhouse. The rain had stopped and it was eerily quiet for two-thirty in the morning.

The trip into the Main Street station took about twenty-five minutes. Traffic was light which allowed Weeks time to wake up and get her thoughts organized.

Weeks scanned her security badge and the electronic door opened. The building was virtually deserted as the night shift was minimal during the week. She rode the elevator to her floor and walked into an empty bullpen. Weeks placed her coffee mug on her desk, took off her jacket and sat down. She opened the bottom drawer of her desk and pulled out a bundle of notepads held together with a wide elastic band. She was surprised how many bundles there were. After she had retrieved all twenty-seven note pads, she began to organize them by dates. She was a voracious note taker, which used to piss O'Dell off to no end, to the point where he would yell at her when she was writing something he didn't want written down.

Weeks sat at her desk staring at the walls of the bullpen that were covered with bulletins, photos, message boards and lined with numerous filing cabinets. She was trying to remember the date of the incident. Weeks settled on late 2008 to start her search and flipped open the first pad. Four hours later and multiple cups of coffee, Weeks found what she thought was the information she was looking for. She read her shorthand notes which began to trigger her memory of the event.

Several detectives arrived early for work, which was a normal practice. It gave them time to socialize and prepare for the day by reviewing file notes. Weeks read and re-read her shorthand notes hoping to glean as much information as she could from the distant recesses of her mind. She was busy reading and jotting down thoughts and ideas and didn't notice Lamp standing over her."

"I guess I missed the memo on the new dress code?" He

said with a grin.

Weeks was startled and took several seconds to formulate a response, "Sorry Sarg, I've been here most of the night. I guess I lost track of time?"

Lamp pulled up a chair, "This is how you grieve the death of your partner by working all night?"

Weeks rubbed her temples, "Hell, I couldn't sleep and something triggered a memory that persisted so I thought I'd come in and try to find the event in my notepads."

Lamp looked at Weeks sitting with one knee crossed beneath her, in a tee shirt and sweat pants, "Did you find what you were looking for?"

Weeks picked up the notepad with the information she thought was relevant, "I think this is it?" She began to read it. 'O'Dell receives call from informant late August 08, re: suspect captured in house, wanted O'Dell to come and pickup. We attended. Suspect found tied up on floor. Informant's name E.H (Elwood Hooper). Suspect was young white male, seventeen-eighteen years old. Name Dustin Ford. Suspect tried to kill Hooper with empty weapon. Suspect needed bathroom break, escaped through bathroom window. Search of immediate area turned up nothing."

Lamp sat in the chair arms behind his head, "And you think this is relevant how?"

Weeks spun her chair to face Lamp, "Like I said Sarg, this just popped into my head and wouldn't go away. Is it related? I don't know? It just seems highly coincidental that both O'Dell and Hooper are killed within a week of each other?"

Lamp held out his hand, "Let me see your notepad." He wiggled his fingers.

Without thinking Weeks handed the notepad to him.

Lamp looked at the notepad and shook his head, "Are you kidding me...shorthand, or whatever you call this?"

Weeks smiled as he watched Lamp lift the pad this way and that trying to figure it out. "You'll go blind doing it that way. I suggest you sit down and hold the pad up like this?" She held up the pad, folded all but one page back, and found the right angle to get the best light. "Sometimes I write something in pencil then erase it and write something over it in pen. My way of hiding information in case I ever lost the pad. I know. I'm paranoid, right?"

Lamp looked at Weeks. "You're shitting me, right? I never realized you were that cunning?"

"Coffee, Sarg?" Weeks said, getting up from her chair. He shook his head no. Walking over to the coffee machine, she rotated her shoulders, hoping to get the kink out of them. She'd give anything for a good massage right about now.

"You remember anything else about the event?" Lamp asked leaning forward.

Weeks returned to her chair and sat down, "Something tells me the kid said something about a gang initiation or something to that effect. We both sort of dismissed it because it sounded so crazy. I mean who sends someone to kill someone with an empty gun. Crazy, right?"

Lamp sat back in the chair, hands again behind his head, "So, are you thinking the kid is involved in this or what? The gang hit both Hooper and O'Dell?'

"I don't know Sarg. I'm guessing anything could be possible; this kid would be nineteen plus now. I understand that Hooper scared the shit out of the kid and know that O'Dell humiliated him while questioning him."

Lamp was sitting upright at the desk, "Any memory of what the kid looked like?" he asked.

Weeks looked around the bullpen and then at Lamp, "Sorry Sarg, I'm drawing a blank. It was dark inside Hooper's house and I think the kid was dressed in all black."

Lamp stood, his towering frame forced Weeks to look upward." Lamp turned to walk away, then stopped and turned back. "After you run his name, you'd better go home and change into some proper clothes…I wouldn't want the Chief to see you so casual.

Weeks entered Dustin Ford's name into CPIC and sat back. The system was slow at the best of times so she scrawled a note, "DO NOT USE" on a piece of paper and taped it to the monitor. She threw on her jacket, grabbed her coffee mug and headed home.

Ninety minutes later, Weeks was back at the station, dressed appropriately and working at her desk. CPIC had done its job.

"Wow, eighteen Dustin Fords in the system." She said to herself, "Let's see contestant number one. Dustin Ford, Laval Quebec, aged forty-seven. And contestant number two is from Edmonton and is fifty-nine years old. And number three is from Regina and is thirty-six." Weeks scrolled through all eighteen names, and no Dustin Ford was listed for the lower mainland.

"Shit, he isn't in the system. I wonder if he told O'Dell and Hooper his correct name. Wouldn't be the first time a perp lied to save his ass."

Weeks continued, "Think, Shelley, think," she said aloud. "How do I find this guy?" She slapped her forehead, "Provincial records. Why didn't I think of that before?"

She ran Ford's name through the provincial registry of births and deaths to see if Dustin Ford was dead. It came up empty. Weeks noticed that Lamp was back in his office, so she quickly got up, stood in his doorway and knocked. He motioned her in.

"What did you find?" he asked.

Leaning on the chair in front of the desk she said, "I found there are eighteen Dustin Ford's in Canada, but none in the lower mainland. I checked Provincial records and there is no record of him being born or dying, so I am beginning to suspect that the kid didn't give O'Dell or Hooper his correct name. So I'm right back where I was yesterday, only minus a night's sleep." She managed to crack a small smile. Lamp saw it and grinned.

"Hey at least we have a lead, a name. Let's see where it takes us."

CHAPTER

14

DUSTIN FORD STOOD among the shadows of the tall cedar trees that lined the greenbelt between Weeks' condo and the freeway. It afforded him perfect cover as he played with his Glock. Ford had tailed Weeks from the police station. He guessed she couldn't sleep, so had gone back into work. He followed her but didn't remain after she entered the station. The drive back to her condo took longer than he thought, due to traffic. Ford figured he would wait for her. He slowly screwed on the silencer, and as he loaded the clip he felt each bullet with his fingers for any imperfections, another trick that Alverez had taught him.

Ford relieved himself among the bushes then lit a smoke with his electric lighter, another trick Alverez had showed him. The electric lighter wouldn't give away his position at night when shielded by his body or hand. He mulled over what he was about to do to O'Dell's partner. Ford was torn between just wounding her and outright killing her. The words of his mentor kept running through his mind. *Make sure the target deserves to die before pulling the trigger. If not, walk away.*

The night in Hooper's place was the source of his desire for revenge. Weeks had been there, but she had at least offered him some respect and civility, something he had appreciated, something that might be the difference between life and death for her.

He looked at his watch. It was nearly three-thirty. Ford slowly inhaled a drag from his cigarette as he watched a vehicle turn onto the dead end street. His attention went into overdrive, and he ground the cigarette out with his foot. Ford quickly raised the night vision goggles, and the headlights almost blinded him. He cursed as the vehicle neared the building. Was it her, or was it somebody else? He watched intently as the vehicle pulled onto the underground parking apron. He relaxed. It wasn't her. Stuffing the Glock into the back of his pants, Ford headed away from the condo, having made up his mind that she wouldn't die, at least not this day. Once he had it clear in his mind, he would kill her like her partner.

He immediately changed his focus to Felix Seven. He couldn't believe his one time friend had turned into such a pantywaist and a coward that would hide behind a woman's skirt. Ford had been taught by Alverez to man up when the time came. It was Seven's time to man up. He needed to let Seven know he was back in town, and it was time to set him straight.

Ford started his car, shifted it into gear, and slowly drove away. The oncoming headlights glared off the wet pavement, so he missed Weeks' vehicle as it passed him by. He decided to sleep first, and confront Seven later.

It was two-twenty in the afternoon, and the sound of the maid knocking on his motel door woke Ford from a sound sleep. Rubbing his eyes, he peered through the peep hole and saw a petite Filipino lady in her white maid's uniform waiting to come in. He cracked the door ajar and told her the room didn't need a cleaning today.

After he had showered and cleaned his weapon, another tip from Alverez, he set out to grab a burger and to find Felix Seven. It took Ford less than an hour to track him down. Ford shook his head, thinking, *if I wanted to pop him, it wouldn't be hard, as he never alters his routine.* Alverez had made that point abundantly clear to Ford by nailing him with a paint ball.

Ford sat outside the Lucky Slipper Casino off Scott Road, where Felix Seven was likely playing his favourite game, blackjack. With two phone calls, he had Seven's location pegged. It was obvious to him that the Numbers Gang were getting sloppy. Its members and associates couldn't keep their mouths shut. He patiently ate his burger and fries, waiting for his former friend to leave for his next stop, which was likely to visit one of his girlfriends.

It was almost five o'clock when Ford noticed a black Lexus sedan pull in ten spots away. It had "gang members" written all over it. The blacked out windows made it difficult to determine who, or how many were inside, but his gut was telling him something bad was about to happen. He quickly pulled his Glock from under the seat and spun on the silencer, then laid the weapon on his lap under his napkin. Ford did a quick check around him, making sure nobody was overly curious. Seeing no one, he relaxed and finished his now cooling burger. It still tasted good. His vantage point gave him a perfect view of the front door to the casino, so he figured Seven had to come out this way. Ford eyed the vehicles in the parking lot's front row and guessed that the white Ford Excursion that was all blinged out was likely

Seven's. He noted that the black Lexus was two vehicles away from it, a prime spot for a hit.

At twenty after five, Ford saw Seven and his buddies coming out of the casino. His eyes immediately zeroed in on the Lexus and saw the passenger window being lowered. His heart rate quickened and his breathing became rapid and shallow. He took a deep breath to calm himself. He started his car and put it into gear, not exactly sure what his next play would be.

His eyes went back to the Lexus and he noticed a small black cylinder protruding from the lowered glass. It was a gun. His eyes flashed back towards Seven, who was basically a sitting duck. Without hesitation, he launched his car from its parking spot and rocketed towards the Lexus while leveling his Glock at the partially open window. He stopped close to the Lexus and opened fire on the passenger side of the car. The passenger window exploded before gunfire was returned from the driver's side of the Lexus. Ford threw his car into reverse and smoked the tires backwards as bullets pelted his front windshield. While backing up, he saw Seven and his cohorts duck for cover behind the valet stand. Ford returned fire on the Lexus as it pulled out of its parking spot. The back window of the Lexus shattered along with the right rear door glass. Smoke was rolling off its rear tires. In a flash it was heading towards the exit, with Ford in hot pursuit, at least that's what he wanted them to believe.

Once outside the confines of the casino parking lot, the Lexus shot to the left, and Ford turned and sped off in the opposite direction. He'd catch up with Seven at his next location, but needed to ditch this vehicle and obtain another as he was sure the entire scene was captured on the casino parking lot video surveillance.

CHAPTER

15

CONSTABLE DAN THURO was the first to arrive on scene at the Lucky Slipper Casino; dispatch had received several reports of gun fire in the parking lot. Thuro pulled his marked patrol car into the reserved parking spot in front of the main entrance. A large crowd was milling about the entrance, which Thuro didn't like. He immediately found casino security and instructed them to get the crowd inside. Once more officers had arrived the spectators would have their statements taken.

"Okay Mike, what the hell happened here this time?" Thuro said to Mike Chambers, the casino security chief.

"Beats the fuck outta me? Some guys wanted to settle something in the parking lot. The video tapes are being secured as we speak, so once you view them you'll know more than me."

Thuro laughed. "Shit, Mike, I already know more than you." He watched as Chambers forced a smile at him. "I see your monkeys have secured the scene. Good boy, Mickey. It shows your apes are learning. What's this, the fourth or fifth time we've had gun fire in your parking lot? I'd say your establishment is attracting a less than savoury clientele, wouldn't you?" He noticed Chambers was about to answer and cut him off. "It was a rhetorical question, Mike. Geez, I guess anyone can be a goddamn security chief. Certainly takes no brains."

Thuro didn't wait for Chambers to come up with a response, instead he made his way towards the taped off parking lot. In the distance, he heard several sirens wailing and knew the forensics team was en route. He squatted down beside a couple of shell casings and, with his pen, picked one up and examined it closely, then placed it back on the ground.

Thuro stood and looked at a Honda Civic in the parking lot with several bullet holes in the right fender and door then he turned back to the casino and looked at the shattered glass in the building. From what he could ascertain, vehicle one was driving through the parking lot, and vehicle two was parked in the spot next to the shot-up Civic.

Thuro walked over towards the casino's main entrance, now clear of onlookers. Several of the rounds had found the columns that held the glass roof up. He turned back to face the Civic and paced off the distance between shots at the casino. He made a mental note; it was approximately twenty-seven feet from impact to impact. Thuro recalled his training with automatic weapons, they were very uncontrollable. The shooter in the driving vehicle likely had a 9mm of some sort, the same weapon as the shooter in the parked car. He quickly reasoned this as a gang spat, but which two gangs, and more importantly, why?

Thuro watched as the forensics' van pulled into the lot and came to a stop a few yards from his cruiser. Two white-suited technicians got out, bags in hand, and walked over to him.

"Nunez and Swift," he said. "What are the odds I'd draw you two clowns?" Thuro stuck his large paw out. They each shook his hand.

"Well, butterball, the feeling is mutual," Swift said, jokingly. "So what yah got this time?"

Thuro pointed to the parked Civic and to the shattered window in the casino as he explained what he thought happened. "The casino security chief said they were pulling the video tapes of the parking lot, so we should be able to get a visual of what happened here. His name is Chambers, and don't let him give you any shit, or he'll have to deal with me."

Nunez picked up his black case and began to walk towards the Civic while Swift went to find Chambers.

Thuro yelled at Nunez. "I've got another call, so if you don't need me, I'm history here." He saw Nunez raise his arm and wave, which meant he wasn't needed here any longer. As he was pulling out, another cruiser pulled in so he stopped. Detective Carol Mertin nodded as he explained what he thought had transpired. She thanked him and took over the scene. Thuro drove away.

CHAPTER

16

FORD FOUND A secluded field half way between Surrey and White Rock that gave him an easy exit and provided enough cover for him to torch his vehicle. After he'd pulled off the plates and removed any paperwork from the glove box, he opened the five gallon jerry can and poured gasoline over the interior and exterior. Satisfied that he had enough fuel on the car, he lit a smoke and inhaled deeply, then flicked the cigarette into the interior of the car. In an instant, the interior erupted into a full blown blaze. Black smoke curled skyward and Ford watched in awe of the destructive power of fire.

During his apprenticeship with the Crypt's in LA, he'd learned how to kill efficiently, with the last five hits being solo jobs, and at full pay for service. In total, he left LA with close to thirty-five thousand. It was one of the things that attracted him to this lifestyle, money. When he returned to Vancouver it had taken him three days and over a dozen banks to exchange the funds from American to Canadian.

He watched the car become fully engulfed in flames before he made his way out of the forested area. Ford lit another cigarette as he walked along the path, contemplating what his next vehicle would be. He knew he wanted something with some pep, but that wouldn't stand out like Seven's vehicle. Then it hit him. He'd get a Mustang, one of those 5.0 liter jobs.

A half hour later Ford hailed a cab just off 200th Street in Langley and headed back to his motel. He knew who he'd call to get another vehicle, a guy he'd met when he was an initiate with the Numbers Gang. His name was Rolf.

When Ford arrived at his motel, it was almost eight o'clock, and he hated being without wheels. Inside his room, he reached out to a contact from his previous life and obtained Rolf's cell number. He quickly punched in the numbers on his burner phone. It rang seven times before a gruff voice answered.

"Hello?"

"Hello, Rolf. It's me, Ford. Dustin Ford. I need to buy a car tonight. Can you help me?"

There was silence on the other end. Then, "Who's calling?"

Ford looked skyward, "For fuck's sake, Rolf. It's me, Dustin Ford. We met at Seven's place a while back. You goddamned near killed me with a pool cue after I beat your ass in Nine Ball. Remember now?" Ford said. He recalled the incident with crystal clarity.

"Ah yah, now I remember. The baby face fucker who got lucky. I should have stuck you with the stick, you lucky prick. What the hell do you want? You said something about a set of wheels. What did you have in mind?"

Ford breathed a sigh of relief. "What I'm looking for is a clean five-liter Mustang. A manual with a sound system and level-three armour. Got anything like that sitting around?"

Rolf was laughing. "Are you fuckin' kidding me? You want a Ford? Hell, I thought you wanted a good car."

Ford sat down on the edge of his unmade bed. He smiled. He liked the idea of driving a Ford. It had a ring to it, sort of like Bond, James Bond, only Ford driving a Ford. He laughed. "And what the fuck's wrong with a Ford? Suppose you're one of those Chevy freaks. Or worse yet, Jap crapper. You got what I want, or do I have the wrong guy?"

There was a long pause at Rolf's end. "Yah, I got a line on what you're looking for. What colour makes you happy?"

"Black would be the only colour of interest to me, with a black interior. Is that doable?" He heard heated voices in the background.

"Look Ford, call me around midnight, should have something for you then. Bye." Then, the line went dead.

Ford shrugged his shoulders and lay down on the bed. He smelled of gas.

"Shit" he said. He jumped out of bed and darted to the washroom, where he shed he shirt and pants. He held each up to his nose trying to find the offending garment. Smelling none, he then smelled his hands, and they reeked of gas. He looked in the mirror and closed his eyes. *If the goddamn cabby is ever questioned by police, he might remember me,* he thought. *Damn it Ford, quit being so damn sloppy.* He slapped himself upside his head. He immediately began to wash his hands with soap. Once he was done, he looked around the room. He wasn't going to take any chances. There were other fleabag motels scattered throughout Surrey, so he'd move in the morning once he had new wheels.

At twelve-thirty, he called Rolf. This time, the phone was answered before the second ring. "Rolf, its Ford. What have you got for me?"

"I have what you asked for. Ninety-nine Mustang GT, five

liter, black on black. All I need is ninety-five hundred cash, and you're styling."

Ford grinned from ear to ear, "Then I guess I'm styling. Where and when?"

"The Denny's on One Hundred Fifty-Second Street in one hour. Don't be late, kid, or I'll stick you the next time I see you," he said, laughing, then hung up.

Ford quickly changed and pulled his duffle bag from under the bed and counted out ninety-five one hundred dollar bills. He divided the wad in half and stuck each half into his front pockets. He didn't like how it looked, so he removed the wads and got an envelope from the desk and put the money inside. He stuffed the envelope into his leather jackets inside pocket and left his room. He walked down the block smoking a cigarette when he saw a cab. He flagged it down and gave the driver his destination and sat back. He couldn't wait to get out as it smelled of curry and it made him shudder.

Twenty minutes later, he was standing on the sidewalk a half block from the Denny's. He checked his weapon in the back of his pants, all was safe and secure. He lit another cigarette and slowly walked towards the all night eatery. He knew he'd identify Rolf in a heartbeat, big red-headed guy with a football player's build and one stupid-looking gold front tooth. Ford guessed nobody would ever tell him that because of his size and his temper.

He stood in the shadows with a view of the interior and spotted Rolf instantly. He was sitting with two other large individuals, all three wearing black leather jackets. Ford shook his head and chuckled at how obvious they were. He took a long drag on his smoke and held it for a long moment before exhaling. Ford pushed the door open with his elbow and walked in as if he owned the place. He didn't look at anyone and walked directly to the three men at the booth. Ford stood directly at the head of the booth and nodded to the two unknown men, who were staring at him.

"Rolf, you haven't changed a bit. Good to see you again," he said, offering his hand.

Rolf looked at Ford, unsure. Reluctantly, Rolf stuck out his hand, and they gripped hard and shook vigorously, each trying to out-do the other. When no winner was obvious, Rolf relaxed his grasp and motioned Ford to pull up a seat.

"Good to see you too, kid. So, did you bring the money?"

Ford eyed the two men across from him. He didn't recognize either, but knew they were connected in some fashion. "Yah, I got the money. And don't call me kid, my name is Ford. Where's the car at?"

Rolf motioned towards the parking lot. "Right there beside the Yukon. You're lucky, this one was for another customer, but he's dead so you get it."

Ford stood. "Let's go have a look-see," He said, and he turned to leave.

"What, no reminiscing? No chewing the fat, so to speak? All business, eh?

Ford stopped at a booth two away from the group. "Hey, all I want is a car. I have all the friends I need, and I only know *of* you, and I certainly am not interested in reliving the past. So, do you want to deal or not?"

Rolf shrugged his shoulders and slid out of the booth. "Well, let's go look at the car then." He motioned to his companions to join him.

Ford led the way from the restaurant out into the parking

lot. He stopped to look at the shiny black car that was parked next to the lamp standard. It glistened. Ford opened the driver's door and slid inside. He checked out the gauges and stereo system then motioned to Rolf for the keys. Rolf tossed them to him and he started the car, sending the tachometer nearly to the red line.

"Hop in let's go for a spin." Ford said, as he dropped it into reverse and held the clutch in. Rolf and one other man hopped into the Mustang as Ford launched the vehicle backwards, then with one smooth motion dropped it into first and hammered it. The rear tires began to smoke as the car careened towards the street.

Ford was enjoying this, but both Rolf and the other man appeared to be nervous. As Ford entered onto the King George Highway, he turned on the lights and sped off towards New Westminster, then at the last minute turned north on 104th Ave. and headed towards the freeway. When he reached the on-ramp, he pegged the tachometer and downshifted into third gear, breaking the rear tires loose. He watched as the speedometer climbed rapidly as all the horses began to work. Within seconds, he was flying east down Highway 1 at close to a hundred miles per hour. Ford saw the off-ramp at 176th Street and guided the Mustang onto it, and before long he had doubled back and was heading west on Highway 1 toward the 104th street exit.

"Nice car, Rolf. We have a deal," he said, reaching into his pocket, pulling out the envelope and flipping it to him in the passenger's seat.

Soon they pulled back into the Denny's parking lot. Rolf got out then stuck his head through the open passenger window. "All the papers are in the glove box. Drive safely kid." He slapped the roof, then he and his companion walked toward the GMC Yukon. Ford quickly installed his license plates, reversed the Mustang, and slowly pulled out of the parking lot. He needed to get some sleep.

The next morning, Ford checked out of the motel. He'd rather be safe than sorry, especially since the car fire had ignited some of the nearby trees and turned it into a media circus.

CHAPTER 17

WEEKS SPENT ALMOST two hours with the sketch artist trying to render what she remembered about the young perp from over a year ago. "I'm certain the informant said he was seventeen or eighteen, so you'll need to make him young." Weeks shifted in her seat.

"I think he was close to six feet tall, and sort of heavy set; you've got him thin and short." Weeks racked her brain, trying to remember even the slightest detail about the remarkably plain youth that she'd encountered for all of fifteen minutes nearly two years ago, a tall order to say the least. In her mind, she only saw a figure dressed in black, no facial features to go by, so the image was just a blob. She could remember that the kid was tall, almost 6', maybe more.

"Do you remember his face shape? Eye colour? Any physical features?" Mander asked. He was becoming frustrated with Weeks.

"His hair was dirty blonde, no wait... maybe brown." Weeks stared at the ceiling. "Did he have eyes…of course he did?" She couldn't believe she'd just said that.

"What colour were they?" Mander asked, drumming his pencil on the desk.

"Don't know?" She silently cursed Hooper for having such shitty lighting in his living room. Then, when the kid went to the bathroom his back was to her. *Christ how could she have been that unobservant*?

Mander Bropal put his pencil down and spun around on his stool to face Weeks. "Look, Detective, this isn't working. We're no further ahead than when we started. You keep changing your mind about every detail. Right now, we might as well draw a stick man for all the good this rendering will do."

Weeks felt somewhat crushed by his bluntness. She closed her eyes and thought back to Hooper's house. She drew a blank.

"Your right, Mander, this is getting us nowhere. Perhaps I can persuade Sarg to sign off on a hypnotist. I'll ask him when I go back upstairs." She stood up and looked at the rough sketch on the easel and shook her head. She could picture his shape, but clarity was lost when it came to describing his features. Weeks thanked Mander for his efforts and apologized, then left the basement of the police headquarters. She rode the elevator in silence up to the fifth floor and the bullpen.

At her desk Weeks held her head between her hands, staring blankly at the scribbles on her desk blotter. Weeks had always been a doodler when she talked on the phone.

Lamp buzzed her on the phone. She didn't pick up. Incensed Lamp slammed the phone down and yelled, "Weeks. Get in here!" His outburst drew the attention of every detective in the bullpen, including Weeks, who sheepishly got up and made her way through the maze of desks to Lamp's office.

"Don't you answer your phone anymore?" he said, sitting down in his high back chair. "I let it ring six times, didn't you hear it? Anyway, how'd it go with Mander?"

Weeks leaned against the door jamb, "Sorry boss, my mind was a million miles away. I wanted to come and see you. Mander isn't able to draw the perp from my recollections. I...thought I might undergo hypnosis to see if I can get a clearer picture of what the kid looked like. But that needs your John-Henry on it."

"So, let me see if I've got this straight," Lamp said, leaning forward in his chair. "You spent almost two hours with him and you can't remember what the perp looked like. Is that correct?"

Weeks stared at the floor. "That's essentially the problem, Sarg. Hey, it was only about fifteen minutes almost two years ago in a room that was dimly lit. If I hadn't made a note of even being there, we'd be at a complete loss. Instead, we just have a minor setback...if we use a hypnotist."

Lamp leaned back in his chair and clasped his paws behind his head. He said nothing as he mulled over the situation, then he leaned forward. "Okay, you've got your hypnotist. But by god, this better be worth it, or you're back writing parking tickets; do I make myself clear?"

"Crystal, Sarg. I'll get it set up PDQ. You want to sit in on it?" She exhaled loudly, "Of course you wouldn't, what was I thinking, you're way too busy."

Lamp grinned, "Go do some police work, instead of holding up my wall."

Weeks returned to her desk. Her spirits were buoyed, so she quickly called Dr. Fuller. The appointment was slated for the next day at ten o'clock, and she hoped that the outcome would be beneficial to the department. She rang Mander to let him know. Then she leaned back and closed her eyes. *Was that kid, that baby-faced kid, the killer?* She ran that idea through her mind time after time and she kept coming back to one central point. Why? *What did Hooper and O'Dell do to this kid that warranted their deaths?*

She was hungry and needed to find something to eat. She looked at the clock. It was almost one thirty, and the bowl of cereal she'd eaten for breakfast had long worn off.

Weeks guided her unmarked police car into the Burger Heaven's drive through lane and stopped at the ordering wicket. This had been O'Dell's favourite place to get a quick bite to eat. The portions were large, the price was cheap, and it was fast. She ordered her usual, double cheese with bacon and mushrooms, no fries, and with a grape soda. Weeks remembered the first time she and O'Dell had come to Burger Heaven after they'd partnered. When she placed her order, he almost gagged. "Grape soda?" she heard him, "That's a kiddies' drink." She also remembered her response, which had been the middle finger.

As hard as Weeks tried to be fair, she disliked O'Dell even more as a cop because his old school ways of doing things grated against her idea of good police work. Still, she found it hard to believe that he was actually dead. A horn sounded from behind her, and half dazed, she drove forward almost hitting the vehicle in front of her. "Christ, Shelley, will you pay freaking attention?" she said.

Weeks opened her purse at the pay window, paid, then grabbed her bag of greasy goodness and sped away. She knew exactly where she wanted to eat lunch, Pioneer Place, locally known as Pigeon Park. It was close, and quiet, and she desperately needed quiet.

Weeks pulled the police car alongside the curb. Grabbing her lunch and cell phone, she locked the car and walked the short distance to a picnic table under some trees. The wind was wafting through the park, causing the trees to sway in a hypnotic motion that put her mind at ease. Birds were singing high in the tree tops, and gulls soared overhead. It was perfect.

Ford parked his Mustang near the entrance to Pigeon Park and shut the engine off. He had a clear line of sight to where Detective Weeks was enjoying her lunch. He lit a cigarette and inhaled deeply and slowly, then exhaled out the window. The slightly overcast day made it easy to pick up her every movement. Out of habit Ford reached under the front seat to make sure his weapon was close by. It was.

He leaned back in the seat and plugged in his favourite Nicole Smack CD, Dark Motion, and hit play. Soon, the rhythmic pounding surrounded his entire body and the singer's voice ground into his brain. Ford grinned, Rolf had said it had a kick-ass sound system, and he'd been right.

Ford watched as other vehicles slowed down then continued on, choosing not to stop at the small park. He was grateful for that. Ford was still unsure if he would do her like he'd done O'Dell.

Weeks watched as two crows fought over some scraps of food next to the garbage bin, and it made her laugh. The smaller crow wasn't taking any guff from the much larger one. Her burger tasted heavenly, and the sweet grape soda washed it down nicely.

Ford was enjoying the music when he spotted a marked patrol car pull in behind Weeks' vehicle. He cursed silently and instantly turned the music down, so as to not arouse suspicion from the tall, uniformed officer who got out of the police car. The officer looked both ways before walking over towards the table. The two crows that were fighting squawked and flew high into the trees. He saw Weeks look up and smile, then give a small wave. Then they kissed. He watched as they embraced for several seconds before separating. The tall officer sat down across from Weeks. Ford watched as she offered him some of her food, but he shook his head. Ford pulled out his binoculars and focused in on the pair. The tall officer wasn't buying whatever she was telling him. He slammed his fist down hard on the picnic table, then stood and quickly walked back to his patrol car. Ford watched as Weeks followed his movements then hung her head down. Something wasn't right between them, but that wasn't Ford's problem.

CHAPTER

18

FELIX SEVEN ENTERED the gang's safe house just a little after two-thirty in the morning. Since his close call at the casino, he had chosen to lie low and only move at night. He had had close calls before, but nothing like what happen earlier on. The identity of the shooters was still a mystery to the Numbers Gang.

Seven pulled a beer from the cooler and sat down on the couch beside Oscar Nineteen, who was watching a re-run of *Baywatch.*

"Man, I love looking at those hard bodies, don't you?" Nineteen said with a grin. Felix Seven smiled and raised his eyebrows. His eyes settled on Chevy, who was sprawled out in the large recliner rocker next to the couch.

"What the hell happened this afternoon? Who were those fucks shooting at me? I could have been fuckin' killed? And who was the dude shooting at them? Shit, it's getting so it isn't safe to go anywhere. Where the hell was our goddamn protection?"

Chevy Three levered the recliner to a sitting position. "If you remember, we agreed that if you went to the casino you'd enter and leave by the rear entrance, not the goddamn front. But no, not you, you've got to do it your way. Jesus

Christ Seven, if you're tired of breathing there's people who will ventilate you. Is that what you want?"

Nineteen leaned forward on the couch. "Okay, both of you knock it off. Seven didn't say it was your fault, but Chevy, you're responsible for security, so it's a legit question. Where the hell were they? Was security even there? If so where? And who the sam hell bailed his ass out? Whoever this guy is, we need to find him fast and pin a medal on his chest, or something." Nineteen leaned back and took a pull on his beer. Three gave him the one fingered salute.

"Oh, that's mature," He said sarcastically to Three.

Chevy Three rubbed his eyes then reached for the beer that he'd started over two hours before and tipped it back, draining its stale contents. He threw the empty can at Seven who ducked out of its path. Seven started to laugh and was joined by Nineteen. Chevy Three pulled his six foot frame off the recliner and stretched.

"Screw both of you. I'm going to bed." He yelled for his girlfriend, Eva, who came from the kitchen, and they went upstairs.

Felix looked at Oscar and shrugged. For the past two weeks, Chevy had been all but impossible to live and work with. He was moody, cranky and belligerent, but most of all, he was mean, often slapping his girl around, to the point where he had to be pulled off of her.

"I think he needs to get lucky more often or something, 'cause he's really starting to piss me off," Oscar Nineteen said, shaking his head. He'd known Chevy Three for close to ten years, and he'd never seen him like this before. Sure, he had his moments, but they usually passed quickly.

Seven pointed to the cooler and nodded at Nineteen, who

shook his head.

“Nah, I think I’ve had enough.”

Seven retrieved another Foster’s from the chest.

“You got any idea who wanted to off you?” Nineteen said.

“I can think of at least a hundred people off the top of my head, but that’s about as specific as I can be. Hell, I never even got a look at what type of car the fucks were driving, and as far as the dude who shot at them is concerned…” He shrugged his shoulders. “I haven’t the foggiest idea who he was, but don’t get me wrong, I’m grateful as all hell for what he did. But you have to ask yourself this: Why was he there? Was he stalking me, or them? Makes you wonder, doesn’t it?”

Nineteen sat cross legged on the couch as he often did ‘to align his karma’. “So, the dude who saved your ass may have been there to kill you? But stopped the other guys from doing it…why? If he wanted you dead why not just let the other guys do it? It shouldn’t matter who does the deed?”

Felix Seven plopped into the recliner. “Christ, don’t sugar coat it or anything. So, what you’re saying is I’m bloody dead either way?”

Nineteen grinned at Seven, “If it’s your time to go, then it’s your time to go. Not a minute before. If I’d be you, I’d either be lying low for a while or be looking over my shoulder, ‘cause you know some bad shit is coming your way. We need to find out who the guy was that saved your ass.” Nineteen inhaled deeply to calm himself; he knew that they were all targets for one reason or another. “If it’s a fuckin’ war they want, it’s a fuckin’ war they’ll get. Tomorrow, have Three call a meeting of our inner circle.” He rose to leave. “And maybe you should contact all our shooters? This could get ugly really fast.”

"What good would an inner circle meeting do? Can't we simply demand? I don't think this is a time to be diplomatic or any of that shit. Just grab your guns and wait for instruction's is all they need to know." Seven pumped his fist.

They bumped knuckles, and Nineteen turned to leave, then stopped. "Well a war right now would be costly. We're finally making good profit. I'd hate to see it all go away over a stupid war among ourselves. Personally, I think we should see if we can get a council meeting and find out if this is a turf war or someone gone rogue."

Seven looked up at his half brother and shrugged, "The last time there was a meeting of the gangs it damned near turned into a war right there at Harrison, remember? Any reason to think it won't happen again?"

"Hey, with all the heat coming from the cops…shit, man," he paused. "How many leaders have been busted, and hell even deported to the fuckin' US? So maybe the time is right to have a meeting to try and survive this. Bad enough the goddamn cops want everyone's ass, the last thing we need is a bloody war amongst ourselves."

Seven levered the recliner as far back is it would go and closed his eyes. "I think I'd rather have a war with cops than the other bastards. At least the cops have to play by the rules. So yeah, if we can prevent a war, I think it would be wise to try that approach. Didn't Hitler say, 'plan for success, but prepare for failure,' or something like that?"

Oscar shook his head. "Where the hell did you read that shit? It wasn't Hitler. He wasn't that smart. Now, if you'd have said Gandhi or Churchill, I'd buy that."

Seven waved him away.

CHAPTER

19

Shelley weeks sat patiently outside the office of Dr. Raymond Fuller, the department's contracted hypnotist, and to say she was nervous would be an understatement. For as long as she could remember, she'd heard horror stories about people who had been put under and made to do all sorts of dumb things without them knowing it. This worried her deeply.

The petite blonde receptionist leaned forward and called her. "Ms. Weeks, the doctor will see you now." She returned to her work, while religious music emanated from a small stereo. Weeks raised her eyebrows as she walked by. She would never have thought the buxom blonde was a Bible-Thumper. Night club queen...maybe, but not the god-squad.

She opened the frosted glass door.

"Come in, Detective Weeks. Sit down." Fuller motioned with his hand. "I haven't seen anyone from the department in ages. What's going on over there? You guys have an in-house shrink or something? He laughed.

Weeks sat down in the black leather chair, "Not that I'm aware of. You know us cops Doctor. We don't like anyone inside our heads, too scary a place." She managed a slight grin. "Just so you know. I'm not a good candidate for being put under. Was told my mind is too strong-willed or something."

"Okay then, good to know. I need to ask some preliminary questions before we start, so get comfortable. It'll make it easier." Raymond Fuller had been contracted by the Metro Police department to assist officers dealing with PTSD and to help victims of crime deal with their loss or trauma. This was a somewhat different situation, but it could work.

Weeks nodded. She removed her black leather suede jacket and tossed it onto the chair next to her. She unbuttoned the top button of her shirt and stretched her neck out of habit. She often needed to make it crack before she could relax. "Okay, fire away, Doc," she said, settling into the plush recliner chair.

Fuller looked up from his paperwork. "Please state your full name and occupation."

Weeks closed her eyes. "Shelley Elizabeth Weeks, Detective First Class, Metro Vancouver Police Dept."

"Marital status and your age?"

"Partially committed, but always on the lookout, and today I'm forty going on fifty."

"How long at the department and do you have a partner?"

Weeks squirmed a bit in the chair. "I've been on the department for five, no, six years and my last partner was Detective O'Dell."

"What was his first name?"

"His first name was Mickey, middle name Aaron. He was fifty-seven years old, a smoker and heavy drinker." She was getting pissed off at the line of questioning.

"Okay Detective, relax, I sense you're getting a little worked up. What I'm trying to do is find your blockers.

Blockers are events in your life that prohibit you from remembering them," he said. "So, tell me Detective, what is it that you want to remember? The memo from the department requested that I assist you in remembering an event. How long ago did the event occur?" He leaned forward poised to write.

Weeks sat straight up and inhaled. "I want to remember what a potential suspect looked like from a ten to fifteen minute meeting almost two years ago, in a dimly lit room."

Fuller jotted the information down, "Do you think you had a good look at this suspect, or was it more general?"

Weeks cracked her neck, "I'm not sure." She paused. "I think I had a good look at him, but can't be certain. Besides, a lot has happened since then, and things sort of run together, if you know what I mean."

Fuller smiled, "I know exactly what you mean." He turned a small dial at the side of his desk and the room lights dimmed. "Okay, Ms. Weeks, relax. Lay back, close your eyes, and start taking long, slow, deep breaths. Clear your mind. Your body is starting to relax."

Weeks followed his instructions. All that could be heard in the office was the ticking of the grandfather clock beside the bookcase.

"That's right, nice long deep breaths. You're becoming calmer. You're relaxing. You feel the tension and stress leaving your toes. Good, keep breathing slowly, deeply. You're becoming more relaxed. You can feel the tension and stress leaving your ankles…"

Weeks could feel her mind and body slipping, falling deeper and deeper into a warm comfortable place, a place she hadn't been to in ages. All her cares began to leave her.

She was relaxed and calm.

After eight minutes of the same mantra, Fuller continued, "You are totally relaxed. You feel good. You feel safe. You are in your warm happy place. Okay, Ms. Weeks we're going back to the time in question. You and your partner Mickey O'Dell are at a house. In that house there is a young man. Can you see him?"

"Yes."

"Good, now carefully look around the room. What do you see?" He leaned closer in case she whispered. Sometimes people under hypnosis would whisper because they were afraid of being overheard. "I see some cheap artwork, a black velvet painting of Elvis. There's a really tacky cuckoo clock on the next wall. Then a stained bedspread hung over a picture window. Then a door next to a closet with no door."

"Good, Ms. Weeks, you're doing excellent. Okay, what else is in the room?"

She paused, cocking her head to one side. "There's a small television sitting on an old milk carton. There's a china cabinet with one of the sliding panes broken, and on top is an overfilled ashtray. The smell of cigarette smoke is overpowering. There's a thrift store rejected couch with a sleeping bag on it in front of the TV. Next to it is a mismatched recliner."

"Very good, Ms. Weeks. Now, who is in the room with you?"

She licked her lips. "My partner, Mickey O'Dell is there. He's upset at Hooper. He's Mickey's CI. And there's a young man laying face down on the floor."

"Excellent. Now focus in on the young man on the floor. What does he look like?"

Again, she moistened her lips. Her mouth was dry. “I can’t see very well, the room is dim, and the man is wearing black.”

“That’s okay. What happens next?”

She shifted her body on the recliner. “Hooper kicks the kid.” She winces. “Then he reaches down and hauls him up. O’Dell laughs because the kid has peed his pants. I can see his face; he’s been crying. He’s tall, over six feet, maybe two hundred plus pounds. Fair complexion, blondish hair. High cheek bones, almost Scandinavian. He has perfect teeth, blue eyes and a small birthmark on the right side of his jaw, sort of a strawberry.”

“That is excellent, detective. Is there anything else about the youth that stands out in your mind? “Fuller asked.

Weeks shifted several times on the recliner and her head moved from side to side. She grimaced.

“I think I see some sort of a tat on his left hand or wrist area. It’s dark, so it’s not entirely clear. It sort of looks like the number eight…only it’s not.”

“Is there anything else?”

Weeks shifted again and smacked her lips. “I’m not seeing anything else. No, that’s all I can see. I’ve got to get out of the house. The smell is making me sick.”

“Okay, detective, when I count to three, you’ll be wide awake and feeling refreshed. You will remember everything that you have told me, down to the last detail. Okay, One…” he paused. “Two…and three and you are wide awake.”

He studied Weeks intently as she rubbed her eyes. “How do you feel?”

Weeks positioned the recliner in the upright position, and instinctively cracked her neck “Wow, how long was I out?”

Fuller smiled. "You were under for about thirty minutes. And you said you would be difficult to hypnotize?" He laughed softly. "Sometimes when a person really wants to find something lost in the mind, they lower their guard and hypnotism becomes easier."

Weeks shrugged. "You're good, Doc, I'll give you that. I was convinced that I couldn't be put under." She leaned forward and placed her head in her hands, elbows resting on her thighs. She ruffled her hair. "I remembered what the perp looked like. That's amazing. Thank you, Doc. You may have helped us find this guy."

Weeks stood up and stretched, her eyes now fully adjusted to the bright light in Fuller's office. She glanced at her watch. "Shit, look how late it is. I've got to run." She reached across the desk to shake Fuller's hand then pulled it back unsure if shaking was the correct thing to do. She paused to look at Fuller with his full head of gray hair. "Thank you, Doc, you've been a tremendous help. If I ever need my head read, I'll know where to come." She turned away and briskly walked to the glass exit door, looked back at him, smiled and left.

CHAPTER

20

THE CONTAINER PUB was a small portside bar off Powell Street, two blocks from the waterfront, and one of Ford's new favourite haunts. Inside, Ford felt at home with the down-and-outs, the hookers, and the dock workers because he knew that none of them were going to kill him. He was surprised that at ten-thirty in the morning there were so many people. As he watched the plump barmaid cleaning off tables, Ford pondered several things. Everything from killing Weeks to getting even with Seven to using his unique skill-set and contracting himself to the highest bidder. He knew that he had a talent for killing that was in demand within the gang world, but Ford also knew that could be short lived if he wasn't careful. He would have much to learn. And then there were the cops. He didn't know how connected they were to the gang world.

He replayed the events of the previous day in his mind. The dustup at the casino was front and centre in his mind; part of him was pissed at himself for not letting the thugs in the car kill Seven, and another part of him patted himself on the back for reserving that honor for himself. Alverez had told him that no self-respecting gang hangs a prospect or a member out to dry, and those that sent him into Hooper's house unarmed had to be held accountable. In Ford's mind, Seven and Nineteen had to pay, so pay they would.

Ford nursed his glass of beer while watching himself in the dusty mirror behind the bar. He knew that Seven or Nineteen wouldn't easily recognize him if they saw him. He had bulked up physically. He had developed a sense of style, and his confidence had quadrupled. He now was a force to be reckoned with.

"Hit me again, Jomo." He slid the empty glass towards the large Jamaican bartender.

"You got it, mon," he replied.

Ford watched as Jomo deftly tapped off a glass, allowing the foam to overflow only slightly before sliding it towards him. It stopped right next to his left hand. Ford nodded his approval. The bartender smiled a toothy grin.

Ford froze as he was about to pick up his fresh drink. In the mirror he saw two Metro cops enter the bar. His heart rate instantly shot up and his breathing became shallow. Were they here for him, or was it just a routine stop?

They approached the bar. The tall, older officer motioned to Jomo, who immediately left the bar through the swinging doors of the kitchen. The two cops followed close behind. Ford relaxed. He guessed they were here to see Jomo. He casually sipped his beer. A few minutes later the two cops emerged and hastily walked out of the bar. Jomo returned a few minutes later. Ford looked at the dark skinned man, his dreadlocks tied back in a ponytail. "Everything okay?" He asked.

Jomo shrugged. He grabbed a cloth to wipe the bar towards Ford. "I see those two leeches once a month, regular as clockwork."

Ford leaned forward. "You doing this voluntarily, or are they shaking you down?"

Jomo looked around; he then made his way closer to where Ford was sitting. "They tell me that if I don't pay them, they're going to have me deported back to Jamaica. And that if I report them then I'm dead."

"So, they're blackmailing you," Ford said after another sip.

"Yep. What can I do?" He shrugged again.

Ford took another swig. "Kill the fucking pigs, is what I'd do. But that's me. They're just a couple of low life bastards who don't deserve to breathe the same air as you."

Jomo looked at Ford. "What do you mean?" Jomo again shot a quick glance up and down the bar to see who was listening to their conversation, then he leaned in. "You know of somebody who can help poor Jomo?"

Ford winked at him. "I might. All depends on the price?" He took another drink. "How much is the shakedown?"

Jomo was uneasy. "You're not a cop, are you?"

Ford shook his head. "Not fucking likely, my friend."

"They first wanted five hundred a week. Then, about three months ago, they raised it to a thousand a week. They're breakings poor Jomo."

Ford grinned at the black man, "Let me look into a couple things, and I'll get back to you. If I can arrange something, it'll cost you ten grand. Can you handle that?"

Jomo grinned. "Jomo will find the money. You let me know anytime soon?"

"Yeah man," Ford said finishing his beer. "Later this afternoon." He clenched his fist and they bumped knuckles. Jomo smiled. "You know the names of these two pigs?"

"Yah mon. The big one is a Wellsley and other one is a

Caterwelt, they work from the East Hastings cop shop."

Ford nodded and stood up. "I'll be back in an hour or two." Then, he turned and walked out into the bright sunshine.

He stopped and put on his sunglasses and looked up and down the street. Ford walked toward his car. The street was busy with all manner of folks going about their business. His eyes were peeled for the cops who obviously worked this part of town. They'd be easy to locate.

Ford pulled onto the street and began to cruise the downtown east side. The radio was playing some righteous tunes as he pulled onto Gore. Just down the block on the left was a small diner, and Ford saw a patrol car parked in the alley beside the building. He found a parking spot nearby and got out. Waiting for traffic to ease, Ford darted across the street and casually walked towards the eatery. He stopped to look at the menu posted in the window, and easily spotted two uniformed cops sitting in a booth. Ford took a deep breath and entered. He walked up to the cashier.

"Can I get a black coffee to go please?" He asked the cute waitress, who nodded. Ford calmly turned to check out the interior and his eyes fell on the two cops eating god only knows what. It looked disgusting. *This is too easy. Cops are so predictable.* Ford pulled a toonie from his pocket and slid it to the young girl.

"That'll be a dollar sixty-eight, please."

"Keep the change," Ford said, grabbing his coffee.

Outside, Ford began to walk back to his car. He passed the alley and saw a homeless man going through the garbage bin. He whistled. The man turned toward him. Ford held up his coffee cup. "Wanna coffee?" The man nodded his head. Ford handed him the coffee and smiled, then left the alley.

Back in his car, Ford patiently waited for the two cops to finish their disgusting looking lunch and get back to work. His plan was to follow them until he got a sense of their routine.

By two-thirty in the afternoon, Ford had learned that Jomo wasn't the only one being extorted. What galled him was they weren't even trying to hide what they were doing. Ford shook his head. He knew he could help Jomo with these two assholes. He found a parking spot just off Powell Street then walked to the Container Pub. It took his eyes several seconds to adjust from the bright sunlight in the dimly lit bar. He saw an open stool and parked his butt on it. Jomo saw him enter and came over to him.

"You found somebody already?" Jomo asked, looking around.

Ford leaned forward. "Yep. Did you find the ten grand?"

Jomo winked at him, "Yes, I did." He grinned. "Who's going to do it?"

Ford just held out his hand and smiled, "Me." Jomo grinned and motioned with his head to follow him. Ford got off the stool and followed Jomo into the kitchen. He followed Jomo through a heavy wooden door that lead to his office. Once inside, Ford couldn't believe his eyes.

Jomo had what appeared to be a luxury suite. Leather sofas, a massive dark oak desk, a state of the art Bose stereo system, marble flooring, and a pool table. The walls were paneled in dark mahogany, and behind his desk he had the flag of Jamaica inlaid with expensive looking tile. It was very striking. Ford instantly thought he should have asked for more money.

Jomo slid into his high back leather manager's chair

and pulled open the bottom left drawer of this desk. "We have a deal, yes?" he said, reaching in and pulling out a fat envelope.

Ford was just settling into the black wingback leather chair in front of the desk, and Jomo's directness took him a bit aback. "Yes. We have a deal, Jomo. Five thousand now, and the other half on completion of the task. No questions asked."

Jomo flashed a wide grin as he produced a fat envelope. He opened it up and pulled out a wad of hundred dollar bills and quickly counted off fifty. "You care to count'm?" he asked.

Ford shook his head no. "A wise man once told me life is much easier if you start from a position of trust and operate that way until you can't."

Jomo bundled up the wad of bills and handed them to Ford. "He's a wise man, indeed."

Ford stood up and accepted the wad of money. "I'll be back for the balance in a day or two." He saluted with his finger and left the plush office. He felt great having a large wad of money in his jeans. The phrase 'I'm the king of the world' zipped through his mind. His step was light and his mood was upbeat as he exited the grubby pub. It was still bright out, so he donned his shades, strutted towards his car, and a grin enveloped his face.

Ford stopped on Robson Street at the Walnut Hut Internet Café and ordered a Venti triple mocha espresso with easy whip. He logged into the computer and punched up Canada 411 and keyed in 'Wellsley' and waited. The computer spooled up thirty individuals with the last name Wellsley. Ford was disappointed. The pimple-faced clerk brought his mocha to the station. Ford thanked him and sat back.

Ford keyed 'Metro Vancouver Police' into the search line and hit enter. He searched the site for several minutes until he found what he wanted. Ford tried to access the site, but was blocked by user ID and password restrictions. Frustrated he slammed his fist on the keyboard, which drew stares from several other users around him. Ford looked around and smiled when he saw a young guy sitting in the back, oblivious to what he had just done. He got up, grabbed his coffee and went over to the guy. "Hey buddy, you think you can help me out?"

The kid looked up at Ford and pulled his iPod ear plugs from his ears. "What did you say, man?"

Ford took a deep breath. "I asked if you could help me out."

"With what?"

"I need to get into the Metro Police web site. You know anyone who has that skill?"

The kid sat up and looked around. "Nope, don't see anyone."

Ford didn't like people who played games. "Look kid, I'll make it worth your while? How much?"

The kid was looking at the screen as he nimbly worked the contents of the site. "That's a fairly easy hack, so three hundred bucks. I've been in there before!" He boasted.

"Deal," Ford said with a grin. "I'm logged in over there.

The kid looked at Ford with his hand out. "No pay, no play."

Ford reached into his pocket and separated a few bills from the wad and handed them to the kid, then pointed to the computer. The kid took the money and moved over to

Ford's computer. With lightening speed, he manipulated the information on the police web site. Then he reached into his pocket and pulled out a small, narrow box, like one that a fine pen set would come in. He quickly extracted a small device that looked like an eraser and plugged it into the back of the computer. He clicked the mouse several times and another screen opened up. The kid keyed a numbered sequence into the device, pressed enter, and sat back.

Ford was amazed at what he saw. "So that's it?" He asked as the computer screen showed a small sub-window open with numbers flashing through it.

"Yep, this little baby will crack that access in ten minutes, give or take, so relax Mister. Your coffee is getting cold." The kid plugged his earphones into his ears, pressed play on his iPod, and sat back.

Ford found an empty chair and a copy of the Sun newspaper then sat down to wait. He hated waiting, and his dislike for nerds hadn't diminished, even though one was helping him. Ford started to read the cartoons and time slipped effortlessly by. Before he knew it, the kid was standing in front of him. Ford saw the small device in his hand.

"It's a flash drive with the access codes for their site. Enjoy," the kid said, before he returned to his own computer. Ford smiled as he accepted the drive.

"Thanks kid, but what do I do with this?" Ford asked seriously.

The kid looked at him in disbelief, "Are you kidding me. It goes into a USB port." He pointed to the four small slots on the front of the computer, "It goes in there. After that just follow the prompts. You know what a prompt is, don't you?"

Ford nodded that he did. He plugged the drive into a USB

port and presto, access was granted to the Metro Vancouver Police employee's web site. He found the employees' screen where names were listed alphabetically; he highlighted the Ws and pressed enter. Instantly, the screen brought up all the police whose last name started with W. Ford ran his eyes down the list until he found Wellsley. There were three of them listed.

Ford cursed under his breath at the parents for naming all the kids with the same first name letter. In this case, they were Lionel, Leonard and Lester. He clasped his hands behind his head and looked skyward. He'd need to come up with another plan. Ford quickly jotted down the home addresses of all three cops named Wellsley then he searched for Caterwelt. This one was easy; there was only one listed. Ford wrote down his address and logged off the computer. He looked to the back of the café. The kid was still wrapped up in whatever he was doing and was three hundred bucks richer for only ten minutes work, but Ford considered it a worthy investment. Ford finished his coffee and was struck with an idea. He quickly wrote down his cell number on a piece of paper then walked over to the kid.

"What's your name, dude? Mine's Ford. I might need your services again."

"Bradley, but they call me The Boa 'cause I can crush any computer's security systems."

"You gotta number I can call, Boa?"

Bradley scrawled a number onto a sticky note and handed it to Ford.

"Tell you what, Boa. How about I put you on retainer? Say, five hundred bucks?" He watched as the Boa's attention peaked. "Sure man, whatever you need." His eyes widened as Ford peeled off ten fifty-dollar bills.

"But you fuck with me and you're dead meat, understand, Boa?" Ford smiled leaning in and placing the wad of money in his hand.

"Don't worry, I only fuck with computers," He said sticking out his hand to shake on the deal. Ford smiled, then turned and left the café, lighting a smoke as he walked back to his car.

Ford knew that he had to figure out which one of the Wellsley dudes was the one shaking down Jomo. He needed to talk to Jomo to see if he knew the guy's first name as he didn't get a good look at the faces of the two cops. But first he would head into Burnaby to Caterwelt's place. He knew the area, so figured it would be easy enough to find.

Rush hour traffic in Metro Vancouver was a bitch at the best of times, and really screwed up when accidents happened. Ford ran into a four car pile-up on the Lougheed Highway, which turned the road into a parking lot. *At least it's sunny,* Ford mused and turned up the volume on his stereo.

It took Ford almost an hour to reach the Royal Oak exit ramp. He sped up the hill on Royal Oak and turned left on Kingsway, heading toward New Westminster. Twenty minutes later he was parked three houses down from Caterwelt's, at the corner of Stride Avenue and 15th Street. The older bungalow with the brick façade had one entrance, and Ford had a perfect view. The large trees separating the adjacent property provided him with the ideal cover. The back yard of Caterwelt's property was huge and wide open. Ford knew he would have to wait until darkness to complete this portion of the contract. He saw a doghouse beside the back door, which meant that the dog needed to be taken out to do his business at some point. He settled in to wait. The tinted windows in his car provided him with enough security to avoid being noticed by nosy neighbors. Ford looked at his watch. It was almost six-thirty so he anticipated that he likely had about an hour until Caterwelt would be home.

At ten after eight, Ford noticed a red Monte Carlo pulling into the driveway. He grabbed his binoculars and focused in on the occupant. *Now it begins*, he thought, reaching under the seat for his piece. He quickly screwed on the silencer and laid the completed weapon on his lap. The sun was almost set, providing enough cover to leave the car. Ford got out of the car, tucked the gun into his pants as he walked swiftly to the trees. He edged his way down the tree-line until he was opposite the rear door. Leaning up against a tree, he waited. He lit a smoke to calm his nerves.

Nine o'clock ran into ten o'clock, and then eleven. Ford was ready to give up when he saw the back door open. His heart rate spiked and his palms became sweaty as he removed the safety from his Glock. Stepping out of the shadows, he had a clear unobstructed firing line at the rear door. Moments later, a large German shepherd bounded out of the house.

Ford froze in his tracks. Taking a deep breath, he moved quickly back into the shadows, his eyes fixed solidly on both the dog and the back door. The dog ran around the yard, happy to be out of the house. Then, Caterwelt appeared in the back door. Ford could see he was watching his dog. The German shepherd disappeared into the front yard, which brought Caterwelt out of the house onto the back deck. He called to his dog three or four times.

Ford sensed his opportunity and stepped from the shadows, leveled the Glock at Caterwelt, and squeezed the trigger three times in rapid succession. All three shots found their mark in Caterwelt's chest. Ford saw him slump backwards against the house, then slide to the ground. He took out his phone and quickly took a picture. Ford knew he was dead. As he was removing the silencer from his gun the German shepherd lunged at him seemingly from nowhere. Its large white teeth bared and the only thing between him and the dog was the fence. Ford was scared so shitless that he fell backwards against a small tree then finally to the ground. He frantically picked himself up, stashed his gun in his pants and bolted for his car. The German shepherd was barking loud enough to wake the dead as Ford hopped into his car, started the motor and sped down the street away from the noise. Moments later, away from the scene he was able to breathe normally. He hated fucking dogs. *One down, one to go, he thought.* He grinned.

CHAPTER

21

THE MORNING BRIEFING of the Metro Police detectives was just underway when Police Chief Walter Von Pleth walked into the assembly room. The room fell silent. He walked to the front where Lamp was going over case assignments.

"Chief Von Pleth...this is a surprise...welcome," Lamp said as he stepped from the dais. He hated when the Chief pulled his surprise visits. "The podium is yours sir." Lamp quickly poured Von Pleth a glass of water.

Von Pleth shook Lamp's hand and quietly said, "I wish it was under better circumstances." Von Pleth had not aged well. He was fifty-eight years old, but looked nearly seventy. His balding head and wire rimmed glasses made his critics liken him to Colonel Klink on Hogan's Heroes.

"Ladies and gentlemen, thank you for the opportunity to speak to you this morning. Our family has lost another member in the most tragic of ways." He paused for effect; all eyes were now fixed on him. "Last night about eleven-thirty p.m. the body of Officer Lesley Caterwelt was discovered shot to death at his residence in Burnaby. I have conveyed our deepest sympathy to his wife Doris and their two children, Andrew and Monica. The Integrated Homicide Investigation Team (IHIT) will assume command, so any leads you develop need to be turned over as soon as possible. As of this minute *everyone* is working this case. Talk to your CIs; see what they know or have heard. No lead will go uninvestigated." He took a short drink. "Detectives, this was a targeted hit. There's no doubt in my mind. So the ramifications of this are enormous, as it affects all of us. We have to assume that someone, or some group, is targeting police. We have, in essence, been dragged into a war, a war that we must not, and will not, lose. Not while I'm in charge." He stopped to look at the bewildered faces of the assembled detectives. "If any media want to talk to you, please don't. Refer them to the Police Information Officer. We don't want distractions on this. Any questions?"

Lamp moved beside the stand to field questions, "Yes, Wheaton."

The young officer in the fourth row stood up. "Is Internal Affairs going to be looking into this?"

Von Pleth looked at Lamp, then at the young officer. "Yes, they will. It's standard operating procedure. When a police officer is killed, especially under suspicious circumstances, IA investigates."

Lamp saw another hand shoot up. "Yes, Officer Healy. What's on the mind of the police union?"

"Will you advise IA that the union will be defending Officer Caterwelt during this investigation, just as we're doing for Detective O'Dell? They cannot run roughshod over our rights as a matter of convenience."

Von Pleth held up his right hand. "Hold on, Detective Healy. Nobody is going to trample on anyone's rights. IA is merely looking into the backgrounds of the officers to see if there is anything that could explain why these two fine officers died. Nothing more, nothing less."

Healy stood up. "With all due respect, Chief Von Pleth, IA has a checkered history of forgetting about the rules and exercising very poor judgment in at least six of their last ten investigations. So, why should the union expect anything different in these two cases?"

Weeks could see that Von Pleth was beginning to get upset with the accusations being leveled by the union representative, but being the Chief of Police required that he handle difficult questions at the worst times.

"Detective Healy, this isn't the place to discuss the merits or shortcomings of IA, but I can assure you and the union that IA will conduct itself with the utmost of professionalism. That, you have my word on." He looked at Lamp, then back at the group. "Sergeant Lamp, if there are no more questions, I have to leave. The mayor is holding a press conference at ten-thirty."

Lamp looked at the group and saw a hand up at the back. He made eye contact with the detective and shook his head. The hand came down.

"Thank you Chief Von Pleth. I'm sure everyone in the room feels sorrow about the death of Officer Caterwelt. I didn't know him personally, but I'm sure he was a fine officer. Thank you for conveying the condolences of the department to the family. Good luck with the mayor's press conference." Lamp extended his large hand to the chief, who shook it vigorously.

Lamp and the thirty-two detectives watched as Von Pleth walked out of the room. When the door closed, Lamp brought his attention back to the revised agenda. "Okay, people, you heard the chief. Put everything on the back burner except for O'Dell's case and Caterwelt's. Leave no stone unturned. No detail is unimportant. No lead is too insignificant. Everything you learn gets run up the flagpole to determine its relevance."

Lamp looked around the room to find where Weeks was sitting. "Ah, there you are Weeks. Have you sat down with Bropal to see if we get some art on your suspect?"

"It's the first thing I plan to do this morning. Any idea when we'll get ballistics on Caterwelt's shooting?" She asked.

Lamp walked to the first row of chairs. "Medical Examiner Montgomery is at the Burnaby morgue as we speak. He's working closely with the coroner and, as soon as the autopsy is complete, the bullets will go for analysis and comparison. Do you think they're connected?"

"Well, Sarg is there any reason to think that they're not? Two cops shot to death within a week can't be coincidence. At least, not in my book anyway?" Weeks looked left and right at her colleagues; she could see genuine concern and fear on almost all the faces. She had known most of the detectives in the room for several years and it was the first time she saw panic in them.

"Well, let's not jump to any conclusions. Keep an open mind. That way, we don't miss anything. Okay people... let's hit the streets and phones. We're now on the clock. I expect that the mayor is going to say something crazy, like 'We'll have the guy in custody by the weekend'."

Lamp watched as the group rose in unison and began to file out of the room. As he watched, his cell phone rang. Lamp unlocked his phone and pressed the icon to answer it. "This is Lamp."

Lamp listened intently, then cupped the phone, and

whistled loudly. “Get everyone back in here right now,” He shouted. Lamp returned to his phone. “Are you absolutely positive about that? When was it discovered?”

The detectives filed back into the room, but chose to stand instead of sit.

“Okay, thanks, Peter. That’s good information.” He ended the call. “Okay listen up everyone, this is important.” He waited for a moment to ensure all eyes were trained on him and the room had quieted down. Lamp knew that the information would be very troubling to most of the detectives as most have families to worry about.

“That was Peter Donner on the phone. He’s with the department’s Technical Support Division. Last night someone hacked into the Metro Police Personnel Department’s web site. It appears the area that was breached was the employee records. They’re trying to track the IP address of the computer that was used.” The noise level ramped up immediately so Lamp stopped talking and held up his hand. “Quiet please.” He commanded. The room became silent again. “At this time we don’t know if any information was taken. It could have been a hacker just poking around or it could be more serious.” He moved to the side of the room, all eyes followed him. “So here’s what you need to do. Talk to your families and let them know to keep an eye out for any unusual activity around your residences. If someone is stalking police, they may get spotted casing your residences. Be aware of where you are. Check to see if you’re being followed. Be vigilant out there and at your homes.”

Lamp looked at a sea of alarmed faces. He could see concern, fear and outright panic and he didn’t blame them. “That’s all people, let’s get to work. One more thing, I know this isn't cool, but everyone wear your vests. That's an order."

He didn't wait around to watch them leave. Lamp exited a side door and made a beeline to his office down the hall. He entered his office, and Jeanie, his secretary, held up a stack of phone messages.

"Not right now, Jeanie. Get the chief for me." Inside his office, Lamp loosened his tie, sat down in his well-worn chair, and took a deep breath, knowing that once he told Von Pleth about the security breach he would explode as the system was his baby. He had convinced the city council to spend over a million dollars on it. The intercom buzzed.

"Chief Von Pleth on line two."

Lamp picked up the phone and punched the line two button. "Chief, not sure if you've heard this, but Peter Donner in tech support said the computer system got hacked last night. It looks like the only area accessed was employee records."

"Are you fucking kidding me? We spent over a million dollars to safeguard against that very thing. Goddamn it to hell, anyhow." Lamp held the phone away from his ear.

"Chief, Donner has got his people tracing the hack. Maybe we'll get lucky and ID the hacker. I'll keep you advised, but thought you'd want to know this in case anyone asks."

"Yes, I want to be kept in the loop. The last fucking thing we need is some whacko out there harassing our people at their homes. Thanks. I'll be making a call to Dylan Technologies to see how this system got hacked. They've got a shit load of explaining to do." Von Pleth ended the call, and Lamp replaced the phone in the cradle. *Wouldn't want to be the CEO of Dylan Technologies,* Lamp thought.

Shelley Weeks rode the elevator to the basement. She had been worried before that she might be a target, and the latest news tore at her very core. More than ever she was now sure someone would try to kill her. This belief added more urgency to what she needed to do, ID the punk from almost two years ago. She pushed the door open with a little more force than required and the door slammed into the stopper, making a lot of noise.

Mander Bropal jumped. He turned to see what was happening and saw it was Weeks. He breathed a heavy sigh of relief.

"Geez detective you scared the living crap out of me." He said, getting up from his workstation. "Don't ever do that again." He shook his pencil at her.

Weeks looked meekly at him. "Sorry Mander. Just a little worked up from our briefing. Did you hear? Another cop was killed last night. Caterwelt. Ever meet him?"

"Are you serious? How?" Mander asked sitting down.

Weeks pulled up a stool at his desk and sat down. "He was gunned down in his backyard at home."

"Holy crap, that's terrible. Poor bugger. Can't say that I ever met the man." Mander said, sitting down and taking a drink of his tea.

"The whole department is on tactical alert. We were also told that the department's personnel files were hacked into last night, so there might be others who're targeted. This scares the shit out of me. First my partner, now this guy? Whose next is what I want to know?" She could see that he was disturbed by the news and she felt sorry for him especially since he was somewhat disconnected from the events by being stuck in the basement. Weeks watched as Mander straightened himself up and assumed his 'proper British gentleman' persona.

"How did your session with the shrink go," he said. "You remember anything?"

Weeks cracked her neck. "Hell yeah! Doc says I nailed his damned ass. So let's get drawing, Mr. Artist," she said, trying to lighten the mood.

Mander shook his head and grabbed his computer pad and sat poised. "Well, go on. What did he look like?"

"Oh, sorry. You want me to start. Well, why didn't you say so? Geez I'm no mind reader," she said. They both forced a short laugh.

"Okay," Mander said. "Was his face round, oval, square jawed, high browed, what?" He exhaled deeply.

Weeks closed her eyes and willed herself to recall the details. "It was oval-ish. His face was oval, and his jaw tapered narrow at the chin." She beamed at the thought of actually remembering what he looked like. Weeks watched as he used the mouse to click on various face shapes, and he stopped on one he liked. "No, no. You've got the cheeks and chin too narrow. Widen them, and then taper it from just below the cheek bone." She studied the image as he quickly made the changes. "That's it! That's the shape of his face."

Mander beamed. "That is more like it. Finally we're getting somewhere."

An hour later, he turned the monitor to face Weeks.

"Is this your suspect?" he asked.

"Hello mystery man-child, remember me?" She smiled at Mander. "That's him. Can you add some small pimples to his face, around his nose area? Oh yah, he's got a small strawberry birthmark on his right jaw, a little larger than a quarter."

Mander nodded and quickly accessed the blemish file and dragged a small pimple file into the frame. In a matter of seconds he had pimples around the nose area and a strawberry on the jaw, "How's this?"

Weeks studied the image, "Fewer. And can you make the pimples smaller?" She watched as he adjusted the image content. "That's it, right there. That's the bastard right there! You nailed him, Mander. Good job."

"Ah, no. All I did was punch in the info you gave me. This is from your memory, Detective. Be happy that you could retrieve it. Here, I'll give you a printout. If you and Sergeant Lamp need me to send it out on the wire, just have someone call me. Glad I could help."

Weeks accepted the copy and safely tucked it into a manila folder, then extended her hand to Mander who shook it weakly. She hated sweaty palms. Smiling, she waved goodbye and headed upstairs to Lamp's office. Weeks looked at her watch. It had taken almost an hour and a half to complete the task, but the results were outstanding. Lamp would be happy.

The ride up to Lamp's office brought the reality of the situation back to Weeks, as her mind instinctively went to the startling revelation that the cop killer had accessed the records of all police members. The thought that she could be next weighed heavily on her mind as she got off on the 6th floor without realizing it. "Shit." She said aloud pressing the 5th floor button. "Come on Shelley get your shit together." She muttered under her breathe.

Weeks stood silently outside Lamp's closed door, waiting for him to get off the phone. He nodded, letting her know he wouldn't be long. She saw Lamp's lips moving and tried to pick up some hint as to what he was talking about. She slid the picture from the envelope. *The guy's just a kid. Where did he go wrong?* Weeks was lost in her thoughts when Lamp opened the door, startling the wits out of her. The image slid back into the envelope.

"You okay?" Lamp said as Weeks grabbed her chest.

"Damn, you scared the crap out of me." She said. She walked into his office and sat down in a chair opposite his large wooden desk. She dangled the folder. "We now have artwork on our suspect." She said proudly, producing the copy and giving it to Lamp.

Lamp studied the image intently, shifting his eyes between the kid in the mock-up and Weeks. "You sure this is the kid who was at Hooper's place?"

Weeks leaned forward. "According to the shrink and Mander's computer program, this is what I remember from our brief encounter with the kid."

"He doesn't look older than eighteen."

"Hooper said the kid told him he was seventeen or eighteen. That was almost two years ago so he'd be almost twenty now."

Lamp leaned back in his chair. "Twenty in gang years means he's likely hardened in ways only that lifestyle can provide. It's also possible he has left the gang or disappeared, or maybe he's dead? Until we find him, we won't really know, will we?"

Weeks looked down at the floor, "The scariest things about this kid that I remember were his eyes. He just stared at O'Dell and Hooper. And he was angry as hell at his situation, and mad at the world or himself. I couldn't tell which. I almost felt sorry for him."

Lamp leaned forward arms crossed on his desk. "So where are we at here?"

Weeks sat forward in her chair, "Where are we? That is a damn good question? We know that Hooper and O'Dell had a connection, so it's plausible that they were killed by the same person. Caterwelt, he's the odd man out here. I don't see a connection to O'Dell or Hooper? And we're looking for a young man who may or may not be involved in this. For all we know O'Dell and Hooper could be gang related and Caterwelt, maybe job related or personal?"

Lamp was still leaning back, "That's pretty much my read as well. You worried about the information breach?"

Weeks sat back, "Naturally, but as you said, we don't know what information, if any, was taken. I'll be careful."

"That's the spirit." Lamp leaned on his desk, "It's important that you get this image out to all police departments in the lower mainland. The sooner they get their eyes on this, the sooner we can locate and bring him in."

Weeks got up and stood motionless for a second. "Let's hope so. If it's not this kid, then who the hell could it be?"

Lamp rose and stood at his desk, palms down on the blotter. "That's why I ordered everyone to wear their damn vests. Nobody knows who the shooter is."

Weeks shook her head and quickly left Lamp's office. Lamp called out to her, "You're going to partner with Mills for now. You two should get along just perfectly." Weeks waved her hand as she headed for her desk. Sitting down, she saw that Lamp was chuckling to himself. *Mills...Not him. His body odor was so bad...Thanks, Sarg.*

She picked up the phone and dialed Mander's number. It

rang three times before he answered. "Hi Mander, this is Weeks. Send the artwork to every police agency in the lower mainland. Also, send it to the Police Information Office with priority one status. They'll need it for the media release." Then she hung up the phone.

Weeks met her new partner, Brent Mills, in the parking lot. It was nearly eleven o'clock, and they needed to get out on the street. She had taken her notebook that contained all the gang contacts she had made in the last five years. It was time to reach out and touch them to see if they knew her suspect.

As the pair pulled out of the police parking lot, they were engaged in conversation, and did not see the Mustang pull out three cars behind them.

CHAPTER 22

FORD MET JOMO before the bar opened up. He showed him pictures of the three officers. "Which one of these is the guy?"

Jomo looked at the three pictures. "This one." he said, pointing to Leonard Wellsley. Ford looked hard at Jomo. "Okay then, I just wanted to make sure I hit the right guy. Wouldn't do my reputation any good if I hit the wrong dude, now would it?" He grinned.

Jomo looked again at the computer printout. "Yes it's him. No doubt about it. How can I forget a scumbag like him?"

Ford stared at Jomo. "As long as we're on the same page, 'cause the next time I come in, this asshole will be dead as a fuckin' door nail and your problem with these two pieces of work will be over." He picked up the picture and walked quickly from the bar into the west coast morning.

He put his toque on to protect his newly shaven head from the driving rain. His mind was rehearsing the hit. The Wellsley that had to die lived in Abbotsford.

Ford nosed his Mustang into the traffic and soon was on the freeway heading east. Traffic was light leaving Vancouver, so he was able to move rapidly without drawing attention. Thirty-five minutes later, he took the McCallum Street exit and headed into downtown Abbotsford. Ford stopped at the first gas station he saw to pick up a Timmy's coffee and to program his GPS with Wellsley's address. Then he headed north towards 2657 Cyril Street.

The street was almost deserted, which surprised Ford, especially since it was almost ten o'clock in the morning. The GPS coordinates led him directly to Wellsley's house, which stood out from the surrounding houses on the street. His eyes were taking in everything about the street. Trees, sightlines from neighboring houses, escape routes, shooting positions, all the things he needed to commit to memory to be successful.

Unable to see the back of the house, Ford drove up the inclined road, making his way to George Ferguson Way, which was higher up the hill than Cyril Street. He parked the car and took out his binoculars. He smiled. Ford saw the perfect perch to complete his task, if he chose to do it here. Ford went back to his car and got his digital camera and quickly snapped off several pictures of the area, then drove away.

By one-thirty, Ford was back in Vancouver and parked off East Hastings Street, three blocks from the precinct where Wellsley worked. He took an old hat and dirty army jacket from the trunk and changed, then walked the short distance to the police station. Across the street from the station was a small encampment of homeless people in an empty lot where a fire had destroyed a small restaurant. Ford settled in against a wooden power pole and waited. Tucked inside his jacket was Wellsley's picture, which was also seared into his mind.

Ford intently eyed every person leaving or entering the

building. As quickly as he scanned their faces, he dismissed them. Wellsley was forty-five years old, stood 6'4", and Ford guessed he weighed two hundred plus pounds. He also guessed that the easy life had left him with a well-established beer gut. Ford deduced that Wellsley wasn't a fashionista, judging from the department store suit he'd been wearing when the picture was taken. It fit him like a sack.

The rain had eased off to a drizzle, which made eyeballing the cops much easier. Ford dared not even go for a pee in case he missed Wellsley, so he held it. At four, there appeared to be a shift change, which resulted in a hoard of cops coming and going. Ford perked up when he saw someone that fit his mental image of Wellsley; he unfolded the picture to be sure. He grinned when he also saw Weeks walking out with him. *Two for one*. He fixed his eyes on Wellsley and followed him as he walked on the opposite side of East Hastings. Two blocks away on Main Street, Wellsley and Weeks parted company. Wellsley entered the four story car park.

Sensing an opportunity, Ford dashed across the busy street, slapping the hood of a car that almost ran him over. The driver gave him the one finger salute. Ford bobbed between two cars that had slowed down and sprinted towards the stairway of the parkade.

He took the steps two and three at a time and exited on the first floor. He quickly surveyed the open garage and didn't see Wellsley, so he made a beeline to the second floor.

Pausing to catch his breath he opened the orange door with a big number two painted on it and stepped through. His eyes shot left then right, he heard footsteps coming from the far end, causing him to look left again. Ford's heart rate elevated. He saw him. Ford checked out the rest of the parkade to see if there was anyone else around. Seeing nobody, he crouched down and quickly moved towards his target.

Ford was four cars away from Wellsley. He watched as Wellsley stashed his bullet proof vest and gun in his safe box in the trunk of his car. Ford pulled his 9mm from the back of his pants, twisted on the silencer and removed the safety. He took a quick look around then fired three shots into Wellsley. The first shot was to the backside of his head. The second shot was to his neck, and the third shot to the upper torso, just for good measure. He watched as the body slumped into the open trunk. Ford smiled. He took out his camera for proof of death evidence, then quickly walked over to the dead police detective and lifted his legs into the trunk and closed the lid shut.

Ford stashed his gun away and walked calmly toward the exit door. He remembered another lesson from Alverez. *If someone sees you looking around, they can assume you're up to something. So whenever you've finished a job, walk away as if nothing happened. No matter how scared you might be, you don't show it.* He never looked back.

Out on the street, the rain was coming down sideways and in buckets. Visibility was almost zero as Ford made his way to the crosswalk at the corner. He saw people scurrying to get out of the rain and wind, but he was content to just pull up his collar and pull his hat down to stop it from blowing away. He blended into the crowd and vanished.

At five-fifteen, Ford casually walked into the Container. It was crowded with people seeking shelter from Mother Nature's wrath. Ford edged his way to the bar and caught

Jomo's attention. Ford motioned towards Jomo's office. Jomo nodded and threw his bar towel at his young attractive barmaid. Ford watched him leave the bar and followed him into the kitchen. Nobody even glanced at them. Inside Jomo's office, Ford pulled out his camera and brought up the image of Wellsley's body with the fatal wound in the left side of his head, and showed it to Jomo. "I think this solves your problem, wouldn't you say?" he said, closing the camera and holding out his hand.

Jomo smiled. "Ah yes, you want your money. You've done your part of the bargain, now Jomo must too." He reached into the top drawer of his desk and pulled out a fat white envelope and tossed it to Ford. "It's all there, man. Count it if you don't trust Jomo."

Ford shook his head, catching the envelope with his right hand. "Thank you, Jomo. I don't think you'd be that stupid, would you?" Ford made a motion towards his back.

Jomo saw what Ford meant and rapidly shook his head. "No way mon! Jomo is not a stupid man," he said, flashing a toothy grin. "Jomo is a smart man. He knows who not to piss off, and you're one of them," Jomo said extending his hand. Ford looked at it and saluted Jomo. He turned away and walked out of his office, stuffing the fat envelope into his jacket inside pocket.

Sergeant Lamp had waited for the rain to subside before leaving for the day. He walked the two blocks to the parkade, where he had parked the family's Nissan Highlander, their only means of transportation. He pulled his collar tight to keep any warmth in where it was needed and put his head down to buffet the wind. Lamp quickly ascended the two flights of stairs to the second floor. All he wanted to do was get home and try to put this miserable day behind him. The parkade was almost empty, except for six or seven cars which Lamp recognized as belonging to the night shift. An unmarked police cruiser caught his eye, causing him to pause. *That car shouldn't be here. Wellsley left over two hours ago, said he had an appointment? Why is it still here?*

Lamp stopped and scratched his head. *Maybe he caught a ride?* Lamp took his cell phone from his belt pouch and brought up his contact list. He found Wellsley's home number and pressed the talk button. Lamp figured he would check with Wellsley's wife just to be on the safe side, considering what had just happened to Caterwelt. The phone rang three times before it was answered.

"Hi Barbara. It's Webber Lamp calling. Is Leo home yet?"

"Webber Lamp…Oh yah, you're Leonard's boss. I'm sorry, but Leonard isn't home yet. He had an appointment at four forty-five, so he's likely stuck in traffic. Why, is there something wrong?"

"No, but when he gets home will you have him call me."

"There is something wrong isn't there? After twenty years of being a cop's wife, we learn these things. Is Leonard okay? Has he been shot?"

"Honestly, Barbara, I don't know. It may be something, or it may be nothing. So could you have him call me when he gets home? Thanks, Barbara. I gotta run." Lamp closed his phone and returned it to its pouch. He slapped the hood of Wellsley's car and walked back to his own. *Maybe Wellsley's got someone on the side. What he does in his private life is none of my business* Lamp thought, as he got into his vehicle.

Dustin Ford pulled his car into the parking spot in front of his motel. It was ten minutes after six. Flush with cash, he was itching to spend it on drinks and women, but remembered another lesson from Alverez. *Don't do anything to draw attention to yourself. It's the surest way of getting caught or killed.* He got a soft drink from the vending machine and went into his room. Kicking his shoes off, he climbed onto the bed and stretched out on several pillows. He lit a smoke and turned on the TV and flipped through the channels. Finding nothing interesting to watch, he selected a local news channel and got comfortable. He allowed his mind to just wander, recalling the events of the day, when a news story caught his attention. He sat bolt upright. A picture came onto the screen, and a news reporter read the following:

"The metro police are looking for the public's help in identifying this person of interest. The person is a male, approximately eighteen or nineteen years old, approximately six feet tall, two hundred pounds, with shoulder length blonde hair and a stocky build. He has pimples around his mouth and a small strawberry birthmark on the right cheek and a tattoo of an eight on his left wrist. If you recognize the person in this picture, you're asked to give Metro Police a call, or call Crime Stoppers. Again, the police are asking for your help identifying this person of interest."

It was if he'd seen a ghost. He quickly sat up on the edge of the bed, trying to make sense of what he'd just seen. He walked over to the mirror and looked at himself. What he saw was someone totally different from the image on the TV, except for the goddamn strawberry birthmark. Gone was the long hair. His face had cleared up, and he had lost about twenty five pounds and grown about two inches. What he saw on TV was how he looked a couple of years ago, and a lot of water had passed under the bridge since then. Ford looked at his tattoo; it wasn't an eight it was an infinity symbol. Dummies?

Ford peeked out the window out of habit. *How did the cops get that image? Did someone rat him out? The gang? Who? And why now?* His mind raced over the possibilities without settling on one that made sense. Ford paced back and forth in the small room. Then it hit him. *Weeks. Detective fuckin' Weeks. She was the only one who had any knowledge of what he looked like back then. That's it. The bitch has put it together. The Numbers Gang wouldn't have ratted him out to the cops, as he was nothing to them.*

He finished his soda and tossed the can across the room, ringing it off the edge of the garbage can. The wheels in his brain were turning a million miles an hour. He needed a plan in case he was made. The first thing he needed to do was change his appearance even more than he had already. He tried to imagine what he'd look like with darker skin and maybe a goatee? Maybe a black goatee, sort of an Anton Le Vey-ish look, dark, mysterious and menacing and some makeup to hide the strawberry. He liked the idea. *Okay genius,* he thought. *How do you darken your skin?* He slapped his bald head. *Of course, idiot. Tanning booths, spray tan.*

Ford liked the plan that was coming together. He'd also need to change his clothes to reflect a totally different persona. Perhaps, all black, sort of gothic? He'd blend into the younger crowd looking like that. And he'd need a new identity. Dustin Ford would have to die, at least on paper, in a way that police would figure it out and stop looking for him, “Nah that’s a bad idea, plus it’s costly, with too many questions requiring answers,” he said aloud. He also needed more money.

Then he’d have to decide what he was going to do with Weeks. Up until now, he’d been willing to go easy on her out of respect, but this latest bullshit changed the whole ball of wax.

CHAPTER

23

WEBBER LAMP PULLED into the parkade at six-thirty a.m. and slowly drove up the ramp to the second floor. He was in a good mood. He had made love to his wife Eva the night before, something that didn't happen that often after thirty years of marriage. The sun shone, turning the west coast into the glimmering jewel that tourists raved about. All seemed right with the world.

He nosed his vehicle around the tight corner coming off the ramp and drove to his parking stall. As he turned the last corner, he caught sight of Wellsley's cruiser still parked where it had been last night. As he approached the rear of the vehicle, he spotted something red. He stopped immediately behind the Crown Victoria sedan and got out, leaving his door open and engine running.

Lamp cautiously walked to the back of the patrol car. Everything about the car looked normal, but his eyes keyed in on the small spots of red down the tail light and on the upper surface of the rear bumper.

His mood instantly changed. Gone were the pleasant thoughts of last night, the sunshine. He knew what blood splatter looked like. Lamp approached the trunk area and knelt down. Taking his pen out, he ran the tip through a spot of the reddish black substance and brought it up to his nose. He inhaled deeply, and then closed his eyes. It was blood. His police training kicked in. He grabbed his cell and called dispatch.

Lamp was leaning on his vehicle when the first police car, sirens wailing, turned into the parkade, followed closely by another. Shortly after, paramedics arrived via the fire department, followed later by an ambulance.

The first car came to a screeching stop a short ways away from Lamp, and two uniformed officers exited the vehicle, guns drawn. Lamp was unsure if the officers knew him, so he'd taken his badge out of his pocket and was holding it in the air. "I'm Sergeant Webber Lamp. I called it in, so you can put your guns down." The two young officers hesitated at first and then followed his instructions. The second police car had arrived and two older policemen got out. They instantly recognized Lamp.

"Put your guns away. He's one of us," The first older officer said as he walked over to Lamp then looked at the two younger officers. "You guys drive like raving maniacs, you know that?" He shook his head and returned his gaze to Lamp. "What's going on, Sarg? Who called it in?"

Lamp was relieved that he knew the two older officers, less explaining to do. "I did Frank. The car was here last night when I went home. This morning, I spotted blood splatter on the back. Something isn't right here. This is Leo Wellsley's cruiser. He was Caterwelt's partner. I'm sure you heard about his death. We need to get into the trunk. I hope to hell that I'm wrong."

Frank Rush was Lamp's age, "You think he's dead?" He said squatting by the rear bumper. "Certainly looks like blood splatter.

As they were talking, Lamp heard the air brakes being applied to the fire truck as it came to a stop at the entrance of the parkade. "What I need Frank, is this parkade sealed off, so get these young pups on security detail. Nobody goes in or out of this place unless they have a badge."

Sergeant Frank Rush had been a member of Metro Police for twenty four years and had been at hundreds of crime scenes, so he knew the routine. "You got it." He nodded at Lamp and went to talk to the younger officers. Within seconds, the officers hopped into their car and squealed away to take up their posts.

Four first responders came up the ramp and headed directly for the flashing lights on the patrol car. Carrying emergency packs, they stopped in front of Lamp and Rush. Captain Willy Jones of the Vancouver Fire Department set his pack down. "What have we got, gentlemen?"

Lamp explained it to Jones and his crew then he kneeled down beside the rear bumper of Wellsley's police car. "Any way of popping this thing?" he asked.

Jones turned to his crew. "Piece of cake. Stand back. We'll have it open in no time." Lamp complied, allowing the four men in turnout gear to assess the situation. There was a short conversation among the three firemen and one of them brought out a small pick from his pants pocket. The fireman placed the pick against the driver's front door glass and gave it a sharp rap with his hand. The glass exploded, sending shards everywhere. The sound reverberated in the empty parkade. The fireman then reached in and opened the door. Jones, being senior fireman of the crew, stuck his head inside the door, located the interior trunk release, and pulled the lever.

Lamp and Rush saw the trunk lid pop up and both quickly stepped forward. Lamp froze. He turned to Rush, who was obviously shocked. "I was afraid this was what we'd find," Lamp said, putting his hands on his hips and looked skyward. "Goddamn it to hell. What the fuck in going on here? He's the third cop in less than a week to be executed."

Rush leaned into the trunk. "If there's any consolation here, it's that he didn't suffer, judging from the shots." Rush rolled Wellsley's body onto his back. "Three shots in total."

Lamp looked down at the blood soaked body of Wellsley. "Fuck. I hate making these phone calls. Three shots you say? That's the same as the other two executions. Frank you think that might be our shooter's signature? Three shots?"

Rush stood over the body still in the trunk, his 6'5" frame made the full size sedan trunk look small. "These guys are pretty proud of what they do, so you might be right…three shots. But I'll bet a week's pay that the first shot was the kill shot, and the rest were to just put an exclamation point on it. You guys got any leads on this case yet?"

Webber Lamp was in a real sour mood, his mind racing at the speed of light considering how they could catch this bastard. "What did you say, Frank?"

"I said do you have any leads yet? You okay old friend?" Rush said, moving over to Lamp and leaning against his car. He knew that Lamp was taking this personally, as would every other cop in Metro command.

"We might have one, but I'm not holding out much hope. Detective Weeks, O'Dell's old partner, thinks she remembers a guy that she and O'Dell met a while back. I have other detectives going through all of O'Dell's cases, see if anything pops?"

Rush shook his head. "Buddy, don't hold your breath on that one. Christ that possibility is even thinner than how my butcher cuts my sandwich meat. So in essence, you've got squat."

Lamp looked at his old friend and smiled. "Right now, if I at least had squat, I'd consider us fortunate."

Fire Captain Jones approached the two policemen. "You guys need us for anything else here?"

Lamp looked at the gray haired Captain. "Nah, we're good. We've gotta wait for forensics and the coroner's office to come, so there isn't much to do here. Thanks for your help."

Jones patted Lamp's shoulder, "Think nothing of it. Just glad we could help." Jones donned his helmet and shouted to his men. "Saddle up." Then confidently strode towards the exit door.

Lamp's phone rang. It was Von Pleth. Lamp marveled at how bad news could travel so fast. "Lamp here. What's up, Chief?" he cradled the phone against his shoulder, while he lit a cigarette.

"I just heard over the radio that we've got another officer down. Is that true?"

"Yes Chief. Officer Leonard Wellsley's been shot in the parkade. Execution style. IA is going to be busy looking into this one as well."

"You sure it was an execution?"

"Yes Chief. Three taps to the head and torso; then stuffed into his own car trunk."

"Shit. The media is going to have a field day with this."

Lamp shook his head and closed his eyes. "I wouldn't

know anything about that, sir." He paused momentarily. "Any chance the media can be turned to be on our side on this one?"

"I don't see how, Webber. Any suggestions?"

"Just one, Chief. These fine law enforcement officers, they were people first and foremost, people who found a calling to serve and protect. Maybe if we presented it in that light, we'd elicit sympathy instead of negative media coverage?"

"That's a good idea, Lamp. Are you sure I can't convince you to work at the Public Affairs Department?"

"Not a hope in hell, Chief. Not a hope in hell. Chief, I gotta run here. The coroner just showed up, and I see our detectives coming as well, so we're going to be busy. I'll call you as soon as I get any new info." He heard the line go dead. He turned to Rush. "Can you believe that guy? He asked if I'd go to the PA Department. Shit, talk about a dumb-ass request." He stubbed his cigarette out in disgust and went to meet his detectives.

Detectives Wheaton, Healy, Rutherford, Weeks, Chou, and Lee stopped beside the patrol car with its lights flashing. Nobody spoke as Lamp approached the group. He could see that they knew and were visibly shaken by what they had learned.

Before he could open his mouth, Detective Healy said, "Is it true, Sarg? Has another officer been killed?"

Lamp eyed the group; all he could do was nod his head in the affirmative, then he inhaled deeply, the anger building within. "It's true. Officer Leonard Wellsley was gunned down right here in this parkade. It happened sometime last night as best, as I can figure."

Wheaton stepped away from the group. "Anything at the

scene to give us something to go on?"

Lamp shook his head. "I looked all over the place, no shell casings. So either the assassin is using a revolver or he's policing his brass."

Detective Eddy Chou, normally reserved, stepped up. "Are we sure it's a targeted hit? Any chance it could be random?"

Lamp lit up another cigarette and exhaled into the air. "Not a chance in hell. Three kill shots, all in the head and torso, same as Caterwelt. So, my guess is we're dealing with the same son-of-a-bitch."

Weeks felt herself welling up. "Was he married?" Her voice trembled.

Lamp heard the sound of Weeks' voice, "You okay Weeks?" He said snuffing out his cigarette. "Yes, he was married. I just talked to his wife, Barbara, last night, to see if he was home. Apparently they have three kids."

Weeks steadied herself. "Yah I'm okay Sarg. This is just getting a little too close to home for my liking."

Detective Danny Lee walked up behind Weeks and patted her on the shoulder. "It's hit us all pretty hard too, Sarg. We're all feeling the same thing. We want to get this bastard more than you know. Any chance his undercover work got him killed?"

Lamp shrugged his shoulders as he turned back to the team, "Beats me, Danny. He and Caterwelt were doing routine undercover work on two unrelated homicide investigations. Hell, I suppose it's possible. Right now, anything is possible. Maybe it was fucking extraterrestrials."

Danny Lee looked at the body in the trunk. "Where do we start, Sarg?"

Lamp surveyed the scene. "Forensics needs to go over

everything first, so as the Chief said, the cop killer is the only case anyone is working on." He eyed each of the detectives standing around the car. "Why the hell haven't you guys got your goddamn vests on? You think I was kidding when I gave that order?" He shook his head in disgust. "You want to end up like him?" He pointed to Wellsley's body.

The detectives looked at each other, sensing it wouldn't be wise to speak.

Lamp saw the Forensic Unit's van enter the second floor parkade. The nondescript white van pulled up alongside the police cruiser with its lights flashing. Two technicians in white lab coats exited the van and both went to the rear to gather their kits. He was glad that they showed up so he could turn the scene over to them and get to work.

Lamp walked the short distance to the station from the parkade.

Inside, the news of Wellsley's murder was on everyone's lips and he was besieged with questions as he walked to his office. Assistant Deputy Chief Peter Duncan came out of his office the minute he saw Lamp pass by the glassed-in office.

"Webber! In my office, now," He barked.

A surprised Lamp stopped short and pivoted around to see Duncan standing in his doorway, hands on hips. Peter Duncan was 44 years old with almost solid white hair. He stood 5'5" tall and was razor thin. The joke within the department was that he suffered from small man syndrome, and that he was a brown-noser. "What can I do for you sir?" Lamp said politely as he walked back to the Deputy Chief's doorway.

"Sergeant Lamp. Inside please." Duncan said waving towards a chair.

Lamp nodded, passing Duncan and taking a seat in an office that could have been used in a magazine. Not a paper clip out of place. He looked straight ahead as Duncan rounded his desk and slid his slender frame into his shiny new manager's chair. There was a long tortured silence that seemed to never end.

"Why is it, Sergeant Lamp that I'm the last to know things around here? Why do I have to hear all about cops getting shot from the Chief? You ever hear of a little thing called the chain of command? I think I've earned that right… that respect."

Lamp didn't like the Assistant Deputy Chief because he would not think twice about throwing an officer under the bus if it meant recognition for himself, and the Assistant Deputy Chief knew it, along with all the other detectives in the department. As far as Lamp was concerned, Duncan was a back stabbing weasel that could not be trusted. "Well, Assistant Deputy Chief, that's something that you'll have to take up with Chief Von Pleth. I was just following his explicit orders that he wants to be the first to know. Especially concerning any deaths of police officers." Lamp stood to leave. "Is there anything else Assistant Deputy Chief? If not, I've got a killer to catch. Unless there's something else you'd like me to do instead?"

Duncan stood to face Lamp, "Sergeant Lamp, the day will come when I'm all you've got to keep your job. I think you know how that will end up. No, I don't have anything else. So please, go catch the killer."

Lamp glared at his immediate boss and bit his lower lip so that he wouldn't speak his mind. Mustering his etiquette, he smiled and said "Thank you," then abruptly turned and strode to his office, knowing that this meeting would be entered into Duncan's little black book. For now, Lamp didn't care, as his next pressing duty was to let Wellsley's wife know that her husband was dead.

CHAPTER

24

THREE DAYS AFTER Wellsley's death, Dustin Ford came out of the tanning salon feeling refreshed and alive. He'd found a tropical themed salon along the Fraser Highway that was new and not too busy. Ford agreed to the spray tan after he had a foundation tan in place. He had dyed his goatee black, and had tanned nearly nine times. He was getting darker. Ford had also frequented the costume stores on Columbia Street stocking up on different wigs, glasses, and teeth inserts. He had purchased multiple changes of clothes from the A&N Department store.

To find out how effective his disguises were, that morning he sat directly across from Felix Seven in an IHOP restaurant in Surrey and he wasn't noticed. Ford had even said good morning to Seven and Nineteen, who just nodded back to him.

After breakfast, Ford tailed Seven and Nineteen as they made their rounds to the various drug dealers, dropping off supplies and picking up bags of cash. As he drove, Ford mused about how easy it would be to take their cash and run. For most of the day Ford drove around in the bright west coast sunshine, following the two gang members and waiting for his chance to force a meeting. He had been working on a strategy for the past week, and the more he thought about it, the better he liked it. He would pretend that nothing happened and get in with them and wait for his chance to deal with Seven.

Ford pulled his Mustang alongside the curb and cut the engine. Seven sat behind the wheel of his black Escalade, while Nineteen went into the stately mansion in a tony Morgan Creek subdivision. Sensing his opportunity, Ford got out of his car and walked directly towards the Escalade. He could see that Seven had taken notice and assumed he had a gun at the ready. To avoid getting shot, Ford lifted his arms about chest high, but kept walking towards the vehicle.

He came to a stop at the front of the vehicle. Ford just stood there and said nothing, waiting for Seven to make the first move. He didn't have to wait long. Seven quickly opened the door and exited the vehicle, gun ready and aimed at Ford.

"What the fuck do you want, asshole?" Seven said cockily.

Ford grinned, but remained silent.

"What's so funny, motherfucker? You want me to shoot your ass?"

Ford shook his head. "Seven, Seven, Seven. You haven't changed one fucking bit, and you're still a cocky little prick. You don't remember me?"

Seven moved even closer to Ford. "Should I, asshole? Who the fuck are you?"

"You sent me to kill a motherfucker with an empty gun. Ring any bells, asshole? I'll bet you thought I was fuckin' dead."

Ford eyed Seven intently for any sign of recognition. Seven shook his head, "Enough fuckin' games, asshole.

Who - the fuck - are you?"

Ford lowered his arms. "I'm the newbie that you sent to kill Hooper about a year and a half ago."

Seven started to rack his memory; then a light bulb came on. "Ah, now I'm remembering your fuckin' name. Ford, isn't it? Yah, Dustin fuckin' Ford."

Ford smiled. "That's right, motherfucker. You guys bailed on me when Hooper caught me. By the way, thanks for coming to get me out, I really appreciated that."

"So, where the fuck have you been? Couldn't have been around here, or my sources would have told me. So where were you?" Seven said, stashing his gun in his pants.

"Been here and there. Mostly there." Ford said, leaning against the fender of the Escalade.

"Ooh, cryptic. Hey asshole, don't scratch the paint." Seven said shoving Ford in the shoulder. "So what do you want? You want in the gang? Is that it?"

Ford looked at Seven. He appeared smaller somehow. "Nah. But maybe I could do some work for you guys."

"What, we're not good enough for you now? So, come on hotshot, tell me. Where were you?"

Ford lit up a smoke and watched the smoke dissipate into the air. "I was in LA. I've been back a month or so."

Seven put his hands on his hips, "LA? What the fuck you doing down there?"

Ford took several seconds before he answered. "I went there to talk to Sanchez, to explain to him that Carlos's death was because of me."

Seven quickly reached and grabbed his gun and leveled it at Ford's head, "You mean you killed Carlos Thirty-Three? You fuckin' scum sucking son-of-a-bitch. He was my fuckin' friend." Seven stuck the gun between Ford's eyes.

Ford's pulse quickened, but he stared directly into Seven's grey eyes and calmly said, "I didn't say I killed him, you dumb fuck. I said he was dead because of me. You sent Carlos to come and help me after I got away from Hooper and those two fuckin' pigs. There were a couple of gang bangers in the café that must have known Carlos and they opened up on him."

"Who the fuck were these assholes? Tell me, so I can go cap their asses."

Ford calmly pushed the gun away from his face and pushed his left hand, holding his gun, deep into Seven's gut. "While you were mouthing off, I could have blown your guts out at least a dozen times, you dumb fuck." He withdrew his gun and tucked it back into his pants, "Don't worry, that problem has been solved. They're both dead. Shot while they watched a peeler."

Seven stowed his gun. "What, you mean you whacked them both? In a public place? And you're still walking around?" He waved at Nineteen, who was now coming out of the posh residence.

Nineteen walked up to him. "Who's this asshole? What does he want?"

Seven reached over and put his arm on Ford's shoulder. "This, my wise brother is Dustin Ford, back from the grave, so to speak. He's done us a solid, and my guess he's here to collect." Seven stopped and looked at Ford. "You here to collect?"

Ford shook his head. "Nah, you guys don't have enough money. But, I've got a business proposal for you, if you're interested." He looked at both Seven and Nineteen to see what the reaction would be. "That's if you're interested in keeping your puny asses alive."

Nineteen turned to Seven. "Let's get the fuck out of here. This isn't the place to conduct business." He turned to Ford. "Follow us. That is, if the piece of shit you're driving can keep up."

Ford smiled remembering another lesson from Alverez. *If you don't want to get caught, don't do anything to draw attention to yourself. Blend in.* Dustin knew where their new hideout was, so he knew exactly where they would be going. As the black Escalade pulled into traffic, so did Ford, following four car lengths behind. In his rear view mirror he saw another car pull away from the curb, coincidence or a tail? His awareness of the situation heightened. He wondered if Seven or Nineteen had noticed. He guessed not; they were getting sloppy.

The convoy turned off 24th Street onto 176th and headed north. The tail was still there, and Ford moved into the outside lane and fell back a few more car lengths. Before long, the tail car had pulled even with Ford on the inside lane. Without being obvious, Ford peeked over at the driver.

The lowered, gold coloured Olds Alero moved ahead of Ford. He felt certain it was an undercover cop, but he had no way of being positive, and he had no way of warning Seven. All he could do was tail the tail. Playing it safe, Ford dropped back a few more car lengths and settled into the routine. Just then the Olds sped up, and rubber peeled off the front tires. Ford upped his speed to remain behind the tail. He wondered if Seven was paying heed to what was behind him. The black Escalade turned east on 88th Avenue heading into the Port Kells area. The tailing car did likewise. Ford followed.

The Escalade turned south on 190th Street and rapidly accelerated. Ford guessed that he had made the tail and was taking evasive action. The Olds turned sharply onto the same street, tires screaming their resistance.

Just before 86th Avenue the Escalade braked hard and spun sideways, blocking the road. The Olds locked up the brakes, trying to avoid the blockade, so to assist Seven, Ford sped up and got right up on the Olds' rear bumper and parked his car sideways. The Olds' driver had no escape. Ford readied his Glock, quickly screwed on the silencer and waited. He saw Seven and Nineteen get out of the Escalade and separate; both walked towards the Olds on opposite sides of the road.

Ford tried to determine the Olds' driver's next move. If the driver was a cop, he'd try to flee the situation. If the driver was a gang member, a shootout may be the next event. The driver of the Olds opened the door. Ford grabbed his weapon, quickly opened his door and stepped out, his gun aimed at the driver's head. To everyone's surprise the driver put his hands in the air. Seven and Nineteen were nearing the driver. Seven yelled out at him.

"What the fuck are you doing? Why the fuck are you tailing us? You a fuckin' cop?" The driver said nothing and remained beside his car.

From Ford's vantage point, he caught the driver making a subtle head gesture. He yelled to Seven and Nineteen, "It's a fuckin' trap! There's someone else in the car." He saw Seven and Nineteen take evasive action as the passenger side window of the Olds was lowered and a shotgun poked out. Without hesitation, Ford opened fire on the passenger, squeezing off five shots in rapid succession. The driver had ducked down behind his open door and pulled his weapon. Seven and Nineteen were concentrating on the driver. Ford crouched behind the Olds. He couldn't see if the passenger was alive or dead. He spun to his left and rapidly emptied his Glock into the driver, who never saw him coming. Leaning against the car he quickly ejected the empty clip and rammed in a full one. "You guys okay out there?" he yelled.

"Yah, we're good. How about you?"

"No worries. Can you see if the passenger is alive?" Ford looked around for something to break the rear window. Spotting a fair size rock on the shoulder of the road, he darted over and picked it up, then in one swift motion launched the rock into the back window, exploding the tinted glass into a million tiny pieces. A scream erupted from inside the Olds. A female scream. Ford peeked up over the trunk lid; he saw a blond-haired woman slouched down in the back seat. Seven and Nineteen advanced to the front of the car, and Ford caught a glimpse of movement from the passenger in the front. He darted around the right side of the vehicle, stuck his weapon into the broken window and fired several shots, then heard another blood curdling scream from the back seat.

The three left standing on either side of the Olds peered into the front seat to see the two dead bodies. Seven looked at Ford, who was standing on the passenger side of the car. "Thanks man, you got both of them. Who's the broad in the back?" He stuck his head inside the driver's door opening. "What's your name, bitch? And who the hell are you?" He waited for several seconds, "Come on, bitch; who the fuck are you? Ford, grab this dumb ho and drag her sorry ass out your side."

Ford stood and looked up and down the road. He silently rejoiced that there wasn't any traffic on the road at this time of the day. "Nineteen, can you help Seven while I move the vehicles off the road? I'm guessing someone in those houses over there phoned it into the police."

Nineteen nodded and reached in to grab her arm. He caught sight of the small .22 caliber pistol in her left hand. It was aimed directly at him. "Shit." He cried out as she pulled the trigger. A pop emanated from within the car. The bullet grazed Nineteen's shoulder. In an instant, Ford turned, aimed his weapon and fired off three quick shots directly into the woman's head.

Then, all was silent. Nineteen looked at Ford who was expressionless. "Crazy bitch winged me."

Ford opened the passenger door and began frisking the slumped over body. Nineteen did the same thing to the driver. Ford pulled out a wallet and flipped it open. His face said it all. "Big trouble. Big fuckin' trouble. This prick is an undercover cop. I'll bet they are too." He grabbed the shotgun and held it by his side. "I'll be right back." Ford darted to the trunk of his car and popped it open. He tossed the shotgun inside and pulled a can of methyl hydrate and a rag from a side compartment, then ran back to the Olds. Pouring some liquid on the rag, he began to wipe down the passenger side of the car. Nineteen looked at him. "What are you doing?"

"Getting rid of any prints. Don't want the cops knocking on my door any time soon. Would have a hard time explaining why my prints are on a car full of dead cops." He finished his side and tossed the rag to Nineteen, "Wipe your side down so we can get the fuck out of here." Ford took his phone and snapped off a picture of each cop.

Seven returned after parking the Escalade and watched as Nineteen wiped the driver's side down. All three vehicles were now parked alongside the road. Nineteen looked at him and nodded. "His idea. Doesn't want any cops coming to his door."

Ford noticed a vehicle turning onto the street at the end of the block, "Guys, we got a car coming. Quick, make it look like we're just stopped to chat." Nineteen and Seven moved beside the Olds Alero with Ford in the middle. All three leaned against the car to shield the bodies from view. The car slowed down as it passed them. Ford waved to the elderly driver and watched him pull away.

Seven looked at Ford, who was going back to his car. "Let's get the fuck out of here in case the cops show up." He looked back at Ford and smiled.

Twenty minutes later, the two vehicles pulled into the well-camouflaged entrance of the Numbers Gang's new safe house. The gated residence looked peaceful and serene. Both vehicles pulled around the back to the designated parking area.

Ford got out of his car and stopped to admire the planning that had gone into its specialized construction. He nodded his head in approval. "Not bad guys, not bad at all."

"Come on in. We have some things to talk about." Seven lifted up a small metal door and reached his hand inside; a green light emanated from the opening. Then, he removed his hand and entered an access code into the keypad. The door clicked open. The trio walked down the concrete-walled hallway down a flight of stairs to another hallway. Their footsteps echoed.

Inside the cavernous room, Ford saw several other members of the gang lounging around, watching television or playing computer games. A large pile of uncounted cash lay on a metal trolley cart next to a counting machine. Ford guessed it was likely in the multiple thousands of dollars. "Looks like business is good? No?" he said as he hopped up on a bar stool. He spotted several brown envelopes bulging with what he figured was cash.

"We've got no complaints. Well not exactly. We've got lots to complain about, but yes, business is good." Seven said sitting next to Ford. Nineteen was behind the built-in wet bar. "Anyone want a beer?" Nineteen watched as both Seven and Ford nodded agreement.

Ford grabbed the beer that Nineteen had set before him and took a long drink. It tasted fantastic. "Not a bad place you guys have here. It looks new."

Nineteen leaned against the bar surveying the lounge area. "Yeah, it's new. We just moved in about three months ago. Cost us plenty to build. Damn near one point five million, but it's worth every fuckin' penny. The cops would need a fuckin' tank to blast their way in here, if they were so inclined. The walls are almost eighteen inches thick, every window in this place is bulletproof. The doors are steel filled with concrete and have deep set hinges, so it's damn near impenetrable."

Ford could see that they were proud of their new digs and he couldn't resist. "A few days ago I watched the cops take down a house that was hardened." He took a pull on his beer, "maybe not as good as this place but hardened. It didn't stand up well when the cops brought out an armoured bulldozer and opened the house up. It was quite the sight."

Seven, now subdued, chimed in. "Yah, but the best part about this whole shootin' match is we're self-contained. We have our own solar power and backup generator, and we have food and drink to last almost three months. Oh, and get this, we also got us a vault to hold the cash. Pretty fuckin' neat, eh?" He beamed as he took a swig of his beer.

Ford nodded his approval. "Yep, not too shabby. Only problem is that once you leave this place you're sitting ducks." He stopped to let that sink in. "You've gotta know that the cops have you guys marked. Why else would undercovers be tailing you?"

Nineteen set his beer down. "Oh, we know they occasionally tail us. We know they are there, and they know that we know they're there…it's sort of a game."

Ford took a sip. "And that doesn't bother you? Knowing that at any time they choose, they could haul your asses into jail. Shit man, that's no way to live. That's more like a rat in a maze than freedom. And the brown envelopes," he said, pointing to the table. "Extortion or blackmail payouts, right?" He paused, "I've tailed you guys three times, twice to an unmarked police car, and once to a newer model Corvette. Each time an envelope was passed. Pay-offs, right? How much a month and to how many cops do you guys pay money? I'm guessing it's more than one crooked cop? Imagine if you didn't have to pay those scum suckers a penny…how rich you would be?"

Seven sat up straight, "Cost of doing business bro. Keeps them off our asses. As for the tails, they don't bother us and we don't get busted like those that don't pay up. Besides, we've got a good lawyer on retainer, so if ever that day comes, we invoke our right to counsel and let the mouthpiece do the talking." He and Nineteen clinked bottles. "Long live the sharks," he said to Nineteen who laughed.

Ford didn't like their smugness. Taking a long drink of his beer, he said, "I suppose after the cops find their three dead undercovers, things will change. Wouldn't you say so?"

Nineteen toyed with his beer bottle. "It's hard to say. Hard to know if they'll figure out who killed them?"

Ford set his beer down hard on the granite counter top. "Wake up, dude. UCs let somebody know what they're doing almost all the time. Fuck man, for all you know they could have told someone that they were tailing the dreaded Numbers Gang. Won't take even the dumbest cop more than ten seconds to figure out who's at the top of their suspect list." Ford shook his head. "Fuck you guys are stupid."

Seven was getting pissed off at Ford's accusations. "What do you mean 'stupid' motherfucker?"

"Just what I said. You're stupid. You know I should have let those two dudes at the casino whack your dumb ass, but no, I had to protect your stupid ass from being blown away."

"That was you that did that?" Seven said, surprised.

"Yeah that was me. Don't ask me why." Ford smiled, not willing to tell them that he wanted that privilege all for himself.

"We've been trying to figure out who had done us a solid," Seven said. "And all this time it was you, the dumb shit who didn't have the brains to check if his fuckin' gun was loaded. Who would ever have guessed?"

Ford smiled at Seven, contemptuously. "Hey, a lot of things have flowed from that fateful night. Best of all, that Hooper is dead, and so is the fuckin' cop that he snitched for."

Nineteen looked surprised. "That was you?" He laughed.

"Here we assumed that he'd been iced by someone he ratted out…and the fuckin' cop as well." He raised his beer. "Salute to a stone-cold killer." To Ford's surprise, everyone in the room raised whatever they were drinking, and yelled out "Salute!"

Seven leaned towards Ford. "So, why now? Why now to make your appearance after nearly two years? What's up?"

Ford looked around the room. He counted at least nine other gang members and immediately wondered why they weren't out doing their jobs. "To be honest, when I came back from LA I wanted revenge for the way you guys abandoned me at Hooper's, but after I took care of the guys who killed Carlos at the strip joint, I changed my mind. I figured that, with my newly acquired skill-set, I could be useful to your organization."

Nineteen slapped his hand on the bar. "That was you that took out those two motherfuckers. Fuck man, we'd heard about that, but figured it was just a normal part of the turf war that's going on." Nineteen took a drink. "Fuckin' awesome, man. Not only did you avenge Carlos's death, but you saved Seven's ass, and you took care of the three cops today. In my book, we owe you big time. Tell you what…" He stopped and walked over to the trolley of cash, grabbed a large wad of fifty dollar bills and stuck them in the counter. The machine came to life and immediately ate up the wad, so Nineteen stuck in another wad. When it was done, the counter registered twenty-five thousand. He quickly threw the money into a brown bag and walked back to the bar and placed the bag in front of Ford. "Twenty-five grand for services rendered. Sound fair?"

Ford looked at Nineteen and then at Seven. "That's what,

eight grand a hit? In LA the average price was fifteen per, with proof of death. Tell you what? Let's call it the introductory allowance, anything else from this point on will be fifteen grand. Half upfront and the remainder upon proof of death."

Seven shifted on his stool. "What's this 'proof of death' shit?"

Ford laughed. "How fuckin' long have you been doing this? In LA, it means proof that the mark isn't alive anymore. Here, let me show you." Ford pulled out his cell phone and quickly scrolled through the images of his many victims. "See, here are Hooper and his cop handler O'Dell." He scrolled further. "Here are the two dudes that got Carlos, and here are the two cops that were extorting money from a friend and here are the three cops today." He closed his cell phone and tucked it back into his inside jacket pocket. "That's how business has to be done. How else would you know if I've actually killed the target or just collected the money and had the victim stashed away?"

By now three other members had joined them at the bar. "See, Seven," Nineteen said, "there are smart people out there. He makes a good point. How the fuck do we know if any of our contractors are actually fulfilling their contracts? Hell, for all we know, the marks are still walking around. Listen up, everyone." He paused for several seconds while everyone stopped what they were doing. "From now on any contract to terminate someone has to be completed with a proof of death, no exceptions. Proof of death is a photo of the contract dead. Any questions?" Nineteen glared at everyone within eye sight. "Okay, then, get on the phone and get in touch with the three contractors currently on assignments and advise them of the new rules. Well, don't just stand there. Get on it," he barked. He watched the members hustle away.

Seven looked around. "Fuckin' amazing. You've been here less than thirty minutes, and already things are changing. You still want to join?"

Ford knew this was coming and immediately recalled his rehearsed response. "Nah, my skill-set doesn't fit well within an organization. It's more conducive to an independent contractor. Besides, you guys have enough members to keep track of." He paused lifting up his empty bottle and waggled it at Nineteen, then smiled. "But I've got a proposition for you guys that I want to run by you. Interested?"

Seven looked at Nineteen who had opened another beer for Ford. "Fire away. Just kidding. I've seen what you can do when you fire." He chuckled.

Ford chose his words carefully, "I've had the opportunity to watch what has been happening here for the past month, and I'd say the cops are gearing up for a war on the gangs, yours included. There are two ways to handle this. First, one could try to weather the storm by going to ground and curtailing operations until the heat dies down. Or two, counter the onslaught with an offensive." He paused to take a drink. Both Nineteen and Seven remained silent, which in Ford's mind meant they were listening. "The problem with the first option is you probably go broke and ultimately end up in jail. The problem with the second option is that the body count will rise and require co-operation between gangs like never before. One gang cannot take on the cops alone and win. But several gangs...would stand a good chance of winning, at least to the point where police would think twice about busting any gang."

Seven shook his head. "Are you fuckin' insane? You can't take on the cops. That would be bloody suicide. They're the goddamn *cops*."

Ford took a drink and looked at Nineteen. "So? What's your point? Who has the authority to put you behind bars? Certainly not the other gangs. The only thing the other gangs can do to you is kill you and take over your turf. Now, try to get your head around this. If the cops were afraid to go after any gang, how would that increase your profits? It doesn't take a rocket scientist to figure out that if you can do your business uninterrupted and without fear of being caught, you'd make a shit load more money." He took another drink. "Here's the beauty of this. If the gangs worked together, they'd soon realize that there's room for everyone and enough money for everyone to make a killing, figuratively speaking." He lit up a cigarette and watched the smoke curl skyward.

"How long before the cops decide to lay siege to this place? A month? Six months? A year? That's just it…you don't know. The cops would back off if their body count began to rise. Hell, haven't you guys watched the news lately? They're freaking out because three cops have been shot in the last week. What does that tell you? Wait till they find the last three, then imagine if that count was ten, fifteen, or twenty dead cops. It's never fuckin' been done before. They wouldn't know how to handle it. You'd find out that cops aren't as dedicated as their posters suggest. They'd be very reluctant to show up for work. Call it a deadly deterrent. Trust me…I know what I'm talking about."

Seven sat forward, beer in hand, "Dude you are fucked

up. Of that I am positive. Nobody in their right fuckin' mind wants to go up against the cops. And as for getting these other gangs to work together forget it. There is little or no trust or co-operation between any of them."

Nineteen set his beer down. "Man, that's a lot of shit to digest all at one sitting. We're going to need time to think about this. You're right, it's never been done before, the gangs working together. Normally we're into turf wars and stuff like that. As for taking on the cops, man, where the fuck do you come up with this shit?"

Ford slid the remains of his cigarette into the empty beer bottle and sparked up another. "When I was in LA I worked for Carlos Thirty-Three's uncle, who taught me the ways of the real world. He told me that back in nineteen ninety-three, the Crypts and the Bluds united for one brief cause in their forty-five year battle, and that was to wage a targeted campaign against the LAPD. In a three month period nearly forty cops were killed. It was front page news across America. The result was that the cops backed off.

"The public wanted the heads of those responsible, but the cops wanted nothing to do with it. Shortly after the campaign, the cops revised their tactics and the Crypts and the Bluds went back to killing each other. Alverez said it was the way of the natural world."

Ford looked at Nineteen and Seven, the brains of the Numbers Gang and silently gave thanks that he wasn't entrusting his life to them. Ford finished his beer. "Well guys, it's been a slice, but I've got to be going. I have a meeting with a guy later and it's in North Van and traffic is going to be a bitch. How the fuck do I get out of this prison?" he said, chuckling as he slapped Seven on the shoulder.

CHAPTER

25

THE METRO POLICE station was in chaos with the news of the three dead police officers found in Surrey the night before. The media had camped out all night in front of the station, wanting to be the first to scoop any story. Chief Von Pleth arrived earlier than normal at the request of the mayor as the Provincial Attorney General was holding a press conference at nine o'clock, and they wanted all hands on deck.

Von Pleth entered the station via the underground entrance, which afforded him the luxury of not having to run the gauntlet of reporters and television cameras parked out front. Safely inside the station, Von Pleth made his way to the fifth floor and the staff briefing room. Sleep had eluded him, so he was operating on pure reflex energy, and his demeanor fit the situation. Everyone was on edge.

Von Pleth exited the elevator and headed straight to his office. Along the way, staff offered their good mornings, but Von Pleth just nodded. Inside his well-appointed office, he closed the door. He needed some time to collect his thoughts, as he knew he'd be put on the hot seat for answers when he had none. Von Pleth sat at his desk and dialed Lamp's extension. It rang four times before Lamp answered.

"You got anything on the triple murder? I need something

to tell the media at the AG's press conference this morning. You are attending, aren't you?"

"Sorry Chief, we're still collecting evidence from the scene. The neighbors said they saw and heard nothing, which doesn't help us one iota. I got their names from Fraser, it's here somewhere?" Lamp calmly searched through the papers on his desk.

Von Pleth slammed his fist on his desk. "Goddamn it to hell. Nothing? No shell casings, no eye witnesses? Unbelievable? Nobody is that perfect. You sure you've got the right officers working this case?" Immediately, Von Pleth wished he hadn't said what he just did.

Lamp became incensed. "Chief, with all due respect, the officers working this case are our very best. If you're suggesting they're not qualified, then we have a problem..."

Von Pleth cut him off. "That's not what I meant to say. I'm sorry. Of course they're the best we have. I was trying to determine if we had any inexperienced officers working the case, which could cause the media to attack us on that front." He massaged his temples.

Lamp butted in. "Chief, we've got nearly every detective on the entire force working this one case, almost everything else is on the back burner. That includes newly minted detectives as well as seasoned pros. Geez, I'd put the goddamn janitor on the case if I figured it would help us. These don't appear random so we're dealing with a pro on this one. Someone who hasn't made any mistakes so far, and we're not even sure if it's one person or a group." There was a long silence as both men stepped back from the edge of a verbal pissing contest. "Ah, here's the list. They are: Officer Sheldon Pratt, Officer Mavis Appleton and DEA agent Marco Aluma.

Von Pleth took off his glasses and dropped them on his desk. "DEA. Christ, now the feds are going to be crawling up my ass…" He put his glasses back on. "You're absolutely sure? No mistake on the agent? And these were targeted hits? No other possibility?"

"We can never be completely sure about anything. IA will do their investigation into the deaths then perhaps we'll know. With one of them being a DEA agent, it stands to reason that it is drug related. Hell, maybe they got too close, or maybe they pissed off one of the gangs. Your guess is as good as mine."

Von Pleth sat forward. "Is that what Fraser from narco told you?"

"Yes, sir, I spoke with him roughly an hour ago. He said something about having to call Washington to let them know they have a dead agent."

"I had better call him to get the skinny so I can inform the mayor and the Attorney General. The media is going to be all over this." Von Pleth replied.

Lamp replaced the phone and looked out at the bullpen. All of the detectives were on the phones, following up with sources and chasing down leads. *For all our sakes we'd better catch this son-of-a-bitch before anyone else gets killed.* He picked up his folder and headed for the briefing room. As he walked through the bullpen, he overheard Weeks on the phone with one of her CIs.

"I don't give a shit if Danny is sleeping, wake the son-of-a-bitch up, right goddamn now, and get him on the phone. Is that clear enough for you, you dumb coke head?" She looked at Lamp as he walked past and shook her head, rolling her eyes skyward. She cupped her hand over the microphone. "Girlfriend." She smiled, "I'd like to slap this silly bitch back to the stone-age. Christ she's stupid."

Lamp smiled. "Do it, if you think it'll help? Briefing room when you're finished."

The briefing room was half full when he entered. All talking stopped as he walked towards the front of the room. He placed his folder on the podium and turned around. All eyes were on him, all looking to him for answers, all wanting to know something…anything. "We'll give the others another few minutes then we'll start."

Wheaton rocked back on his chair. "Sarg, what the hell is going on? Are we at war with someone? That's six cops in less than two weeks…I'm beginning to wonder if I made the right career choice."

Lamp leaned against the small two-person table in the front row. "Phil, if I had the answer to that, I'd be a wise man. You know as much as I know, which isn't much." He saw Harbach stand up. "Yes Mike?"

"Sarg, between you me and the doorway, you think we're being targeted?"

"I honestly don't know Mike. I wish I had the answer?"

He turned to see Weeks sitting down. She was smiling. "What's going on Weeks? You're the only one in the room that's smiling?"

"Well Sarg, we may have caught a break. One of the CIs saw Pratt's Olds Alero following a Black Cadillac Escalade yesterday afternoon. He was going west on Eighty-Eighth Avenue in Surrey, when he saw Pratt turn off One Seventy-Sixth and follow it eastbound on Eighty-Eighth. So the question we need to be asking is does the Escalade ring any bells with anyone? That is a popular gang symbol, so we should check that with the gang squad."

Lamp forced a small smile "That's using your head, Weeks. Run with that idea. Contact Hedley in the gang unit and then check with the insurance company for a printout of all the registered Escalades in the lower mainland. It should be easy then to cross reference that list with known gang members. Good work indeed." His smile broadened.

Weeks saw her mentor smiling. "Ah, boss. Gang members never put their vehicles in their own names. It's either in their wives', girlfriends' or parents' names, or some bogus numbered company, so I'm thinking that it might not help us that much, at least on the insurance angle."

"You know, I hate it when you're right Weeks. Well, at least check with Hedley. Their intel might be valuable."

"Okay, everyone put a lid on it and listen up." Lamp paced between the podium and the north wall. "As you have all heard, three more police officers were killed yesterday in Surrey's Port Kells area. That's six in the last ten days. Their names are: Officer Sheldon Pratt and Officer Mavis Appleton. And to complicate matters more, one of the three killed was DEA agent Marco Aluma, so we can expect a lot of heat from the feds on this one. And, as usual, there is squat to go on. Whoever is doing this isn't an amateur; he's a goddamn pro, so I suspect we're going to have to work our asses off to find this bastard." He took a sip of water; his mouth was dry.

"One other thing you need to know is that the AG is holding a press conference at nine, and I'm invited. So if you learn anything, I don't care how small, give me a heads up, as I'm sure the Chief, the mayor, and the AG will want to know where we're at." He leaned against the podium, "I don't have anything else to tell you, except get out there and pound the bushes. Something has to break. We have a picture out there of a possible suspect, but it's dated, so we might be tilting at windmills, but at least it's something." He watched as most detectives rose. "And people, be safe out there. Wear your vests. No exceptions. Travel in pairs. And be smart. I don't want to make any more phone calls to grieving family members."

The AG's press conference started at exactly nine a.m. The area in front of the station was packed with every media outlet in the area as well as a large crowd of ordinary citizens wanting to know the latest. Von Pleth stared silently out over the crowd, glad that the rain had stayed away. He tapped the microphone.

"Okay ladies and gentlemen this is what we know so far. First, condolences go out to the families of the three fallen police officers. We have lost three more valuable members of our extended family, which brings the total to six in the last ten days. We have very little to go on except for some vague clues that are being tracked down as we speak." He paused to collect his thoughts. "Metro police have every available officer working this case and it will only be a matter of time until we get the break we're looking for and put this person, or persons, behind bars where they belong." He paused again, looking down at the sea of cameras all pointed at him. "To the individual or individuals that are responsible for this senseless tragedy, we will find you. You can be sure of that, and when we do, rest assured we will be more civil to you than you've been to our members."

The press conference lasted for nearly an hour. Weeks

and her new partner, Mills, left the station after the briefing and were on the street when their radio chirped, “One Delta Five, this is dispatch.”

Mills, who was riding shotgun, grabbed the mic. “Dispatch, this is One Delta Five, go ahead.”

“One Delta Five, your presence is required at twenty-nine-o-one Robson Street, a place called the Walnut Hut Internet Café. See Detective Rutherford. Over.”

Mills looked at Weeks with a puzzled expression on his face. “Roger, dispatch. twenty-nine-o-one Robson Street, Walnut Hut Internet Café. Over.” He replaced the mic in the cradle. “What the hell’s this about?” he said, and without looking at Weeks he flipped on the lights and siren.

“Don’t know, but I’m sure Rutherford has a reason for requesting us. Hang on.” Weeks floored the Crown Vic. It took them twenty-five minutes to make it to Robson Street.

The ritzy shopping district, even at this early hour, was bustling with tourists and locals looking for bargains, some just looking to be seen. Weeks and Mills entered the spartanly adorned café that consisted of a small counter that sold specialty coffee and pastries, but their main business was internet time, which sold by the minute. Weeks saw Rutherford and Chou talking to a man and woman behind the counter.

“What’s up, Stan?” Weeks said, stopping in front of Rutherford.

“Hey, you guys got here quick. The tech division traced the hack of the personnel files back to this joint. That’s Devon, and she’s Amber. They own this place. She works mostly during the day, and he works mostly at night. They’re open until midnight, seven days a week.”

Weeks looked around the café. It was deserted except for three Asian youths playing online video games. "Are they regulars?" she asked, pointing to the youths.

Devon Service stepped from behind the counter. The grey streaks in his long red ponytail gave away his real age, although he did whatever he could to look the part of a young man. "Them, yah, they're in here every morning, playing online video games with their friends in Hong Kong. Time difference, you know."

Weeks looked at Rutherford. "So, what's the deal with the hacker? They able to ID him? Is there any video surveillance in here?" She shot a quick glance towards the multicoloured ceiling.

Service was quick to answer. "Yes, we've got constant surveillance, which is digitized and stored on our mainframe. Detective Rutherford has already requested a copy of the last ten days. My technician is downloading it as we speak."

Weeks pulled out the composite rendering of Ford. "Does this guy look familiar?"

Service took the printout and studied it intently. Then shook his head, "Can't say that I've ever seen him in here. Why, who is he?" Weeks wasn't surprised.

Mills looked Service in the eye. "Maybe somebody, maybe nobody. We just want to talk to him. So he hasn't been in here?"

"That's what I just said. I don't recall ever seeing him. Have, you Amber?" Service said to his partner. She looked at the picture and shook her head no. "There you go detective. Is there anything else we can help you with?"

Rutherford turned to Chou. "Yeah, you can tell your customers to get out. As of now, this place is under investigation.

Our tech squad is coming down with a search warrant to find out which computer was used to hack our server."

"Oh, wonderful," Devon Service said snidely. "They won't find much. We run a hub system here. All these computers are linked into one central hub that splits the signals going outbound. They won't be able to ID the exact computer that was used."

Chou was standing against the counter. "You'd be surprised at what they can find. We don't hire idiots to work in that department. If there's anything here, they'll find it."

Service laughed. "If it's the same group that I trained when I was an instructor at BCIT, then I'd surprised. They couldn't find their asses with both hands and a flashlight."

Weeks was in no mood for school yard bravado. "Okay, guys, zip it back up. I'm sure they all have excellent computer skills, you included, Devon. So just relax. They'll be out of here in due time." She turned to Mills, "Let's go. There's nothing that we can do here. Rutherford and Chou have it well in hand." She held her hand up to her ear as if using a phone, then looked at Rutherford who knew what she meant, and nodded yes. Then, she turned to leave the café. Outside she donned her sunglasses, as the sun stabbed brightly through a small opening in the cloud cover.

Inside the car, Weeks rolled down the window to let in some fresh air. Mills began working the keyboard on the onboard computer system. "Where we going?" he asked.

"Station, we need to talk to Hedley. He said he'd have a list of known gang vehicles for us."

Looking straight ahead Mills said. "I'll bet any money it's either the Big Valley Gang or the Golden Dragons. From what I've heard they're the most ruthless of all the gangs operating down here. What do you think?"

Weeks kept her eyes on the road ahead. Traffic was light, and she was wasting no time getting over to Main Street. "Well, you can't discount the smaller gangs who want to make themselves a name. Hell, for all we know, it could be a new gang, sending a message to other gangs that they've arrived." She turned onto Water Street, heading east, and as she turned, the tires squealed their resistance to the speed. People on the sidewalk stared at them as they made the turn.

Mills hung on for dear life, he hated being the passenger. "So, are you happy that you're partnered up with me? I sense that you have something on your mind?" He looked straight ahead.

Weeks couldn't believe what she'd just heard, "What? You want to have that type of discussion while I'm driving? Are you crazy?"

"It's the body odour thing isn't it?" Mills said turning slightly to Weeks.

"Hey as long as it's under control, I'm fine. Besides from what I know of excessive body odour, it's genetic." She smiled at him, while braking for the corner.

Weeks turned south on Main Street and pulled next to the curb directly across from the Main Street station. "Wait here, I'll be back in a jiff." She opened the door and got out before Mills could reply.

Fifteen minutes later, Weeks returned with a folder. Getting in, she tossed the folder onto the dash. She started the car and began to pull away. "Have a look at the list. I took a quick peek, looks like it's the vehicle of choice for a lot of gangs."

The blare of a horn got her attention. "Shit. Where did

that asshole come from?" she said, as she watched a gray minivan swerve around the cruiser's front end.

"We should pull the asshole over for speeding," Mills said. "Or at least give him a talking to. Fuckin' jerk."

Weeks smiled. It was the first time that Mills had said anything that indicated he was normal.

"Nah, that'd be a waste of time." The cross breeze that blew through the open car windows carried the strong scent of the cologne Mills was using to hide the odour. She had smelled it before, but figured he must have put more on while she was in the station. "I'm getting hungry, how about you?"

"Yeah, I could use a bite. What did you have in mind?"

Weeks looked left as they turned onto Renfrew. "There's a little diner just up ahead. They serve a mean Salisbury steak."

Jimmy Chan beamed his broad smile when he saw Weeks and Mills enter his diner and quickly rounded the counter to meet them. "Ah, Detective Weeks, you not come in long time. Good to see you. Please come this way. I bring you coffee, no?" he said standing by the corner booth table.

"No, Jimmy, I'll have a root beer. And you, Mills?" she said, scanning the menu.

"How's the coffee in this joint?" Mills said flatly.

"Ah, yes, coffee very strong. Just like mama made, yes?" Chan said smiling even wider.

"Okay, Jimmy, I'll try a cup of your poison." Mills smirked. He watched as Chan disappeared into the kitchen through the swinging doors.

A few minutes later Chan arrived at the table with the drinks. "You know what you want to eat? All food very good."

Weeks noticed Mills wince when he saw Chan's deformed teeth.

"I'll just have a cheeseburger and fries," Mills said.

"Ah, yes. Best cheeseburger in town, no?" He wrote it down quickly. "Detective Weeks, the usual? No?"

"No, Jimmy, I think I'll have your Greek salad with garlic toast, please."

"Ah, very good choice Detective Weeks. Best Greek salad in town." He smiled, jotted it down then disappeared from the table.

Weeks picked up her root beer and took a sip. The bubbles tickled her nose. She watched as Mills poured sugar into the coffee. "That bad, eh?" she said with a chuckle.

"Boy, he wasn't fooling when he said 'coffee very strong'. This stuff could be used for paint stripper." He opened the folder and handed several sheets to Weeks. "Seems like everyone drives a bloody Escalade." Mills ran his eyes down the typed list of names. "Shit, half of these bastards drive black Escalades. How the hell do we figure out which one was the one they were tailing?"

Weeks scanned her portion of the list. "You're right. Hell, over half of these are black as well." She took a drink then set the glass forcibly on the table. "I know, let me make a call. Maybe there's a way to narrow this list down." Weeks took out her cell phone, unlocked it, and keyed in a number. It rang four times. "Hi Sarg, Weeks here. Sorry to interrupt you, but we need your horsepower."

"What do you mean my horsepower?"

"Well Sarg, Hedley's list has half of the gangs driving black Escalades. Is there any chance you could call your contacts in undercover to see if they radioed in who they were tailing? A license number would make this a lot easier."

"I'll see what I can do. I'll get back to you."

Weeks saw Mills's face contort with displeasure as he took a drink of his tar black coffee. "Sarg said he'd make some inquiries from the guys in undercover to see if they recorded the license number of the car they were following. If that doesn't pan out, we're back to square one, which is zilch."

Mills looked into his coffee, then up at Weeks. "All we can do is wait for them to make another move. Sooner or later, they're going to slip up."

"Oh, fuckin' wonderful, another cop has to die. And who would you like that to be?" Weeks was disgusted at what she had just heard.

Mills sensed her indignation. "Well, Miss Smarty, how else do we track them down, pray tell? Come on, you've got all the answers."

Weeks was ready to launch her glass of root beer at Mills, but fought for self control. "Ever wonder why everyone dislikes you so much? Ever wonder why nobody in the whole department wants to partner with you?" Mills was about to speak when she cut him off. "Well let me tell you, it's not only your smell, but it's because you're a real, honest-to-goodness jerk." She inhaled. "You have the sensitivity of a charging rhino."

He stared at her. "You finished, Your Highness?"

She cracked her neck.

"You're not the easiest person to work with either," he said. "Both you and Healy think you're God's gift to detectives. Well let me tell you this…you're not. What I said makes logical sense, as cruel and distasteful as you believe it seems to you. But if there's nothing else to go on, all we can do is wait for the next event to happen. I don't like it any fuckin' more than you, but it's the reality of the situation, so deal with it for Christ sake." Weeks frowned. She knew she should have kept her mouth shut.

Chan placed their orders in front of them and smiled broadly. "You eat. Jimmy makes special food for Metro's finest."

Weeks looked at him. "Thanks Jimmy. All your food is special." She picked up her fork and stuck it into the salad, all the while envisioning it was Mill's heart.

CHAPTER

26

DUSTIN FORD PURCHASED a carton of cigarettes at the grocery store on 6th Avenue in New Westminster and made his way to his car in the underground parkade. Now that he was flush with cash, he felt like he was on top of the world. Inside his car he checked his face in the rearview mirror. The tanning sessions were darkening his skin tone to that of a Southeast Asian person, the strawberry was covered up with makeup and he was happy with how his goatee and moustache were filling in; a little black hair dye, and they would be perfect.

Ford liked how his specific skill-set was developing, but what he had yet to do was expand his methods of accomplishing his tasks. He had heard Alverez speak of a sniper rifle, something called an M40A3 that took a 7.62 round that had an effective kill range of 800m and accepted a five-shot cartridge. Ford mused at the possibility of getting his hands on one of those bad boys, as it would make his job easier and safer, especially with a shot that travelled 2,756 feet per second.

The only problem he had was where to get his hands on one. In LA it would be a matter of a phone call. If he couldn't find one, he'd have to settle for something similar.

Ford remembered another thing Alverez had told him. *It isn't the weapon that makes the hitman. It's what isn't in his heart that determines how well he'll do.* This had puzzled Ford at first so he had Alverez explain it more clearly. He remembered Alverez poking him in the chest with his stubby forefinger finger. *The target is just a piece of meat. A hitman cannot care anything, and I mean anything, for his target. He has to be cold and ruthless, and treat the entire task as no big deal.*

An hour later Ford found himself in his favourite haunt. Jomo was behind the bar as usual. Ford motioned him over. Jomo's attire made him stand out from everyone in the bar. His brightly multicoloured Jamaican shirt was loud, but it suited him.

"What's up?" Jomo said.

Ford beckoned him to sit. Jomo complied. "I need something, and I'm hoping you can help me."

"What is it?" He asked, looking side to side.

Ford pulled a piece of paper from his shirt pocket and slid it across the well-worn table. "This."

Jomo picked up the paper and unfolded it. The shocked look on his face told Ford that Jomo knew exactly what Ford wanted.

"No problem man, give Jomo some time and Jomo will find out where you can get this."

Ford threw back the rest of his beer and stood, "Well then, I'll see you tomorrow or the next." He slapped Jomo on the shoulder as he passed by him, heading to the door. Pushing it open, the bright sunlight blinded him for a second. He knew if Jomo came through, he'd need to find a place to practice and the lower mainland didn't offer anything like that.

Ford pulled into a parking lot just off Commercial Drive and parked. Three doors down was a small bookshop. Inside the bookstore, Ford found what he was looking for so he paid for it and promptly found a coffee shop where he could study the map. He remembered that when he was younger his foster family took a trip inland and he recalled that around Cache Creek it was semi-arid desert, which could provide the isolation he needed to hone his skills with the long rifle.

Sitting in the sunshine, he unfolded the map and located the area. Ford was delighted that it presented several good possibilities. He sat back, sipping his usual coffee, trying to figure out how best to do this. Ford knew one thing from looking at the map, and that was his car couldn't make it to either of the two areas he was considering.

On his way back to New Westminster via Kingsway traffic was light, which afforded his mind time to wander. He knew he needed a four-by-four with a canopy or camper so he could spend several days practicing. When Alverez had taught him to shoot, they'd driven for two hours up into the mountains and spent four days just shooting.

Ford had just entered his apartment when his cell phone rang. He flipped it open, but didn't recognize the number. "Hello?"

"Ford, it's Seven. You able to talk?"

Ford walked to his fridge and grabbed a beer. "Yeah, what's on your mind?" He walked to his balcony, slid open the glass door, and stepped outside. From the balcony Ford had an unobstructed view of the Fraser River Docks; he counted four ships unloading.

"Nineteen and I were wondering if you wanted to do a job

for us."

Ford took a pull on his beer. "Depends? What have you got in mind?"

"We want a rival gang leader eliminated. He's become a royal pain in our ass. The fuckin' prick thinks he's God's gift."

Ford looked over the Fraser River at a log-boom being slowly pulled by a tugboat. "Sounds to me like you want to start a turf war."

"Hey, if that happens, fuck them all. There's too much money at stake to let this asshole horn in on our territory."

Ford sat down on the only chair on the balcony. "So, who's the unlucky prick?"

"He goes by the name of Freddy Pham Lee"

Ford looked at his phone. "Freddy Family? What kind of fuckin' name is that?"

"Not 'family' dipshit, Pham Lee. P-h-a-m L-e-e. Got it?"

Ford shook his head. "Oh, Pham Lee. Now I got it. You have a picture of this guy?"

"Yeah we do. I'll have Sixty-Eight send it to your phone. So you'll do it?"

Ford took another swig. "Sure, I'll do it. When do you want it done? I'm going out of town for a few days. Can it wait until I get back?"

"The sooner the better; and we haven't forgotten your proposal. Nineteen is meeting with Wilkinson from the Los Demonios. We have a working association with them."

Ford finished his beer, "Tell you what, when I get back into town, I'll call you and let you know when it can be taken care of. Does that work for you?"

"Yeah, it'll have to. You haven't asked the price."

Ford closed his patio door. "I'm assuming it's what we talked about, or is this something special?"

"I'm authorized to offer it to you at twenty-five grand."

Ford opened another beer and stood staring into the fridge. "Consider it done. Half up front, the rest on proof of death."

"Deal. Gotta run." Seven cut off the call.

Ford flopped onto his couch, remote in hand. He found a ballgame on a sports channel then closed his eyes and drifted off to sleep.

The ringing of his cell phone woke him. He groped around trying to find it. It kept ringing. Finally he laid his hand on it and flipped it open.

"It's Jomo. I have what you're looking for. He wants eight-thousand dollars. Says he can have it here at midnight. You still want it?"

"He can supply everything, yes?"

"Yes, he says everything that's on your list."

"Fantastic, Jomo, see you at midnight." Ford ended the call and leaned back, closing his eyes. *It begins.*

The next day, Ford picked up his rental at the Econo Car and Truck Rental and stopped at a gas station to pick up some essentials. Ford then drove to his apartment where he loaded everything into the back. Buried deep inside the box of the truck was the black case that contained the M40A3, the silencer, nearly a thousand rounds of 7.62mm ammo, and a spotting scope. Also in the back were three mannequins that he'd bought from the local thrift store. He chuckled as he remembered the stunned look on the clerk's face when he offered to pay a hundred bucks apiece for the dummies. He had stopped at the local surplus store on Columbia Avenue and stocked up on the necessary camping supplies. The way

Ford figured it he might as well be comfortable while he learned the art of the long rifle.

Three hours later, Ford was descending the hill into Cache Creek. On his map, he'd found two areas close to town that would afford him the privacy he needed. The first was west of town, near McLean Lake. That would be his first area to check out. The map showed a large plateau area north of the lake. The second area was north of town and was a transmission tower right-of-way that stretched for miles.

As Ford drove towards the lake, he tried to recall what he'd seen when he was last in the area, but the memories wouldn't come. All he could remember was the ill treatment and beatings he received at the hands of Wilbur Daniels, his foster parent. He liked Thelma Daniels. She tried to make it a pleasant place, but her efforts were futile.

The lake was a short drive down a poorly maintained gravel road. Ford was glad he opted to rent a truck. When he rounded a corner he met a truck loaded with logs that was taking up almost the entire road. Ford quickly swerved onto the loose gravel on the shoulder and the truck narrowly missed him. He came to an abrupt stop because the dust that was kicked up by the big truck completely hid the road. Ford quickly raised the window to keep the dust out.

He waited.

The still air allowed the dust to hang over the road for fifteen minutes. Finally Ford was able to see. He continued slowly.

Ford saw the lake from the crest of the hill and slowly eased the truck in that direction.

It took Ford about forty-five minutes to scout the two areas that he was considering. About a mile down the road he caught sight of a gated area and pulled in. The area was fenced off with a metal pipe cattle gate. He nosed the truck into the driveway and proceeded up the incline.

Once he got to the top he stopped and got out. Binoculars at the ready he scanned the hillside in all directions looking for any telltale signs of prying eyes. He found none. Ford drove further along the plateau going cross country, as the trail had ended half way up the hillside. He reached down and engaged the four-by-four feature then headed across what looked like level ground. Ford soon learned his eyes had deceived him, and the truck bounced from depression to depression, throwing him violently into the air so that he hit his head on the roof of the truck. With one hand, he did up his seat belt.

A short time later, he was well into the back country. The scrub brush was thicker, which made travel more difficult. He plowed the four-by-four through the bushes until he reached a clearing. Outside, the temperature was hot, nearly thirty-five degrees. Ford grabbed his water bottle and got out, the hot air nearly took his breath away and he instantly started to sweat. He began to walk around the clearing area, checking sightlines, imagining where he would set up the mannequins and targets, and where his nest would be. Satisfied that he would be completely alone, he walked back to the truck and began to set up.

It was a little past two-thirty. He figured he had at least seven hours of good daylight, and he wasn't about to waste it.

He had assembled the weapon and he stood back to admire its shape. Just sitting on the ground with the tripod extended, the weapon looked menacing and deadly. Ford walked out about one hundred yards and set up his first target. He then proceeded to place a paper target every hundred yards until he reached the limit of the M40A3 rifle, twelve hundred yards. Each target had a bull's eye on it with a small black centre, and a small piece of orange ribbon attached to the top. He checked the wind at each target and made mental note of its approximate speed and direction.

He attached the silencer to the end of the barrel and ensured it was tight. Then he carefully loaded the five-clip magazine into the underside of the rifle. Removing his sunglasses, Ford lay down on the blanket and nestled the rifle into position. Ford sighted in the first target and adjusted the scope so that the target was in focus, then he checked the wind, it was blowing from his left. At three hundred feet Ford knew that the bullet would fly straight, so no need to compensate for wind drift. He steadied his position and relaxed his breathing, remembering what Alverez had told him, but never showed him. *Exhale, then fire.*

Ford squeezed the trigger and the rifle gave a gentle kick-back, he inhaled. He quickly switched positions and focused the spotting scope on the target and frowned.

Three inches off centre.

He took a deep breath; his body tingled with excitement. He loved being in control of such a powerful weapon. Ford relaxed then took aim at the same target. He checked again, this time it was almost the bull's eye. He repeated the process until he hit the target dead centre. His plan was to shoot all twelve targets from his current nest then move to another nest and repeat the process. The change of angle on the target would present unique challenges, which he had to master.

On the eighth target, which was up the grade of the hill at seven hundred and fifty yards away, he missed the target completely. He slapped himself on the forehead. "Dummy," he said out loud. "You didn't take the wind into consideration."

He quickly settled in to retake the shot. Taking careful aim, he fine-focused the scope, this time allowing about a quarter inch to the left of centre he exhaled and squeezed the trigger.

Ford looked through the spotting scope at his second shot. "That's a little better," he said smugly, seeing a gaping hole four inches from the centre. Ford repositioned to retake the shot. On his third shot he hit the target about an inch from dead centre. The next three targets each required two shots to hit near the centre bull's eye. On the eleventh target, which Ford could barely make out with the naked eye; however, the rifle scope brought it close enough that it seemed he could reach out and touch it. The twelfth target was eleven hundred yards up the slope, which was nearing the outer limit of the kill range of the rifle. The rifle scope showed Ford that at this distance the orange ribbon was straight out from the target which meant the wind was blowing quite strongly further up the hill.

Ford fired four shots at the twelfth target, missing the bull's eye each time. "Shit," he said after the fourth shot. "Come on, concentrate." He refocused his mind and scope and settled in for the fifth shot. The upward angle of the rifle was presenting some unique challenges. Frustrated, Ford backed away from the shot. Then he realized that he needed to raise the tripod, which elevated the barrel of the rifle. He raised it three inches then sighted the target again. This time the angle seemed more natural and more comfortable. Ford refocused the weapon and exhaled. The gentle kick of the rifle told him the shot was away. He peered through the spotting scope. "Yes, damn it, yes." After Ford had hit the twelfth target in two shots he stood up and took a rest.

The shooting exercise had drained him of energy, so he sat back and enjoyed a warm beer and a smoke, satisfied with how he had progressed. He knew that shooting the targets was far more demanding than killing a person. Ford knew that even the shots that missed the bull's eye would have, in all likelihood, killed his target, but he wanted them to be perfect shots. As Alverez had told him, o*ne shot, one kill.*

The next day Ford was up early and repeated the entire process. This time he started from the top target and moved down, which presented a different set of challenges. After he had completed the twelve targets, he realized that he had only used eighteen shots.

In the afternoon he repeated the entire process and this time he used only fourteen bullets, a number he could live with.

His next exercise was the mannequins. Ford placed the three plastic replicas at different positions on the hillside. He paced off approximate yardages then returned to his shooting position.

Ford fired only two shots at each mannequin. One shot in the head and the other in the heart. On all three mannequins, his aim was deadly. All would have killed the target instantly. He marveled at the amount of damage the shell did to the target, going in small and coming out large it left a gaping hole in the back of each mannequin.

Feeling that he was fairly proficient with the long rifle,

he took a quarter from his pocket and scrambled down the slope, past his encampment, towards a small grove of trees. He selected one on the outer edge and wedged the quarter in a limb junction about five feet off the ground. He then moved back up the hill to see if he could see the coin. He turned and climbed back up to his nest.

Ford figured if he could hit the quarter from over twelve hundred yards, he would consider himself a true sniper. He settled into his nest and sighted the rifle on the tree branch.

Fine tuning the scope, he found the quarter. Ford swung the rifle from left to right to visually determine how the wind was blowing. At the target there was little or no wind, but between him and the target there was a steady gust blowing across his bullet's trajectory. He had not tried this type of shot before. Ford focused on the coin that glinted in the early morning sunlight. Satisfied that he had taken the wind into consideration, he exhaled and squeezed the trigger. Ford was excited; he wanted to see if his marksmanship in real life matched that of his mind. He eyed the tree through the spotting scope and couldn't find the coin anywhere on the tree limb. Ford leapt up exuberantly, pumping his fists in the air.

Ford spent the next hour cleaning up his mess. He picked up every shell casing, along with the targets and destroyed mannequins. The drive back to the lower mainland was uneventful; he elected to take the back way through Agassiz. As he drove past the Federal Prison, he promised himself that he would never end up being an inmate. That was for those who failed at their purpose.

Ford returned the truck to the rental agency and loaded everything into his car. The camping gear he gave to Good

Will. The targets and mannequins he threw into an out of the way dumpster. Back in New Westminster, he parked at the Riverside Quay and bought a coffee in the food court. He found a bench far away from the market and opened the bag containing the shell casing. One by one he tossed all of them into the Fraser River, confident they would never be found. When the last task was completed, he called Seven. It went straight to voicemail.

"Seven, I'm back in town, so send the down payment to me at the Container Pub in Vancouver. Have them ask for Mr. Ford. I'll be there between three and four, so if you want this done, have the money there." Ford knew that Seven would likely send one of his gangster wannabes. He had been one of those guys nearly two years ago, a gangster wannabe. *That whole incident seemed to be a lifetime ago.* Ford found humour in that thought.

CHAPTER 27

IT HAD BEEN three days since the press conference with Chief Von Pleth and the AG, where they'd asked the public for any support they could offer in the way of tips or leads. The response had been overwhelming, and the 9-1-1 switchboard had been flooded with potential leads. The downside was that police were chasing ghosts, as most of the tips proved to be cases of mistaken identities, or in some cases, vendettas.

Weeks and Mills parked the police car next to the curb on Main Street. They had just finished their fifth false lead from the tip line that day, and they were getting frustrated.

"You know if O'Dell was still here, he would have beaten on something. I'm glad you're more evolved than he was." Weeks grinned.

The radio crackled to life. "One Delta Five, come in." Weeks looked at Mills and the radio crackled again. "One Delta Five, this is dispatch. You there?"

Weeks picked up the hand mic. "Go ahead dispatch, this is One Delta Five. Over"

"One Delta Five, meet the man at the Mountain Cement plant on Granville Island, tach three. Over."

"Dispatch, One Delta Five, meet the man at the Mountain

Cement plant on Granville Island, tach three, copy. Over" She turned to Mills. "Wonder what this is about?" Weeks started the car and turned on the lights. "Meet the man" was a code that meant see the detective on site, and get there ASAP. Weeks tore down Main Street, then hung a hard right onto West Second Avenue, then down Second onto West Sixth, taking another hard right on Granville Street. Due to heavy pedestrian traffic on the island, Weeks kept the lights on but slowed down considerably.

She pulled into the driveway at the Mountain Cement plant with its wildly painted silos, while Mills scanned the parking lot for a police car.

"Over there," he said, pointing. "That's Healy and Wheaton's car. I recognize the damaged trunk lid."

Weeks stopped next to the other police car and they both got out. "They must be inside," Weeks said. They made their way into the well-lit office, but didn't see them. Back outside Mills picked up the car mic. "Tach three to Wheaton. Over. Where are you guys? Over."

The radio came to life. "What took you guys so long? Look up. Waaaay up," Healy said. "And I'll call Rusty." Wheaton added.

Mills looked up at the towering cement silos. High up on the catwalk, he saw three people, Healy, Wheaton and a worker. The radio again came to life, "There's a ladder at the north end. Hurry up. I think you'll want to hear this."

Before long, Weeks and Mills joined Healy and Wheaton on the catwalk some seventy feet above the ground, where it commanded an unparalleled view of the tourist area on the island. Mills was panting from the exertion. "This better be important." He said, gasping for air.

Healy looked at the other detectives. “Mills, Weeks, meet Zolan MacCreedy, number one snitch; low life; stab you in the back; piece of garbage.” She turned to MacCreedy and winked. “Did I overlook any of your strong points?”

MacCreedy looked at Healy. “You’re funny. Follow me.” He turned away and started to walk the tee intersection of the catwalk. The four detectives followed him down a steep ladder onto another catwalk that led to a small shed beside the number two silo. When all were inside, MacCreedy closed the door. It was dimly lit and it was dusty. “I suppose you wonder why I called this meeting.” MacCreedy said with a chuckle, as he ran his hand through his greasy shoulder length brown hair. His sleeveless shirt showed a wide array of tattoos on his muscular arms. He looked at Healy and Wheaton. “Over to you.”

Healy was standing next to MacCreedy. She placed her hand on his shoulder, “I would like you to meet Constable Wayne Troy, RCMP undercover. Troy is undercover with Los Demonios for what, two years now, or something like that?”

MacCreedy looked at his feet. “Yeah seems like a lifetime. Two years, five months, eighteen days, eleven hours, and forty-one minutes…but who’s counting?” He lifted his head and a wide grin engulfed his face. “And I love it.”

Weeks stood facing MacCreedy “So, what’s this about?”

MacCreedy looked at Healy. “Boy, I’ll bet she’s a lot of fun at parties.”

“Cute asshole, really cute,” Weeks retorted.

“Hey, I don’t get to talk to my fellow law enforcement colleagues very often, so indulge me.” He reached into a barrel and brought out a tape recorder wrapped in plastic.

MacCreedy unwrapped the device and set it on the lid of the next barrel. "What you're about to hear was recorded two days ago. It's a meeting between Wilkinson, big cheese with the Los Demonios, and some guy called Nineteen with the Numbers Gang. The quality isn't that great, because I couldn't get close enough to them, plus the bar was a little noisy. He pressed play and the tape came alive. "Oscar Nineteen, as I live and…haven't seen you…what the fuck…on?"

"Dante Wilkinson…you haven't…a bit. You're still ugly as I…ber. How's…ness?"

"Same ole…ame ole, and you?"

"…complaints. Hey I know you're…A hit…has suggested that…heads of all the…portant gangs get…gether for a council…ing. What…you th…k? Is this some…the Los Demonios…trested in?"

"What…to talk…out?"

"The hitter is…gesting th…we take on the…ops. Says the six dead…ops is only a pre…ude of what could happen if each gang sent their hitters after the cops."

"Are you…tting me Oscar?"

MacCreedy paused the tape. "It gets a little clearer because I just got them another round for their table and I left my pen there. He pressed play again.

"Nineteen, is your fuckin' hitter nuts? A war with the fuckin' cops? That's fuckin' suicide."

"Don't dismiss it that quickly, Dante. The proposal has some merit. Check this out. Let's say we did go to war and the body count rose dramatically on their side. How eager do you think the cops would be to hunt us down? I would venture a guess that none of them are that ready to be shot to death. To most, it's a job, not an obsession that they're willing to die for."

"Wow, that's fucked up…really fucked up. Oscar, you guys have to stop using your product. Who is this hitter anyway? Is he on drugs, or just plain fuckin' stupid? How does he think we could win this war?"

"He's known to us. Personally, I think the idea has merit. I've got a meeting set up with three other leaders this week. I want to see what their take on this is, so I'll get out of your hair. Think about it, Dante. We can always meet again if you want."

"What I'd like Oscar is to meet this fuckin' idiot and see if he's actually from this planet. Tell you what, I'll think it over and talk to the boys about it. We'll be in touch."

MacCreedy pressed stop. "The Numbers guy walked out after that and I retrieved my pen. Personally, I'm not sure if the gangs could ever work together, let alone start a war with the cops."

Weeks shook her head. "Are these guys serious? Aren't we already being targeted?"

MacCreedy looked at Weeks. "Don't underestimate these guys. To them, you're just an obstacle. They watch the news like us and they like what's happening." He paused and lit a smoke. "Beside, most of the gangs don't do their own dirty work. They hire hitters to do their dirty work…and most of them would shoot their own mothers."

Healy reached over and grabbed MacCreedy's smoke and took a long drag, then handed it back to him. "He's right. The scuttlebutt coming from upstairs about the six shootings is that it's one shooter. Apparently, the prelim on the bullets is that they're all shot from the same weapon."

Wheaton opened the door to let in some fresh air and to let the smoke out. "So, you figure the gangs will go for this bullshit, or are they smarter than that?"

"It's hard to say. It largely depends on which gangs get involved. At last count, there were what, sixty or seventy gangs operating in the lower mainland? Hell, all they'd need is four or five to join forces and, presto, you've got a gangland onslaught on all police forces. Yah, I can see them doing that." MacCreedy took one last drag then snubbed out his cigarette. "Well, boys and girls, it's been fun, but I've got to get back to work. I'll try to get in touch with you if I hear of anything." He stepped out of the small shed and immediately went down the next flight of stairs.

Weeks stepped out of the small enclosure, determined that if a war broke out she was going to be on the winning side. Or so she hoped.

CHAPTER

28

FORD WAS SITTING at the bar nursing a glass of draft beer when a young Asian girl walked up to the bar. She flagged the bartender over. "Is there a Mr. Ford here?"

Jomo looked at her "Who do you want?"

"Mr. Ford," she politely said again.

Jomo looked around the bar and nodded at Ford then pointed to the girl.

Ford threw back the rest of his beer and slid off the stool. "You have a package for me?" he said, walking towards the girl. Ford liked what he was looking at. He guessed she was in her late teens or early twenties, approximately five-three, with a slender build, nice body, and a really pretty face.

She turned to face Ford. "Yes, I have a package and the information for you. If you have any questions, you're to call Seven or Nineteen immediately." She reached into her purse and produced a bulging envelope, then handed it to him. Without saying anything further, she turned and left the bar.

Ford watched her walk away. *Nice butt.* He stuffed the envelope into his back pants pocket and waved at Jomo. "Thanks."

In his car, Ford opened the envelope and saw a large wad

of cash, a mix of twenties, fifties, and hundreds. Also in the envelope was a sheet of paper with hand written information on it. Ford looked around him at the people walking along Powell Street. Deciding this wasn't the place to sit with a large amount of cash he stashed the envelope in the glove box and started the engine.

Ford was back in his apartment shortly after six-thirty. Rush hour traffic had been a bitch, and he was feeling a little agitated. On his small kitchen table, he placed the down payment into individual stacks. Seven had kept his part of the bargain; the money totalled twelve thousand, five hundred dollars, as agreed. He took a small pull on his beer then lit a smoke. Ford unfolded the piece of paper and read it over. It was sketchy information on the target. It gave him several addresses for Freddy Pham Lee and a few known associates and possible hangouts. As he was reading the information for a second time, his phone beeped an incoming message.

The screen popped open and there was a picture of Freddy Pham Lee standing in front of a restaurant. Ford took a drag of his smoke and zoomed in, bringing the face closer. He studied the image intently, burning it into his mind. He set the phone on the table, and pointed his finger at Lee's head. "Pow," he said, and closed the phone.

Ford finished his second beer, and then called Seven. It rang three times before it was answered. "Hello?"

"Seven, it's me, Ford."

"What's up, Ford? You get the package?"

"Yes, I did. Your delivery girl was pretty hot. Who is she?"

"Ah, you liked that did you? I kinda figured you would. She does odd jobs for us. Her name is Melissa Chow. You want her number?"

"Maybe later, when all this is done with. The reason I called has to do with the text. Lee is standing in front of a restaurant. Do you know where it is? I looked in the phone book and there are over a hundred of them, so I need some help narrowing it down."

"Hold on." Seven cupped his hand over the phone mic. Moments passed before he removed his hand again. "Sorry dude that was taken over a year ago."

"Shit. So it may take a while to find this mark?"

Seven took a deep breath. "Hey, I thought you were the professional killer. It doesn't bode well if you can't find your target." He laughed, "Hold on," he said. "Let's see, he's the head of the Golden Dragons. They're based out of Chinatown. I think it's around the corner of Keefer and Taylor. There should be a little café called the Jade Dragon, or something like that. Aside from that I don't know anymore. It's been a while since we checked this guy out. Maybe try tailing him?" Seven laughed again.

Ford had all he could do to keep from reaching through the phone and strangling the cocky little prick. Under his breath he swore he would get him. "Well, that will give me a starting point. Thanks, I'll be in touch." He ended the call. He shook his head. *If Alverez saw how sloppily these gangs operated he'd be shocked.* He remembered Alverez showing him their intelligence gathering operation. It had every gang member identified, where they worked and lived, their favourite restaurant, their girlfriends' places…the works. It was obvious to Ford that the gangs here didn't yet understand the importance of good intelligence. Ford walked over to his fridge and took out another beer. Maybe when this was finished, he could make some extra cash doing the leg work. That should be worth a pretty penny.

The next morning, Ford drove down to Columbia Street; he was in the market for a digital camera that had a zoom lens on it. He found a camera shop just up from the A&N Department store. The shop was mostly hidden by a large maple tree. It was one of the things Ford liked about New Westminster, how they kept the old buildings and lined streets and avenues with trees. It made the entire area stand out from the rest of the urban madness.

Within an hour, he had found what he wanted, and when he paid cash the salesman took an additional ten percent off, which delighted Ford. Outside on the street, the sun was shining brightly, without a cloud in the sky. Ford walked into a Greek restaurant, and requested a seat on the outside balcony overlooking the Fraser River a long way down. He ordered lamb souvlaki with a bottle of Mythos lager and sat back and studied the camera. Ford was amazed at how close the telephoto lens brought images, the autofocus feature was slick; he liked the results from his practice shots.

In the twenty minutes he had to wait, he took multiple close-up pictures of tugboats and log booms on the river. The camera would be perfect for getting to know Pham Lee. Seven gave him the impression that the method of the kill was entirely up to Ford, so he wanted to make the right decisions.

Ford finished lunch then headed for Chinatown to check out the area around Keefer Street. He had been there years ago when he was much younger on another dreadful family outing. Ford had just been placed with the Daniels; they already had another boy, Alex Thompson, in their care.

They came into Vancouver to give the boys some 'culture' as Wilbur Daniels called it. Neither Ford nor Alex had ever eaten Chinese food before. It tasted horrible and both of them spat it out. This infuriated Wilbur Daniels who made the two of them stand in the middle of the restaurant and eat a heaping plate of leftovers that Daniels scraped off other patron's plates. Both of them threw up, which made other patrons throw up. Ford remembered it as if it happened yesterday. Now, he parked just down the street from David Lam Park and grabbed his camera, sunglasses and hat. He became a tourist.

He walked the short distance to the corner of Keefer and Taylor and looked north. Seven was partially right. The Chinese restaurant was the only business with a garish neon sign. It read Pagoda Dragon. Ford casually strolled up the street, stopping every so often to appear to be window shopping. He stopped directly across from the restaurant and brought out his camera. Zooming in on the upper windows, he found them to be old and almost never used. They were covered with dingy curtains that allowed in little or no light. He continued up the street to the corner of Taylor and Main, then crossed over and went back down the opposite side of the street. What Ford saw wasn't very appealing to him. There wasn't one good nest that afforded him a clear shot at his target.

Standing in front of the restaurant Ford looked across the street at the low rise, likely offices or some sort of condominiums. He dismissed that site outright, as there wasn't a good escape route after the shot was taken. Ford was looking for an unobstructed vantage point with a well concealed exit onto an adjacent street or laneway.

Ford began to walk back to his car when a noisy Honda Prelude whizzed past him and braked suddenly in front of the restaurant. He calmly turned to see what was going on, camera at the ready. Three Asian men piled out of the black import car, laughing and speaking Mandarin, not seeming to care who saw them. Ford removed the lens cap and from the hip pressed the button, snapping off several pictures of the three young men. None of them matched his image of Pham Lee, so he guessed they were gang soldiers or just careless youths.

Back at his car Ford reviewed the images on the tiny two by two view screen. He looked up the street and saw a car leaving a curbside parking spot, so he hastily started his car and sped towards it. Just then, a police cruiser rounded the corner. Ford slowed down immediately and pulled into the vacant spot. The police car pulled up beside the black Honda, and two officers got out, donning their uniform caps. The shorter of the two poked his head into the open driver's window and turned to his partner, shaking his head. They then looked at the restaurant, and in unison, unhooked the safety strap on their weapons and entered the eatery.

Ford wished he was inside the restaurant to see what was going on. He sat patiently, when all of a sudden the front door of the restaurant burst open. The taller cop had one of the youths by the scruff of the neck and one arm twisted behind his back. Ford instantly sat up his pulse and breathing quickened. He watched as the cops muscled the youth into the back of the squad car. The two other youths stood in the doorway, and Ford could see they were mouthing off to the cops, who ignored them. Once they had the youth in the back seat, they took off their hats and got into the car, then sped away. The smaller youth gave them the finger as they drove away.

Ford relaxed and sat back. He had quite enjoyed the free show and wondered if they were Golden Dragons or just unlucky punks. It was obvious to Ford that, in order to find this Lee dude, he'd have to start at the base, and that was the man's crib. Ford pulled out the piece of paper with Pham Lee's addresses then started his car. Ford located two of the three addresses Seven had given him, neither of them were possible. The drive to the trendy Southwest Marine Drive and the third location would take a half hour, so Ford put in a CD and pulled away from the curb.

Ford was surprised that Pham Lee didn't live in Richmond. It had the largest Asian population in Western Canada, and would have allowed him to blend in more easily.

Twenty-five minutes later, Ford pulled alongside the curb about a half block from Pham Lee's gated property. This was what he was expecting for a gang leaders residence. The property overlooked the ocean and was well over two acres in size. Ford could only imagine how much it must have cost. He knew he couldn't get into the estate, nor did he want to. Security would be tight. The gate was reinforced, and there were security cameras everywhere. Ford took out his own camera and snapped a couple images of the gate and surveillance cameras, then sat back to wait.

Ford hated staking out targets; he would rather just walk up, blast them and leave. He had been sitting there for twenty minutes, but it felt like a couple of hours, when a black Mercedes Benz 750 sedan pulled up to the gate. All its windows were tinted dark, so Ford wasn't able to see who was in the car, but he hoped it would be Pham

Lee. He quickly wrote down the license plate number for future reference.

Ford watched as the large gate swung open and a stocky, bald Asian man dressed in all black stepped out to meet the car. He was carrying what looked like an Uzi. The car stopped and the driver's window came down. An Asian woman's face appeared. There was a brief exchange, then the window went back up and the car pulled into the tree-lined driveway.

A sharp rap on the passenger window startled Ford, who spun sideways to see an elderly lady peering into the window. He exhaled and relaxed. She motioned to him to roll his window down. Ford pressed the button, bringing the glass down. She raised her finger at him.

"What are you waiting for, sonny?" she said in a British accent. "You a cop, or are you casing the area?"

Ford looked at her; she could be just about anyone's grandmother. "Ma'am, I just got off work and I'm tired, so I'm just sitting here for a rest before I head home. Is that okay?"

"That's fine. As long as you're not a cop or a crook; I don't like either of them."

Ford smiled at her as she turned to continue down the sidewalk. He grinned and shook his head. *Stupid woman. Could have gotten herself shot*. Ford didn't like the idea that someone had noticed him, so as soon as the old woman was out of sight, he started his car and pulled away, his eyes fixed on the gate as he drove by.

Ford headed for the Container and a cold one. He'd need to revise his plan on how he'd find Pham Lee.

CHAPTER 29

DETECTIVE MICKEY O'DELL'S funeral at the Pastoral Meadows Cemetery drew a large crowd of police officers from every jurisdiction, including many from the United States. It was part of the blue tradition to attend the funeral of a fallen colleague, wherever they were located. O'Dell had no family except for the police and a few guys that would begrudgingly admit to being his friend. Throughout his police career he had pissed off just about everyone he knew, or who had taken the time to get to know him. O'Dell had been a loner, which was his main excuse for never getting married. A variety of speakers praised O'Dell for his many years of service and his dedication to the force. Very few said anything about him as a man, which reinforced everyone's opinion that he was basically an asshole.

The police chaplain, Rev. Mark Oberfeld, opened the service with the Lord's Prayer, followed by the police choir singing Rock of Ages, which had become a Metro Police tradition over the past twenty years. He then read from the Bible.

The service ended with the traditional twenty-one gun salute, which sent shudders through Detective Shelley Weeks' body. She looked toward the pale gray clouds that seemed to befit the mood on this day and wondered if he was in heaven or hell. She could guess.

Police Chief Von Pleth walked away from the gravesite followed closely by all ten division commanders who were to have a meeting instead of attending the wake. That did not go well with some of the commanders, who said it broke tradition. Von Pleth had asked that Lamp be in attendance to update the commanders on the progress in tracking down the killer of the six dead policemen.

The conference room at police headquarters was posh by any standards with oak paneling from floor to ceiling and a large oval table capable of seating thirty people. The table was inlaid with brass around the edge, and engraved in the centre was the metro police emblem. Each chair had a microphone, which also recorded everything said in the room.

Von Pleth sat at his usual spot at the head of the table in front of the large screen that was used for presentations. The room looked almost full with the ten commanders, their deputy commanders, and Lamp.

Lamp felt like a fish out of water at these briefing, not because he was the low man on the totem pole, but every word spoken was dissected by each person and things said often came back to bite the orator in the ass.

Von Pleth poured himself a glass of water and momentarily waited for the chatter to subside. Setting his glass down with deliberate force caused the room to become silent, and all eyes turned to him.

"Hello, everyone," Von Pleth said. We have five more of these to attend in the next week to ten days, and quite frankly, I'm not looking forward to that at all. Some of you have told me that by not going to the wake we're breaking tradition. Well I'd like to address that right here and now. I don't give a rat's ass about tradition right now, especially when I have people whose lives may be in danger. We can raise a glass to the fallen on any given day, but protecting our people has to take priority. Now, if some of you disagree with that outlook, well…tough. My door is always open if this doesn't sit well with you. Now, I've asked Sergeant Webber Lamp to join us. It's his job to get his people to catch the son-of-a-bitch and he'll give us a progress report." He paused to take a sip of water.

"As you may or may not have heard, the AG is going to endow the Metro Police with special authority to get this perp. By that I mean we can wiretap anyone we think may be connected using one blanket warrant. We can detain whomever we need to. Now the AG wasn't very clear on this point, but she didn't specifically say we *couldn't* use extraordinary means. So we can assume that we can use whatever means necessary. We also have expanded search and seizure authority, whereby we can enter any establishment with one blanket warrant. She wants to nab this bastard as much as we do, and she's willing to play ball with us, so we'd better produce some tangible results." He took another sip. Von Pleth looked at the faces looking at him and knew that he had their support. "Okay, at this time I'd like to hear from Sergeant Lamp." Von Pleth leaned back in his chair to listen.

Lamp pulled his chair closer to the table and adjusted the microphone. "Thank you, Chief Von Pleth. Good afternoon commanders and deputy commanders. I wish it was under different circumstances that we were meeting. Currently there isn't much to go on. We have a sketch of a person of interest that may or may not be linked to the murders. As of this morning we've had no hits on the image. Ballistics has confirmed that all six dead officers, plus the informant Hooper and two gang members, were killed with the same weapon. The investigation into the hack on the police database has not produced any results. The video surveillance of the café has been secured and detectives have questioned everyone who uses the Internet café."

Lamp paused to reorganize his papers. "The report of a black SUV being followed by the undercover team also has not provided any leads. We are working with the Integrated Gang Squad and we're questioning every gang member who drives a Black Escalade." He took a sip of water. "I have another piece of bad news, and some of you may have already heard this. My detectives have learned from an undercover RCMP officer within the Los Demonios motorcycle gang that the Numbers Gang has someone who is trying to start a war with the police." He stopped to look at the faces of those in attendance. Lamp was able to read a few of their expressions, some showed amazement, some showed contempt, while others shook their heads in disbelief.

"All available Detectives are working to track down those taking part in this insanity. If this information is correct, we could see more bodies in the days and possibly weeks to come. The undercover officer told detectives that he'd try to contact them if he heard anything else about the subject." Lamp flipped the last sheet of paper over. "Well that's about all I have to report at this time. You will be kept posted about any new developments. Lamp turned off his mic and leaned back.

"Thank you, Sergeant Lamp," said Von Pleth. "I know your detectives are doing the best that they can and hopefully they'll catch the break they need to crack this case." He looked at the group around the table. "Okay, any questions for Sergeant Lamp?" Von Pleth saw several hands shoot up in unison, and he sighed. "Charlie, what's your question?"

Lamp spent the next half hour answering a variety of questions from all the attendee's including Von Pleth. When the last question was answered he turned off his mic and leaned back.

Von Pleth acknowledged his old academy buddy, Mike Tillsberry. "What's your question, Mike?"

Tillsberry leaned into his mic, "Is there any consideration of bringing in the military to declare martial law if this whole thing goes horribly wrong?"

Von Pleth didn't know exactly how to respond. "Let's just say this, Mike, and I'll be perfectly candid, we will use whatever force is necessary to keep our people safe, protect this community and, get this bastard. I'm sure the mayor has already made overtures to Ottawa to flush out any interest in providing military assistance should we require it. But we have to be realistic, if this is a single shooter martial law would have a hard time intercepting him, but it's something we have to consider seriously should another body show up."

CHAPTER

30

FORD ARRIVED AT Commercial Drive and Renfrew Street and found a parking spot. He darted across Renfrew Street and entered the Emperor's Tea Room to check out a lead provided by Seven. Ford's eyes quickly adjusted and he scanned the room. Not seeing his target, he motioned to the elderly lady behind the counter and asked, "Could I get a can of Coke, please?"

While she shuffled to the cooler, Ford visually cased the seating arrangements and determined he couldn't do the job from the inside, as it was too open. He paid for the coke and left. Once outside, he pulled the tab and took a swig of the cold beverage. His eyes searched the roof tops of the adjacent buildings looking for a suitable nest should Pham Lee show up. Ford's eyes came to a stop at a three story condominium that was under construction about a block away.

Ford looked at his watch. It was nearly two-thirty. Taking another swig, Ford strolled up Renfrew toward the condo site. He spotted a security guard sitting in his shed near the locked gate. He continued to walk the perimeter of the work site, ending up in an alley that exited onto Renfrew. Ford spotted a hole in the fence which would allow him access if necessary. Making his way back to his car, he felt his plan was coming together should Pham Lee actually make an appearance.

Ford sat back and relaxed. He spotted a black Mercedes Benz that was making a turn onto Renfrew. His eyes followed the luxury car as it pulled up to the tea room. Was it Pham Lee? He checked the license plate number; it was Pham Lee's ride. Ford quickly checked under the driver's seat for reassurance that his weapon was there. It was. Three Asian males exited the luxury sedan. None of them was Pham Lee. Ford grabbed his binoculars from the glove box and focused them on the sedan. The three who got out first were already going toward the tea room. One entered the tea room while the other two waited outside.

Ford grabbed his Glock and his baseball cap. As he got out of his car, he donned his sunglasses and stuffed the gun into the back of his pants. Ford darted across the street, about a hundred feet or so away from Pham Lee's car.

Ford instantly recognized Pham Lee who was just exiting the car. The two Asian men stood beside the doorway into the tea room. Obviously they were bodyguards. Ford approached the tea room, weapon drawn, safety off. He dispatched the two bodyguards with two single shots to their heads. Ford aimed the weapon at Pham Lee who had a look of shock and horror written all over this face. Ford fired three shots, two to the chest and a third between the eyes. He hurriedly took out his cell phone and snapped a picture, then bolted back to his car.

Ford's heart rate was pounding as his car rocketed up the adjacent alleyway. He checked his rearview mirror to see if he was followed. He was not. Ford guessed that people had seen the execution and were in the process of calling 9-1-1, so he knew he had to ditch the car in a hurry. He felt fairly safe that he couldn't be identified; all that people could report was a brown skinned man about 6' tall, with a ball cap and sunglasses and a black jacket.

His mind was clear as he pulled onto Commercial Drive and headed east towards First Avenue. He wanted to put some distance between him and the event, so the freeway was the fastest route. Twenty minutes later, Ford took the Brunette Avenue East exit off the freeway then hung a left on Cumberland. The industrial area would provide an excellent hiding place for his car. Ford found an abandoned warehouse that had the door open enough to get his car into the cavernous building. He'd leave it sit for a while before taking it to a discount paint shop. Ford stood silently looking at his glossy black Mustang, musing about what colour it should become. He favoured red. He waited across the street at a mom and pop café for nearly three hours until he felt it was safe, and then went back to the warehouse to retrieve his car.

A short while later he was back in his apartment enjoying a cold Corona and a smoke. He called Seven. It went instantly to message. He hung up then sent a text message to him with the attached photo of Pham Lee lying on the sidewalk, and included instructions about where he'd be waiting for the remainder of his money. He lay down on the sofa and closed his eyes.

Ford couldn't remember when he fell asleep, but he was awakened by his cell phone. He rubbed the sleep from his eyes and checked the phone. No caller ID. He pressed the talk button on his phone. "Hello."

"Hey, it's Seven. I got your text message. Nice picture,

dude. You want me to send your money via courier to the same place?"

"Sure. Is there a problem?" Ford said sensing something wasn't right about the question and the tone in Seven's voice. Normally he was cocky and full of self importance, but now he seemed rushed, somewhat panicky and inpatient.

"Well, yeah, as a matter of fact. We seem to be having a small problem right now."

Ford's senses went into full alert. Was the phone being tapped? Was he compromised? "What seems to be the problem?"

"Well, from looking at our security monitors, I count at least twenty fuckin' cops around the house. They're just waiting for something? So it's going to be a little tough for me to get you the cash."

"Fuck. I told you this was going to happen, didn't I? Fuck. So, what's your plan?"

"Our plan is to get the hell out of here once we've removed anything incriminating, then I'll contact you with a drop-site. Does that work for you?"

"What? You said the place is surrounded. How are you getting out?"

"Ha. Remember when we told you we had this place built. Well we had an escape route built into it. We're just about finished wiping the computers and the cash is all but boxed up. Then we're splitting. If all goes well, I'll give you a call in an hour or so."

"I guess that will have to do."

Ford looked out his window, the tugboats were working and pleasure boats were zipping along; all normal for the waterfront. "Okay. I'll talk to you when I talk to you." He pressed end on his phone and tossed it onto the sofa.

Ford looked in his fridge. Nothing looked edible. He threw on a different jacket and grabbed another ball cap and headed to Gito's Italian restaurant on East Coloumbia. It was three twenty-five. He couldn't remember when he'd last had a proper meal. Ninety minutes later Ford was back in his apartment feeling stuffed by the delicious meal of lasagna with chunks of New York steak. He clicked on the television and watched the early news. Ford paid close attention to the segment about three bodies shot dead in front of a tea house. The reporter talked over the photograph of a rough drawing of the suspect, calling the shooting a brazen act of gangland activity. Ford chuckled. It didn't look anything like him.

It wasn't until eight-thirty that Seven called back. Ford picked up the cell and pressed talk. "Hello."

"Hi, it's Seven. We're back in business. So where do you want the money delivered?"

Ford mulled that over. "How about the Westminster Quay? Let's say…in an hour?"

"Done. We'll send the same delivery person as the last time. Oh, I almost forgot. Nineteen has discussed your idea with three other gang leaders. Two of them are in. The third is sitting on the fence. He has two more meetings soon, so with any luck we should know by tomorrow night whether we do this or not."

"That is very good news. If this happens, you'll see. The cops will cave and you guys should have unimpeded access to your product and network." Ford smiled, fingers crossed. This venture was fraught with problems, but he figured he could handle it as long as he was in charge…his plan… his rules. He liked the idea of living on the edge and hoped he wasn't biting off more than he could chew. The idea of taking on the cops would keep him on the edge and make him a boat load of cash in the process. *Let the mayhem begin.*

"Well let's cross that bridge when we get to it. In the mean time, I'll get the twelve and a half grand out to you. Well gotta run, we've got things to do." With that, the line went dead.

At nine-fifteen Ford's cab pulled into the deserted parking lot and he walked the short distance to the Quay. The steady rain had chased all but the most ardent outdoor enthusiasts inside, so he knew they would be left alone. He dashed toward the empty casino lobby and hugged the wall to escape the drizzle. Ford didn't like waiting, but knew the money made it worth it. He lit up a smoke and waited. About ten minutes had passed when a grey Lexus iS350 pulled up and stopped. His attention piqued when he watched the beautiful Asian girl get out of the passenger side. She gracefully deployed her umbrella then scanned the area. Spotting Ford leaning against the building she casually walked toward him. When she was within ten feet, she asked, "Mr. Ford?"

Ford flicked the cigarette towards the parking lot. "Yep, that would be me. Are you Melissa? That's what Seven told me that was your name."

She just smiled and looked back at the car. "Yes, it's Melissa, and that's my boyfriend. Any more questions?"

Ford lit up another smoke. "I guess not. Do you have a package for me?"

"Yes, I do." She reached into her shoulder bag and produced a white envelope that she handed to Ford. "It's all there. Do you want to count it?"

Ford shook his head and took possession of the money,

"Nah, I don't think Seven or Nineteen want to fuck with me. Thank you, Melissa. Hope to see you again." He winked at her then smiled. She smiled warmly then turned and ran towards the car. Ford stuck the envelope into his jacket pocket. He turned up his collar and headed for a cab.

Out of the corner of his eye, he spotted a marked patrol car coming down the road toward the parking lot. He froze and his heart rate increased, while his breathing became shallow. He wondered if this was a set up. Not wanting to be obvious, he walked past the cab toward the pedestrian gate, while keeping an eye on the cop car. It turned off Begbie Street onto Front Street and headed south. He breathed a sigh of relief and headed back to the cab stand.

CHAPTER

31

WEEKS AND MILLS returned to the police station after chasing down another dead end from the tip line. It was the fifth they had investigated that left them with nothing. They walked the short distance from the parking lot to the station. The rain had subsided into an annoying drizzle, which pretty much matched their mood. “You know,” Weeks said, as she opened the door to the station, “If I didn’t know better, I’d say this guy is a ghost. Nobody can disappear that well without leaving some kind of trail.”

“He’s good, but I know for a fact we’re better. We’ll catch a break and we’ll nail the bastard. It’s just going to take time.” Mills said, going through the doorway without waiting for Weeks.

“Some gentleman you are!” She laughed.

“I’ll get the next one.”

In the bullpen area they saw most of the team working the phones. Even the officers with CIs were coming up empty, which had them second guessing themselves, all the while hoping and praying that nobody else got killed.

Lamp came out of his office. “Listen up, everyone.” He paused for a brief moment giving them time to focus on him. “Ballistics just got back to us. The three dead bangers that got shot yesterday…Well guess what? Our shooter has returned. So it looks like our shooter is working both sides of the street."

"Sarg, how can that be? The description from the latest shooting isn't anything close to resembling the image we have of the suspect? Is he a bloody chameleon?" Weeks poured a cup of coffee. A shred of doubt crept into her mind. She resisted it and reassured herself that she had gotten the image correct.

Lamp leaned against a desk. "Again you want answers from me that I don't have. Maybe the witnesses got it wrong; maybe your image is wrong. At this point in time the shooter could be one of you guys for all we know. As much as I hate to be insensitive, until this guy makes a bonehead mistake, I think he's free to roam around and kill again pretty much with impunity."

"Uh uh no way. This guy is good but not that good. The image out there is correct, of that I'm positive. Mander said it was unlikely anyone can lie under hypnosis, so it's accurate." Weeks said confidently.

"Geez, thanks for the pep talk Sarg. You really know how to pick us up." Wheaton said, tossing a wad of paper into the garbage can next to Lamp.

Lamp watched it hit the floor next to his feet then looked at the faces of his detectives. "Sorry people, but I call it as I see it. Besides, we've had tough cases before, just not this close to home. We all know somebody who's been killed, which makes this harder to swallow. Its times like this that I wish Canada still had the death penalty. Hell, even death is too good for this bastard."

"Sarg, I think I can speak for every member of the force

in saying that we don't like the idea of being sitting targets. I mean, we're the goddamn police department and we can't even feel safe doing our jobs…shit, man. I don't know about the rest of you, but I didn't sign up to be picked off by a whack job with a grudge or a death wish." Wheaton crossed his arms and rocked back in his chair.

Lamp rose to his feet. "Good, get it out if it makes you feel better. I'll bet there are twenty-two hundred other officers who have similar feelings as you do Gerry, but they're coping with it and doing their jobs. That's all we can ask and, you're right, none of us signed up to be a target. But, this is the reality of the job. There are nut jobs out there that hate cops, but they don't shoot us. And then we have our current shooter who doesn't value human life and thinks nothing of killing someone, cops included. So, long and short, we have to deal with it and continue to do what we're paid to do, serve and protect. Remember, wear your vests and travel in pairs and get eyes in the back of your heads. This guy could be anywhere. So let's get this bastard."

Weeks looked at Mills and Wheaton; she could see fear on both their faces. She wondered if they saw the same fear on her face. Weeks toyed with her coffee cup until her phone rang.

"Hello, this is Weeks." She flipped her notepad to a blank page and readied her pen.

"Detective Weeks, this is Troy. We met a few days ago. You're the first one that has picked up the phone."

"Ah yes, I remember you."

"Hey, you guys need to know something. I overheard Wilkinson and one of his lieutenants saying something about four or five of the larger gangs agreeing to this war against the cops. From what I overheard, they're calling their shooters together to map out targets. Shit, gotta run. Someone's coming."

Weeks sat stunned, staring at her notepad on which she'd scribbled *war is coming,* the phone still held to her ear. She snapped back to reality. "Sarg, you're gonna want to hear this," she said, standing up. "Hey, everyone listen up." Weeks waited for everyone to stop talking. When she was satisfied she had their attention. "I just got off the phone with a RCMP undercover who said he overheard the Los Demonios leader talking to his lieutenants about the impending war. The undercover said four or five of the larger gangs have agreed and they're getting their shooters together to select targets. Sounds like it could happen at any time."

The room fell completely silent. Calls were cut off, and phones were hung up.

Lamp stood beside an empty desk. "Who is this undercover? Is he reliable?"

Weeks sat on the edge of her desk. "Yes, he's completely reliable. He's the undercover that we met with a few days ago. He's RCMP. We met him at the Mountain Cement Plant. Remember Pam?"

"Yeah, I remember, but why's he calling you? He's my contact." Pam Healy seemed a little defensive.

"He said he tried, but your number was busy. I just happened to answer my phone."

Healy leaned back in her chair. "This guy is solid, Sarg. If he says shit's about to happen, wear your rubber boots."

Lamp shook his head. "Now that's a visual I can do without. Weeks, give the Gang Unit a call. Let them know what you've just told us. Maybe their sources can pinpoint which gangs are in on this. I think it's about time for some pre-emptive police work. I'll let the chief know what's about to come down, then hopefully the AG will invoke the Police Protection Act."

Healy looked at Wheaton and shrugged. "What's that, Sarg?"

"Didn't you read the memo I send out? The Police Protection Act gives the police the power to take anyone into custody that has the potential of committing a felony and hold them. This will allow us to pick up gang members without a warrant and hold them incommunicado for seventy-two hours. Longer, if there is a viable threat."

Weeks looked around the room. Most of the detectives were nodding their heads in approval. Her eyes darted around the room. "Sarg, I have a question, and I don't mean to rain on your parade but…"

"What is it Weeks?"

"Well Sarg, the Protection Act will only help us if it's the gangs themselves that are doing the shooting. But they're using outside hitters, so unless these scumbags roll, we'll never know who the shooters are."

Lamp walked to the front of the room. "Glad to see someone was paying attention. I was wondering if anyone would pick up on that. You're right, but if we hold these low-life idiots incommunicado, maybe we can sweat out the names of their hitters and put an end to this insanity. Even the dumbest criminal gang leader knows who's doing his dirty work, even if it's just a first name or an alias." Lamp sat against the desk edge. "Here's our plan, and this doesn't leave this room, understood?" He stopped and looked at each member of his squad. He watched as heads nodded.

When he was satisfied that everyone agreed, he continued. "Those that we pick up will be brought into the station where they will be apprehended. They will not be booked. They will not be fingerprinted. They will *not be abused* in any way shape or form. Then they will be taken out the back door into a waiting van and moved to an undisclosed location. That way, if any of their lawyers make an issue of it, we have no paper trail linking us to them. We expect…*no*, we *demand* that nobody talks to their media contacts. If we see one fuckin' news van outside hoping for a scoop, it'll blow this whole goddamn thing up in our faces. Everyone clear on that?"

Weeks shot her hand up. She had visions of Abu Ghraib prison in Iraq or other CIA black-ops camps in third world countries. "Sarg, an undisclosed location? What? Are we copying the USA? Are we privy to the location?" Weeks looked around the room and got the immediate sense that her co-workers didn't see a problem with the arrangement.

Lamp stood up. "No, that's why it's an undisclosed location. Plausible deniability, and all that. Suffice it to say, we've got a location that is central to all divisions that we'll be using to obtain the information we're seeking. The Chief along with Crown Council will be putting together a team to interrogate anyone that is picked up. I will of course be putting my recommendations in to the Chief, but it will be solely his decision if you're asked to participate or not. Okay, people, we've got our work to do, so let's get our butts moving. Remember, don't be a hero, call for back-up if you're in any trouble, understand?"

As if on cue the group stood. The shuffling of chairs made considerable noise. "One other thing people, I've asked the

Gang Squad to send us a list of names of the leaders of all the gangs in the lower mainland, and I've asked SWAT to start rounding these suckers up. So maybe check with your CIs for their exact whereabouts and relay that info to SWAT."

CHAPTER

32

FORD SPENT THE next day chasing down a discount paint shop to have his car repainted. After much haggling, he settled on Big Bob's Auto Painting Shop. For nine hundred and fifty dollars cash he'd get a complete exterior paint. Ford chose Diablo red.

He gave Big Bob fifty percent down and hopped into one of the shop's loaner cars, a Chevy Sprint that was basically a piece of crap. But it worked, and Ford didn't have anything pressing to do anyway.

The next morning Ford pulled the loaner car into the driveway of Big Bob's Auto Painting. He saw his car sitting inside the doorway, shining brightly. He liked what he saw. Ford walked into the office and saw Big Bob sitting behind a cluttered desk.

"Looks good, man," he said, pulling out the rest of the money he owed. Ford walked over to Big Bob and handed the wad of twenties and fifties to him. "I think that squares us up." Big Bob took the wad and quickly counted it, then refolded the bills and stashed them in his pocket. Ford knew that money would never be entered into the company's books, which suited him fine. *Screw the government.*

Big Bob got out from behind the desk and stuck his head

through the side door, whistled and nodded his head to someone inside. Within seconds the car started and slowly pulled outside. Big Bob motioned to Ford to follow him. Outside, the young driver tossed the keys to Big Bob, who in turn handed them to Ford.

"Enjoy your ride, *amigo*," he said, turning back to his shop.

Ford walked around the car. Now, all he had to do was find another set of plates on the off chance that someone had seen him leaving the Pham Lee hit and had written it down. And he knew of the exact place, Metrotown Mall.

Ford fired up the five-liter. He liked the sound the engine made. He popped it into first and purposely rode the clutch, allowing the rear tires to put on a smoke show for the guys in the shop. He laughed as the car tore off down the street. At the light, he inserted a Nicole Smack CD and cranked up the volume.

About a mile down Kingsway Avenue, Ford pulled into the left turn lane. Across the intersection was the prime place to find a new set of plates. He pulled into the parkade and slowly drove up and down the lines of vehicles, looking for another red Mustang. It took him over twenty minutes to cover the entire parkade, and as he was about to leave he spotted one. There was even a parking spot beside it. Ford quickly pulled in, retrieved his screw driver from the glove box and hopped out. He checked both ways and was sure he was alone. Seeing nobody close by, Ford quickly removed the plates.

Ford had just finished taking the plates off when a woman carrying packages came walking between the rows of vehicles toward him. Ford froze. He was squatting at the rear of the other car. He hoped like hell that this wasn't her car. He quickly stood up and moved to his car. He opened the trunk and tossed in the second set of plates. Ford then bent over as if he was looking for something. The woman looked at Ford as she passed by enroute to the next row of vehicles. He breathed a sigh of relief. Within minutes he had finished the swap. "Stupid ass," he said aloud, "why didn't you wait until dark. Go to fuckin' jail over a set of goddamn plates. Dumb ass." He hopped into his car and sped off.

Back out on Kingsway Ave., Ford headed towards New Westminster. He was hungry and bored; he needed something to take his mind off of the current situation. Since he'd been back from LA, he hadn't had a day off and he felt he deserved some down time. The first place Ford visited was The Brass Pole in the Billy Barker Hotel, an "A" circuit peeler bar in New Westminster. It was eleven in the morning. He was surprised that he could have breakfast and a beer while he watched beautiful women take their clothes off. Life was good.

Ford stayed to watch the entire stable of women strut their stuff on the small stage; he particularly liked the swing they had above the stage.

A little past two, his cell phone rang, so he quickly left the stage area and went to a quieter area by the main door. "Hello?" he said, plugging his other ear to shut out the hoots and hollers from the crowded room.

"It's me, Seven. Where the hell are you? Sounds like a wild party going on. Can we meet? We've got some things to iron out."

Ford craned his neck close to the corner beside the defunct pay phone station. "You want to what? I didn't hear you."

"Can we meet?" Seven repeated.

Ford still couldn't hear. "Hold on. I'm going outside. This fuckin' place is a zoo." He cupped the phone and made his way to the glass swinging doors and exited the historic hotel. "Okay. What did you say?"

"I said can we meet? We've got some things to iron out."

Ford quickly eyed his surroundings. Nobody was within earshot. "Sure. When and where?"

"Let's say around four at our new place. I'll text you the address and directions if you can make it."

Ford looked at his watch. Two hours. "Sure, that's doable."

"Okay, see you then. Enjoy the party," Seven ended the call.

Ford grinned and returned to the scene inside. Twenty minutes later, he made his way back to his apartment. He needed to change clothes and let the effect of the beers wear off.

At three-twenty, Ford's alarm woke him. He stumbled to shut it off, cursing when he couldn't find the off button immediately. "Shit," he yelled when he stubbed his toe.

The text message, which included the map to the new control centre for the Numbers Gang, showed Ford that he needed to drive across the Pattullo Bridge into Surrey.

Their new digs were located in the Port Kells area on a sprawling acreage just off the freeway. The trip there took Ford all of twenty minutes, so he arrived earlier than expected. He sat in his car smoking a cigarette watching the non-descript rancher-style house. Ford could see a small corner of the back yard where the gang members parked their expensive vehicles out of sight. He pulled into the driveway at four p.m., stuffed his Glock behind his back, and walked up to the door. He pressed the doorbell and stood back. Ford knew that someone was looking out the peephole, so he instinctively gave a one finger salute which resulted in the door being hastily opened.

Ford walked into the house as if he owned it. He could see Seven and Nineteen sitting around a large dark dining room table that was piled high with cash.

"What's up?" he said, walking towards the table. Ford saw Seven motioning him to sit down.

"Right on time, dude, how was your party? Sounded like it was really rocking?" Seven said as he tossed a wad of fifties to a young girl operating the counting machine in the kitchen.

"Oh that. I was at a peeler bar in New West. You know they've got some gorgeous girls working there. You guys should get out some night and go have a peek." Ford smiled.

Felix Seven leaned onto the table with arms crossed. "Maybe we'll do that when things slow down. Wanted to bring you up to speed on this war of yours…" he looked at Nineteen and nodded.

Oscar Nineteen deliberately finished sorting a stack of hundred dollar bills then wrapped an elastic band around them and tossed them to the young brunette running the counting machine. He removed his glasses and leaned back. "Seems there's an appetite for what you've proposed among the other major gangs. I've talked to most of the leaders, which was no easy feat let me tell you. As you've guessed, we don't like each other very much, so getting them to even listen to your insane proposal has been a challenge."

He stood and rubbed his neck. "The long and short of it is this…five gangs plus ours are in so far. Los Demonios are in and have committed their associate gang, the Black Widows to do their bidding. The International Brotherhood is in; Bondrah Bros are in; Big Valley Boys are in, and the Two-Sixty-Fourth Street Gang is also in. I'm still waiting to meet with Brendelson from the Scratchy Crew, and Tolls from the Wedge Gang. All in all, I'd say we're assembling quite a bit of firepower for your little war." Nineteen sat down and took a sip of his coffee.

Ford sat back in the chair, rocking it on two legs, hands behind his head. He set the chair back down with a thud. "This isn't my war. This is the gangs taking control of their respective turfs. All I'm doing is facilitating such a position. Did these guys tell you how many hitters they're going to commit? It's one thing to say yes, it's another to have people step up to the plate."

"From what I've been told, there will be at least ten hitters. How many do you think will be needed to pull this off?" Nineteen walked to the window overlooking the backyard and stared out.

Ford closed his eyes. "I was thinking that five or six good hitters could make life totally hell for any cop, but any more than that might become uncontrollable."

"That few?" Seven said with surprise. "I would have thought you would want twenty, maybe thirty hitters. Get in there, bang, bang, bang, and get out."

Ford shook his head. "This isn't going to be a one shot deal. It's going to be a sustained effort for about a week, as the opportunities present themselves."

Other members of the Numbers Gang had gathered in the dining room area, keen on hearing what was going to happen.

"You'll need to explain the logic of that." Nineteen said sitting down. He held up his hand to silence the members who were talking.

Ford leaned forward elbows on the table, arms crossed. "Simple. If you want to drive fear deep into their hearts, you need to sustain the attack. That way they'll never know if today's the day. If they know the risk of being killed is always present, that'll affect them in ways they don't even know, and it'll give your soldiers the ability to move about more freely, as long as they're using their heads. A one-time attack will just piss them off and then they'll come at every gang full tilt. Trust me Nineteen, this is what was done in LA, and there's no reason why it won't work here as well."

"So let me get this straight," Seven chimed in. "You figure five, maybe six hitters can bring the Metro Police to their knees? Doesn't make any sense."

Ford looked at Seven. *What an idiot. Have to explain everything to him.* "Let me explain. Let's say you're a cop, and in the past week there has been...let's say ten cops killed. Your dick sergeant tells you to go out there and get the bad guys. So you, being a dumb cop, say 'sure, Sarg'. But the minute you walk out of the station what's on your mind? Well, I'll tell you what. 'Am I next? Where's the bullet coming from?' That's what's on your mind. And if you're married with kids; what do you think your wife or husband will say to you. 'Have a good day dear'. Knowing that you might not come home? You think that wouldn't add just a little pressure? Do you think you'd be an effective cop out on the street with that on your mind?" He paused. "I don't think so. There'd be a severe case of the blue-flu."

The room was silent, except for the counter who continued

to add up the large amount of cash stacked on the table and kitchen counter. Nineteen looked around the room at the faces of his crew, then down at the money on the table. "So, you figure the cops are going to just roll over on this? Or is there something that you're not telling us?"

Ford figured this would come up. "Oh, I've thought about this a lot, and this also had come up in LA. The cops down there began hunting anyone and everyone who they thought might be involved. Rounded them all up and threw their sorry asses in jail for weeks, months on end. Sanchez even said they had to move gang bangers into other city jails. But the war continued because the cops didn't know who was doing the shooting. The gang members that got thrown into the jug had perfect alibis for the time of the shootings that kept on, day in day out, night in and night out. Oh sure, the cops figured that the Bluds and the Crypts were behind the killings, but they couldn't prove it because everyone clammed up. Which, I might add, you might want to advise the other gangs that this is how they'll have to act. I think some English dude said it best…'loose lips sink ships', something to do with the Second World War, and all that."

"So what about SWAT? You think these guys will just sit around waiting? Those bastards will be front and centre," Chevy Three added.

"Who's to say they aren't first on the list?" Ford smirked.

Nineteen laughed and shook his head. "Man, you've got balls the size of…fuck…just big balls. Taking on SWAT, now that's ballsy. And just how the hell does this happen?"

Ford didn't like being questioned. "If I told you that then I'd have to kill you. Are you sure you want to know?"

"Seven, he's your brother. Is this making any fuckin'

sense to you? If so, please explain it to him?" Ford said, somewhat frustrated.

Seven stood with his hands on the table. "Ford are you bullshitting me? Or are you for real? You're either as stupid as a rock or as good as you pretend to be? Nobody goes up against SWAT and comes out alive. They're mean motherfuckers and they don't mess around. So what makes you so special?"

Ford stood and moved his face inches away from Seven. "Because, asshole, they don't know I'll be coming. You think I haven't thought about every scenario regarding this matter? Well, if it's a demonstration you want, it'll be a fucking demonstration you will get. SWAT doesn't mean shit to me. They're just a bunch of amped up motherfuckers in dark clothing. No more, no less. They bleed out just like a regular beat cop."

Nineteen held up his hands. "Okay, guys, dial it back a few notches. We're all on the same side here, remember? Ford, if you say you can do this, and so far you've proven you can…if you take out a SWAT member that will be proof enough for me and Seven, as well as the other guys in this war. And as an added bonus, you take out a SWAT member and I'll give you twenty grand, just for the pure hell of it. How does that sound?"

Ford shot Nineteen a menacing glance. "You're on. Then maybe we can get down to business and dispense with the cockfighting." He stubbed his smoke out in the full ashtray. "I'll be in touch. Oh, and here's a freebie for you. You guys might want to try driving something less obvious. Fuck, just look out back and tell me what you see doesn't scream gang banger." He watched as Seven and Nineteen looked at each other, then at the other members around the room.

Nineteen moved to the window, paused, then looked back at Ford. “Makes sense man. Now that you mention it, it makes fuckin’ good sense. We’ll see what we can do.”

CHAPTER

33

IT HAD BEEN two days since Lamp gave the detectives their marching orders to find out the locations of every gang leader and member and relay that information to SWAT. In two days, SWAT had rounded up sixty-two gang members and leaders from eight different gangs.

In an undisclosed location were the leaders of the Red Dragons, the Black Widows, the Golden Dragons and the Medieval Thrust, as well as soldiers from the Wedge Gang, 264th Street Gang, and the International Brotherhood Gang.

Weeks and Mills were out pounding the pavement, looking for the leaders of Los Demonios. The gang unit had provided known locations and associates, so it was their task to find Wilkinson and Durant, the number one and two of the motorcycle gang. The two detectives had stopped at six of the locations on their list, but nobody had seen the two bikers, or at least they weren't talking. Even their CIs could not pinpoint their exact location?

Detective Weeks nosed the unmarked police car onto Main Street, coming off Second Avenue. "Dispatch, this is Detective Weeks, can you patch me through to the gang unit please?"

"Detective Weeks, this is dispatch. Patching you through."

Weeks waited as the call was transferred to the Gang Unit command office in the basement of the Main Street Station. Moments dragged on.

"Gang Unit, this is August. How can I help you?"

"This is Detective Weeks. We need some assistance."

"What are you working on, Detective Weeks?" Brenda August asked.

"We're trying to track down Los Demonios head honchos. So far we've hit six of their known locations, but no joy. Have any of your people been able to put eyes on these two? Over."

"Weeks, let me make a call to Hanson; he's been working their file for two years. If anyone knows where they are, he will. Over."

"We're pulling up, going on tach two." Weeks cradled the mic on the dash and pulled the police car next to the curb. She turned to Mills. "Let's hope Hanson has had better luck than we did. Almost like chasing a ghost. Something's got to be in the wind. Normally these guys make no bones about being seen? What do you think?"

Mills undid his seat belt and got out. "Makes sense. But what are they up to? Are they part of the gangs' war on police, or are they just conducting normal business?"

Weeks leaned against the car, elbows on the roof. "That's what I wondered as well."

The pair walked into the Main Street Station and ID'd themselves to the desk officer, who buzzed them in. Weeks and Mills hastily descended into the bowels via the staircase, their footsteps echoing their presence. They entered level three and proceeded down the brightly lit corridor, looking for room 315B.

The door was open, so Weeks and Mills walked in. Several officers who looked nothing like policemen sat around their desks, phones plugged into their ears.

The young officer sitting at the front desk addressed them. "You must be Weeks and Mills. Officer Hanson is waiting for you in the lunchroom, down the short hallway, on your left. Or, just follow the smell of food," she laughed as she pointed them toward the hallway.

Weeks nodded and they walked toward the hallway. "Boy, she wasn't kidding when she said follow the smell. What on earth is someone cooking in there? Smells like dead rat."

"Dead rat?" Mills said. "Nah, that smells more like fried running shoe with old sock sauce." They both laughed.

Entering the lunchroom was a shock. It was comprised of a fridge, microwave oven, coffee pot, a small sink, and lots of boxes. Boxes everywhere. The lunchroom obviously doubled as a storage room. Weeks spotted a guy with long, greasy black hair and a goatee sitting at one of the small tables. She walked up to him. "Are you Hanson?" Her nose puckered up from the smell of the food he was eating. "No offense, but what the hell is that smell?"

Hanson looked up at the two detectives standing in from of him. "This, to you unenlightened jerks, is Afghan beef. You should try it before you 'yuck' it. Have a seat. We don't stand on ceremony here." He pointed at the plastic chairs around the table. "So, you want to know where you can find Wilkinson and Durant. I'm assuming you've checked all their regular haunts already with no luck, right?" he asked, taking a mouthful of the beef.

"That about sums up the last two days," Mills said. "We've got a big fat zero. Is there any light you can shed that might help us find these dumb bastards?"

Hanson began to chuckle. "These dumb bastards, as you call them, are likely more educated than both you and me. Wilkinson has a master's degree in business administration from the U of A, and Durant has a degree in mathematics from the U of T, so dumb, they are not, stupid, yes. Guess they figured they could make more money on the other side of the law than toiling in the corporate or academic world."

A stunned look came over Weeks' face. "You're bullshitting me, right? These two are university grads?" She shook her head.

"Hard to believe, isn't it? So, when I tell you they can hide in plain sight, believe me. When they take off the leather vest and blue jeans and put on a suit, they look just like everyone else in the corporate establishment. In some cases…better. Did you know they have a corporate office in the Bentall Centre? That's where all their legitimate businesses are run out of." Hanson rocked back on the chair as he wiped his mouth and took a drink of water. He grinned.

"I'm blown away that these guys are that sophisticated." Mills said.

"Hell yeah. Most of the larger gangs have legitimate businesses as covers for their illegal stuff. Some are better than others, but they pay their taxes and contribute to the economy just like us regular folk." Hanson sat up to the table. "I'll bet you don't have a clue how much these gangs and their legal businesses contribute to the provincial economy, do you?"

Weeks had heard that some gangs ran legitimate businesses as covers, but didn't know the extent of it. See could see that Mills didn't either.

"Thought so? Well, according to the AG, the gangs contribute close to four-hundred-sixty million dollars to the legal economy. That's wages, goods and services, taxes at all levels. But at the same time, their illegal activities generate up to two billion dollars, and that's a conservative figure."

"I always heard crime was lucrative, but to what extent I obviously had no idea," Weeks said. So, would our boys be at their office downtown?"

Hanson played with the toothpick in his mouth, tonguing it from side to side. "That's a good question. Best thing to do is stop by and pay them a visit you might get lucky and they'll be in. But chances are the front door to the office will be locked, and you'll be on video." He quickly scribbled down the address on a piece of napkin and handed it to Weeks. "That's the best I can do. But if I hear anything, I'll let you know."

Mills looked at the paper. "If you guys know where they are, why haven't you picked them up? You know we've got what looks like a war going on."

"Yeah, we know what's coming down, but we've been told not to blow our covers or risk losing our CIs. That way, once this shit storm blows over, we'll still be working to put all their asses out of business." He smiled.

"That makes absolutely no sense. You're sitting on info that could save a cop's life and you're okay with that? I just wish someone would have told us this useful little tidbit before." She turned to leave. "Thanks, you've been a great help." She shook her head then said to Mills. "Let's go check out these expensive digs. Maybe we'll get lucky."

The trip to the Bentall Centre in downtown Vancouver didn't take long. Weeks pulled into the parkade and piloted the police car into a designated police parking stall. Together, she and Mills made their way up to the tenth floor office of Three Coasts Developments, the front company of Los Demonios.

They waited with others for the elevator car to stop at the marble-tiled lobby of the building. Hanson was correct; it would be hard to blend into this crowd unless you wore designer duds. The ride to the tenth floor was fast and silent, with everyone looking up at the indicator lamp as they ticked off each floor. The door opened on the tenth floor, and Weeks and Mills elbowed their way out of the crowded car. The clashing scent of perfume and cologne in the elevator had been overpowering to say the least, so Weeks was glad to get out of there.

The oak door frames had small name plates below the frosted glass doors, so they walked up and down the hallway looking for the right office. Mills spotted it.

"Down here," he said. Mills tried the door knob; it was locked. He looked at Weeks, who now stood beside him.

"Let's see if they're home." She knocked on the door. Weeks saw what she thought was someone moving behind the frosted glass, but no one came to the door. "I'm guessing they're watching us on video right now." Weeks said, casually gazing at the ceiling. High above them was a small black bulb attached to the ceiling. She waved at it and smiled.

The two stood there, waiting. Finally, Mills started pounding on the door. "This is the police; open up right now. Don't make me get a battering ram to take this door out. Now open up." Several other office doors opened up and surprised occupants peeked out.

"It's okay, everyone. Go back inside. Nothing to see out

here," Weeks waved her hand at them. People stared at her then disappeared behind closed doors. She stuck her face against the frosted glass. She could see someone coming towards the door. She stepped back, hand on her weapon. Mills did the same.

The door to Three Coasts Developments slowly opened, and a scared young secretary asked to see their badges. Weeks thrust her badge into her face, while at the same time pushing the door wide open. "Step back, please," she demanded. "Who else is here?"

Mills caught Weeks' nod and pulled his gun, then began to check out the office's rooms.

"What's your name?" Weeks barked at the frightened girl.

"Monica. Monica Belzwick." She said stepping backwards.

"Who else is in this office? Now! Ms. Belzwick, who else is here?" Weeks shouted.

"Nobody. They left about twenty-five minutes ago. They got a phone call then they left. They didn't say when they'd be back."

"Who was here? What are their names?" Weeks said, glaring at the girl.

"Dante Wilkinson and Roland Durant. They own the company. Am I in any trouble?"

Mills returned after sweeping the small office. "There's nobody here."

"Ms. Belzwick, you're not in any trouble. If anyone asks, you didn't tell us anything. Understand?" Weeks said, relaxing her grip on her weapon. The scared girl nodded her head in agreement. Weeks reached into her pocket and pulled out a business card. "Would you please see that Mr. Wilkinson gets this? Ask him to call me." The girl took the card and placed it on her desk.

"I'll tell him as soon as he comes back," she said, somewhat calmer.

"Let's go, Mills." Weeks turned and walked to the door, stopped and turned back to the girl. "You might want to erase the surveillance tape, if you know how. Could save you some trouble?" She smiled and walked out into the hallway.

CHAPTER

34

FORD SPENT THE next day developing his plan to take out a SWAT officer. Of all the police, he disliked SWAT the most. They were the cockiest, most arrogant of all the cops. On his way back from his meeting the day before with Nineteen and Seven, he'd stopped by an electronics store and purchased a police scanner. The salesclerk also convinced him to buy a frequency scanner and an inverter so that he could find out what frequency the police were using. He'd given a large tip for the good suggestion.

Ford took the radio and scanner on a field test. His plan was to find a SWAT operation underway and scan the airwaves to get their frequency. The police scanner gave him the general police radio traffic, but not SWAT.

Ford followed police cars, dialing in the scanner to pick up calls, and once he had a frequency, he wrote it down. It took him a good solid day of cruising before he hit the one he was after, the frequency for New Westminster Metro SWAT. He headed home to listen to the calls that came in over that frequency, trying to pick up their lingo. His plan started to take shape. Ford would call in a report of shots fired in an area of his choosing. There he'd lie in wait for them to complete their quick and dirty contingency plan then he'd pick off a member.

If they did the same thing as SWAT teams on TV, they'd deploy an elevated sniper who'd have a bird's eye view of the scene. Ford figured that would be his target, as the sniper would be alone and likely unarmoured.

A day and a half later, Ford got his wish. A 9-1-1 call came in which would involve SWAT, so he listened to get the address. On his way to the scene, he followed the incident on the handheld radio he'd purchased. Ford nosed his car onto Sixth Avenue from Twentieth Street, and headed east toward the call location, some kind of hostage situation, which meant they'd deploy full resources.

Ford pulled into the parkade at the Royal Centre Mall and drove to the farthest end. He got out of the car, bounded up the single flight of steps to the mall entrance, and calmly walked out to the street. The police had cordoned off the intersection and uniformed patrol officers were on crowd control duty. He tried to see past the throng of people lining the barricade, but couldn't see the action. Binoculars in hand, Ford walked swiftly down 6th Avenue to 7th Street, then to the next intersection.

It too was blocked. He continued around to come at the scene from the opposite end, but it too was blocked. Irate, he scanned the surrounding buildings, and spotted a hi-rise condominium building at the north edge of the mall, twenty-four stories tall. Ford quickly backtracked to his starting point and headed north towards the condominium. He waited for a couple to enter and quickly walked in behind them. He wanted the roof.

The couple got into the elevator, so Ford took the stairs. He knew it would be a challenge to climb up that many flights of stairs, but he didn't want to answer any questions from strangers. Ten minutes later, and totally out of breath, he reached the top floor. He quickly found the door indicating roof access. It was locked. He checked left, then right, then pulled out his Glock, screwed on the silencer, and fired one shot into the lock. He grabbed the handle and twisted. The lock yielded and the door opened.

Ford closed the door behind him and sprinted up the stairs to the outside door. It was locked and alarmed. He shrugged his shoulders and fired a shot into the lock, fully expecting the alarm to sound, but all he heard were the air-conditioners humming on the roof. He grabbed the handle and slowly eased the door open. Nothing. No sound, no alarm bell going off.

Outside, Ford pulled out his binoculars and trained them on the action far below. He couldn't hear what was being said, but he could see a man holding a woman hostage in the front of a pharmacy. The man was waving his gun and shouting at police. His eyes panned the surrounding buildings, looking for the sniper who would surely be in place. He stopped when he saw the black-garbed figure lying on an adjacent roof top, sniper rifle aimed at the man holding the woman. He smiled. Ford knew that his plan would work.

Two days later, Ford had worked out every last detail of his ruse, and set the plan into motion. He dialed 9-1-1 on his burner phone and reported a hostage situation at 389B Columbia Street, right next to a small diner. He told the 9-1-1 operator that he saw the man pull a gun on a young girl. Ford said his phone battery was dying and ended the call. He quickly shut the phone off in case they tried to call back. Once he had completed the call, he sat back and waited high atop a condominium on Columbia Street.

He'd scouted the location the day before and found that the roof had an access door that led out onto the steeply pitched roof. From his perch he could see all the action below from six blocks away. He knew that SWAT would most likely put a sniper across the street on the government building. As the sirens wailed, his heart rate quickened.

He caught a glimpse of the first police car coming up Columbia Street. It braked hard in the centre of the intersection. Within minutes there were police cars everywhere, and the entire street was taped off. True to form, the SWAT team deployed their members, four were sent around back, while others flanked the doorway into the building. Ford propped open the access door just enough to see the roof of the building six blocks away. He watched as a solitary figure emerged onto the roof of the three story government building across from the action. Through the scope, Ford watched the sniper position himself.

He smiled as he removed his rifle from its case. Slowly he assembled the weapon piece by piece, with the silencer being the last item.

Ford trained his scope on the street below; all SWAT members were in position, waiting for something to happen. Again Ford smiled. He needed them to know this was real, so he aimed his rifle at a plate glass window in the building and squeezed off a shot. The window exploded, sending shards of glass everywhere. Ford was happy at the effect of the bullet hitting the glass on a slightly downward angle. It revealed to him the power of the weapon. The stunt got their attention; he could see guns were drawn and ready to fire.

He listened intently to the radio as the police were ordered to adopt a holding pattern. Ford wanted them to start firing on the building so all eyes would be pointing in the direction of the action. Ford spotted a police car midblock with an officer standing beside the driver's door. He aimed at the windshield, just beside the officer's head, and pulled the trigger. The glass in the police car erupted, causing the officer to jump backwards. On the radio, he heard "Shots fired. Shots fired."

Several officers directly across the street from the building opened fire on the broken window. Ford saw his window of opportunity. He shifted his sight to the sniper on the roof and took aim. When everything was just right, he pulled the trigger. In a millisecond the bullet travelled the short distance and hit the sniper right in the side of the head. He died instantly.

Ford quickly dismantled his weapon, put everything back in the case, and closed the access door. Then, he remembered he hadn't taken a picture, so he took out his camera, propped open the door, and zoomed in on the figure lying on the roof. He zoomed close up on the officer's head and pressed the shutter. The image was saved. Ford closed the door.

Within minutes, he was walking down Columbia Street towards the Pattullo Bridge and the parking lot where he'd left his car. He stowed his gear in the trunk and calmly pulled out onto Columbia Street, then headed north away from the action. Within fifteen minutes Ford was back in his apartment, decompressing from the rush of the job. His weapons were stashed in the back of his ensuite dryer, safely away from any prying eyes, should any ever enter his apartment.

He lit a smoke, kicked back, and turned on the news. It

was on every channel. He picked up his cell phone and dialed Nineteen. It went straight to message. Ford paused for a second, determining what to say. “This is Ford. I’ll be by to pick up the twenty grand.”

CHAPTER

35

WEEKS SAT AT her desk in total shock as she and all the other detectives watched the six o'clock news. The lead story was about a SWAT team member who was shot in the line of duty. They had no suspects or leads, and forensics was at the scene trying to develop information about the shooting.

Lamp stood in his doorway watching the news, unable to comprehend what had just happened. He walked into the centre of the bullpen. All eyes turned to him.

"Okay, people, here's what I know, and this doesn't leave the room. Investigators believe the entire hostage incident was a hoax, or 'swatting'. They also believe that a member of SWAT was the target. They believe this was a hit carried out by a trained assassin using a high-powered weapon. It is too early to tell if this is related to the threatened war with the gangs, but logic says we shouldn't discount that possibility. If it is a prelude to the war, we have to determine why. My bet is on intimidation." Lamp paused letting the information sink in, because if he was right it would profoundly affect each and every one of them. He took a sip from his water bottle. "Any questions?"

Weeks looked around the room. She stuck up her hand. "Sarg, are we being hunted? If so, what is the department doing to protect us?"

"Hunted? I doubt it, targeted perhaps. We're doing pretty much all we can do right now. You're wearing your vests, you're travelling in pairs, and you're being hyper vigilant. Aside from that, what else can we do? If anyone has a suggestion, I'd be happy to hear it." Lamp said leaning against a desk.

An unidentified voice in the back muttered loud enough for others to hear, "Stay home."

"Sarg, any word from the locked up gang bangers as to who is doing this? Are we really at war with the gangs, or is this just a scare tactic?" Wheaton asked.

"It's pretty much like we expected. We talk, they listen, they don't respond. Each and every one of those bastards has asked for their mouthpiece. We keep stalling them. Sooner or later they'll figure out that we're not calling their lawyers, and then they'll clam up for good, either that or some will start to talk?" He could feel the sweat start to run down his brow and down his back. He wished he could tell them something that would reassure them, because he knew the possibility of death had spooked everyone, all the way up to the chief.

Pam Healy stuck up her hand. "Does the Protective Act allow us to use chemicals to extract the truth from these slime bags?"

Lamp waited as the group hooted and hollered their approval of the question. He held up his hand. "People, this is Canada. People still have rights here, which we can't overtly violate. Trust me, the less you know the better off you'll be. That's all I can say on the subject." The murmurs became louder as the detectives talked amongst them-selves.

Stan Rutherford normally didn't say much in meetings, but today was different. "I take it from the way you phrased that last statement that using chemicals to obtain the truth isn't being ruled out by upper management. Is that a safe assumption to make?"

Lamp felt himself getting a little defensive. "Stan, you can make any assumption you want."

CHAPTER

36

OSCAR NINETEEN RETURNED to the safe house early in the morning after a meeting with other gang leaders. Due to the constant rivalry among the gangs, it was difficult to meet face to face; everyone feared a set up.

At 3 a.m., Nineteen retrieved his messages from his smart phone. He had to replay the message from Ford four times and look at the picture full screen before he believed what he was seeing.

"Son-of-a-bitch." He said to the empty room. "That crazy bastard actually did it." Nineteen looked at the stippled ceiling and shook his head, wondering if he'd made the right decision to go along with Ford's far-fetched idea. Or, as the other gang leaders called it, the "fuckin' hare-brained idea." Regardless of what they thought or said, the Numbers Gang was now committed to seeing where this war would go, and for all their sakes, Nineteen hoped he was correct.

Nineteen sent a text to Ford saying the payment would be made as agreed upon and let him know where and when to pick up the twenty grand. He also said the last two gangs had said no, too risky. He asked what Ford's next move would be. Nineteen inhaled a cold KFC drumstick and a glass of beer before going to bed. He was mentally exhausted.

The next day, Nineteen awoke around one-thirty in the afternoon. He showered, dressed, and walked out into the kitchen. It was a buzz of activity, as money was being counted and stacked. He looked into the living room, saw who was there, and yelled, "Where's Seven at?"

"He's downstairs," Came the reply from a member watching television.

Nineteen poured a coffee and walked downstairs to the pool table. Seven and Randy Forty-One were playing a game of cutthroat poker pool. Nineteen's favourite game was Texas hold 'em poker; although he rarely won, he enjoyed the element of chance involved in it.

"Seven we need to have a sit down. You guys just about finished?" Nineteen said, setting his coffee down on the small table beside a recliner rocker.

"Just give me a minute, I'm just about to kick Randy's ass here." He concentrated on the bank shot and executed it. Seven watched as it bounced off two rails and hit the eight ball, then the eleven ball sending both into the corner pockets.

"You lucky bastard," Forty-One said tossing the cue onto the table and shaking his head. He pulled out a wad of bills, peeled off two fifties and tossed them onto the table. "This guy's got horseshoes up his ass, you know that Nineteen? Big fucking horseshoes." Forty-One shook his head and walked away.

Felix Seven picked up the bills and stuffed them into his jeans. "Not bad for fifteen minutes work eh?" He laughed, sitting down on a bar stool. Seven turned to his brother. "What's up?" he said, taking a pull on his can of beer.

"I spoke with the last two guys last night. They're not

interested in this little endeavour we're embarking on, said we're out of our fuckin' minds if we go to war. You think we are? Out of our minds?"

Seven played with his can of beer, twisting it around and around on the bar. "There's a part of me that says yes, we're totally fuckin' nuts to even consider this…" he took a sip of his beer, "but then there's a part of me that says, if we do this, and it turns out like Ford said it would, it would mean more money and power for us, which isn't a bad thing. Is there a risk that this could blow up in our faces? Big time! But there's a chance that this could just work out, too…so it sorta balances things out. Why? Do you think we should bail on this?"

Nineteen was playing with his phone. "You haven't seen this yet have you? It's a picture of the dead SWAT guy that Ford nailed." He hopped up and walked over to Seven's stool. "Have a look and tell me that this whole situation isn't becoming too real?" He watched Seven's face light up in amazement.

Seven took the phone and enlarged the image. "That crazy bastard actually did it. Boy, I guess I've underestimated this guy from the get go. Ford's a one man killing machine. Maybe we don't need the other gangs to join in on this, maybe we just go it alone and turn Ford loose on the metro cops and the other gangs? What do you think of that idea?" He handed the phone back to Nineteen, who had sat down on a stool next to him.

"Only problem with that is it's all us. There's nobody else to blame if this goes south, plus the cost factor. If he killed a dozen cops at twenty grand a pop, that's a quarter million bucks we'd have to pay out. That's some serious coin. So

I think it's better to spread that around among the five that want to join in. I sent him a text this morning, but he hasn't got back to me yet."

Seven stared at his beer. "What you say makes sense. I suppose if we're only responsible for a part of the whole, then as you say, this thing goes south then it'll come back on whoever's hitter screwed up and got caught. And who knows, maybe working with these other guys will lower the hatred and maybe put an end to the ongoing turf war." He raised his beer to his brother. "Here's to the war against the cops and to hell with them all."

Nineteen lifted his coffee mug and toasted his brother. "To hell with them all," he echoed.

Just then, they heard a commotion upstairs.

Seven was the first to exit the stairs from the basement and dart towards the kitchen, where the noise was coming from. He stopped beside the fridge. "What the fuck is going on?" he yelled.

"We caught this asshole looking into the window," Ninety-Nine said, grabbing the male by the neck and spinning his head around for Seven to see.

Seven began to laugh. "Ford. What the hell are you doing here? Let him go Ninety-Nine, he's one of the good guys."

Ninety-Nine complied, shoving Ford's head down.

Everyone in the room watched as Ford got up off the floor. "Well that was quite the reception. Hate to see what you'd do if I wasn't one of the good guys." He said laughing. He saw Nineteen standing behind Seven. "Got your text and was in the neighborhood, so thought I'd stop by for tea."

Nineteen stepped around his brother and came face to face with Ford. "Your goddamn cockiness damned near got you killed, you stupid ass." He slapped Ford across the back of the head. "What, a wig. Are you kidding?" Nineteen laughed. "You're lucky these guys showed some restraint; they could have just as easily filled you full of lead, and then where would your little war be? Dumb ass."

Nineteen looked around the room. "Okay everyone, relax. This is Ford. He's working for us. We have a few guys here from our Coquitlam location; they don't know you. Go back to whatever you were doing. Don't some of you guys need to get out there and do some collecting? Christ do I need to babysit all of you? Come on, get with it." He clapped his hands and watched as bodies disappeared into other parts of the house.

Ford sat down at the counting table, as did Nineteen and Seven. He lit up a smoke and repositioned his long-haired wig. With his dark tan he looked Southeast Asian. "So, the last two don't want to play, eh? No problem, more fun for me. Say, did you like the pics I sent you? I'll bet you right now the cops are beside themselves trying to figure out what's going on. Poor slobs don't know what's about to hit them."

Nineteen picked up a wad of uncounted cash and began thumbing through it. "So, what's your plan of action? What happens next?"

Ford extinguished his cigarette in the ashtray. "Well, the logical thing to do would be to meet with the five that are in and map out who does what and to whom. Is that something you can set up fairly quickly?"

Nineteen pulled out his phone and scrolled through the contacts page and tabbed each of the five phone numbers then pressed dial. "Why not try a conference call?" He waited for the rings to begin. His phone showed him all five numbers, and when the call was answered, it would glow green.

The phone would automatically say, "Hold for a conference call," not allowing the recipient to speak. When all numbers were green, Nineteen pressed talk.

"This is Oscar. I'm sure you've all seen the news about the dead SWAT member. Well, that's just a prelude. We need to meet to discuss who's bringing which hitters and who the potential targets are. Can we meet tonight?" Nobody spoke for several seconds.

Chessy from International Brotherhood was first to respond. "This is Chessy, IB. What time tonight? Have a thing I gotta attend at midnight."

"Wilkinson, here. Tonight's not a problem."

"Sangrah, here. Tonight's okay."

"Kleek, here. What time? I've also got a thing."

"It's Carver. Have a thing earlier on, but anytime after nine-thirty would be okay."

"That works for me as well," Oscar Nineteen said. "Okay, we need a neutral site. How about the Edgemont Hotel? It's central, fairly high-end, and is always busy. Any objections?" Nineteen waited, but none came. "Okay, Edgemont it is. Ten-thirty." Again he waited, but no objections came. "The room will be in the name of Ford. Hold on one more second, guys." He cupped the phone in his hand and turned to Ford. "Who needs to be there? Quick?"

The question seemed to catch Ford off guard.

"Uh, let's see…the head of each gang of course, maybe their seconds. No more than three per gang?" He shrugged his shoulders.

"Okay, I'm back, can we limit those attending to a max of three members per organization. Otherwise, it becomes difficult to manage. What we'll need to do is determine how many hitters each group will need to employ and what targets they'll need to hit. Hold on another second." He cupped the phone and looked at Ford who was signaling for a time out. "Now what?"

Ford leaned in towards Nineteen. "The list of cops should likely start with those that are shaking them down for money. You know, the cops on the take."

Nineteen nodded, knowing that would be a long list. "Okay, back again. Let's say we start by hitting those cops that are shaking us down. That should be quite a few, if our organization is any indication. Any objections to that?"

"Yah, it's me, Carver. Can we hit that fuckin' chief of police? That asshole has had his guys up my ass for the past three years."

"Don't see any reason why not. It'll certainly test their resolve won't it? If nobody has anything else, we'll see you tonight downtown." A silence fell on the line, so Nineteen ended the call and turned to Ford. "Downtown by ten-thirty. Doable?"

Ford looked at them. "Hell yah, that's doable. Can you have that Asian chick that brings me the money, Melissa or whatever her name is, there to serve drinks? Make sure she's wearing something slinky. I'd love to get into her pants." Ford grinned.

Nineteen looked at Ford and shook his head. "She's already going out with a pledge." He laughed out loud. "Don't worry, Ford, Melissa will be there."

Ford smirked at Nineteen. "Who's her boyfriend?"

Seven chimed in. “What do you need to know that for? Isn’t it enough to know that she’s off the market?”

Ford spun around to look at Seven. “Just like to know who the competition is bro, if that’s okay with you? You know, in case I need to kill him? Or something like that?” He enjoyed pushing Seven’s buttons. Ford laughed and turned towards the door. “I’ll see you turkeys at ten-thirty. Don’t be late.” He pointed his finger at each one like he was firing a gun, then winked and opened the door.

Nineteen looked at Seven, who had a confused look on his face. “Do you trust this bastard? I think he’d kill both of us without any reservation whatsoever. So we need to keep a close eye on him, and I think I’ve got the perfect solution to this problem.”

Seven looked at his brother and grinned. “Melissa, right? You’re going to hook her up with Ford. You sly bastard. That’ll keep Ford happy, especially if he’s getting into her pants. Maybe he’ll tell her what he’s up to. I like it.”

At ten-fifteen, Ford opened the door to the Edgemont suite to allow Nineteen, Seven, and Melissa to enter. He stuck his head out into the hallway and saw others coming toward the room so he held the door open.

Nineteen made the introductions as Melissa opened beers and set them on the table. Ford was happy to see her in a very tight fitting black cocktail dress that was low cut and short. She was a vision. Ford had called down to housekeeping to have additional chairs brought up. At ten-forty, the last of the guests arrived.

Ford took a beer and sat down, looking over the assembled group. The guys from the biker gang were tough looking, and he guessed they used that aspect to their advantage.

Nineteen started off the meeting. "Thanks for coming, guys and gals. Hopefully this won't take long. Did you put together a list of cops that are giving you trouble? If you have, give the list to Melissa. She'll be in touch with Ford here so that it can be evenly shared among the hitters, thereby maximizing their skills."

Wilkinson from Los Demonios was the first to speak. "As I said earlier, we've told the Black Widows to take part in this job. MacCreedy here will be our go between, and Miller here is head of the Black Widows. Any communication will be through MacCreedy, who'll tell me or Miller."

Ford looked at MacCreedy. Of the three, he was the least biker looking. He watched as MacCreedy got up and walked over to Melissa with a piece of paper. MacCreedy stood in front of Melissa, all tough and tall. "You wanna ride on my hog, sweetie?" he laughed, then tossed the paper onto her lap.

Within twenty minutes, Melissa held six pieces of paper. Ford walked over to her chair, took all the papers, and quickly scanned them. All eyes were on him, which made him a little uncomfortable. "I see that some of these cops are on everyone's lists. These fucks must be making a pretty penny off you guys. Let me guess, if you don't pay these fucks you get busted right and that gets expensive, right? Just a show of hands. Who has been busted lately?" Ford watched as two hands were raised. "I can see why you want them done away with. Of all these names, who's the biggest prick?" He sat down and looked around the room. He could see each gang leader was trying to formulate an answer. As if rehearsed, three of the gangs uttered, "Pastorelli."

Ford had his own paper and scribbled down Pastorelli.

"He should be on the first wave of hits then." Ford took a pull on his beer. "Who else? There can't be just one prick in the entire police department." That brought a laugh from the room.

"Sergio Deplume, that French speaking son-of-a-bitch that works out of vice," Chessy from the International Brotherhood said.

"Okay, Deplume is next," Ford answered. "Who's next?"

Sangrah from the Bondrah Brothers spoke. "I have a real problem with Cheevers; that bastard has his hands so far into my pockets I think at times he's playing with my junk. If he can be dealt with, that would be righteous."

"Cheever's it is." Ford said, after taking a swig of his beer. "Anyone else?"

Nineteen cleared his throat. "We'd like to see Mickey Taylor on that first wave. Like Cheevers, he's been bleeding us dry for the last two years."

"Taylor it is. Okay, Two-Sixty-Fourth, who's your main target?"

"Hammerlin, that son-of-a-bitch is relentless." Carver said shaking his head.

"Okay, Hammerlin it is. Big Valley Boys, who's your favourite cop?"

"Zamanski. That piece of work has not only been cleaning us out financially, but we have to supply the lazy fat fuck with broads as well. Kill the asshole, I say."

"Zamanski it is. Okay, here's what is going to happen. Before you go, I'll need a list of your hitters. Then I'll go over this list and divide the names up, so that each hitter has an equal opportunity to do right by you guys. It should take about a week to clean off this list; then, depending on how far we take this, others will be selected at random." Ford sat back and took a pull on his beer. He raised his empty bottle towards Melissa, who immediately got up and got him another.

Miller from the Black Widows shifted in his chair. "What makes you the boss of this operation?" he said, staring at Ford.

Ford felt multiple eyes fix on him. He lit a smoke and inhaled. In his calmest voice, he answered. "Because you wouldn't be here if it wasn't for me. Who, besides me, can organize this with enough precision to pull it off?" He looked into the faces of those assembled. "What no volunteers!" His pulse quickened and he could feel beads of sweat forming on his brow; he loved the adrenalin rush. "When was the last time you guys actually worked together on anything? I'll bet never. If you don't want me, then who do you suggest, oh wise one?" Ford instantly regretted his last comment, fearing they might actually pick someone else and he'd be out.

Nineteen sensed things could quickly get out of hand. "Okay, let's calm down. Does anyone else have a problem with Ford here running this? If so speak up." He looked around the room and saw several heads being shaken. "So that's solved, Ford's in charge. If he fucks up then we kill him. Agreed?" He paused for effect. "Okay, leave your hitter's phone numbers with Melissa before you go, unless there's some other business we need to talk about."

Wilkinson looked at the other gang members. "I don't know about the rest of you guys, but we're okay with this to a point. Do I trust this guy…not one fucking bit, but we're willing to go along because it will help us. I'm sure not everyone else here trusts Ford either, but also will go along with the crazy fucking plan…for now."

Carver cleared his throat. "Amen Dante, amen. You know the cops have picked up other gang leaders and are holding them in custody. We heard that they're being held somewhere other than at the cop shop. Seems a rather odd coincidence that they'd be picked up and here we are talking about a war. Any thoughts on that?"

Dante Wilkinson spoke up. "Our sources within Metro Police said something similar, but we haven't been able to prove it. If they are rounding up leaders, perhaps we all should lay low for a while until this thing gets going. Once the bullets start to fly and cops are dead, they'll be beating down our doors as sure as I'm sitting here."

Prospo Miller from the Black Widows chimed in. "I wonder if that's what happened to Jefferys. I haven't seen hide-nor-hair of him in the last couple days. If he's in the slammer, he won't talk. Son-of-a-bitch doesn't know anything anyway." He laughed.

Ford looked around the room. "It stands to reason that my handiwork over the past few weeks or so has them wondering what the fuck's going on. So it's reasonable to think they're reaching out to anyone who can further their investigation, and unfortunately you guys are at the top of their lists. My suggestion would be to either lay low as Dante suggested, or better yet, get the fuck out of town for a while. Go on vacation with your squeeze or your old lady, and let us take care of the dirty cops." He paused and watched as heads nodded agreement.

"Just so you all know. This war isn't against all cops. The regular cops won't be targeted. Our beef is with the crooked bastard's and them only, because if we target *all* cops, rest assured that J. Q. Public would rat us out in a heartbeat. My plan is to let the media know that the beef is with crooked cops only. The other thing about being out of town is that it gives you guys a perfect alibi, or at least plausible deniability, if this ever were to go to court."

Sangrah spoke up. "The kid's right. If we're here, they'll be coming for us. We all know that to be true. So the less we tell others in our respective organizations, the less they'll know and the less they'll be able to tell if they're picked up."

Ford looked at Freddy Sangrah and nodded acknowledgement. "Thanks. Let your hitters know that I'll be calling them within the next day to set up a schedule." Ford took a long drink from his beer. It felt good going down, but he knew that tomorrow he'd have a hangover. He watched as the group stood and made its way to the door. Ford chuckled and thought, *even in a situation like this, these boneheads don't really trust each other.* He wondered what Sanchez would have to say about this.

Dustin Ford rocked the chair back and rubbed his neck. He looked around the seven-hundred and fifty dollar a night suite and saw the mess that nine people in a living room area could make. Ford shifted his weight forward until the chair sat level. There were beer bottles everywhere. *What a bunch of slobs.* He took off his leather jacket and tossed it onto his chair, then set about picking up the empties.

He heard a noise coming from the bathroom. He stopped to listen. His senses immediately went into high alert. He thought he'd seen everyone leave. Who had he missed? Ford reached behind him and quickly extracted his weapon from his belt and removed the safety. Slowly, he edged towards the bathroom. There was no way someone would get the drop on him. He leveled the gun at the bathroom door and took a deep breath. Sweat began to bead on his forehead.

"Okay, whoever's in the crapper, you'd best come out, right fuckin' now." He waited for a response, but none came. He felt his heart rate quicken. "I said get the fuck out of there right now, do you hear me?" Again he waited.

The door opened a crack, then a little wider. He readied his weapon. Then a scream erupted that Ford was sure they would have heard down in the lobby.

"Are you nuts? Put the gun down, it's only me," Melissa said, as she emerged from the doorway looking like a dream. Ford breathed as huge sigh of relief.

"Damn girl, I could have shot you. Thought you'd left with Nineteen and Seven," he said as he tucked his weapon into the back of his pants. "What are you still doing here?"

Melissa walked past Ford to the lounge area, and the spicy scent of perfume wafted through the air. Ford was transfixed on her hips. She sat down. "How long do you have the suite?" She asked.

Ford wasn't worldly when it came to women, so he had to ask again, "What are you doing here?"

Melissa smiled and patted the sofa beside her. "Come, sit down."

Ford felt his pulse rising when it finally dawned on him why she was there. He pulled his weapon from his pants and put the safety on. He laid it on the end table, and sat down at the other end of the sofa.

"I don't bite, Ford. Oh, I get it. You want me to come over there." She stood up.

Ford's mind raced through all the possibilities that her

being here presented. Failure to satisfy was right at the top of the list. "Whoa, girl. Did Nineteen or Seven put you up to this? 'Cause the last time you pointed to your boyfriend in the vehicle. Has that situation changed?"

Melissa sat down beside Ford, put her hand on his thigh, and slowly moved it up and down. She could sense Ford's muscles tightening up. "Why do we need to discuss him? He's not here, but you are." She moved her hand to his crotch; she could feel he was aroused. She smiled then moved in to kiss him.

Ford eyed his watch; it was twelve-thirty. He wondered how long this would take.

At six-thirty the next morning, Ford rolled out of bed. He looked to see if Melissa was asleep, but discovered she had left sometime during the night. Ford grinned and made his way to the bathroom. He flipped on the light and was surprised by what was written on the bathroom mirror. *Had a great time. I'll be in touch. Melissa.* She'd drawn a little heart. Ford touched the mirror.

He ordered breakfast from room service, and while he was waiting, he found the number for The Boa in his wallet. He dialed the number, but it went straight to message. "Hey, it's Ford. I need you to get into the police computer and get me a list of all active cops who were or are currently being investigated by Internal Affairs. I need their names and addresses, and I need them yesterday. Call me." Ford hung up. He sat back, still grinning about last night. He was happy and life was good and if all went as planned, life would be great.

CHAPTER

37

SHELLEY WEEKS' PHONE rang several times, before she rolled over and answered it. She looked at the clock on her alarm; it was three-thirty in the morning. She rubbed her eyes and answered, "Hello."

"Detective Weeks, it's me, Troy. We met the other day at the cement plant. I've got something that you need to see. I tried to call Detective Healy but she didn't answer her phone, so I called your station and spoke with the duty officer who gave me your number. They're very protective. When can you meet me?"

Weeks rubbed her eyes again, trying to become awake enough to understand what the hell was going on. "Do you know what time it is, Troy? What's so important it can't wait?" She remembered the RCMP undercover agent. She had heard from Healy that he had a handler within E Division and wondered why he wasn't calling them?

"Yes, I know what time it is. It's the only chance I've had to call. So, when can we meet? This is life or death."

"Life or death. Does your handler know you're calling Metro Police?"

"Who do you think told me to call you guys? I don't have that latitude."

Weeks sat at the edge of the bed, "Where are you right now?"

"I'm sitting in a dumpy little café in Surrey."

"What's it called, asshole?" Weeks said rolling her eyes.

"It's called The SamDee Café, just off One-Hundred-Fourth and King George Highway."

Weeks held the phone to her ear as she dressed throwing on her blue jeans and sweat shirt. "I know the place, okay, I'll be there is fifteen minutes."

It was close to four when she arrived at the SamDee Café.

As she parked the car, she looked at the front of the building. Troy was right, it wasn't a Class A eating establishment. Weeks walked up to the dirty glass door and swung it open; she was surprised that, at this hour of the morning, the place was busy. She racked her brain, trying to remember what he looked like, as she eyed the patrons, many of whom were drunk or stoned. She caught sight of a guy sitting alone near the back and began to walk toward him, when she heard her name being called. She spun around and saw Troy sitting at the counter; he looked different than she remembered.

She shook her head as she walked to where he was sitting. "Didn't recognize you." She sat down beside him.

Troy was nervous, he had done this multiple times, but it still made him anxious because he didn't want to be made; he looked around the café multiple times. "Let's get a booth back there." He said, pointing towards the door at the back. He got up and Weeks followed him.

They found an empty booth away from prying eyes and ears. Weeks ordered a coffee.

"Okay, what's so ultra-important that you're depriving me of my beauty sleep," she asked.

Troy reached into his pocket and pulled out his Blackberry and set it on the table. "This." He said pointing to his phone. "There's some video that you need to see." He stopped mid-sentence as the waitress set a coffee in front of Weeks.

"You want some more coffee?" the waitress said to Troy, who shook his head.

"No thanks, I'm already floating." He watched her disappear then turned back to his phone. Troy picked it up, turned on the video replay, and handed Weeks the device. "I guarantee you'll find this interesting. The guy that's speaking is the guy who's bringing the war to your doorstep. Sorry the picture is out of focus, but the audio is crystal clear."

Weeks eyed the images that flashed before her on the tiny screen. The audio was clear. She couldn't believe her eyes or ears. "I need a copy of this," She said before she'd even finished watching the entire video. "When did this take place, and why were you there?"

Troy looked at Weeks as she continued to watch the video. "This meeting, for all intensive purposes, was a targeting session. The guy doing the talking, his last name is Ford. He's the architect. There were six gang leaders there, and each one provided the names of cops that they want dead."

Weeks had a hard time believing what she had just heard. "Are you serious? You were there?" Her mind was spinning with what she had just learned.

"I was there playing my part as the representative for Los Demonios. Wilkinson had me and his second from the Widows attend this meeting last night downtown."

Weeks cut him off. "Who else was there?" she asked then took a sip of her coffee. Her face contorted.

"That bad, eh?" He smirked, "Let's see, there were guys

there from International Brotherhood, Bondrah Brothers, Big Valley Boys, the Two Sixty-Fourth Street Gang, Numbers Gang, and Los Demonios. Six in all."

"These sons-of-a-bitches are actually going to war with us. Are they crazy? Don't they know we've got a hundred times more manpower and resources than they do? What, in their wildest dreams, makes them think they can win this?" She took another drink while watching the small screen.

"What makes you think it's about winning? Maybe they're getting tired of the graft and corruption that comes from within your police department?" Troy said leaning forward.

Weeks played with the Blackberry. "Corruption, graft? Are you kidding me? What, within our police department?" She smirked.

Troy sat up straight. "That's why I'm risking it by contacting you. My handler figured you guys needed to hear this from me instead of through the channels.

"Are you sure you're safe, do you want to come into the station?" Weeks asked.

"I think I'm good, everybody is sleeping. That's why I called you at this time of the night. I want to bring these assholes down more than you do. That's why I haven't seen my family in nearly eighteen fuckin' months."

Weeks leaned in. "You've been undercover for a year and a half? How do you do it?"

Troy looked down at his coffee cup and spun it around. "By believing that what I'm doing will make a difference. My fiancé told me she understood, and we keep in touch electronically, so she knows I'm still alive and thinking about her."

Weeks picked up the cell phone. "Can you send this file to

my cell phone? I need to show this to my boss. He's going to shit himself." She slid the phone to Troy. "How did you get the video?"

Troy reached into his pocket and took out his pen. "This little sucker has a camera in the end, and inside the pen is a transmitter that sends the image to my phone. It also writes very nicely," he said, laughing quietly. Troy took out his smart phone, unplugged the earpiece jack, and separated the cord. "Let's see your phone."

He connected his phone to hers, and began pushing buttons on his touch screen. "You're getting the entire file, should only take a few moments." Troy looked around to see if anyone was paying too much attention to them. He saw no one. His phone beeped and he slid her phone back to her. "I've gotta run, I have to be at work by six-thirty. You guys have to warn your people." He stood. "If I hear anything else, I'll be in touch."

Weeks sat motionless, staring at her cup of coffee, trying to absorb what she had just seen and heard. She remembered her uncle, a cop, telling her about the days of Al Capone and Eliot Ness and the war they had. He told her that something like that would never happen again. She wished her uncle was still alive, but figured he'd be rolling over in his grave if he knew what was happening. She took another swig of coffee, put three loonies on the table, and left the dingy little diner. As she walked out she could feel the eyes on her.

An hour later, she pulled into the parking garage just down the street from the Main Street police station. The rain had not let up since she'd left the café, her mind still trying to comprehend what she had learned from the RCMP undercover agent. She desperately wanted to call every one of the detectives working the case and tell them to get their asses into the station, but knew that wouldn't be a wise move. Instead she elected to work at her desk until the others arrived.

It was five-thirty in the morning. Weeks sat down at her desk. Even at this early hour, the phones were ringing. She thought of answering them, but decided to let them go to message. By 6 a.m. she found herself in the gym in the basement. She wrapped her fists and began working on the heavy bag. Within minutes anxiety and stress decreased, and she began to relax. She worked out for about an hour then hit the showers. When Weeks returned to her desk, it was nearly eight, and other detectives were already at work. She shot a glance towards Lamp's office; the light was still out. Weeks knew she had to tell him about this before letting the other detectives know.

At ten after eight, Lamp came into the bullpen, speaking to each detective that wasn't on the phone as he made his way to his office. He stopped at Weeks' desk. "Good morning. Did you sleep here last night?" he asked, pointing to her damp hair.

"No Sarg, just came in early and did some work in the gym. Sarg, I've got something that you need to see, and you should see it in private."

Lamp looked puzzled. "Sure, come on, before they start to line-up." He chuckled, pointing to the empty detective desks.

Weeks grabbed her phone and followed Lamp into his office. Lamp pointed to a seat in front of his desk while he took off his coat. "Okay, what have you got?"

Weeks played with her cell phone to get the file to open

up. "I got a phone call early this morning from the RCMP undercover, Troy, that we met a while back at the cement plant. Remember? He called me because he couldn't reach Detective Healy and his handler said it was urgent. Anyway, he called me this morning and asked me to meet him at some rat hole of a café. So I met him there and he told me about this meeting he was at with Wilkinson of the Los Demonios gang. He showed me this video he'd taken. They're actually planning to go to war with us. Can you believe it? Here, watch this. And he told me that we should warn our people." She pressed play and handed the phone to Lamp, then sat back down.

Lamp's eyes were fixed on the small screen. "Piss poor quality video," he said. After about ten minutes, Lamp had seen enough. He handed the phone back to Weeks. "You figure the guy doing most of the talking is your perp? Did Troy give you that impression?"

Weeks pocketed her phone. "From what he said, and what I could surmise, that would be correct. Too bad it's so grainy. We can't really get a good look at his face from the angle of the pen camera. What should we do with this?"

Lamp scratched his chin. "Let me make a call to our tech department. I want all detectives to see this, as well as those up the food chain, so they'll have to put it online. I'll talk to the Chief about letting our people know. Can you leave me your phone? Once it's online, we'll show it to everyone. You're right; I can't believe they're going down this road, but who said gang members were smart?" They both laughed.

Weeks picked up a coffee and returned to her desk. She couldn't help but wonder why someone would want to go deep undercover risking life and limb, especially with an organization like the Los Demonios. They were reportedly ruthless to both their enemies and members. She admired what Troy was doing and silently wished him well.

The impending war with the gangs scared the crap out of Weeks, and she was doing her best to keep a brave face.

She saw Pam Healy coming back into the bullpen and waved her to come over. Shelley liked Pam; she was a good detective, a year ahead of her in seniority.

Healy pulled up a chair, coffee in hand, and sat down. "What's up?"

Weeks leaned toward Healy. "I got a phone call from your RCMP CI this morning. He said he tried to call you but you didn't answer. He had a video that he said we needed to see. Boy was he right. I still can't get my head around it? "

Healy spoke quietly. "What phone call? What video." She pulled out her phone and brought up the call log. "Shit. He's right. He called at three-thirty. I must have been out like a light."

Weeks took a sip of her coffee, "The video is about a meeting. Sarg wants to show everyone at the same time. It's scared the shit out of me."

"If it scared you then I have this awful gut feeling that things are going to get a lot worse before they get better, if that's even possible." Healy said.

A cold shiver ran up her spine. "Why do you say that?" Weeks fixed her eyes on Pam.

Healy leaned in toward her. "Like I said, if you're scared then it must be bad and my gut is seldom wrong."

"Pam, maybe your gut is wrong this time. After all you're sort of a half empty instead of half full kinda a gal." She smiled at Pam, when suddenly they both heard a loud whistle. All eyes turned towards Lamp's office, and the bullpen fell silent.

"Listen up. I need everyone in the boardroom p.d.q. There's something that I have to share with you, and this right here isn't the place." Lamp's personality and policing history made everyone in the office respect him, and when he said jump, the usual answer was how high on the way up. Lamp followed up the rear to ensure there were no stragglers. Once everyone was seated inside, he went to the head of the table. "Okay people, this is Nigel from the IT Department. We have about a twenty minute grainy video that you need to see, as it affects everyone in this room. The audio will send chills up your spines." Lamp walked over to the wall and flipped the light switches off. "Okay, Nigel, hit it."

The screen that hung from the roof came to life with the video that Weeks had obtained earlier.

At the end of the video, Lamp walked over and flipped the lights back on. "Interesting little piece of video, don't you think?" he said to the room. "What are your thoughts?"

Nobody spoke.

"Okay then," Lamp said. "Weeks, does the kid in the centre of the room look like your suspect? Is that the image of a cold-blooded killer?"

Weeks shifted in her seat. "Well, Sarg, it's a pretty crappy video. But the guy in the video looks almost Caribbean or East Asian. Our suspect is Caucasian."

Lamp looked at Weeks, "Maybe he's altered his appearance?"

"Perhaps." Weeks looked down the table. "Nigel, can the video be cleaned up a bit?"

"It's worth a shot. We'll see what we can do?"

CHAPTER

38

FORD WAS SIPPING a triple mocha espresso at the local Starbucks when his phone rang. He looked around and saw that nobody was watching him. "Hello, who's this?"

"It's me. I have the info you wanted. Plus, I've got something else that I think you'll enjoy viewing. When can we meet? And this will definitely cost you additional dollars."

Ford sat up; it was Bradley the computer kid. "Something I'll enjoy watching…let me guess, you've found Sasquatch?" he laughed. "Tell you what. If I like what I see, there'll be an extra grand in it for you. Sound fair?"

"Hell yeah."

"Thought that would pique your fancy. Tell you what? I'll be there…" Ford looked at his watch. It was just after eleven. "I'll be there at two." He didn't wait for the reply. Ford's mind raced, trying to guess what the kid had found that could be so interesting. He leaned back and took a long slow sip of his coffee.

At one-thirty, Ford pulled into the parkade just off Burrard Street and walked the short distance to the Walnut Hut Cafe. Robson Street was busy even in the rain, which was normal for Vancouver. Ford liked watching people.

The Walnut Hut Café had its awning fully extended so

patrons could sit outside. Ford shot a quick glance at each one and determined that nobody looked like a cop, so he entered the café and walked into the internet lounge.

He spotted the Boa sitting by himself in the corner. Ford pulled up a chair and sat down, which startled the young whiz kid, who quickly removed his ear buds.

"Let's see what you've got," Ford said, reaching into his pocket and pulling out a wad of cash. The kid's eyes widened and he stuck a flash drive into the USB port and launched it.

"I found this video while I was poking around, thought you might find it interesting. Looks a lot like you?" Bradley said eying the wad of cash.

Within seconds, a video began playing. Ford couldn't believe what he was seeing. He furrowed his brow, trying to figure it out…then it hit him. "Son-of-a-bitch. Here's your grand kid." He peeled off twenty fifty-dollar bills. He tossed the wad onto the keyboard then held out his hand.

"The info about IA is on the stick as well," the kid said. He grabbed the money once Ford had the flash drive and quickly put it into his pocket. "Hey, you need anything else, give me a call."

Ford nodded, then quickly turned and left the café, his mind reeling with what he'd seen on the video. Some son-of-a-bitch had taped the meeting, and somehow it ended up on the goddamn police computer. But who? Ford was pissed off. He needed to contact Nineteen and Seven immediately. Within minutes, Ford was back in his car. He quickly paid the parkade fee and pulled out into traffic. Who was it? He didn't know, yet.

Once he was heading towards the freeway and he'd

calmed down he called Nineteen. It rang three times.

"Nineteen. It's Ford. You'll never fuckin' guess what I saw this afternoon."

"You're right. I'll never guess, so why don't you tell me."

"All right, I will. I saw a goddamn video of our meeting last night, and I got it from the goddamn Metro Police computer. How the hell is that possible? I'll tell you how. Somebody at that meeting was a fuckin' cop, that's how."

"You saw what?" Nineteen's voiced rose several decibels. "Are you positive it was of our meeting?"

"Hey, I know what I look like. So yeah, I'm positive. We have to meet. This puts everything we've planned in the toilet."

Nineteen looked at Seven sitting on the sofa and made a slicing motion across his throat. "Okay, tell us where and when and we'll meet with you."

Ford wheeled around slower cars heading for New Westminster. "Well, I'm fifteen minutes away from New West and you guys are in Surrey. Why don't we meet in Coquitlam, say the Lougheed Mall, in forty-five minutes? I have to stop and get my laptop."

"Forty-five minutes it is, at the Lougheed Mall food court." He ended the call.

Ford checked his speed and immediately slowed down, realizing that he was travelling way over the limit. He slowed down and fell into line with other cars doing the same speed. Ford let his mind wander and consider the possibilities. Who was the cop in the meeting? He was fairly certain that it wouldn't be any of the gang leaders, unless the cops had flipped one of them. Hell, for all he knew, it could be Nineteen or Seven. Ten minutes later, Ford pulled off the freeway at the Brunette Avenue South exit, and before he knew it he was home. He picked up his laptop and headed to the mall.

The mall was busy for this time of the afternoon, school kids meeting to swap stories and tell lies about how exciting their day had been. Ford remembered back when he had done the same thing. Only what they had talked about was their foster parents, their bruises and who had it rougher. Ford stepped onto the escalator that went down to the food court; the smell of the assorted foods always captured his senses. He walked over to Mr. Bean's and ordered a strong coffee, then found a seat near the back of the food court. Sitting with his back to the wall, he fired up his laptop computer and placed the flash drive in the port. He saw two files. He clicked on the video file. The video popped up on the screen. He took out his ear buds and plugged them into the computer, then clicked play.

His blood boiled as he watched the video. He fast forwarded it in several spots then rewound it, trying to figure out where the camera was located. He racked his brain trying to figure out who was sitting where in relation to where he was sitting in the video. Ford hoped maybe Nineteen or Seven could shed some light on the seating arrangements.

Time had flown by and out of the corner of his eye he saw Nineteen and Seven coming down the escalator, so he closed his laptop and stuck his hand in the air to catch their attention. They sauntered over to the table as if they hadn't a care in the world. He motioned them to sit down. "You guys want a coffee?"

Nineteen turned a chair backwards and sat down. "Nah, we're okay. We just want to see this video." Seven sat down opposite his brother. Ford nodded and opened his laptop, unplugged his ear buds, then turned the sound down and pressed play. All six eyes were fixed on the screen. The blurry image was clear enough to make out who was at the centre of the video. "Ford, that's you," Seven said sounding surprised.

Ford chuckled. "No shit, Sherlock. Why else would you be here? I know it's me. What I want to know is who's the motherfucker taking the video? Do you guys remember who was sitting where?" He noticed Nineteen looking at his brother with confusion written all over his face.

Seven looked at Ford. "It would be easier if we had a piece of paper."

Ford walked over to the Sandwich Baron and grabbed a hand full of napkins. He tossed them into the centre of the table. "Who's got a pen?" Nineteen fished one out of his jacket and handed it to Seven.

"Okay," Seven said, sketching the outlay of the room. "We were sitting here, you were sitting there." He drew boxes and put initials inside each box.

Nineteen looked at the drawing. "Wilkinson was sitting right there. And wasn't Sangrah sitting between you two?" Ford looked at the drawing. "What's the freaky guy's name? Wasn't he sitting beside the guy who was with Wilkinson, right over here?" he pointed to an area beside Wilkinson.

"You mean Chessy? Yeah, he was sitting beside… MacCreedy." Nineteen said.

Seven pointed to another spot. "Wasn't Carver sitting there?" Nineteen's head nodded, as did Ford's. "And I think Kleek was sitting beside Chessy, over here." Seven filled in the boxes. I think that's where everyone was sitting." All three looked at the screen, trying to get a fix on who was sitting off at an angle to Ford's spot.

"Where was Miller sitting?" Ford asked.

"Here, next to MacCreedy." Nineteen said looking at Seven, who nodded.

Ford was the first to offer a suggestion. "From what it looks like, could be Wilkinson or MacCreedy, or Miller or Chessy." He played with the pen, "It wouldn't be the first time somebody was turned by the cops? I'm just saying."

Nineteen and Seven both looked more closely at the video, then at the drawing. Seven turned to Ford. "Are you fuckin' nuts? You're going to accuse these guys of being a stoolie… you're crazier than I thought."

Ford rocked back on his chair, his eyes fixed on Seven. He let the chair slam back to the floor. "See, Seven? That's your problem. You've got no balls. Just like when you were downtown on the strip and some bangers came around the corner, you moved your girl to the curbside, so if they shot at you, they'd hit her first." Ford inhaled deeply to control his anger, cracked his knuckles then spun the laptop towards Seven. "What do you think this is, Seven? Fiction? A collective dream we're having. This, asshole, is reality. Somebody is working both sides, and if we don't find out who it is, then this whole exercise is off. Get it?" Ford spotted Seven making a move towards his back pocket area. Instantly, Ford grabbed his other hand. "I wouldn't, if I were you." He said threateningly. He then tapped Seven's knee with his gun barrel. Seven's eyes widened in disbelief.

Nineteen erupted on Seven, "What the fuck is wrong with you. You want to take Ford on in here, a goddamn public place, are you nuts. I should take you outside and give you a good shit-kicking. You've had this hate on for Ford since he's been back. It's fucking time you grow up or I'll let Ford deal with you." "Now, Ford is correct, if there's someone on the inside, we need to figure out who, and fast. If I was Wilkinson or Chessy, I'd want to know if it was one of my guys, not that either of them would ever admit it. But it could be either of them, as well. Either way, if we don't find out who is the snitch then this little foray into a war with the cops is over before it's started. Get it, Seven?" Nineteen looked at Ford. "What's our next move?" Nineteen watched as Seven got up and walked away from the table, he kept an eye on him in case he did something stupid.

Ford was calmer now, playing out different scenarios in his mind. "Well, I think the first thing we need to do is to meet with Wilkinson and Chessy. Show them the video and see what they have to say." He took a sip of his cool coffee. "If they will meet, it has to be in public. Just them, you and me. The fewer, the better."

Ford turned his computer back to himself, closed the video down then opened the other file. He was surprised to see how many cops had been, or were being, investigated by IA. He scrolled through the names and guessed there must be at least fifty or sixty cops who were dirty, or thought to be. Ford smiled.

Nineteen turned to Ford. "So, what do you want to do with this info?"

Ford kept looking at the screen. "It's a no-brainer. We have to find out whose leaking info to the cops and eliminate the bastard, pure and simple."

Seven returned from getting a pop. "So what's the deal here? We good or what?"

Ford looked up at Seven and shook his head. "No, we're not *good here*. Fuck man! How you have survived as long as you have I'll never know. Of course we're not good. We need to find the asshole snitch and send him and the cops a message. Christ, do I have to do all the thinking here?"

Nineteen held up his hands to Seven and Ford. "Okay, you two, I've had about enough of this shit. Either you kids learn to play nice, or I'll have to shit-kick both of you, understand? Now Seven, park your ass down, and Ford, stow that fuckin' attitude of yours until this is over. Got it? Well?" He said, and watched as both Seven and Ford slowly nodded in agreement. "Okay, I'll get in touch with Wilkinson and Chessy and see if they can meet tonight. I agree with Ford, we need to find out who the snitch is and get rid of him or call a halt to the war.

Ford started laughing as he closed his computer.

"What's so damn funny, Ford?" Nineteen asked.

"Oh, I just had an idea. Check this out. Let's say we find out who the asshole is. Then why couldn't we use him to feed the cops bad information? That's assuming that either the Los Demonios or IB let him live." Ford cracked his knuckles again.

"It's a tall order to ask these two guys to let a snitch live and breathe among them. Hell, if it were someone in our organization, we'd cap his ass in a heartbeat, so I just can't see either Wilkinson or Chessy letting the asshole stay alive. No, my guess is that if that person is named, they're as good as dead."

Ford grabbed his computer and stood. "Okay, I'm outta here; there are some things that I need to check out. Call me when and if a meeting is set up for tonight. Later." He turned and walked briskly toward the escalators.

Fifteen minutes later, Ford was at home. He opened a beer and plopped down on his couch. He rubbed his neck, then put the flashdrive into his laptop and opened up the list. He grabbed the piece of paper with the names from the meeting and began comparing the two lists, then started to laugh. He shook his head. "Dirty bastards." Every cop named in the meeting was on the IA list, which didn't surprise Ford. Alverez had once told him that if a cop was dirty it was a safe bet that the other cops knew about it and either covered it up or took forever to gather enough evidence to kick their asses off the force. He remembered something else that Alverez had told him. Some dirty cops worked for the gangs as informants, tipping them off about raids and investigations. Ford mulled over this last possibility. He remembered the expressions on some of the faces at the meeting when a certain cop's name was given by another gang. He suspected some of the cops were extorting from more than one gang. If so, this would present a challenge when the time came to make the hit.

Ford leaned back, beer in hand, trying to sort out the politics that might come into play. His mind was going in circles. He hated doing this type of thing. Planning and organizing were never his strong suits, except when it came time to acquire the target and pull the trigger. He mulled over the idea of being the only hitter instead of using those offered up by the other gangs, but quickly dismissed the idea as unworkable.

The sound of his cell phone ringing brought him back to reality. Ford picked it up, the LED screen showed the time; it was four forty-five. Caller ID came up unknown caller, which meant it was likely a burner phone. He pressed talk.

"Ford here. Who's this?" he asked before he took a swig of his beer.

"Nineteen. Talked to Wilkinson and Chessy. They're very interested in seeing the video. They can meet tonight at eleven. Does that work?"

"Eleven is fine. Where at?"

Nineteen paused for a long moment. "I don't know, man. Where would you want to meet that is public yet private?"

"How about the Container Pub downtown? I know the owner, and he's got a private office in back that I'm sure he'll let us use."

Nineteen laughed. "Shit, I haven't been in that rat trap in ages. Will be fun to see how bad it's become. Okay, Container it is. I'll let the other guys know."

Ford punched in Jomo's number and pressed send, it rang several times before being answered. "This is Jomo. Who's this?"

"Jomo, it's me Ford. Need a favour, pal."

"Ah Ford, what's the favour, mon?"

Ford paused trying to figure out how to ask it. "Jomo, I need a very private place to hold a very important sit down. Nobody can know about this, get it?"

"Ah yes, Jomo has a place. When is this meeting?"

"It's tonight at eleven. Can you take care of this? I'll make it worth your while."

"Sure, Jomo can take care of it. Who's coming to this meeting?"

"Three guys. That's all you need to know."

"Yes, Jomo doesn't need to know."

"You're right. I'll be there around ten-thirty, so I'll take care of them. You just have the place ready. Got it?"

"I got it." There was silence on the line, so Ford hung up and smiled.

CHAPTER

39

THE BULLPEN OF the Metro Police Department buzzed with activity more so than usual. Every detective was actively trying to develop leads to catch the shooter. Lamp was sitting at his desk when his phone rang.

"Yeah, Lamp here." He rocked back in his chair.

The voice at the other end of the line was tiny, or so it seemed. "Detective Lamp, this is Mander in the lab. I've cleaned the video image up as much as I can. Who should I send it to?"

Lamp's heart began to beat more quickly. "Send it to me. I'll be waiting. Thanks Mander, you don't know how much this helps us. Good work."

"Detective Lamp, perhaps you should view the video before you start praising my efforts."

The comment caught Lamp off guard. "Okay, I'll call you back once I've seen it. Is that fair?"

"Yes, that's fair. I'm sending it to you right now."

Lamp patiently watched the hourglass icon as the computer loaded the large file onto his computer. When it stopped rotating, he opened it up. Lamp racked his brain trying to figure out which version of the video was better. He guessed Mander had done the best he could with what he was given, so he couldn't be held accountable. Lamp picked up his phone, pressed the intercom button and punched in Weeks' number. It rang once before she picked up. "Got the video back. I need your eyes on it." He saw Weeks look up from her desk; he waved her over. She nodded.

Weeks walked into Lamp's office leaving the door open. "What does it look like now? Did Mander have any luck cleaning it up?"

Lamp turned his computer monitor towards Weeks. "You be the judge. I think it's only marginally better but that might still be enough."

Weeks leaned forward, hands on the desk, and stared at the images on the screen. "Well, you can see the guy in the centre a bit clearer, but it's still hard to tell what nationality he is. Asian, Indian, Mexican? Who knows? I think we can deduce from the audio that he is likely our perp, and I think Mander cleaned it up enough that we can get the image out to the press to see if the public can help us locate this bastard. And maybe, if we find this asshole, we can avert this war that's coming our way."

Lamp looked at Weeks. He could see the concern on her face. "Wouldn't putting his face out there alert him? Then all he'd need to do is change his appearance again and we'd be back to square one. But, if we keep this under our hat and work the back channels with the gangs, we might get lucky and nab his ass before the bullets start flying."

Weeks sat down and rubbed her neck. "You're right there, Sarg. Never thought of it that way. That's why you get the big bucks." She managed to get a small chuckle out of Lamp.

"Yeah, I get so much money that I'll be working here until

I'm ninety-five to pay off my mortgage." They both laughed.

"Any luck with the bangers we've rounded up?" She asked.

"Funny thing about those assholes, they know something is coming down the pipe, but they're not saying one damn peep, which makes me wonder why? Normally we can persuade one of these scumbags to roll, but they seem to have a new sense of purpose, a new-found loyalty to the cause, or some other damn reason for keeping quiet."

"Who's doing the main interrogating?"

Lamp rose and walked over to the water cooler in the corner of his office. "Oh, you know. The usual. But we did bring in two experts from the feds who are supposed to be the best in the system. We'll have to wait and see how good these two are."

"What kind of deal are we offering to get one of them to roll?" She said getting up and walking over to the wall of certificates.

"Why do you ask?" Lamp said returning to his desk.

"'Cause it would be nice to know so that when we round up more of these guys we can drop that carrot in front of them. Maybe by the time the feds talk to them, they will have considered all the options and maybe one of them will talk."

"The commissioner and the AG are offering total immunity to whoever is the first to give us credible info on the events that have happened and or will happen."

"Total immunity? Christ, that's generous. And still no takers, eh? Makes you wonder, doesn't it. Either they don't know what's going on, or they've been threatened with death if they do talk."

Lamp rocked back in his chair. "Likely a little of both. So far we've got a few smaller gang leaders. Mostly it's soldiers that we've rounded up, but the Gang Squad has leads on the whereabouts of some larger gang leaders, at least the ones who haven't gone into hiding."

"They can't all be in hiding. Can they?" Weeks said returning to the chair.

Lamp leaned on his desk. "That's another funny thing. Normally, these guys are strutting their stuff for all to see, all blinged out and badassed. But now they're nowhere to be seen, which suggests to me that they know we're rounding them up, so they're laying low."

"What's Hedley's take on this? Surely the Gang Squad has files on all these creeps." Weeks asked.

Lamp smiled. "That's a damn good question. So far, the gang squad has been helping round up the one's we've got in custody. I realize that they have a tough job to do and gang bangers don't trust anyone so it's hard for our guys to get close. And they are chronically understaffed. I know the Chief ordered all departments to help us. Maybe if we put more pressure on the gang members, they'd give up the locations of the safe houses, hideouts, lairs or whatever these assholes call their places."

Weeks took a swig from her water bottle. "You'd think that Guns and Gangs would give up their info freely, considering we're on the same team, right? But no, we have to scratch and claw to get anything from these guys. Are they special, or what?"

Lamp sat forward on his chair. "It's a classic case of turf protection. Damn it Weeks, you're right. Time to shake the tree and see what falls out!" Lamp picked up his phone and punched in Hedley's number. "Martin, Lamp here. Can you come to my office? We need to talk." He listened intently then hung up.

"He's coming right up. Maybe we'll finally get some intel we can use."

Weeks and Lamp chatted for five minutes before Martin Hedley's muscular body filled the doorway into Lamp's office. Lamp waved him in, and offered his big hand. Hedley sat down beside Weeks.

"What's up, Webber?" Hedley said, repositioning his body in the small chair. He pulled up his sleeves revealing several tattoo's on each arm. Hedley looked and dressed the part of a badass gang banger. He wore a black Harley-Davidson crew neck sweat-shirt, a black vest with a skull embroidered on the back, blue jeans, and black engineer boots.

Lamp looked at Weeks then back at Hedley. "Martin, we need some straight answers, and we need them fast. No bullshit. It's the opinion of those investigating these hits that the Gang Unit isn't fully co-operating with the investigating officers. What we need is a list of all the gang hideouts, safe houses, lairs, dens, whatever, and we need it yesterday."

Hedley squirmed in his seat. "Webber, we've given your detectives all that information already. You need to talk to your people."

Weeks interjected. "No, all we got from Guns and Gangs is the last known addresses. We didn't get the whole thing. You know that, and I know that, so don't sit here saying you've given us all the information. We're not stupid."

Hedley shot a damning glare at Weeks. "I don't know what you're talking about Detective; all we've got is their last known addresses. We don't have complete lists of their safe houses and the like. That's part of our job to find out, and when we do, we enter it into the system. Gathering info on these bastards is not easy. They move from location to location and just because they go to a place doesn't make it a safe house or lair. We have to establish a consistency of use before we deem it a safe house, lair or clubhouse. All in all it's a work in progress and it's constantly changing. "

Lamp slapped his hand on his desk. "Yah, yah. Bullshit, Martin. When I was in the Gang Unit years, ago, we had the official logs to update and the unofficial ones that were kept within the Unit. I'm guessing that practice still goes on today. I want the unofficial info on my desk within the hour, is that clear enough?"

"Whoa, Webber. I'm not prepared to compromise my Unit's intel by giving you addresses. A lot of these guys are working with us. No way, no how. You want that info then Von Pleth is going to have to order me to give it to you. And, if he does, all the work we've done in the past four or five years goes out the window."

Lamp stood up, hands on his desk, and leaned towards Hedley. "What the hell are you guys smoking down there? Von Pleth already told every department, including yours to co-operate fully with our investigation. Do I have to make a phone call upstairs? Because if I have to, I will, and you my friend will be back writing parking tickets. In case you haven't noticed, we've got a fucking war going on with your goddamn gangs, and you try to pull this protocol bullshit with me?"

"Yeah, but…" Hedley began to say.

"Don't you 'yeah but' me, Martin. We've got cops dying, and you're stonewalling me to protect your goddamn CIs?

What the hell?" Lamp sat down hard in his chair.

Hedley looked at Weeks, then at Lamp. "Okay, which gangs do you need the info on?" he asked.

Lamp leaned forward. "Now that's more like it. I sense that you only want to give me certain information, is that correct?"

Hedley rested his arm on his knees, head slumped down. "I understand what we're up against, don't get me wrong. But I would like to keep as many of the CIs protected as possible, because this little dust-up won't last forever. So you tell me which gangs you need info on, and I'll see what I can give you. Does that sound fair?"

Weeks entered the conversation. "Well, not really, Martin. Because if we need gang info that you're not prepared to share, then we're no farther ahead than we are now." Weeks looked at Lamp. "Sorry, Sarg."

Lamp looked at Weeks then Hedley. "She makes a good point, Martin. So, tell you what…these are the gangs we're especially interested in...Los Demonios, Numbers, International Brotherhood, Black Widows, Big Valley Boys, and Two-Sixty-Fourth Street. We think these are the main groups in this 'little dust-up', as you call it. Which I might say is a piss poor choice of words."

Hedley looked sheepishly at both Weeks and Lamp. "Yeah, I knew that the second it crossed my lips. Why these six? They don't even like each other."

"It's obvious you haven't seen the latest video that we've been given by an RCMP undercover agent." Lamp said, as he accessed the file on his computer. Once it was up he spun his monitor towards Hedley. "Watch this. Maybe you can identify the voices?" Lamp clicked on the play button and sat back.

"The video, yah the Chief called me about this, but the way he explained it didn't make it sound all that urgent. So I was going to watch it later." After several minutes, Hedley's eyes grew wider with amazement. "Who the hell is this guy?" he said, after watching for a few minutes. "Is he nuts? Wait, I know that voice. Can you go back?"

Lamp hit the back button.

Hedley cocked his ear towards the screen. "Ah ha, thought so. That's Wilkinson of the Los Demonios, a real scumbag, back-stabbing son-of-a-bitch. The guy he's talking to here… Stop!" Hedley held up his left hand. "Go back a bit." He waited then listened again. "That's Oscar Nineteen from the Numbers Gang. We don't know much about him, cagey son-of-a-bitch. Always in the shadows. We've trailed him and a guy we think is his brother, but haven't got anything on them." Hedley listened intently to the voices on the tape. "That's Chessy from International Brotherhood, another real scumbag."

Lamp played more of the recording.

"I don't know this guy. He sounds French." He listened again. "What's that asshole doing with the big boys? Stop it here. This guy is with the Two-Sixty-Fourth Street gang… oh, what's his name? Think, Hedley…of course, Carver, Brandt Carver. Nice guy who took a wrong turn. They're a small gang with a small turf. No real bad asses, unlike Los Demonios."

He continued to listen as several minutes passed. "Well hello. Haven't heard that voice for quite some time. Good old Kleek, head of the Big Valley Boys. Now this guy is a real piece of work. Keep your eyes on him; this bastard would kill his own mother just for the hell of it." Hedley leaned back in the chair and closed his eyes. "This one here, I don't know his name, but I've heard that raspy voice before; he rides with the Black Widows, a wanna-be biker gang that works for the Los Demonios." Hedley opened his eyes and sat up.

"What an odd combination of assholes. The ones to worry about are the Los Demonios and the Big Valley Boys. They're the bad ones in this group."

Lamp turned his computer around and closed the file. "Can we get the intel you have on all of these gangs? If we can get one of those leaders into custody, maybe they'll rat each other out and we can end this before it gets really ugly."

Hedley looked at Lamp and shook his head. "Even if you get Wilkinson, Kleek, or Chessy, they'll just lawyer up and spit in your face. My suggestion would be to go after the other three gangs, and try to get them to roll on the big boys."

Weeks leaned in. "Then we just need the info on the last three." She looked at Lamp. "We have some good intel on Los Demonios and the Big Valley Boys."

Hedley squirmed in his seat. "By good intel, what do you mean, exactly?"

Lamp butted in. "Show us yours and we'll show you ours. Quid pro quo…and that sort of thing."

Hedley frowned and shook his head. "That's a visual I can do without. I'll have to go downstairs and collect notebooks and bring 'em back here. I'm sure my guys will protest, but last time I looked, we all took the same oath." He stood and stretched. "I'll be back in ten."

Lamp and Weeks watched as he left the office then looked at each other. Weeks rolled her eyes. "I think Hedley's been doing that job too long. Either he's on a power trip or something illegal, or both." They both laughed.

"I went through the academy with him and we both worked in several precincts together. Deep down, he's not a bad guy. He's a typical Type A personality, but basically a good cop. What have we got to give him?"

Weeks put her left foot on the edge of her seat and scrunched into the chair. "Well, if he asks, we've got names and addresses of safe houses, chapter houses, vehicle storage places, and Wilkinson's legit company info." She paused. "We've only got a rough list of known associates and addresses."

Lamp took a swig of cold coffee from his Vegas mug, "That should keep Martin interested. We'll soon learn what info they have that we don't have. Should be helpful?"

Fifteen minutes later, Hedley walked back into Lamp's office carrying a small cardboard box. He plunked it down on Lamp's desk then sat his 6'1", two-hundred and ten pound frame into the chair.

"It took some arm twisting, but the guys gave up their unofficial logs, and from what I've seen so far, you should be able to work with the info." Hedley reached into the box and tossed each of them a packet of note books.

Lamp caught the packet tossed his way. "Can Weeks and her partner go through this stuff? I've got a shitload of paperwork to do." He tossed it to Weeks.

"I'd prefer if nobody else saw this. I know a little about Weeks. I don't know her new partner from a hole in the wall, so if it's all the same, I'd rather he didn't."

Lamp wasn't pleased with Hedley's answer. "I can understand that. So, let's get at it then." Lamp began leafing through the first notebook. He couldn't believe how bad the handwriting was from this officer. “I thought legible handwriting was a prerequisite of becoming a cop, or did that one go by the boards?” Weeks and Hedley both laughed. “What’s your take on this, Martin? Are we in a war, or is this just a revenge thing by a whack job?”

Hedley looked up from the notebook and a puzzled expression came over his face. “That’s a damn good question. We’ve discussed this at length, and it’s no secret that we’ve been hitting them hard where it hurts, their wallets. Prison doesn’t scare these guys, but losing money is a whole other matter.” Hedley paused and took a drink of his coffee. “Personally I think its revenge.” He stood to stretch his back then sat down again. “You have to admit, we’ve had some big dollar busts and a large number of gang members have been locked up. Anyone in the know can see that the gangs wouldn’t put up with this for long without retaliating.”

Lamp leaned on his desk. “Well I’m in the know and I for one didn’t see this coming. Shit, I never even dreamt of this possibility.”

Hedley leaned back and clasped his hands behind his head. “Don’t you guys study history? Capone had enough and lashed out at the feds, and lots of people died. And the two gangs in LA banded together to take on the LAPD back in the eighties. A hell of a lot of good cops died there as well. But the feds and LAPD survived and learned from that experience, just as we will learn from this when the dust settles.”

Weeks looked off into the distance. “So, this is about honour, money and prestige. Perhaps if they legalized the drug trade it would serve two purposes. First, it would put the gangs out of business, and secondly, it would save the medical community tons of cash, not to mention save countless lives."

Lamp grinned. "Well we all know they'll never do that. Especially if they want to keep the border with the US open. If drugs were legalized in Canada that border would be slammed shut in a heartbeat."

CHAPTER

40

THE CONTAINER PUB was packed with its usual customers. Ford had difficulty making his way to the bar and an even a harder time getting Jomo's attention. He edged his way between two patrons at the bar and tossed a peanut toward Jomo. The peanut bounced off Jomo's head and he instantly spun around with a look of a madman on his face. He recognized Ford and grinned. Jomo motioned him over and Ford made his way to the end of the beer-soaked bar. Jomo leaned across the bar. "Things are ready mon. You will have nobody bothering you, mon," Jomo grinned.

Ford nodded and pulled a folded up wad of cash from his inside jacket pocket. "This should take care of any incidentals." He stuffed the wad into Jomo's hand and winked. Ford looked at his watch; it was quarter to eleven. "Give me a beer, Jomo. The others should be here in a few minutes." Ford lit a smoke and leaned against the bar, surveying the patrons that had come to party. It was a real mix of characters. There were dock workers, streetwalkers and zonked out druggies. He chuckled as a more than past-her-prime hooker gave him the eye. Ford shuddered at the thought of anyone having sex with her. He turned away and downed his beer. Ford caught the sound of his cell phone ringing and opened it up.

"Hi, who's this?" he said, looking towards the door. Ford plugged his other ear to shut out the noise.

"It's me, asshole. Nineteen. We'll be there in about five minutes. Is everything ready?"

"Yes, everything is ready. I'm just going to check it out now. Jomo said we'd have all the privacy we need. He's got a fifty-five inch screen that we can use."

"Okay, see you in a bit." Nineteen ended the call and Ford held up his empty glass signifying another, which Jomo promptly delivered.

Ford nodded acceptance and motioned towards Jomo's office. Jomo knew what he meant and waved him to follow. Ford glanced around before going through the swinging door into the kitchen. It smelled of French fries and greasy fish.

Jomo unlocked his office and ushered Ford in, then closed the door. Ford looked around Jomo's office. He liked that Jomo had not lost his connection to Jamaica; every wall had some kind of memento from his homeland. Ford envied Jomo's ties to his country, but wondered about his new found friend. For some reason Jomo was very eager to help him. Was it out of friendship or was he up to something? Ford mused about the question for a few moments then took his laptop out of its case and plugged it into the back of the big screen television. He then queued up the video file for the others to watch. When that was all set, he took a sip of beer. Ford looked around the room; it was almost ready. He opened the closet bi-fold door and pulled out a stack of plastic chairs. Taking another swig of his beer Ford returned to the bar and hopped on a stool. He signaled to Jomo to bring another beer. He wondered how Wilkinson and Chessy would receive the news that they had a leak within their organizations.

Ford was watching in the mirror behind the bar when he saw Wilkinson enter the bar. Ford had a hard time believing that Wilkinson was a biker; he didn't fit the profile. Wilkinson surveyed his surroundings. Ford saw him looking around and turned to look in his direction. As Wilkinson walked toward him, he saw Chessy walk in from the side entrance. He too made his way toward Ford. Nineteen was the last to arrive. Ford got them all a beer then showed the trio into Jomo's office.

"We meet again," Wilkinson said, sitting down in the black leather chair beside the equally overstuffed sofa.

Ford nodded. "Seems that way, doesn't it?"

Chessy flopped down onto the sofa, spilling a little beer on his pants. "Shit. Goddamn thing's too soft." He took a drink. "So, what's this I hear about a video of our last meeting?"

Nineteen sat down at the other end of the sofa, next to the chair Wilkinson occupied. "As I mentioned Chess, seems our last meeting was videotaped and we're trying to figure out who did it." Nineteen could see that Chessy was getting tense. Ford noticed it as well and quickly interceded.

"I met with Nineteen to try and figure out who was sitting where at the last meeting." He reached into his pocket and pulled out the napkin with the seating arrangement on it. "I thought what we'd do was recreate the seats from the meeting, so I'll need your help." He looked at the trio and watched as heads nodded. "We'll arrange the chairs the way they were in the hotel room." He quickly took nine chairs off the stack and began placing them in a semi-circle." Ford handed the napkin to Wilkinson, who looked at it with Chessy.

Within a few minutes, the chairs were arranged. "Okay." Ford said, "You've seen the rough layout of the meeting; do we have the seating arrangements correct?" He looked at Wilkinson and Chessy, who nodded agreement. "Okay, then, I'd like you to sit in your seat as per the meeting, and I'll start the video." The group watched the video on the big screen TV. Wilkinson looked at Chessy then at Ford, "What the fuck gives? That's you sitting there. How in the hell..." Wilkinson stopped and looked at Chessy, who was just as dumbfounded.

"Hey don't look at me. I'm as surprised as you." Chessy said staring back at Wilkinson.

Ford, playing peacemaker, said "Okay, okay! What we need to do is figure out who was sitting in the two seats beside you.

Wilkinson looked at Ford, "MacCreedy was sitting next to me and Miller was sitting next to him and Chess."

Ford looked at Chessy, "From your angle can you tell whether it was Miller or MacCreedy that took the video?"

Chessy studied the stopped image on the big screen. "From here it seems that it's being shot from closer to Dante than me? What's your take Dante?"

Wilkinson stood and moved towards the TV. "You might be right, Chess, it looks like it was shot by MacCreedy. That son-of-a-bitch is a fucking undercover? The fucker's dead." Wilkinson slammed his fist into the wall next to the television, leaving a fairly large hole in the wood paneling.

Ford jumped up, "Ah fuck man, look what you did to Jomo's wall, shit."

Wilkinson spun around and glared at Ford as he rubbed his fist, "I'm pissed off and when I'm pissed off I hit things.

Don't worry I'll leave some money to fix it."

Nineteen stood up. "I agree. It looks like its MacCreedy. How long have you known him Dante?"

Wilkinson returned to his chair and grabbed his beer. "MacCreedy. For the better part of a goddamn year. He came from an affiliate chapter in Montreal. Marcel Gillespie vouched for him, so I didn't think much about it because I've known Gillespie for years. We rode together in Toronto for…shit, had to be four or five years. Did a lot of shit together, so he's solid."

"So it's MacCreedy?" Ford leaned against the wall next to Jomo's desk. "Instead of killing him, why don't we use him? I mean it would be perfect. We feed him a load of bullshit, he reports the bullshit back to the cops, and we do something totally different. They'll soon learn to not trust him, but once we've used him to our advantage, you can cap his ass."

"Nah, I don't want that fuck anywhere near me or knowing what we're going to do. If he's still with us, who's to say the cops won't be right behind him, throwing our asses into the slammer. No, I want the motherfucker gone…tonight." He watched as three heads nodded agreement.

"Okay, then, looks like we've got this problem sorted out," Ford said, putting his beer down. "I've gotta run, have to meet with your hitters to work out who's doing what and to whom. We shouldn't have to meet anymore, unless something comes in out of left field."

At the door, Ford turned back to Wilkinson. "I just had an idea. If you get your guy Miller to get rid of this asshole, you should consider sending a message to the cops. Make it horrible, ugly, full of anger…and make it public. Then, have a sign nailed to his chest that reads 'snitch,' or something like that. That will make every undercover think twice." Ford grinned then nodded and left the office.

CHAPTER

41

FORD WAS EARLY for his meeting with the group of hitters. He parked his car in the stall furthest away from the entrance to Bear Creek Park in Surrey. From where he'd parked, he could see anyone driving into this section of the parking area, another little tidbit of information from his mentor Alverez. As he waited, he went through the list of cops that were in shit with IA. It was quite the list of who's who. Most were on the list for discreditable conduct, abuse of authority, improper off-duty conduct, neglect of duty, corruption or extortion. The last one piqued Ford's attention. He read the names on the list that were in the IA's doghouse for corruption and extortion and wasn't surprised that the list dove-tailed nicely with the list given to him by the gangs. Thirty-four cops were either corrupt or suspected of being corrupt. Ford smiled; he knew this was the target list. He checked to make sure each name had a photo to go with it. He relaxed when that task was complete.

Ford's attention shifted when he saw a black Lexus GS-450 pull into the parking lot and back into a spot several stalls away. He could make out three occupants in the car who were checking him out at the same time. Ford nodded to them, and they returned the nod. Moments later, a black

Mercedes-Benz G55 AMG pulled in and parked across the lot facing the Lexus. Ford saw two bodies in the front seat area, but couldn't tell if anyone was in the back due to the tinted window. The three occupants of the Lexus got out and stood at the front of the vehicle. The two in the front of the Benz got out, then two more got out of the back seat. Ford wasn't exactly sure who these people were. Were they the hitters, or were they just Surrey punks out looking for a good time? He checked his weapon, his eyes fixed on the vehicle as a tall male got out and nodded to Ford.

Moments later, a white lowered GMC Denali entered the lot and backed into a slot across from where Ford was parked. Three people exited the vehicle and moved to the picnic bench a few feet away. So far there were ten hitters with still two more gang teams to show up. All eyes turned to the driveway to watch a green Chevrolet Impala pull in and park between the Denali and the Lexus. Ford glanced at the shooters. Each group was eyeing the others suspiciously.

Two occupants got out of the Impala and leaned against their vehicle. Several minutes later a red Subaru Impreza WRX pulled into the lot and stopped in the middle of the road. Ford motioned them to pull in between the Benz and the Impala. Ford started his Mustang and moved it to block the entrance. He grabbed the package that he'd put together, tucked his gun into the back of his pants, and exited the car.

As he walked toward the vehicles, he grinned. He liked how much he had grown in the past two years. The new Ford, as he called himself, was less naïve, more confident and worldly, bigger, stronger, meaner, wiser, fitter and better looking. If this situation had happened before he'd gone to LA, the old Ford wouldn't have had the guts or smarts to do this. He was glad that Ford didn't exist anymore.

Ford strutted his way toward the gazebo, motioning with his free arm to those standing by their vehicles to join him. He ascended the three steps to the entrance and plopped the folder onto a well-used picnic table, then leaned against the railing. Soon, the rest of the group was gathered under the shelter. Ford slowly panned the group. They were all young like him. He guessed early to mid- twenties. He slowly removed his weapon from his back with two fingers and laid it on the folder, knowing that if anyone hadn't been sent here by a gang, they would surely freak out and want to leave. None did.

"Okay everyone, if you're packing, put it on the table." He watched as eyes darted left and right, shoulders shrugged. His order was obeyed. Soon after, there was a small arsenal on the table. Ford smiled.

"My name is Ford. I don't need to know yours. The less I know about you the better. All I need to know is that you can follow directions and won't cowboy up on the rest of us. I'm also going to assume that your employers have discussed financial compensation for this task. If not, you should contact your employer before accepting your assignments." Ford looked at their faces and could see that a few had yet to resolve that issue. "Okay show of hands. How many have yet to finalize your payment with your employer?" Two hands shot up. Ford grinned. "Give them a quick call to make those arrangements before we continue. I need to know that everyone is committed to completing their assignments once we leave here…so make those calls now." A young Asian male pulled out his cell phone and quickly placed a call. A young East Indian woman did the same thing. Not wanting to be overheard, both left the gazebo and walked a few yards away.

Moments later, both rejoined the group.

"Okay, now that everyone is committed to being here, let's get started. Does everyone know what 'proof of death' means?" He didn't wait for answers. "Whenever you complete an assignment, you must take a picture of the target, showing that the assignment is indeed successfully completed. Once you've done that, you'll send me the picture so that I can keep tabs on our progress. Does anyone have a problem with that?"

Ford heard no objections.

"Great. So we have an initial target group of seventeen really rotten cops. These assholes are responsible for our employers' financial suffering and they're going to be the first wave."

Ford noticed a hand go up. "You don't have to raise your hand, just speak up. What's on your mind?"

"You said initial target group. Does this mean there will be more?"

Ford looked at the young Asian male who had just made the call. "That depends on what reaction we get. If cops continue to harass our employers or lock the city down, then the answer is yes. If, on the other hand, they back off, then the answer may be no. A lot of this will depend on how much pain our employers want to inflict on the Metro police."

Ford surveyed the assembled group. All eyes were fixed on him. He loved being in charge of such a deadly group. "The plan is to divide the initial targets evenly among you. I too am participating in this for my employer. Ideally, what I'd like to see is a coordinated attack in two waves over two nights, so you'll have to do your own intel gathering. Today is Wednesday. I'd like the first wave of attacks to happen no later than this Saturday, so you'll have to get busy scoping out your targets. I've prepared five packages. Each group will receive a package of their assigned targets. I would prefer that you don't complete your assignment in front of any family members. Any other place is fair game." Ford paused. "Any questions?"

"Yah, I got one." Ford looked around for the voice. "My employer told me that you were in charge. Why you?" Ford watched as a well-built guy, about 6' edge his way from the back to the front.

Ford sensed a challenge. "Because, my friend, this was my idea, and it has been agreed to by all of our employers. Does anyone else have a problem with this arrangement?" He felt his palms sweating and his face going a little flush.

The well-built stocky guy looked around at the others assembled. "I don't like this plan. I've never heard of anyone going to war with the cops and winning. Personally, I think this is a really fucked up idea. The fucking cops are going to come after anyone involved, shooting first and asking questions later. This is suicide." He paused and again looked around at the group. "Anyone else feel the same way I do?"

Ford eyed the group. No one agreed. "Perhaps you should contact your employer and ask to be relieved of this assignment. If you're not committed to its success, you could be responsible for its downfall."

The stocky man wheeled around to face Ford. "Look, pipsqueak, I'll do my fucking job as per my employer's request. It doesn't mean I have to like it. As for my commitment, I'll remove the targets you provide, and I'll do it in a fashion of my choosing. Not yours, not this group's, and not my employer's. Get it, half pint?"

It was all Ford could do to keep from laughing at the pompous ass. He laid his folder down and walked directly to face the mouthpiece. When Ford came eye to eye with him, he looked down. "Here I am tough guy; as you can see I'm no fucking pipsqueak or half pint. I'm taller, stronger, and faster than you, so if you want to take me on let's get this shit out of the way so I can wrap this up." Ford stared at the guy as he backed away.

"Buddy, I don't know you from a hole in the ground and personally I don't give a shit about you one way or the other, but I will tell you this my friend, you fuck this operation up and I will personally fucking blow your fucking brains out and not lose a minute of sleep over it. Is that fucking crystal clear?" The guy nodded and cowered to the back of the group. Ford exhaled. He refocused on the group

"Now, I've put a lot of time, effort and money into this operation and I will not let anyone, and I mean *anyone,* fuck it up by going rogue or endangering those who participate in this task…is that clear? If this is beyond anyone's skill-set, then I suggest you talk to your fucking employer and be relieved." Ford took a deep breath to steady his nerves. He looked at the stocky man in front of him. He could tell this wasn't over by a long shot, and at some point in the future they would settle this, but not now. Ford leaned on the picnic table and with one hand opened the folder. "Okay, assignment time."

He grabbed the first packet held together with a paper clip. "Who's with Los Demonios?" The stocky man signified he was; Ford wasn't surprised. "Here's your target list. Your first target is Pastorelli. Who's with IB?"

The young Asian male raised his hand.

"Here's your list. DePlume is your first one," Ford said handing him the packet. "Okay, Bondrah Bros?"

The young East Indian woman raised her hand. He handed her the packet. "First on your list is Cheevers. Big Valley Boys? First on your list is Zamanski. Two-Sixty-Fourth Street? Hammerlin."

"Okay, you have your target lists. Before you leave, are there any other cell numbers I need, so I can provide additional targets should our employers wish to take this to the next level." Nobody offered anything so he closed the folder. Ford turned to the group. "I don't think I need to remind anyone that if, by some fluke you get busted, you have no knowledge of the war or the participants. Once I've received proof of death for your main targets, I'll let you know about the others on your list. Happy hunting. "

He picked up his weapon, stuffed it into his pants, and walked briskly towards his car. Ford grinned; knowing that by Saturday hell would begin to befall the Metro Police Department. He looked at his watch. It was a little past seven-thirty and he was hungry.

The stocky well-built hitter for Los Demonios looked over at Ford. "So, who's your target, Mr. Big Shot?"

"Fair question, I have lots of targets. A low-life named Taylor, and maybe the fucking Chief, plus whomever else I deem necessary to further this endeavour." Ford stared hard at the assembled group. "Any other questions?"

"The Chief of Police, are you fucking nuts? That'll piss off every cop in the province, let alone Metro Vancouver.

Are you trying to get us all fuckin' arrested?" The stocky man blurted out.

"Exactly, he's controlling all these assholes so it makes strategic sense to take him out. Let me guess, you never read the Art of War?" Neither had Ford, but he didn't wait for a response and continued walking to his car.

CHAPTER

42

MACCREEDY, ALONG WITH the two collection goons from the Black Widows, pulled into the parking lot behind the Pop and Whistle Pub in downtown Surrey. This was the second to last stop on their nightly collection run, and MacCreedy was looking forward to getting back to the clubhouse and getting rid of the buckets of cash they had collected that evening. He guessed it was close to a hundred grand.

The two goons were the muscle in case an owner decided not to pay. MacCreedy felt safe knowing that they had his back, although his black belt in karate meant he had no problem dispensing hurt if it was needed to maintain his cover. The owner of the pub knew they were coming and nodded to them when he saw the trio enter the bar. MacCreedy casually walked toward the man behind the bar, Marty Shurman, a man of questionable character.

His eyes surveyed the patrons; he found it difficult to tell if anything was out of the ordinary, as he didn't know what type of cliental frequented the joint. The two goons were right behind him.

Shurman opened the classic replica till, lifted the coin drawer, and extracted a fat envelope. He stuffed the folded envelope into his shirt pocket and motioned MacCreedy to follow him.

Shurman turned and walked through the swinging door into the back of the bar. MacCreedy followed, goon in tow.

Shurman turned as MacCreedy came through the doors. “Here’s your goddamn money, you blood sucking parasite.” He tossed the envelope to MacCreedy.

“Do I need to count it, Marty?” MacCreedy said grinning.

“Screw yourself. You got your money now haul your fucking ass out of my bar.” Shurman glared at MacCreedy and brushed by him as he went back to the bar.

MacCreedy shrugged his shoulders, laughed, and pocketed the envelope that contained five thousand dollars. He pushed back the double swinging doors and entered the bar. *Where is the other goon*? His eyes darted left and right to assess the situation, and seeing no visible threats, he made his way through the bar towards the exit. Outside across the street he spotted their vehicle. He looked up and down the sidewalk. All was clear.

He crossed the street and walked up to the driver’s side rear door and hopped in. He was instantly met by a large fist encased in brass-knuckles being rammed into his jaw, knocking him out.

Miller saw the lights flash twice from the vehicle behind him. He exited his vehicle and quickly walked back and hopped into the passenger side rear seat. “I see that you’ve got things well in hand. Any ideas on how he should meet his maker?”

“Wilkinson said we should make it horrible and public,” the goon behind the wheel offered.

Miller slapped the back of the passenger seat. “Fucking eh, man. He did say that, so let’s make it happen. I have an idea. How brave do you guys feel?”

“What do you have in mind, Miller? Am I gonna hate you

for this idea?" The passenger said.

Miller laughed. "Hell, Ronny, you already hate me, so what else is new." He turned to the driver. "What about you, Sid? You hate me too?" he laughed again.

"You are a sick mother, Miller, you know that?" Sid replied.

"Ah, love you guys, too. Okay, here's what we're going to do. Kill this asshole and hang his body off the cop shop on Main Street."

Both goons looked at each other in disbelief. Ronny quickly turned to Miller, "Are you fucking crazy? Hang a fucking body off the cop shop?"

Miller looked at both of them. "What's the problem? You guys aren't chicken are you?" He grabbed both seat backs and began shaking them. "Come on, guys, it will be a trip. It will be poetic justice for this pig to be displayed where all the other goddamn pigs hang out." Miller leaned back. "Drive, motherfucker. Drive." He laughed. "We'll need to stop and get a few things, so swing by Marlow's place. You guys gonna do him in here, or is there some other place you had in mind?"

Sid turned to face Miller. "Just how much of a statement does Wilkinson want to make here. I mean, there are multiple things we could do to him that would really piss the cops off. How far does he want us to go?"

Miller studied Sid's face. "What do you think?"

The answer caught Sid off guard. "That's why I'm asking you. I have no bloody idea. Does he want us to chop off his fucking head? De-limb the asshole? Gut him like a fish? What?"

Miller laughed. "Any and all of the above. Take your pick.

Whatever gets you off."

Sid shook his head and muttered. "Just great."

"What was that?" Miller asked jokingly.

"I said, JUST GREAT," Sid shook his head again.

"Relax, Sid. As long as we nail a sign to his chest, anything else we do will be icing on the cake, so relax and take a deep breath."

"Why don't we just shoot the bastard and be done with it?" Sid said looking in the rearview mirror at Miller.

"Okay, screw it, let's just shoot him." Miller laughed sadistically and pulled out his silenced Beretta and fired two quick shots into MacCreedy's chest. "Done…see, easy peasy." Miller looked out the window and ordered, "Drive."

An hour later, the black SUV pulled off of Terminal Avenue onto Main Street. The cop shop was only a few blocks away. At Marlow's place, they had acquired two lengths of rope, a grapple type hook on a nylon rope, three large spikes and a sledge hammer.

Miller looked at his watch; it was ten past three in the morning, only a few people were out and about. "Drive around the cop shop. I want to find the best possible place to get onto the roof."

"The roof. Are you nuts? How the hell do we get up there without being spotted or shot?" Pete asked, as he turned onto Hastings Street.

"Drive, Pete. Leave the planning to me." Miller looked out the window. "Ah-ha, that's it. Let me out here and park up ahead." Without waiting for the vehicle to completely stop, Miller opened the door and stepped out, almost falling on his face.

He watched as the SUV pulled into the first available

parking spot. Miller walked to the corner and looked up at the building right beside the police station. The alley between the two buildings would be the only challenge. He crossed the street and walked toward the alleyway, only stopping to light a smoke. Craning his neck upward, he checked the power poles. The power transformers were on a catwalk between the poles that held it up. He smiled as he walked down the alley to the back of the adjacent building. The alley lights provided enough visibility to see that there weren't any outside stairs to the roof, so he guessed the entry was inside. Miller walked back to the front of the building, stepped up to the front door, and pulled on it. To his surprise, it opened. Miller quickly turned and crossed the street. Inside the SUV he detailed his plan to the two goons.

"Are you nuts, man? If we touch one of the transformers, we'll be cooked!" Sid said visibly shaken by the thought of death by electrocution.

Miller laughed sarcastically, "Well then I guess you'd better not touch any of the wires. Let's go before the cops change shifts.

Pete drove the SUV two blocks up the street then made three left turns and a right back onto Hastings. He pulled up in front of the building.

Miller leaned forward, hands on the seats. "Okay, like I said, pretend he's our buddy and he's passed out." He watched as two heads nodded. "Okay, let's do this."

Sid turned to Miller. "Is this a business building, or do people live here?"

Miller snapped back. "I don't give a rat's ass, so why the hell do you?" He shot a glance up and down the sidewalk; he could only see one person way up the block. "Okay let's go." Miller opened the door and stepped onto the sidewalk. His part of the plan was to be the lookout and holder of doors. Miller watched as the two goons easily manhandled the corpse into a standing position and carried him toward the door. Miller closed the SUV door and darted to the door of the building. He held it open as Sid and Pete moved the very dead MacCreedy in front of the door. Miller closed the door, dashed to the elevator, and stabbed the up button. He checked the back of his pants; his gun was still there, just in case things went south.

It seemed like forever before the doors opened and Miller stepped inside. When they all were in, he pressed the fourth floor button. A minute later the door opened, and Miller stuck his head out and checked both left and right. *Good, nobody around.*

Miller walked left to the end of the hallway looking for a service door, finding none, he ran back down the hallway. The second to last door had a small sign on it. *Roof is off-limits to residents.* Miller leaned into the door to test its resistance, took a step back, pulled out his silenced weapon, and fired two shots into the lock. The door swung open.

Miller quickly went through, followed by the others and quickly closed the door. He motioned for Sid and Pete to go up the stairs to the roof door. Miller cracked the door ajar to see if any resident was nosey enough to check. He didn't see or hear anybody, so he joined the others on the stair. At the roof door, he saw a small bolt and handle lock. Miller slid the bolt back and shoved the door open. The night air was refreshing, as they all were sweating. Miller ventured onto the roof and found the power poles and motioned the others to join him. Pete and Sid dropped the body of MacCreedy onto the graveled roof. Pete removed the backpack and opened it up to expose the ropes and other gear they had brought along. Miller checked the roof for an anchor point. He spotted a sewer vent pipe in the middle of the roof and quickly grabbed a length of rope. In no time, he had the rope securely around the vent pipe and knotted, then rejoined the others.

"Okay, who wants to go first? No volunteers, okay Pete, you're up." He handed him the end of the rope. "Tie this around you and go to the edge. Come let's move it."

At the edge of the roof, Miller looked down. It was about fifteen feet to the catwalk, and he was glad the city had elected to put the poles right beside the buildings so the alleys could handle large delivery vehicles. He and Sid grabbed the rope and pulled it taut as Peter lowered himself over the edge. Slowly, they let out the rope, lowering him down to the catwalk.

Once down, Pete untied the rope, and Miller quickly hoisted it back up. Hastily, they secured it around MacCreedy's arms and lowered the dead weight over the edge. Pete grabbed the body, lowered it to the catwalk, and removed the rope. Miller pulled it up and handed it to Sid, who secured it around his waist. He slowly slipped over the roof edge as Miller kept the line tight. He struggled to keep himself from being pulled over, as there was a substantial weight difference between him and Sid. The rope burned through his jeans. He grimaced in pain, but kept lowering him. Within seconds, the line went slack.

Miller hurriedly tied the rope around his waist, grabbed the backpack, and went over the edge. He slid down the rope, landing with a thud on the catwalk. Miller let his eyes adjust to the darkness. He could see the outline of the three transformers and he could see enough of the catwalk edge to know that with care they could safely pass by them. Miller made his way across the catwalk and tossed the grappling hook onto the roof and yanked it taut. He instructed Pete and Sid to pick up the body, which they did.

Miller was surprised at how much heat and noise the transformers emitted. In no time, the three were past the last transformer and were at the wall of the station. Miller climbed the rope to the roof and looked back down. He instructed Sid to tie the rope around MacCreedy's chest then climb up the rope to the roof. Pete followed Sid up. Miller ordered them to haul the body up. He grabbed the end of rope and tied it around the power pole and walked to the street side of the building. Miller got onto his stomach and crawled to the edge of the building. He carefully peered over the edge to see if there was any activity on the sidewalk below. Miller motioned for them to join him. Sid opened the backpack and took out the cardboard sign that Miller had made up and chuckled at what it said, *FUCKING STOOLIE.*

He then retrieved the sledge hammer and two spikes and proceeded to attach the sign to the body. Pete took the rope and tied it around MacCreedy's arms and neck. Miller motioned them to get ready. He held up his hand, palm flat out, checked the sidewalk then waved them forward. The two goons had no trouble getting the body over the edge, and lowered it down between the third floor windows. Miller had sprinted to the power pole and quickly tied the rope off, so the body would hang where it was intended. He then darted to the edge of the roof and checked where the body was hanging. He grinned.

CHAPTER 43

WEEKS NOSED HER unmarked patrol car onto Hasting Street, heading towards the station. The Main Street intersection was blocked off by police cruisers. She turned onto Gore and headed to the parkade on East Cordova. Pulling inside, she could see cops milling around their patrol cars. Weeks found her parking spot and pulled in. On her way to the elevator, she spotted Mills talking to another detective and made her way towards them.

Mills waved when he spotted his partner. “Hey, Weeks, hell of a morning, eh? This ugly bastard is Danny LePointe. He’s working Surrey Metro. Danny, this is my partner, Shelley Weeks.” He watched as they shook hands.

Weeks eyed LePointe. He had sandy blonde hair, dark rimmed glasses and was tall with a muscular build. “What’s all the activity on the street?” she said.

Mills looked at LePointe, then back to Weeks. “You haven’t heard?”

“Heard what?” Weeks replied.

“Shit, I thought everyone was called about this. About three-thirty this morning, they found a corpse hanging from the roof with a sign nailed to his body. ‘Fucking Stoolie,’ it said.”

Weeks was stunned, “A body hanging from the roof of our police station…yah right!”

“It’s the gospel truth,” LePointe said. “He had a sign nailed to him with large spikes. The guy had been shot two times in the heart. They cut him down around four. It turns out the guy was an RCMP undercover. What was his name again?”

“I think it was MacCreedy.” Weeks felt the colour drain from her face. “You know this guy?”Mills said.

Weeks, stunned, struggled to reply. “Yeah, you know him too. His undercover name was Zolan MacCreedy and in real life, his name was Wayne Troy. He was the CI who gave us the video of the gang meeting. We met him down at the cement plant.” Weeks inhaled deeply. “Damn I hope he and his fiancée didn’t have any kids?” Shelley Weeks felt herself tearing up.

LePointe shifted uneasily. “Maybe what we’re hearing about a war is true. Never thought I’d see this happening. The gangs are little piss-ant cowards. Too stupid to know better, and too dumb to do anything about it. They whine when they get caught.”

Weeks couldn’t believe that bullshit. “Are you kidding me? You think these guys are stupid cowards? Boy, have you got these guys wrong. Some of these guys are well-educated, well-financed, well-connected, and for the most part don’t give a fuck whether you, me, or Mills here gets killed. Our biggest mistake will be to underestimate just how fucking ruthless these bastards can be.” She paused to catch her breath. “Furthermore, the scary part is that I think this is just the beginning. So if I were you, LePointe, I’d start wearing my fucking vest because nobody knows who’s next.”

LePointe was taken aback by Weeks' onslaught; he was lost for words momentarily. "Dial it down a notch, Weeks. Fuck, the last time I looked we were all on the same side. You sound like you admire these fucking animals."

Weeks' rage exploded and she deliberately got into LePointe's face. "Look you smug son-of-a-bitch, I don't admire these assholes, but I am well aware of what they can do, what they did to my last partner, what they've done to all the other cops who have been gunned down in the last few days, so when you try to blow smoke up my ass about these guys being dumb cowards, you're only showing us just how ignorant you are." Weeks backed away. "Come on Mills, we've got work to do." She turned and headed to the elevator, not seeing the many eyes that followed her.

Mills slapped LePointe on the shoulder. "Don't worry about it; she's a damn good cop who's going through a rough patch. Hey, was good to see you again. Once this shit storm ends, we can get together for a beer." Mills turned and trotted to where Weeks was standing waiting for the elevator.

Weeks stared at the door. "You don't have to make excuses for me, understand? The arrogant asshole needed exactly what he got."

Mills recoiled a bit. "Hey, lighten up. He's a good cop. He's got one of the best arrest and conviction rates in Surrey Metro, so you might want to cut him a bit of slack." He wished the door would open as things were getting awkward.

Moments later the door opened and they waited for people to get off before silently getting on.

Lamp was sitting in his office with the door closed as Weeks and Mills walked by. He saw them from the corner of his eye and tossed a yellow highlighter at the window to get their attention. The thud against the glass startled Weeks and she turned. She caught Lamp's wave to come in.

"Mills, Sarg wants to see us," she said, opening his office door. Weeks walked in and she could smell that Mills was right behind her. She had become somewhat accustomed to his odor problem and knew it really wasn't his fault.

Lamp was on the phone and made the gesture with his hand that whomever he was talking to wouldn't shut up. He motioned them to sit down.

Both detectives sat down and tried not to listen to the conversation Lamp was having. From what they could tell, it was someone high up the food chain.

Moments later, Lamp replaced the receiver and shook his head. "Christ, the media is all over this murder. As if we didn't have enough goddamn problems, now we have to kiss their butts." He leaned back. "Are we any closer to nailing these animals? Weeks, do you have any new info on your suspected perp? Please tell me you've got something."

Weeks composed herself. "The answer is no. We're working our CIs, but this guy is a ghost. People say they've seen someone like him here or there, but nothing we can hang our hats on. Sorry, Sarg. Until this guy slips up, we're spitting into the wind."

"Damn." Lamp slammed his fist on his desk. "Mills have you got anything?"

Mills was startled. "I'm getting the same info. The guy seems to be able to vanish into thin air. If I didn't know better, I'd say he doesn't exist. Sorry."

"Well, what the hell are you two sitting here for? Get out there and find this bastard before someone else dies." Lamp burst out.

Weeks and Mills beat a hasty retreat from Lamp's office. They heard the phone ring again as they closed the door. Weeks looked back at Lamp. She didn't envy his job. "I'll meet you in the bullpen. I gotta talk to Mander downstairs." Weeks said heading for the stairwell.

She arrived at Mander's office and walked in, startling him with her abruptness.

"Hello, Detective Weeks, what can I do for you?" Mander said, visibly surprised.

"I'm just looking for anything new on our suspect. You were going to try again to clean the images from the video?"

"No luck. I've pushed the pixels as far as I can, sorry. It's as good as it'll get."

Weeks slapped her thigh in frustration. "Well, it was worth the trip, thanks." Weeks stood up and left the office. She paused for a moment then turned toward the stairs going to level three in the basement; perhaps Hedley had heard some chatter from one of his CIs. It was worth a shot.

The smells in the lower levels always made her feel queasy, so she took a deep breath before walking into the Gang Squad bullpen. She spotted Hedley and wound her way through the clutter to get to his desk. "Hi Martin, remember me?"

"Hi Weeks, to what do I owe the pleasure of your company?" Hedley said with a devilish grin on his face.

"Three guesses and the first two don't count. You heard anything about Troy?"

Hedley glanced around the room and leaned toward Weeks. "Nothing definitive. CIs normally don't get up 'til the afternoon. Hell, my guess is that most of them just got home, wherever that might be. But rest assured, come this afternoon we'll be burning up the phone lines to see what we can find out. The consensus in the bullpen is that Wilkinson and the Los Demonios iced him, so it's also safe to assume that his cover was blown. We can forget about getting anyone else close to Wilkinson. From what I've learned, it took the GRC almost a year and a half to get someone into his organization."

"GRC?" Weeks asked.

"Gendarmerie du Royale Clip-clop. That's slang for RCMP!" He laughed. "I would have thought that every city cop knew what GRC meant."

"They've told me I've lived a sheltered life," Weeks grinned. "Seriously though, would Wilkinson be that brutal."

"There's the odd thing. He's not a violent guy by nature, but can be when needed. I remember dealing with him years ago before he became head honcho. He was an easy guy to talk to, was civil towards us beat cops, and had a real soft spot for kids. You know the annual toy ride at Christmas? Well, one year Wilkinson and two other bikers went out and bought five-hundred stuffed animals and handed them out to every biker before the ride. I asked him why he would do this, and you know what his answer was? He said it made him feel human and that kids deserved toys at Christmas. Go figure." He turned to face Weeks. "I'll call you as soon as I hear anything. These bastards can't remain clammed up forever."

Weeks patted Hedley on the shoulder and beat a hasty exit from the awful smelling area. She rode up the elevator lost in thought. Her mind was reeling with possibilities, and she came to one inescapable conclusion, if it was her turn to die, she hoped it would be a glorious death, not like

MacCreedy's. She struggled to get the image of Troy's body with spikes driven into it out of her mind.

She arrived at her desk moments later to find the normally loud and busy bullpen quiet, almost like a church. It was unnatural. She looked around at her colleagues; everyone was quietly sitting, reviewing files or simply staring into space. Weeks guessed that each was thinking about his or her own family and the tremendous price this job could extract. She remembered the wisdom that her drill sergeant imparted to the class on graduation day.

This job has to be a calling, as you will see, hear, smell and feel things you never in your wildest dreams ever thought you'd encounter. You will see your fellow officers go bad, make mistakes, excel, and yes, even die. But know this, if they've chosen this occupation for the correct reasons, they will not feel a moment's regret. When you get out on the streets, you have to put aside the fear that, at any given moment, you could be knifed, beaten, pelted, spit on, stabbed or shot because police work is out there, among the people, the good ones and the bad ones, the smart ones and the stupid ones, the honest and dishonest, the gentle and the brutal. Keep your heads up and your wits about you and you'll all do an excellent job. Good luck, everyone. May you have a long and successful career, with more good days than bad ones.

Weeks shook her head. She had to get her mind back to the task at hand, identifying her perpetrator. She kept asking herself, who is this guy and how can someone disappear so completely with all the eyes they've got out there looking for him? Where is he hiding?

CHAPTER

44

FORD PULLED INTO the U-Rent storage facility in Queensborough. He quickly entered his storage locker and removed two Glock 9s, his break-down sniper rifle, and two boxes of ammunition. He took off his shirt and put on the bullet proof vest that he had acquired from Jomo. *Better to be safe than sorry.*

He thought about how many crooked cops were about to go down. Knowing full well that the police would never tell the media that all the dead cops were corrupt, Ford's plan was to let the media know exactly who had been killed and why.

Ford quickly stashed the weapons into secret compartments that he'd found inside his Mustang and programmed Taylor's address into his GPS. Ford crossed over the Queensborough Bridge and headed down Marine Way toward Vancouver and his intended target's home.

Traffic was light for a Saturday night, and thirty-five minutes later Ford eased his Mustang off Marine Way onto Ash Street and headed toward West 69th. He slowed as he entered West 69th and looked for the house on the west side of the street. He spotted the split level older house with the huge trees in the front yard. *Taylor had either bought the property long ago, won the lottery, or he was crooked.* Ford suspected it was the latter. He drove around the neighborhood, completing a figure eight so that he could drive by the house from the other direction. He noticed that an unmarked police car was parked on the street as well as a newer BMW and a Mercedes Benz in the driveway.

Ford pulled into the back alley that divided the block and cruised towards Taylor's house. It was easy to spot with the large trees out front and the nearly seven foot fence in the backyard. Back out front, Ford found a parking spot several houses away and pulled over. He decided to wait and see if Taylor stayed in or went out. Personally, he hoped Taylor would come out. Taylor's police records didn't indicate any immediate family members, but they could be wrong. Ford pulled out his digital camera and attached the zoom lens, focusing it on Taylor's front doorway. It was nine thirty-five, and the street was quiet at this time of night. Ford guessed that was why Taylor had chosen to live in this neighborhood.

Ford hated waiting, so to ease the stress, he lit a smoke. It was all he could do not to kick in the door and start blasting, but he remembered the wise words Alverez had told him, 'inhale deeply and hold it if he felt too amped up and the feeling would pass'. Ford inhaled deeply and held his breath. As usual, Alverez was right, the feeling passed and he calmed down.

For nearly an hour, Ford waited for Taylor to do something, and at ten-twenty Taylor's garage door opened and Ford could see a newer red corvette. Ford shook his head. *How the fuck does this guy afford these cars on a cop's salary? Is nobody in Metro seeing this?* He watched as the back-up light's came on. Ford quickly put the camera on the seat and pulled out his silenced weapon. Starting his car, he waited for the Corvette to pull out onto the street.

Ford knew he'd have to take out Taylor before he got onto the main highway as his Mustang was no match for a Corvette in a street race. The Corvette backed out and headed west. Ford's Mustang did likewise and hung back three car lengths so as to not arouse suspicion. Six blocks later, Ford made his move. There were no other vehicles coming, so he gunned his car and pulled up alongside the Corvette. He readied his weapon and aimed it directly at Taylor, who looked shocked when he saw the weapon. Ford fired off three quick shots; all hit their mark, which sent Taylor's car careening off to the right as he lost control and slumped in his seat. Ford calmly circled the block. As he passed by the Corvette piled up on the bus stand a few people had started to gather to view the accident scene. He quickly aimed his autofocus camera at Taylor and snapped a picture, then casually drove away. From what Ford could tell only one person briefly looked his way.

Ford quickly headed down Marine Drive toward New West. He needed to keep a level head. Soon the others would be letting him know their progress, but he felt no need to let the others know that he had already successfully eliminated his main target.

Twenty-five minutes later, he was back in New West. It was just past eleven-thirty and he was thirsty, so he pulled into an all night diner on Sixth Street. His phone began to light up with text messages from the other shooters. Ford smiled, the cops wouldn't know what the hell had hit them.

Ford laughed. It was just before midnight, and already five of the six had been taken care of: Pastorelli, Cheevers,

Zamanski, Hammerlin, and Taylor were dead. He had to confirm the additional targets with the hitters so that they could complete their tasks and get out of town before the city was locked down tight, which he knew would happen. Ford finished his coffee, promptly left the diner, and headed for his apartment. The rain pounded down, making travel difficult due to the reflection of headlights on the wet street. Ford took his time. The last thing he needed was to be in an accident.

He arrived home close to one o'clock and quickly began to assign targets to the various hitters. Ford gave the Los Demonios hitter Peter Wilson and Charn Damansk, two real pieces of work. The International Brotherhood got Gary Thorsen and Silvia Lee; Bondrah Brothers got George Fellers and Winston Chambers. Ford gave Sara Farnsworth and Randy LaRouch to the Big Valley Boys, and the 264th Street Gang got Steve Manters and William Bender. In total, fifteen crooked cops would be taken off the street, plus those that Ford chose to get rid of personally. He'd get rid of Von Pleth last?

Ford closed the notepad and switched on the television to the local twenty-four hour news channel. As he guessed, the news of the eliminated cops was breaking news. He flipped the channel to other local outlets, and it was breaking news on all of them. Ford went back to Channel 21 and his favourite news anchor, Debra Patton.

CHAPTER

45

DETECTIVE WEEKS, ALONG with every officer in the Metro Police force was summoned into work early. The news and events from the previous evening had every cop on edge, looking over his or her shoulder and wondering, *am I next*? She nosed her unmarked police car into the parkade and spotted Mills leaning against another squad car, Timmy's coffee in hand. Weeks parked, grabbed her Starbucks and briskly approached Mills. As she neared him, they both began shaking their heads and shrugging their shoulders. "What the fuck is going on here?" Weeks asked him.

Mills again shrugged his shoulders and raised his eyebrows. "I believe we're in a bloody war with somebody who doesn't give a rat's ass whether we live or die." Mills took a large swig of his coffee as they walked towards the door. "I heard three cops got killed, as if it was open season on us or something."

Weeks walked slowly with her head down. "I heard there were five. I guess it depends on who was doing the talking. My guess is we'll find out exactly how many as soon as Sarg briefs us." The pair made their way to the squad room, which was half full of detectives that were in the same state of disbelief as they were.

"Okay, people," Lamp said. "Let's button it. We can't wait for the few stragglers to show up." The room fell silent instantly as Lamp's large frame stopped in front of the whiteboard. "As you may have heard, several of our fellow officers have been shot and killed. He scanned the room to gauge the effect of what he was saying.

Weeks looked down at her hands, they were trembling and her heart rate was elevated. The pit of her stomach roiled.

"If any of you doubted that we were at war, I think this is your answer. We are at war! Not of our choosing, but you can be damn sure we will end this on our terms. Reports are still coming in, so we don't know exactly how many are dead or even who they are. It is safe to say that we don't know who the shooters are. We have the name of one man so far, whom we believe is the ringleader, Dustin Ford. We have a rough idea of his height, skin colour, features, but other than that, he's a ghost. We should not underestimate this individual because he has proven that he is an excellent marksman with both short and long weapons. We've been trying to find this son-of-a-bitch, but we keep hitting dead ends. We don't have any solid leads as to his whereabouts. Hell, we're not even sure exactly what he looks like, so we can't put out a bolo on him."

Lamp paused again to take a quick gulp of his cold coffee. "We have several other gang members in custody at a secret location, and they're being questioned, but so far none of them have given us anything. I would like to say this will be over soon, but I can't, just like I can't tell you that none of you will be killed in this war. As of this minute, we have no idea what their plan entails, so all I can tell you is that when you're out there, make sure you have your vests on. This is not optional, people. Wear them." Lamp noticed small groups chatting among themselves.

"People, one meeting please." He waited until they'd shut up. "As you may have figured out, we don't know shit at this point, and we need to change that the second we leave this room. Von Pleth has been on my ass about this whole war thing, and he's demanding answers. So guess what, people? Consider me on your asses until I get something to pass up the food chain." Lamp walked over to where Weeks and Mills were standing. "Okay, you two. You're up. Tell us what you know about this Ford asshole, whatever you have."

Weeks stretched and motioned to Mills to join her up front. She walked slowly to the whiteboard, her mind reeling with possible information she could share. Weeks turned to face her co-workers, all of whom were staring back at her. "Thanks, Sarg, wasn't expecting to be at the head of the class this early in the morning." She looked at her watch. "Crap, it's only four-fifteen. Okay, here's what we know, or what we think we know. Dustin Ford is about twenty-ish, over six feet, stocky with a fair complexion and he has a strawberry birthmark on his right cheek. We have no idea where he lives. We believe he's associated with the Numbers Gang and that he's the one who started this war.

"We think this all started because of a botched hit on an informer named Hooper, two years ago. We also believe he drives a red Ford Mustang, year unknown. We think that he frequents a place called the Walnut Hut Cafe downtown. We have video surveillance that the Information Technology (IT) department is currently analyzing. She looked at the faces looking at her and she could see fear in everyone's eyes.

"We believe that he's the brains behind this war, but we're not sure how the other gang members fit into it. According to Gangs and Guns, these gangs have never agreed on the weather, let alone a war, so how they all mesh we don't know. If they're all working together, the guy who arranged this should work at the United Nations. We have a video of a meeting that Ford had with several of the gang leaders. We know this because an undercover RCMP agent got us the video before he was executed. We believe Wilkinson of Los Demonios had him killed, but no proof of that yet. Hell we can't even find Wilkinson. It seems some of the gang leaders have gone into hiding and likely will be there until this madness is over. Basically, as Sarg said, we know shit and this has to change before the body count rises. We know that Ford isn't doing this alone, but we don't know who the other shooters are. We suspect they're imports who'll leave town as soon as the shooting stops." Weeks turned to Mills. "You got anything else to add?"

Mills stepped toward the whiteboard just as a panicking clerk rushed into the room and blurted out. "Two more dead. Two more cops killed."

Lamp held up his hand to stop Mills. "Two more…WHAT THE HELL is going on? A war with the gangs. The ones we try everyday to bring to justice…totally unheard of in a civilized society. I must be missing something…either these guys are idiots or they just don't care, either way it makes them extremely dangerous. As of now, I want this town torn apart to find these animals. We must assume that it's more than one shooter. Leave no stone unturned, check and recheck your sources. Dig until you can't dig any more, then dig some more. We cannot afford to lose another cop to these assholes, do I make myself clear?" Lamp looked around the room, all heads were nodding in agreement. "Okay, everyone, get out of here. Go do what you do best and remember, no more dead cops."

Weeks and Mills entered the elevator and descended into Mander's realm. Weeks turned the knob and walked in, "I sure hope the fuck he's got something."

Mander was sitting at his desk, eyes glued to his computer screen. She leaned on the counter. "Hi, Mander," she said loud enough to break his concentration.

Mander was startled by the sound and looked up. "Christ all mighty, can you guys just once use the damn bell instead of scaring the crap out of me?" He stood up and went to the counter. "What is it you want?"

"The video from the Walnut Hut Cafe, did you finish analyzing it yet?"

"Ah yeah, the rush job, like everything else down here. We finished it last night. Let me bring it up on the screen." Mander queued up the video and pressed play.

Weeks and Mills stared at the images for several minutes. "Stop there," she barked. "Who are these two?"

Mander interjected. "You'll see in just a bit, there's a good image of the kid and another guy together." He pressed fast forward. The image blurred as he pressed play to resume the regular viewing. The image on the screen showed the young kid and an older male at a computer terminal in the corner. "Here's what I was referring to."

Mills and Weeks stared intently as the image played. "Stop there, please. And can you back it up a bit, then go slo-mo." Mander quickly made it so.

Weeks squinted at the screen. "Could the older guy be Ford? Too grainy to tell?" Her adrenalin was pumping, "We need to talk to this kid."

Mills stared even more intently. "There, did you see that? Back it up."

Mander backed up the images then pressed the super slow motion feature.

Weeks and Mills both stared at the somewhat grainy images. "Freeze there," Mills said. "Correct me if I'm wrong, but that looks like a wad of cash changing hands. Can that be enlarged?"

The three watched the image multiple times in slow motion to be sure they were all seeing the same thing. Mander zoomed in on the hands of the person standing next to the kid sitting at the computer.

"Yep, that looks like a money exchange to me," Weeks said excitedly.

Mander pressed the screen print button then went over to the printer to retrieve the image. He handed it to her and smiled.

"Finally! A solid goddamn lead in this nightmare. Let's hope this kid is a regular. Let's go Mills." She smiled at Mander. "Good job." Twenty minutes later, Weeks pulled the unmarked police car into the corner parking lot adjacent to the Walnut Hut Café. Armed with the image, Weeks and Mills entered the café and quickly scanned the occupants. Weeks recognized the owner from their previous visit and signaled for him to come to the vacant booth. Moments later, a somewhat bewildered owner stood beside the booth and Weeks pulled out the image and handed it to him. "Is this kid a regular, or a drop in?"

The owner looked at the image for a long moment. "He's a regular."

"What's his name?" Mills demanded.

"Don't know. Why don't you ask him? He's sitting at the computer by the back wall."

Weeks looked at Mills, then at the owner and motioned him away. She drew her weapon and Mills did likewise. Weeks kept her weapon close to her body and went down the left side of the café, while Mills took the right side. They converged at the computer where a young kid was wearing ear buds and playing a game.

Weeks tapped him on the shoulder, her weapon by the side of her waist pointed right at the kid.

The kid looked up and freaked out. "Holy Shit, don't shoot!" His eyes were big as saucers and his pimpled face flushed red.

Mills joined Weeks at the computer desk. The kid looked at him with a bewildered expression. "Holy shit, two cops with guns! Am I in trouble?"

Weeks put her weapon away and grabbed a chair. "Okay, young man, let's start with your name. Who are you?"

"Okay, okay. My name is Nathan Bradley. What did I do?"

"That depends, Mr. Bradley," Mills said, towering over the kid. "You may have helped a cop killer."

Weeks produced the picture and placed it in right in front of Bradley. "That's you there. What we need to know is who's the guy next to you and why did he pay you?" She studied his face and could see he was visibly shaken.

Bradley stared at the image. "I only know him as Ford. He never told me his first name…Is he the cop killer?" Bradley said, his voice quivering.

"Let's just say he's a person of interest. How do you contact him?" Weeks said as she jotted notes. Her heart was racing and her palms were clammy, excitement welled up within every pore of her body. She wanted to scream out to the world that she was right, but managed to subdue her enthusiasm for now.

Bradley squirmed in his chair. "I have a phone number, but I haven't talked to him in a while."

Mills pulled his chair next to Bradley's. "Okay Mr. Computer nerd, what did Ford want with you?"

Bradley shot a glance between Weeks and Mills, a childish grin enveloped his face. "Okay, who is the good cop and who is the bad cop here? I need to know."

Mills kicked his chair, sending Bradley backwards onto the floor. "Wise up, asshole," he barked. "This is serious. What did Ford want you to do?"

Nathan Bradley cowered. "Okay, okay. He wanted me to hack the Metro Police computer." He looked at Weeks. "I told him I could, but it would likely be suicide."

Weeks leaned towards him and asked softly, "And did you?"

Bradley sat there somewhat stunned. Weeks could see by the expression on his face that he was thinking it over and was scared.

She leaned back. "You know I can call our tech department, and they'll tell me if anyone has hacked in or even attempted to hack into our system. How long do you think it'll take me to get that info? You know it's a federal offense to hack into a police computer." she smiled at Bradley who just sat there stunned. "You didn't know eh. Too bad as it'll take them less than five minutes if they're not too busy. So that's how long you've got before we run you in." Weeks sat up and pulled out her phone and punched in the number.

"Hi, this is Detective Weeks, badge number Bravo four-nine-eight-three, can you put me through to tech services please?" She looked at Bradley. "They're putting me through…not much time left." Weeks watched as Bradley squirmed a little more.

"You're running out of time, Mr. Bradley," Mills chimed in. "You ever been inside a Metro police cell? They're pretty rough. You know any self-defense? No? Too bad."

Bradley turned to Weeks visibly shaken. "Okay, what do you want to know?"

Weeks closed her phone and leaned in. "Everything. Don't leave out a single fact, or so help me you'll be in the worst cell we have with the meanest bastards in town. Are we clear?" Weeks leaned back, pulled out a tape recorder from her pants pocket, and placed it on the computer desk. "Okay, kid. Talk."

Weeks kicked his chair, sending Bradley over backwards again. "We're waiting." The commotion caused everyone to look their way. She couldn't believe how young he was and how obviously gifted he was. Weeks thought about Ford being just a little older than this kid when he tried to kill someone.

Mills stood up and pulled out his badge and held it up. "Nothing to see here people."

Weeks extended her hand to Nathan Bradley, who grabbed it and pulled himself up. "Anything else to delay this?"

"Nope, nothing else!" Bradley blurted.

Mills grabbed his forearm and squeezed. "Mr. Bradley, we're running out of patience. Either you begin talking, or we're through here. Do you get my drift? In case you haven't figured it out, I'm the bad cop, and she's even worse, so start talking."

Bradley tried to move his arm, but it was pinned to the desk. "He said he wanted to get into the Metro data base to find a cop who had humiliated him a couple of years ago."

"That's it? Were you able to get into the system?" Mills pressed.

"I broke into the system and created a working back door so he could enter the system undetected anytime he wanted to." Bradley said, his head hanging low.

"Jesus Christ, kid, you know what the fuck you did? You put close to two thousand cops' lives in danger. Did you ever think about that?" Mills was fuming.

Bradley mustered some backbone. "How was I to know he wanted to kill cops? All he told me he was looking for a cop who made him feel stupid."

"So why did you do this for him?" Weeks asked.

"Because the guy scared the shit out of me. Plus, he had money, lots of money. Can you let my arm go? It hurts."

Mills removed his paw from the kid's skinny forearm. "How much did he pay you?"

"He paid me a grand, all in fifties."

"Do you have any of that money left that we can check for finger prints?" Weeks asked.

Bradley shook his head. "Are you kidding? I lived large. I was popular for three days."

Weeks motioned to Mills to follow her. She stood and went towards the counter. "Stay put," she barked at Bradley.

Mills leaned on the counter and looked at Weeks, then the kid. "What are you thinking?"

"How old are you, Nathan?" She asked.

"Almost fifteen."

Weeks looked back at Mills. "Here's what I'm thinking. Let's see if we can draw Ford out and get him to come to the kid." She looked skyward for a second. "There must be something that Ford needs. But what?"

Mills looked around the café, "Information would be my best guess. Ford's been doing a lot of shit. I'll bet he'd like to know what we know about him."

Mills and Weeks returned to Bradley. "Okay, Nathan," Weeks said putting her hand on his shoulder. "If you were to text or call Ford and tell him you found some really juicy info about him, do you think he'd come and see you here?"

Bradley looked at Weeks, "He has access to the police database system, so it would be unlikely he'd come here, all he'd do is ask for the file extension and go in himself to look at it."

"Shit," Weeks said. "I forgot he had access to the system."

Mills again looked around the room then down at Bradley. "Try this on for size. What if the kid here shuts down the back door so Ford can't get in? Then, he calls Ford and let's him know he's found something he should see. Ford tries to get in, but can't. Ford either calls the kid or comes here to find out why he can't access the system. If he calls, we could get the kid to go in and provide another access door for him. Ford would have to come to get the info from the kid, and when he does, we'd be waiting for him."

Weeks looked at her partner; she was awed by the plan. "That's pretty damn devious, and a good plan, in theory. We'll have to get our tech people involved, as this has to become seamless and natural." Weeks turned to Bradley.

"Okay kid, we're going to take a ride downtown to the station. You'll have to give every detail to our techs as to how you broke into the system and where you put the back door."

CHAPTER

46

FORD WROTE DOWN the names of all the dirty cops that had been killed or were about to be killed in the next few days. His plan was to contact Channel 21's Debra Patton once the killings were completed. He felt that the public had a right to know why this action had taken place and that at no time were they in danger contrary to what the media was warning. He wasn't looking for salvation or anything noble like that, he just wanted his side of the story out before he was either arrested or killed.

Dustin Ford lay back on his bed, wondering whether Von Pleth should be shot or not. He had a day to figure that out. He was also unsure whether Detective Shelley Weeks should die for her part in his shaming years back. Likewise for Felix Seven. *How stupid was I back then*, he thought. He sat up abruptly. "Felix Seven needs to die." *If it wasn't for that asshole, none of this would have happened. But, all in due time, all in due time.*

Ford shut his eyes and drifted into an uneasy sleep. His mind wouldn't shut off completely as he relived the events of the past week. He wondered how it would end for him. Whatever scenario he ran, he couldn't see a happy ending. No white knight to save the day. All he could see were bullets hitting his body and him going out in a blaze of glory.

He awoke three hours later. Looking at his alarm clock, he figured he had at least two hours before he met up with Oscar Nineteen and Felix Seven to work out the payment. Ford had told Oscar that he wanted twenty-five thousand from each gang leader, plus the cost of the hits he did for the Numbers Gang. He figured he should get it beforehand, because he may not be alive to collect after the killings were completed, if things didn't go well. Oscar Nineteen protested, but to no avail and said he'd need a few hours to round up the money from the others. They would meet in New Westminster at the Quay parking lot at eight o'clock.

Ford calculated that by the end of the night, he should have at least one-hundred and fifty to one-hundred and eighty thousand in his jeans, plus what was left in the rented storage facility, maybe two-hundred and twenty-five thousand all together.

Ford left his building around six-thirty p.m. and went to the Starbucks on 6th Avenue for his caffeine fix, a venti triple mocha espresso. Every time he ordered it, the baristas would look at him as if he was crazy, shaking their heads. Ford checked the back of his leather jacket to make sure it was covering his Glock. Reassured that it was, he grabbed his coffee and sat outside under the awning in front of the building. He placed his back to the corner and slowly sipped the sweet goodness.

Ford watched people come and go and overheard snippets of conversations, some were even talking about the cops that had been shot. Most were saying that whoever was responsible should be shot to death like the animals they were. He chuckled to himself. *If you only knew how crooked some of those bastards were, you'd change your tune*. He looked at his watch; it was seven-thirty. He finished his coffee, tossed the empty cup into the trash bin, and walked across the street to his car. Just as he was about to open the door, he heard his name being called by someone behind him. He froze momentarily. His mind was telling him to be careful.

Slowly, Ford turned in the direction of the voice, his hand twitching with anticipation. Then, he caught sight of a figure darting across the street. It was Alex Thompson, his old foster brother. "Shit man," he said. "You scared the crap out of me." Ford gave him a big man hug and slapped him on the back. "Haven't seen you in a while. How've you been?"

Thompson stepped back and looked at Ford. "I thought it was you, but I wasn't sure so I took a chance. Look at you! Leather jacket, hot car, and it looks like you've been working out. And you shaved your fucking head, how cool is that?" They both laughed. "Christ, the last time I saw you was a couple of years ago. What the hell have you been up to?"

Ford instantly felt awkward. He knew he couldn't tell Thompson about what he was doing, so he went into liar mode. "I've been working construction here and there for the past year or so. Money's good, so I bought some wheels. Been pissing most of it away on booze and broads, but a guy's gotta have some fun in this life, right?" He punched Thompson in the shoulder playfully. "What about you?"

Thompson grabbed his arm, "Me? Not much. Rachel and I got married last year. She's expecting here in a couple of months. I work for the City of New Westminster in the planning department. Kinda boring, but the pay's good and the benefits add up." Thompson looked at his watch. "Man I'd love to yak with you longer, but just had to pop into the drug store to pick up a few things before going home, so I gotta run." Thompson stuck out his hand and Ford grabbed it and shook it hard. "We should get together one of these days for a beer," Thompson said, as he began to walk away.

Ford smiled broadly. "You know it, pal. One of these days…when you least expect it." He laughed and got into his car, his heart rate had returned to normal. Ford looked at his watch, it was quarter to eight.

Sunday traffic was light. It was only minutes before he was pulling into the Quay parking lot. He immediately spotted Nineteen and Seven leaning against the railing overlooking the Fraser River. Ford pulled his car next to theirs. He lit a cigarette and hopped out of his car. "Gentlemen and I use that term loosely. How the fuck is it hanging?" he said, walking toward them.

Oscar Nineteen had turned around to see who had parked next to them and smiled at Ford as he approached, "Always the entrance, hey Ford? Always the entrance." He turned to his brother, "Look who's here. It's Ford, gracing us with his presence."

Ford may not have gone far in school, but he knew when he was being dissed. "Fuck yourself, Nineteen. And while you're at it, fuck that brother of yours too."

"Okay Ford, calm down. I was just joking. Fuck, you need to lighten up."

"Back at you, Nineteen. I will when you do and he does." Ford pointed to Seven who had now turned around. "I believe you're here to reward me for a job well done. Am I correct, or does Mr. Glock have to be called to sort this out?"

"Always the big man, hey Ford? What are you covering

up? Oh, I know…a small dick?" Felix Seven sneered at Ford then laughed.

"Fuck, who pissed in your cornflakes this morning? Nineteen, you'd better rein in your pet there before he becomes very dead very quickly." Ford quipped.

"Okay, both of you, this ain't a cockfight. We've got business to conclude." Nineteen glared at Seven. "Don't make me smack you, little brother, cause I will if you keep pissing me off. Now cool it." Nineteen looked at Ford. "We got your money from the others, plus from our hits. All in all, its two hundred thousand in a duffle bag in the back of the car. All you need to do is open your trunk and toss it in."

"Do I need to count it?" Ford said, laughing. He saw that Nineteen wasn't laughing with him. "Just kidding. I'd prefer if you tossed it into my trunk" His eyes did not move from Seven.

"Whatever floats your boat, Mr. Glockman," Seven said, snidely.

Ford wanted to push his Glock 9 deep into Seven's throat and empty the magazine, but he figured that would be a waste of good ammo. He just smiled, knowing that before long Seven would be dead. Ford triggered the auto trunk release and lifted up the hatch lid and stood beside the car as Seven tossed the black duffle bag into the trunk.

"Thank you, gentlemen. It has been a business doing pleasure with you. If all goes well tonight, you likely won't hear from me, as the cops, according to my scanner, are starting to lock down the region." Ford nodded at them and opened his door.

Oscar Nineteen came around the front of the Toyota Camry. "Ford, take care of yourself. I appreciate what you've been able to do. How many are left on the list?"

Ford was somewhat taken aback. "Thank you, Oscar. Tonight, another ten will fall if all goes as planned. That'll bring it to a total of fifteen crooked cops off the street and out of your lives. It should make for easier business for a while until the next batch of scumbag cops hold out their hands."

Oscar Nineteen laughed. "I think it'll give all the other cops a good reason to stay clean and leave the crooked stuff to us," he laughed again and stuck out his hand to shake Ford's. "Keep your head down." He slapped the roof of the car and turned away.

Ford started his vehicle and pulled away before Nineteen and Seven did. He wanted to *get over to Queensborough to get the duffle bag out of his car. Ford laughed as he* envisioned trying to explain to a cop why he had two-hundred thousand in a duffle bag in his car.

Normally, Ford liked to drive above the speed limit, but tonight he followed it to the letter. Twenty minutes later, he pulled into the mini-storage yard, which was open until ten at night. He pulled up in front of his unit and quickly opened the door. Ford grabbed the duffle and went inside.

He had never seen what two-hundred grand looked like, so he closed the door and locked it, then went to the table at the front, opened the duffle and dumped out the excessive amount of cash. He let out a whoop! Ford revelled in the moment then it dawned on him...*How was he going to move around this much money?* He couldn't carry a large black duffle bag around wherever he went, and he couldn't leave it here in case something happened to him and he couldn't pay the storage fees. The last thing he wanted was some asshole to bid on the unit and reap a windfall. Ford grabbed the green duffle bag that he had tucked in the corner. He opened it and dumped that money onto the pile. It was a spectacular sight, nearly two-hundred and twenty-five thousand stacked over a foot high and two feet wide, and it was all his.

Ford pulled up a stool and sat at the table. Where could he hide this much cash, yet have easy access to it if he needed it? Then it struck him...Jomo. He didn't exactly trust Jomo, but he was the closest thing to a friend that he had. He thought about Alex Thompson, but he was too straight-laced and would ask too many questions, plus he didn't want to involve him. Jomo it would be. Ford scooped almost all of the money up and put it into the black duffle bag and locked it. He went to his car and grabbed a smoke off the dash then took out his phone and punched in Jomo's number. It rang several times.

"This is Jomo. Who is this?" he answered.

"Jomo, it's me, Ford. I need a favour."

"Ah, yes, another favour?"

"Jomo, I need you to look after something for me, can you do that? I'll even make it worth your while. Say five grand to hold something for me?"

"Yes, Jomo can do that for yous. How big is this thing?"

"It's just a duffle bag, but it's very important to me, so you need to swear that you'll protect it at all costs. Agreed?"

"Ya mon, but it'll be ten grand if I have to protect it at all cost."

"You thief. Seventy-five hundred, and not a penny more. Deal?"

"For you, a deal. Bring it by. I have a place for it."

"Okay, I'll be there in an hour." He cut off the call and smiled.

A little over an hour later, Ford pulled his car into a parking spot along Powell Street and walked the short distance to the Container Pub. As usual, it was a busy night with the regular riff-raff that frequented the pub. Jomo was his cordial self behind the bar, barking orders to his servers. He flashed a big grin when he saw Ford walking towards the bar carrying a large black duffle bag. An old guy sitting at the bar saw Ford and piped up, "What ship you come in on matey?"

Ford grinned and replied, "The Good Ship Lollipop." He laughed. "Jomo, give this man a pitcher of beer on me." Ford slapped the old guy on the back as he walked by.

Jomo complied and slid a full pitcher of beer down the bar to the old man, then motioned to Ford to follow him into his inner office. Ford nodded and made his way to the other end of the bar and through the swinging doors. Jomo had done a few renovations since the last time Ford had been there.

Ford entered the dimly lit inner office and remembered the large black leather chairs that seemed completely out of place.

Jomo offered his big hand to Ford, who took it and shook it hard. "Good to see you, my friend," Ford said. "How have you been? I see you've made a few improvements since I was here last."

"Yes, Jomo did some improvement. Had a bad fight here two days ago, place closed for a day. Very bad." Jomo smiled and beckoned Ford to sit in a chair in front of his large desk.

"Thanks, Jomo." He lifted the duffle bag and placed it on his lap. "Here it is, Jomo. This is very important to me. It contains some things that I do not want anyone else to see or get at, do you understand?"

"Yes, Jomo understands. Very important to you. Jomo has place for important things. Follow me." Jomo stood up and went to the middle of the wall across from his desk and pressed on the wooden panel. Ford heard a small click as the wall section popped outward and Jomo swung it to the side then motioned for him to follow.

Jomo turned on a light that illuminated the very narrow staircase that descended into the basement. Ford guessed that not many people knew about this feature of the heritage building.

Ford put the duffle bag on his head to make it down the narrow staircase then at the bottom swung it down to the floor. He stood for a long second, looking at the surroundings; it was a storage room that had an inch of dust on everything. He saw Jomo standing before a large safe with a massive steel door. It was an obvious relic of the past. Jomo bowed as he presented his storage solution. "What do you think, Mr. Ford? Will this suffice?"

Ford was stunned, confused. "Ah, what happened to your accent? You're not Jamaican?" Ford asked.

"Hell no, man. Never been out of Canada. Born and raised in Toronto, moved out here twenty years ago. Leased the bar about five years ago from a company called Three Coasts Developments. The accent, well, that's for my customers. People think I'm a simple Jamaican, so they talk freely around me. I learn things that can be useful. Since you're entrusting me with something of great importance to you, you're no longer a customer, you're a friend." He grinned and stuck out his hand. "Name's Neil Anderson."

Ford was flabbergasted. "Man, you had me completely

fooled. Fuck, you should be an actor. You'd win an academy award hands down. Nice to meet you, Neil Anderson."

Anderson spun the old tumbler then swung the heavy door open, revealing a small room behind the door. The room was lined with shelves that contained an odd assortment of items, presumably being stored for other "friends". Ford was impressed. Anderson cleared a spot on the upper shelf and held out his hand for the duffle bag. Ford handed it over to him and watched as he easily hoisted it up onto the upper shelf.

"Your possession will be safe here. Nobody except me, my wife and a few other friends even know about this place." He held out his hand palm up. Ford reached into his coat pocket and pulled out the wad of cash and placed it in Anderson's hand.

Ford looked at objects on the other shelves; most were covered in dust, which meant they hadn't been touched in years. "I guess I should explain how this will work," he said. He walked to the doorway then turned around, "I have no relatives that I know of. I have no family that I care about, and I have few friends. If you don't hear from me within a year, or have proof of my death, whatever is in the duffle is yours to do with what you like. Agreed?"

"Agreed, my friend, but you'll be back here within a year to claim your possessions and Jomo won't have to deal with it." He laughed as he ushered Ford from the vault. Anderson swung the heavy door closed and spun the tumbler. He patted the steel door, "She's an oldie, but a goody. Rumor has it that his place burnt to the ground around nineteen-twelve. It's said only the safe was salvaged, so they rebuilt the building around the safe. Yep, she's a solid old girl."

Ford smiled. “That’s very reassuring; let’s hope that I’m back here within a year.” Ford bounded up the stairs two at a time. Anderson was right behind him. Anderson closed the paneling shut and assumed the role again. Ford stuck out his hand and they shook. “I’ve got things I have to get done tonight, so I’ll let myself out. It was very nice to meet you Neil Anderson; your secret identity is safe with me.”

Anderson nodded and Ford spun around and left.

Outside the Container Pub, Ford’s phone lit-up with incoming texts from the other hitters; they were having a very productive night. Peter Wilson, Silvia Lee, Winston Chambers, and Steve Manters had all been eliminated, and it was just past ten. Only six remained. Ford smiled as he walked toward his car, his mind running through possible ways to eliminate Felix Seven.

CHAPTER

47

NATHAN BRADLEY SAT alone in the interrogation room where the temperature was turned down to make perpetrators uncomfortable. He shivered uncontrollably for what seemed like hours, while Weeks and Mills attended to other matters, or so they'd said.

Weeks and Mills waited in the IT Department for a meeting with William Behr, the manager of all information technology for the Metro Police Dept. He was running late from a meeting with the Chief of Police. It was all hands on deck since the killings started, so everyone was called in on OT. Fifteen minutes passed, and Weeks saw an older man dressed in a tweed jacket with patches on the elbows rushing through the door. Behr acknowledged they were there, made a beeline to his office to rid himself of his satchel then beckoned them into his office.

"Please sit. I must apologize for being late; the Chief likes to talk. How can I help you?" Behr said leaning back in his chair.

"We have a kid who said he hacked into our system and placed a usable back door in it for a civilian to access the system at leisure. Is that even possible?" Weeks asked point blank.

Behr stroked his goatee for a moment then answered, "Unfortunately, it's very possible. But there are a few things that have to occur. First you need an unfiltered access portal, that's a portal that has been cleared by us or by the programmer. Secondly, you would need to name a password on the list of acceptable passwords approved by us. Third, you need to know what side of the system to install the back door on. That my friend's is the tricky part; you need to know our system intimately. So you need to ask this young kid how it is that he acquired this knowledge of our system. My money is on the original programmer, perhaps a friend, family member, employee of the contractor or through someone with connections to the programmer. This system was designed to be triple redundant, which means you need three passwords to get in to do any upgrades. We're safer than most of the big banks."

Mills looked at Weeks with a blank expression on his face, which told Weeks he didn't understand anything Behr had just said. She chuckled.

"Can you tell if our system has been hacked? Are there any traces left by a hacker that would give us a clue where he went inside our system?" Weeks asked.

Behr shifted in his chair. "That would take time. We'd need to go through all of our systems to see when they were last accessed, and by whom, then cross reference each access point with our known computer log-ins. As I said, it would take a long time."

Mills furrowed his brow. "You mean you can't just type in some command that would bring up all those who have accessed the system say in the last month? They do that on TV."

Behr removed his glasses and massaged the bridge of his nose with two fingers, then shook his head. "Detective Mills, you watch too much TV. Not everything you see is based on facts. What I will do is get in touch with our contractor, perhaps they know something that I don't, and I'll have to get back to you. Meanwhile, you should talk to your young hacker to see where he acquired his skills. Maybe he can tell you what you need to know."

"Can you give us some kind of time frame? Twenty minutes, half hour? We have cops being killed and a kid sitting on ice. We just want to know how long to keep him there." Weeks said as she stood.

Behr stood as well. "Give me a half hour. Leave me your cell number, and I will text you when I have this figured out."

"Okay, half an hour it is." Ten minutes later, Mills and Weeks were back in the interrogation room. They had stopped at the cafeteria to pick up coffees and muffins for themselves, and a pop and chocolate bar for Bradley.

As soon as they entered, Bradley demanded they turn up the heat. Weeks set the snacks on the small table and went out and turned up the thermostat. Closing the door, she returned to her chair. Bradley was still shivering wildly, so much so that he could hardly hold the can of ice cold pop. "Did you consider bringing me a coffee instead of a pop?" Bradley said.

"No," Mills responded. "You're too young for coffee."

"Actually, sir, there is more caffeine in a can of pop than in a cup of coffee. I offer that for future reference only," Bradley said.

Mills didn't appreciate the comment and kicked the chair out from under Bradley, sending him crashing to the floor.

Weeks turned to her partner. “Mills, take it easy, he’s just a kid.” She reached down to help him up. “We need his help here, so let’s not kill him before we get what we need.” Weeks winked at Mills. She felt Bradley’s arm. It was ice cold. “I’ll get you a blanket; that should warm you up.”

Bradley nodded, “Thank you. That would be appreciated.” He looked at Mills then said, “You’re not going to leave me with him, are you?”

“You boys going to play nice while I’m gone?” Not waiting for a reply, Weeks left the small room.

She returned a few minutes later with a gray and blue blanket with the words Metro Police Dept stenciled in white letters on it. She placed it around Bradley’s shoulders then sat down. “Okay, let’s get down to brass tacks here.” Weeks opened the manila folder she had set up for Bradley and began to write. “So where did you learn about hacking?”

Bradley nibbled his chocolate bar and looked straight ahead. Mills slapped the table. “Hey, the Detective asked you a question!”

Bradley jumped. “Sorry, when I’m under stress my mind wanders to calm me down. What was the question?”

Weeks again asked where he had learned the hacking skills needed to hack Metro Police.

“I learned a few little things here and there, mainly in school, they teach coding you know.”

“‘Here and there…don’t play games with me.” Mills yelled, “I’d say they’re rather big things. Did it ever dawn on your pea brain that what you were doing was wrong?” Mills said loudly.

Bradley, intimidated by Mills, looked at Weeks as if for help in dealing with her partner. “I didn’t think anybody would get hurt. He was just looking for the cop who shamed him a couple of years ago. I didn't see any harm in that. I guess I was wrong, eh?"

"You might say that." Weeks said quietly. "Okay young genius I'm taking you upstairs to the tech dept, there you will show the manager exactly where Ford got in and then we'll see what he was looking for."

Twenty minutes later Mills, Weeks and Bradley returned to the interrogation room. It was just as cold as before, so Bradley immediately wrapped the blanket around his shoulders.

"Sit," Mills barked to Bradley. "So now that we know he was looking in IA for dirty cops, how do we reel in this bastard?" He looked at Weeks for the answer.

"Well, we know he can't access the system to gain any more information on any more cops, so that might be a way. Or, maybe we get the kid here to call him and tell him the cops found the access portal and shut it down, but he can create another one if Ford is interested." Weeks began to pace the room. "Whatever we do it has to be good. We're only going to get one shot at this. If we fail he's in the wind knowing that he's been made and we'll never find his bastard." She turned to Mills, who had a dazed look on his face.

"What kind of plan are you thinking of?"

Weeks sat down, she looked at the tiled ceiling, "Perhaps…" she stood, "perhaps there's another video of Ford that the kid here just found that he might want to see. Ford will try to access the system but will be blocked." She paced looking at the floor, "then since Ford can't get in he'll phone or text the kid, who'll tell him that they found it in a security sweep, but he can reestablish another portal if Ford would like to see it. If Ford says yes then he'll have to go to the café to get the flash drive with the access codes. Then we nail his ass." She punched the air.

Mills wasn't sure about the kid, and the plan seemed hokey, too many ifs and maybes. "Hell if you've got nothing else, then let's try it." He looked at Bradley. "Are you a good actor kid?"

Bradley looked at Mills. If looks could kill, Mills would be dead. "Don't need to be an actor when you send a text." He gazed at Weeks who had a smirk on her face.

"Nathan, do you have the number that Ford gave you in your phone?" Weeks asked as she signed the evidence bag then opened it to remove the phone.

"Yeah, it's there, but Ford said it was a burner so I don't know if he's still using that number, or if he's already got another phone?"

"For your sake, kid, let's hope he isn't as smart as you are." Mills added sarcastically.

Weeks handed Bradley his phone. "Okay, here's what you'll will text him. Tell him you were snooping around Metro's database and you came across another video about him and that he should take a peek when he gets a chance." Weeks watched Bradley as she spoke. He seemed to be understanding. "Then we'll wait for him to try to access it and find out he can't get in. Then, we'll just have to play it by ear."

Bradley understood exactly what to do, he tapped his phone to life and scrolled his contact list until he found Ford's number, then tapped it open and began typing in the message. In no time, he pressed send and sat back. "Done."

Weeks turned to Mills. "Do you want to run this list that Ford has accessed up to Sarg? Tell him we're trying to set a trap for Ford and that I'll be up as soon as it's been set." She didn't wait for a response from Mills, just handed him the printout. Mills took the printout and left the small room.

Weeks looked at her watch. It was 11:15 p.m. and she realized that she was starving and she assumed the kid was as well. "You hungry?" she asked.

"Starving." Bradley said. "Is he always such a dick?"

Weeks laughed and nodded. "He's just a little on edge. This cop killer has everyone wound up pretty tight."

"Is this my fault? What's going to happen to me?" Bradley asked.

"Well, if you tell us where your parents are, we'll call them to let them know where you are." Weeks said sympathetically.

"Nah, my foster parents don't give a shit about me or any of the rest of us. They're just in it for the money from the government. In fact, I can guarantee they're not even home. It's Sunday so they'll be at the casino gambling away our government cheques."

"How many others are there?" she asked

"In all, there are six of us living in a house in Burnaby."

"So where are your parents? How long have you been in foster care?" Weeks asked.

"Don't know my real parents. Can't remember ever seeing them. I've been in foster care all my life."

Weeks stood and put her hand on Bradley's shoulder. "I'll be back with something to eat. At this time of the night the cafeteria has a limited selection, but I'll try to find something you'll like."

Five minutes later, Weeks returned with two foil wrapped packages of food, she handed one to Bradley and kept one for herself. "They're hamburgers, and trust me these were the best looking things on the menu, so dig in." She laughed, and noticed that it brought a smile to Bradley's face.

"Nothing for your partner?" he asked.

"Nah, he's a big boy. He knows where the cafeteria is." Weeks unwrapped the burger and dug in. She was famished.

Several bites into his burger, Bradley's phone went off. "It's him. What do I say?"

Weeks put her burger down and rearranged her mouthful so she could speak. "Let's see the phone?" She quickly read the text. '*tried to get in, system blocked me. What was vid abut*' Weeks closed her eyes for a moment, then began to respond to Ford's text. '*don't know didn't open it. You want another access portal'* She turned to Bradley who was enjoying his burger, "Now we wait and see if he bites."

Within seconds Ford came back, *'yes I do'*. Weeks spun sideways to face Bradley, "how much did he give you to hack the system the last time? Quickly?"

Bradley chewed faster, "He gave me a grand."

Weeks smiled. He wants to know; this is good. She answered, '*no prob, same $ as last time*'. She sent the text. Weeks took the last bite of her hamburger, just as another text arrived. '*ok, when can I get it'*

Weeks responded, '*tomorrow afternoon'*

Ford's reply was, '*see you tomorrow'*.

Weeks leaned back in her chair. "I think we might just catch this bastard."

Bradley forced a smile. "So, what about me? What happens to me now?"

Weeks stood and looked down at Bradley, "Well, you'll have to spend the night in juvy, then tomorrow morning we'll bring you back here to complete this trap. You up for that? Then I'll talk to my Sergeant and see if there's something we can do for you."

Bradley nodded. Weeks opened the door and motioned for the duty officer to come into the room. The burley officer filled the doorway, "Can you see that young Mr. Bradley here gets over to juvy tonight? I'll call ahead to let them know he's coming. Thanks, Mike," Weeks said as the officer led Bradley away. "Oh, Nathan, I'll need your phone."

Bradley winced as he handed over the phone.

Weeks wasted no time getting upstairs to the bullpen to meet with Lamp and presumably Mills, who had vanished. She bounded up the stairs two at a time because it was faster than the elevator. Weeks walked straight over to Lamp's office and stood in the doorway. Lamp was on the phone, so he motioned her to sit down. Moments later, he hung up. "Well, how did it go? Did the perp take the bait?"

"Hook, line, and fucking sinker," Weeks beamed. "Kid's on his way to juvy for the night, and tomorrow we'll set the trap and maybe nail this bastard."

Lamp reached across the desk to high-five Weeks. "Good job. Damned good job."

Weeks looked around. "Where's Mills?"

"Gone to get something to eat. He dropped off this list of files the perp looked at. What's your take on it?" Lamp said leaning back.

Weeks mulled over the information for a moment. "From what Behr said, all the files were from officers that were on IA's list. He didn't say why they were there, but we all know that you have to fuck up royally to get onto that list in the first place. Do you think Dietrich would break the rule and tell us what these cops did wrong?"

Lamp leaned forward and put his elbows on the desk. "He will if either Von Pleth or Aldridge tells him to." He paused then picked up his phone, "I'll make the call."

Weeks saw Mills return to the bullpen and motioned him into Lamp's office. She leaned toward him and quietly said. "The rat's taken the cheese; we'll nail his ass tomorrow. Lamp's getting IA to unseal the list of guys Ford's been looking at."

Mills smiled and offered his fist to bump with Weeks, but she just sat there. She remembered what Bradley said. *Is he always such a dick?* She smiled and held up her fist.

Moments later, Lamp hung up the phone, "Mills, glad you could join us. Aldridge said we'll have access to whatever we need within minutes." Lamp rubbed his temples. "Any guesses as to what we'll find?" He stopped abruptly. "Oh, you two need to see this. It's the list of who has been killed so far." He handed Weeks the paper, then sat back.

Weeks accepted the paper and looked for the first name; she saw it was O'Dell, then Pepper from SWAT, then Pastorelli, DePlume, Cheevers, Zamanski, Hammerlin, Taylor, Wilson, Lee, Chambers, Farnsworth, and Manters, thirteen officers in all. Weeks wiped the tears from her eyes. She used to work with Sara Farnsworth. *What could she have done? She was a good officer*. Weeks handed the list to Mills, not saying a word. She looked at Lamp; he too looked distressed.

Lamp picked up the phone after the first ring. It was Dietrich. "Hi Vern, what do you have for us?" Vernard

Dietrich was head of IA, and had been for the past five years. He enjoyed his job, even though every cop in Metro hated his guts. He seemed to like the negative attention, for some unknown reason.

"I just emailed everything to you. You should have it now. Call if you need something else." Dietrich hung up the phone. Lamp quickly opened the email and found the attachment. He studied it for a minute not saying a word, then hit print and waited for the printer to spit it out. While he waited, he turned to Weeks and Mills. "You're going to love this." Lamp stood and reached to retrieve the printout. He checked it over, then handed it to Weeks and sat down.

Weeks quickly scanned the document. "Are you kidding me? This bastard is killing cops on IA's shit list?" Weeks ran the list of names through her mind, trying to link each of the death's to Ford. O'Dell humiliated him. Pepper no idea, the cops on IA's shit list for getting rich off the gangs, it all was making sense. Ford was trying to rid the city of corrupt cops and in so doing he was helping the gangs. Pepper was the odd one; she knew no reason why he'd been killed. Same for Caterwelt and Wellsley. She also struggled with Sheldon Pratt, Mavis Appleton and the DEA agent Marco Aluma. Perhaps they were killed for being too good at their jobs.

Lamp opened the file for Pastorelli and began to read. "Wow, this guy's a piece of work."

"Who is, Sarg?" Weeks asked.

"Pastorelli. Says here that he's been accused of taking bribes, blackmail, excessive force, unlawful search and seizure, the list goes on and on." He opened the next file. "Another winner. DePlume, same shit. Christ, these guys are the worst of the worst. Any bets the rest are the same?"

"I think I got it figured out Sarg." Weeks said proudly. She told them about her theory, "The ones I can't figure out are Pepper, the SWAT sniper, Caterwelt and Wellsley, Pratt and Appleton the undercover cops, as well as Aluma the DEA agent."

Lamp eyed the list of names trying to determine if Weeks was correct. "You could be right."

"I know I'm right, and here's why." Weeks leaned on the desk, "I'd venture a wild-ass guess that Pepper was killed to convince the gangs of his ability. It makes sense. Ford would have to show them that he was serious…the man, and all that bravado crap that the gangs love. If O'Dell humiliated the kid then that would be revenge on Ford's part. As for the dirty cops, maybe this is just a job for him. The gangs pay, he shoots, cops die…sick bastard. As for the undercover cops, maybe they just got too close. When we lock his ass up we'll have to remember to ask him. That's if he doesn't get killed first."

CHAPTER 48

OSCAR NINETEEN STEPPED into the brightly lit corridor with the fine imported carpet and white marble wall paneling carrying a tan satchel under his arm. He walked the hallway to suite 2019, swiped his key on the door pad, and entered the room. Cigarette smoke, noise, and laughter greeted him as he set the satchel down on the kitchen counter.

The chorus of "Oscar!" rang out from the four guys sitting around a large wooden table surrounded by stacks of cash. Felix Seven came out of the bathroom and saw his brother. "I was about to send the posse out looking for you," he said walking over to the kitchen to pick up the satchel. He returned to the table and emptied the contents onto the pile of uncounted cash. Seven smiled at his brother. "Not a bad take for one day. Sixty grand, give or take?"

"I believe the count is seventy-three-five," Oscar grinned. "A damned fine day." He walked around the mess that was on the floor to look out the window overlooking Central Park in Burnaby. He turned to the others. "Ever since that blood sucking cops were eliminated, our profits have gone up an additional twelve and a half percent, which equates to about an extra sixty to seventy Gs per week. Those bastards would have bled us dry had it not been for Ford. He's one cold-hearted motherfucker; I'm glad he's on our side." Oscar grabbed a beer from the fridge and sat down in the high back leather office chair.

Felix Seven scoffed. "I don't trust the asshole as far as I can throw him. I think he's up to something."

Oscar looked at his brother and shook his head. "You fucking idiot. Don't you get it? According to Melissa when she slept with Ford, she said he told her that he can't stand you, that you're just a little prick. So you're the reason he's pissed off. Besides you sent him to ice Hooper with a fucking empty gun. Hell, I'd be pissed at you too. You keep pushing the wrong buttons with Ford and he'll take you out, and it'll be your own goddamn fault."

"Ah, you're full of shit. He doesn't have the balls to take me on face to face. That fucking coward hides behind his Glock. Without that, he's nothing."

Steveo Twenty-Three chimed in. "If this guy's as good a shot as you guys have said, I wouldn't be doing anything to piss him off. Fuck, he could take you out from a mile away…if he's as good as you say."

Felix Seven retorted. "You're just a chicken shit like he is."

Twenty-Three looked at Seven, cocked his head slightly and said, "Really? You think I'm a chicken shit? How many fucking times have I bailed your skinny ass out of trouble? Or have you forgotten about that?"

Stu Forty-Two piped up. "I have to agree with Steveo there, Felix. He's had your back on more than one occasion, and you know it, too. So why are you disrespecting him? If your bitch is with this Ford guy…then man up, and deal with it girl." Stu Forty-Two stood up and showed off his twenty-two inch biceps as if to challenge Felix Seven.

Oscar Nineteen was enjoying the banter; he often worried that his little brother relied too much on him, especially when he went off on fellow members. He had talked to Felix multiple times about keeping his mouth shut, but to no avail. Nineteen knew it was only a matter of time until someone stood up to Felix and beat him down, or worse.

The third member of the counting team voiced his opinion. Eddie Sixteen was the quiet one who rarely said anything to anyone, let alone enter into a disagreement. "It strikes me as funny that you guys call yourselves brothers in arms, then you disrespect each other the way you do. Seems to me that you guys are more alike than you are different, so why are you fighting?"

A refrain of, "Shut the fuck up" rang out, followed by laughter.

Barry Fifty-Five offered up, "Now that's more like it ladies…peace, love and all that shit."

Oscar walked to the counting table. The three counting machines were silent. "This stuff isn't going to count itself, you lazy butt-plugs. Come on, let's get it done. Seven, Forty-Two can I see you in the boardroom?"

The boardroom happened to be the master bedroom of the three bedroom condominium that the Numbers Gang currently used as a counting house. Nineteen grabbed another beer and headed for the boardroom, followed closely by the other two. Once inside, he sat down at the oval table and motioned for the other two to do likewise.

"Okay, some serious shit. We need to be clear about this, so I want honesty without emotion. Ford will be finishing up his hit list tonight. Hell, he may have already done it, which presents a potential problem for us. If Ford were to be nabbed by the cops, we don't know if he'll roll on us or not. I, for one, am not willing to take that chance. Now my question to you two is this…do we put out a contract on Ford?"

Seven and Forty-Two sat in silence. Forty-Two shifted in his chair, then placed both hands together on the table. "I say whack his ass. Up until a few months ago I'd never heard of this asshole, now he can walk on water and do no wrong. Sounds too good to be true. This fuck is up to something, and I'm with Oscar. We can't take a chance on an outsider."

Both Oscar and Stu looked at Seven, who blurted out, "What? Can't I take a second to think about this stuff?" He stood and went to the balcony window. "Hey, it's no secret I don't trust him one bit. Should he be killed? Maybe, maybe not. Have either of you thought about whether he might want to join our merry band of misfits? He has a unique skill-set, one that fits well within our group, and it would be a shame to see that talent gone." He returned to his seat. "I think we should discuss it with him to see if he wants to join us. If he doesn't, then we can do as Oscar suggests, but if he wants to join us, the other gangs would think twice about fucking with us."

Oscar Nineteen looked at his brother, then at Forty-Two. "Where the hell did that come from? That was logical and thoughtful. Where's the real Felix Seven?" He laughed. "You bring up some valid points to consider. So, here's my solution. Seven, you've got until Friday. Two days to talk to Ford and see what his plans are, and if he doesn't want to join our group, then I want him dead by Saturday morning. Agreed?"

"Agreed," the other two replied in unison.

The three all stood and left the boardroom, returning to the counting table. "What's the count at so far?" Oscar asked.

Eddie Sixteen looked up at Nineteen. "So far, we're sitting at just under two hundred, and we still have this much to count yet," he pointed to the other half of the table with the uncounted money. "There could be at least a hundred grand there."

Oscar Nineteen smiled. "It's been a good week. Lock it up in the vault when you're done and call it a night. I'll have the pick-up crew come by tomorrow to take the duffle bags away."

CHAPTER

49

FORD AWOKE AT seven-thirty. It seemed like he'd just gone to bed, and already it was morning. *It isn't fair*. He checked his phone. There were several text messages. He quickly opened up the texts, knowing that they were from the hitters. Ford scrolled through the texts and saw Damansk was gone, and so were Thorsen and Fellers. LaRouch and Bender remained alive, but he was advised they would be dispatched soon.

Ford lay back on his pillow and smiled. He could just imagine the panic and anger that was erupting at the Metro Police Department. Ford reread the text from the young hacker Bradley. He didn't like where this could lead, and needed to make a plan to complete his tasks. The first thing he'd need to do was get his car painted. If the police were looking for a dark coloured two door, then he'd make his car white. If they had him down as bald, then he'd wear wigs and hats. He realized he couldn't change his height or his build, so he'd wear bulkier clothing to hide his body.

Dustin Ford dragged his body out of bed and into a hot shower. Twenty minutes later, he was at the IHOP at 6th and 10th Avenue enjoying his first cup of coffee when his phone came alive. It was a message from the Big Valley Boys' hitter letting him know that LaRouch was taken care of. Ford smiled. Only one crooked cop left, then he'd contact Debra Patton to let the entire Lower Mainland know what had been going on. He wolfed down his stack of pancakes and thought of ordering another, but elected to leave instead.

Outside, the sun was trying to peek through the cloud cover, and Ford needed to alter his appearance. He had one good wig, but he wanted to broaden his choices, so he figured a trip to the A&N Department Store was in order. He'd also need to get a few hats. It was 9:30 a.m. when his phone buzzed. It was the kid. *Have the portal, can you p/u at W/H Cafe 2 p.m. today, plus a grand?*

Ford texted back, '*ok*'. That would give him time to make arrangement to have his car painted in Langley. He scrolled through the internet listings for body shops until he found what he was looking for then placed the call.

"Hi, is Marty there?" Ford asked. "Yes I'll hold."

Less than a minute later, Marty came on the line. "Hi, this is Marty."

"Hi, Marty, Dustin Ford here. I'm a friend of Rolf's, who said if ever I needed anything done fast and cheap, you're the guy to talk to."

Marty paused. "Any friend of Rolf's is definitely not a friend of mine, but I'd be happy to do business with you regardless. What do you need?"

"I need my car painted a different colour and I need it yesterday. Can you help me?"

"What kind of car, and what colour?"

"Five Liter Mustang, white."

"When can I get the car?"

"How about five today, and I'll need it back tomorrow

around noon. You got a loaner for me to use? And what's the freight?"

"Yah I got a Hyundai you can drive, and the freight is twenty-five hundred, cash."

Ford smiled. "Okay, Marty. See you at five."

Ford made his way to A&N Department store and found a wig that made him look like a rock star, and he also found one with dreadlocks. He was able to find two cool hats that made him look somewhat stylish, as well as a pair of red running shoes. Ford paid for his purchases and drove back to his apartment to change, as well as grab his second burner phone to make the call to Channel 21 news desk.

Dustin Ford stood in front of the mirror, admiring his new self. The long hair suited him, and his dark suntanned complexion made him look Southeast Asian. He tossed on his hoodie jacket, black Levi's and red running shoes. It made him look like a hipster, and not a cold-blooded killer. The hat he'd chosen was a gray fedora with a red feather on the side…very stylish and only twelve bucks. Then, the *coup de grace*, he inserted a gold cap onto his front tooth.

Happy with his new appearance, he left the apartment and drove into downtown Vancouver. Something about the text from the kid worried him. He had questions. *Why was the kid poking around in the Metro database? I never asked him to do anything else. And why did he text me? I don't know him; we're not friends? Was there something else going on here? Was the kid working for the cops?* He needed to figure this out before he walked into something he couldn't get out of.

The trip into Vancouver only took thirty-five minutes, as the traffic was really light at this time of the day. Ford found a parking spot off Robson and Burrard. He checked himself in the rearview mirror to make sure his disguise was in place, then left the car and walked the short distance to where he could see the Walnut Hut Café. Ford bought a bottle of water and sat down on a tree planter box to watch the café. He carefully scanned cars parked along Robson to see if any were occupied with cops. None were. Ford then shifted his gaze to the roof-lines to see if any spotter nests had been set up, and again, nothing. He wondered if his gut was wrong. Feeling brave, Ford walked toward the café. They had tables out front, so he ordered a coffee and sat down to see who all entered, confident that his disguise would fool them.

He slowly sipped his triple mocha espresso with easy whip for almost twenty minutes. Then out of the corner of his eye, he caught site of the kid walking down the sidewalk. Ford casually moved inside to a computer near the back wall. He wanted a good vantage point. He watched as the kid entered the café and found a computer by the window. *This wasn't right. The kid said he always sits in the back.*

Ford rose and walked up to the counter. He recognized the guy working from before, but he didn't seem to recognize Ford, which was good. "Hey bud, anyone here who can help me with a computer? I can't remember how to log onto a site. If there's a cost, it won't be a problem."

The guy looked around. "Hey, kid. You, by the window, want to earn a few bucks showing this guy how to log onto a site?"

Bradley looked at Ford; he didn't recognize him either. "I'm waiting for someone…but sure, show me what the problem is." Bradley got up and walked back to where Ford had been and sat down. "What's the problem?"

Ford moved the mouse and the screen lit. "I want to print this page, but it won't let me. Am I doing something wrong?"

Bradley right clicked the mouse, and up popped the page protocols. "Ah, here's the problem, they've removed the print option on the page, so you can't print it."

Ford leaned back and fished a ten dollar bill from his pocket and handed it to Bradley. "Thanks, kid, appreciate your help."

Bradley took the ten dollars and went back to his window seat. Ford leaned out a bit to watch him. Bradley subtly shook his head side to side for no reason. Ford's senses perked up. It was a trap after all. *Those sneaky bastards, using a kid.* Ford looked around the café; he had learned enough about police procedures that somebody in here was likely an undercover cop. He had six to choose from and they all looked ordinary. He ruled out the two young girls, that left four, he seemed to remember the two younger Asian males from a previous visit here. So in Ford's mind it was either the woman three computers over from him or the guy sitting near the front.

Leaning back, Ford sipped his coffee. His mind spun, trying to figure out his next move. He was certain that the cops had a spotter across the street, and there were likely cops in the businesses next door as well. He was also certain he was being watched on surveillance cameras. He was surprised that he wasn't panicking. If this would have been a couple of years ago, he would have pissed his pants. Ford wanting to see how far he could push this, stood, and took his near empty cup to the counter, "Can I have another please?"

"No problem. I'll bring it to you when it's ready."

Ford returned to his seat with no clear exit strategy in place. A few minutes later the owner brought Ford's second triple mocha espresso. Ford gave him a five dollar bill and a toonie as a tip. He watched as the owner walked away, looking for any kind of tell that he had been made. Ford looked at his watch; it was quarter to two. He wondered how long the cops would wait before they called off their trap.

Did he really want the new portal into the police database, now that he knew that they knew about him? If the meeting was at two and he got up and left before two, would they follow him? If he called the kid over and quietly demanded the flash drive and gave him the money, would the kid rat him out? Ford looked around the small café to see where the rear exit was in case he became trapped; he didn't see one. *If I call the kid over, it shouldn't draw suspicion, because he has already signaled them that I wasn't the guy, so would they believe him the second time. Was the kid helping them voluntarily, or was he being forced?* Ford was sure that even Alverez would have struggled with this problem.

"Hey kid, can you help me again?" Ford said. Several other patrons looked to see what was going on, then quickly went back to what they were doing. He watched as the kid lazily walked across the café. Ford had the twenty, fifty dollar bills in his palm ready for the swap that he'd make as soon as he had the flash drive.

Bradley neared Ford's computer station and stuck his head into the cubical, "What's the problem this time?" He asked sarcastically.

Ford raised his finger to his mouth. "I want the flash drive," he said quietly, showing Bradley the thousand dollars. "And I'm not here. Understand? I know the cops are outside."

Bradley was stunned; he quickly fumbled in his pocket for the flash drive and laid it on the desk, then quickly pocketed the grand.

"Okay, go back to your seat and signal the same way as before," Ford said. He watched as the kid walked away. "Hey, thanks kid. Appreciate your help." Bradley got to his seat and shook his head side to side again. Ford smiled. He took several big gulps of his coffee then stood up and started walking to the front door as if nothing happened. He paused momentarily at the door then pushed it open. Nothing! No rush of cops with guns drawn and no shots were fired, nothing. Ford walked down the sidewalk past the kid sitting in the window.

Across the street from a second story window, Weeks saw the kid patting his head, which was the signal that the deal had been done. She panicked. "Where the hell is he?" She shouted into the radio. "Has anybody got eyes on Ford? The kid signaled he was there," Within seconds, six cops flooded the small café from stores nearby. Weeks darted down the stairs and out the front door and across the busy street. She barged her way into the café and over to Bradley. "Where is he?" She demanded. She stared at the undercover cop in the café, "Did you see him Barbara." Weeks saw her shrug her shoulders and shake her head.

Bradley was visibly rattled by all the police, "He just walked out the front door." He said defensively.

"What did he look like?" She added.

"He was just here, hat, long hair, hoodie jacket, gold tooth." Bradley grinned.

"You mean the guy you signaled wasn't Ford?" Weeks said angrily.

"Yah, that was him. I didn't know it the first time I helped him, but the second time he said 'give me the flash drive' and he handed me the money and told me to signal that he wasn't the guy. That's why I could only do it after he left. I was going to do it as soon as he went out the door, but then he walked in front of the store and would have seen me so I had to wait until he passed by to signal you. Sorry. Did I do something wrong?"

Weeks took a deep breath and stood hands on her hips. "No, Nathan you didn't do anything wrong. You did good. We were just outsmarted by a killer, that's all." Weeks took out her radio, "Okay, listen up everyone. I want a three block radius locked down around this location ASAP. Ford is in this immediate area. He's wearing a gray hat, has long brown hair, gold front tooth, a black jacket with a white hoodie, and is wearing red running shoes. This guy should stand out like a sore thumb."

Ford heard the sirens wailing. He knew that meant reinforcements were on the way and a probable lock down around the café, he guessed at least a couple of blocks. Ford darted into a Japanese restaurant and went directly to the men's bathroom. There he quickly removed the hat, wig, black hoodie jacket, and the gold tooth. Ford then calmly walked out of the restaurant as a bald guy with a white tee shirt, black pants and red running shoes.

Within minutes he was in the parkade where his car was parked. He quickly exited the parkade and made his way towards West Georgia and out of the downtown core. Ford crossed over the Georgia Viaduct and turned onto Main then onto Terminal, heading for Highway 1. As Ford neared Commercial, he pulled into a back alley and found a place to park. He reached into the back seat and pulled out his laptop and plugged in the flash drive. Ford guessed that it was equipped with a tracking device of some kind as part of the trap. Within moments he was in. Ford tried the usual way to open up the file but nothing appeared. He tried again. Again nothing. He panicked, 'Goddamn kid screwed me over, there's nothing on this fucking thing." He said aloud. Ford quickly pulled the drive out of the computer and threw in out the window. He got out and put it under his shoe and ground it around until it was crushed. Ford got into his car, turned around, and got back onto First Ave., heading north.

Just as he pulled onto First Avenue, a police car entered the alley without lights or sirens. Ford sped up and began weaving through traffic to put some distance between him and the tracking device. As he tore away, the Metro Police helicopter arrived over the area.

Ford pulled onto the freeway and wasted no time getting out of Vancouver and into New Westminster, where he parked the car. He phoned Marty to let him know he'd be a little late for the paint job, and that he'd make it worth his while.

CHAPTER 50

WEEKS AND MILLS returned to the station, miserable in the knowledge that Ford had been within their net, and yet somehow he had outsmarted them and gotten clean away. She knew that Lamp would be pissed as a wet hen that Ford had gotten away and that they had intentionally put a child's life in danger, exposing him to a suspected killer. They both walked into the bullpen, which instantly fell silent, all eyes were on them. She could tell this wasn't going to go well.

"Get in here you two," Lamp bellowed from his desk. "Not now, but right goddamn now." He was standing with his hands on his desk.

Weeks and Mills sheepishly walked into the lion's den and sat down.

"Please tell me what the fuck just happened out there?" He didn't wait for a response. "How the hell can a dumb kid without education outsmart a pair of Metro's finest? Please tell me how this happened with all your training, experience and resources. Outsmarted by a twenty something little piss ant." Lamp's fury waned and he sat down.

Weeks had seen Lamp do this in the past; the tirade was short, but venomous. She looked at Mills then at the red-faced Lamp. "Well, Sarg, it's like this." She paused for a moment to organize her response. "We didn't know that Ford suspected anything from his texts with the kid. Something must have spooked him. The fact that he even showed up tells us plenty. He is cocky, arrogant and conceited; a real risk taker, but a strategic thinker, all rolled into a twenty something piss ant. Who knew that he would be there before we even had the bait there, and the fact that he wore a disguise that even his mother wouldn't recognize didn't hurt either. Fuck, Sarg, we're good, but I doubt if anyone would have seen that coming?" Weeks took a deep breath to calm down.

"We also placed a tracker in the flash drive, but he figured that out and we found it in a back alley just off Commercial Drive. Metro had a helicopter in the area just after the tracker stopped, so we've got the footage being scrutinized by Mander and his team downstairs to see if we can find any images of the vehicle he's driving. Did we screw up? I don't think so. Did we handle this right? Based on past experience and cases, I'd say yes. Did we learn something? You bet your ass; we won't underestimate a perp again." She turned to Mills. "Did I leave anything out?"

Brent Mills looked at her, then at Lamp. "No I think you covered everything quite well."

Lamp leaned forward arms crossed on his desk. "Okay, I'll buy some of this as being played by a perp. What about the kid? How is he doing?"

Weeks stood and walked around the room. "That's a matter of opinion. The kid is a bit strange, raised in foster care all his life; he has no support system to help him through tough times like this. It's almost wrong to send him to juvy where he'll really learn how to be a delinquent. Right now, he's just adventurous, but six months or more in juvy and he'll be on his way to becoming a real criminal. If I were sitting in your chair, I'd cut him loose and tell him to stay out of trouble."

"I agree. If the press got hold of the fact that we put a child's life in danger, we'd be strung up by the nuts on every news channel. Cutting him loose is the right thing. Get a draw from petty cash for cab fare and send him on his way."

"Cab fare from petty cash? No way, the little bugger got paid a grand by the perp. Let him keep it for all his effort," Mills piped up.

"Okay, get out of here and go see what Mander and his people have found," Lamp said, waving his hand at the two of them.

Weeks and Mills walked through the bullpen, several of the officers gave them the thumbs up sign, while others nodded approval. Outside the bullpen Weeks pressed the elevator button and stood back to wait.

"Does Lamp always get that rattled when things don't go right?" Mills asked.

"That? Nah. That was nothing. You haven't seen Sarg get mad yet. And for your sake, let's hope you don't. It ain't pretty, trust me." The elevator car arrived and they entered. Mills didn't say a word.

In the basement Weeks led the way to Mander's world. She opened the door, walked in, and rang the bell. "Mander, are you here?" she called out.

"Thank you for using the bell! Back here Detective. Come on back." He replied.

Mills bulled his way through the swinging door as if there was a prize for being first. Weeks just shook her head and walked in casually.

"What do you have for us?" Mills demanded.

Mander looked at Mills with disgust. "What we have Detective, is an aerial shot of a dark coloured car leaving the area at a high rate of speed, just after the beacon went silent." Mander used the mouse to open up the correct file and typed in the right destination. "Okay, it's up on the big screen."

He sat back and watched the image from the helicopter's camera pan the area. "Here's where we first see the dark coloured two door car on First Avenue. It pulled out of the alley moments before our cruiser pulled into the alleyway. And now watch, the dark car begins to weave through traffic at a high rate of speed."

"That's all we got?" Weeks asked plaintively.

Mander grinned. "You know me better than that, Detective Weeks. I took the liberty to check the feeds from two news helicopters and the traffic helicopter, and look what I have found." He clicked play again. The big screen lit up, "Here, we have our dark car still travelling at high speed on the freeway, just past the Kenningston off ramp. So we know he's heading east towards either Burnaby or New West."

"Now from the News One helicopter, we see the same dark coloured car driving like a flipping idiot. Now, this next bit is from the Global helicopter. Here again is the dark coloured car taking the Brunette Avenue exit off the freeway. I believe it would be safe to assume that your perp went to New West, unless he took the Pattullo Bridge and went into Surrey."

Weeks stared at the images on the big screen, "Yeah, but if I lived in Surrey, I would go across the Port Mann. I wouldn't go through New West. You may be right, Mander, perhaps our perp lives in New West." She paused, "Okay, Mills, let's head down to the situation room. Mander, can you call Lamp and let him know where we're going?"

Mander nodded. "Good hunting."

Weeks and Mills showed their badges at the door to the situation room, where Metro Police planned all of their operations on a giant electronic whiteboard.

Weeks had been there before, and even now after all her years with the police, she was still in awe of this room and the people who worked there. She saw Assistant Deputy Chief Sandra Fenton, who was the tactical officer in the room. Every move made by Metro had to go through her. Weeks and Fenton took their basic training together, but had chosen different paths up the ladder.

Sandra Fenton spotted Weeks and Mills and waved them to come over. Weeks and Fenton exchanged a brief hug and Fenton shook Mills' sweaty palm. "Sounds like you guys have your hands full out there. Too bad about your sting op, damn near had him I hear. How can we help here?" Fenton said.

"Sandra Fenton, meet my new partner Detective Brent Mills. Brent Mills meet Sandra Fenton, tactical officer here in 'the hive.' That is what they call it, isn't it?"

Fenton laughed. "I've heard it called a lot worse." She ushered them to her desk. "So, how can the hive help?"

Weeks turned to look at the electronic whiteboard. "Can you bring up New West? How many exits are there to cover?"

Fenton quickly keyed in the information, and instantly the whiteboard changed, showing only New Westminster. "Looks to be roughly fourteen exits, not counting the alleyways." She turned to Weeks. "What's going on in New West?"

"We have credible intel that our cop killer lives there and is there right now. How long to get all the exits blocked off?"

Fenton took a deep breath. "We can have it locked down in ten minutes. But you'll need someone up the food chain to sign off on that. This will really screw up traffic."

Mills looked at Weeks, "Has to be done, the cop killer is top priority."

Weeks grabbed her cell phone and keyed in Lamp's desk number.

"Sarg, Weeks here. We're in the hive, and Assistant Deputy Chief Fenton needs some juice to lock down New West. Can you talk to her?" Weeks listened for a moment then handed the phone to Fenton. "Your juice."

Fenton listened intently. "Okay Sergeant Lamp, you got it. Lock down New Westminster in ten."

Fenton smiled. "That was easy." Fenton ran her fingers deftly over the computer keys, entering information on the fly. She then picked up her radio. "Attention all cars in sector four this is command, proceed Code Red. Shut down all primary and secondary access points. Be on the lookout for a dark coloured two-door Mustang. Driver is a twenty-year-old male, dark skinned, long hair, heavy set, about six feet tall; detain and question if located. Backup is coming from sector three. Over." She keyed in further data. "Attention sector three, units twenty-five through thirty-five proceed Code Red to assist sector four lockdown. Over."

Weeks was impressed, the revised whiteboard instantly started showing where cars were and where they were heading. Within a few minutes, twenty Metro police cars where blocking every access point in and out of New West, checking every car. Metro Helicopters began circling the city, their eyes peeled for the target vehicle.

CHAPTER

51

FORD LEFT HIS apartment fifteen minutes after arriving dressed like someone from Jamaica. He got into his car and drove onto McBride Avenue and went over the Pattullo Bridge into Surrey, then up 104th to the freeway, bypassing the damn toll bridge with its cameras. Fifteen minutes later, he was in Langley at Cando Paint and Body, the shop Rolf had recommended.

He pulled the Mustang through the gate of the chain link fence and parked near the office. Ford made sure all his compartments where locked and nothing incriminating was visible then he walked into the office. A strikingly beautiful woman greeted him. "Can I help you sir?"

Ford shifted his gaze. "Why, yes. I'm here to see Marty."

She quickly looked at her computer screen. "He doesn't have any appointments booked today. Are you sure it's today?" She asked politely.

"Yes, it's today. I spoke to him not long ago and told him I'd be a little late getting my car here today. I don't have an appointment; he's going to paint my car tonight. I told him I'd be here after five. It's now five twenty and I'm here, but I don't see Marty. Can you call him up front please?"

The receptionist paged Marty to the front for customer

service then went back to her duties. Moments later, Marty entered the office from the shop.

The receptionist said, "This gentleman is here to see you, said he doesn't have an appointment."

"Ah, yes, Mr. Ford. Glad you could make it. So, you want your car painted. I believe you said white? Was there a specific shade of white you wanted? There are about fifty different varieties available," Marty said professionally.

"Nah, just pick one and make my car white." Ford reached inside his jacket and produced an envelope with two-thousand dollars in it. "This should get you going on it." Ford smiled.

Marty accepted the envelope and handed it to the receptionist. "Wendy, put this in the safe and can you see which loaner we can give to Mr. Ford here." He turned back to Ford. "Did you have any trouble getting out of New West? I hear on the scanner that they've locked the city down and they're checking every car. Something big must be going on."

Ford's heart rate jumped a little. "No, I didn't have any problems. Must have happened after I left?"

Wendy produced a set of keys for a Hyundai Sonata and handed them to Marty.

"Come with me, Mr. Ford. I'll show you our loaner." Outside, Marty led Ford to the red, four-door sedan loaner. It wasn't new, but it was clean. Ford transferred some of the items from his car trunk into the loaner and handed his keys to Marty. "So she'll be ready around noon tomorrow?"

Marty nodded then returned to the office. Ford started the loaner and drove away. He elected to return to Surrey via the Fraser Highway, less traffic than the freeway. Ford wondered if it was wise to go back into New Westminster, or if he should stay in Surrey for the night and go back later. He reasoned the cops couldn't lock the city down for another day without people getting really pissed off and screaming at the media.

Ford soon arrived in Surrey's Guilford area and checked into the Rampart Hotel, the only hi-rise hotel in Surrey. He'd make the call to Channel 21 from there then go for dinner. Once inside his room, he checked his phone and there was a text from the 264th St. hitter. Bender was dead. Ford fist-pumped the air. All targets were now eliminated, and technically the first round finished.

Ford's phone beeped, it was a text from Nineteen, *'other gangs don't want to continue, end the assault.'* Ford was pissed with their decision. He looked out his seventh floor balcony window, *'They've chosen to only eliminate the worst of the bunch leaving the other cops on IAs list alone.* He thought.

"Cowards" He said aloud. Now he only had Seven to contend with, but that was personal. He'd deal with Weeks later. Von Pleth would be spared.

While Ford watched the news, he found the number for Channel 21 on his phone's web browser and jotted it down. He then retrieved his second burner cell from his knapsack and dialed the number.

"May I speak to your news director or Debra Patton? Whichever one is handiest."

The news channel receptionist said, "Sorry sir, they're all busy. Can I take a message?"

"No, you cannot. Listen, you talk to either one and ask them if they're interested in speaking with the cop killer.

You go do that. I'll wait," Ford said angrily. There was dead silence on the line; then the music began to play.

Moments turned to minutes before finally an exhausted voice came on the line.

"Hello, this is Debra Patton. To whom am I speaking?"

"This is Ford. I'm the cop killer. Do you want to talk?"

Patton paused to compose herself. "Yes, I'd love to talk to you. What do you want to talk about?"

"I want to let the people of Metro Vancouver and the honest cops of the Metro PD know why there's a war going on. Can you make that happen live on the news right now?" Ford said calmly.

Patton again paused. "I think I can make that happen. I'll have to okay it with my news director. Can you hold on for a moment?"

"Yes, but only for a minute. Any longer and I hang up and call another station, got it?"

"Got it," Patton replied.

Ford again had to listen to the electronic music on the phone. He hated it. He preferred classic rock and roll.

"Okay, Mr. Ford, my director has okayed the live feed, stay on the line while I transfer to the news room. I'm at my desk right now. Hold on."

CHAPTER

52

THE BULLPEN OF Metro Police was busy as usual. Weeks and Mills were taking a coffee break at their desks when Lamp came darting out of his office. "Listen up everybody, our cop killer is going to speak on Channel Twenty-One, so whoever has the remote for the TV, turn it to Twenty-One right now."

"This is a Channel Twenty-One exclusive. We interrupt the evening news for this special bulletin." The screen showed Debra Patton sitting at the anchor desk.

"This is Debra Patton reporting. A few minutes ago this station received a call from a man purporting to be the cop killer, the most wanted man in Vancouver history. We have verified some details that only the killer would know, and are confident we're talking to the alleged killer. The alleged killer's name is Ford, no first name given, nor age, or any other personal details. Ford, the alleged killer, wants to speak directly to the Metro Police Department and the general public. Ford wants to provide his side of the story. Okay, Mr. Ford, go ahead. You are on the air."

Several seconds later, Ford spoke. "Thank you. To the people of BC and Metro Vancouver, you have nothing to fear; your lives are not in danger, they never were, nor will they be. Our fight is with the Metro Police." Ford paused to light a smoke. "To the honest, everyday police officers of Metro, you too have nothing to fear. We are not after you, never were, nor will we be. Our fight is with the infestation of corrupt cops that your own Internal Affairs department chooses to do nothing about. Well, we did something. A few of us have had enough of being blackmailed, bribed, harassed, and even killed by a select group of rotten cops. We've accessed the IA personnel files and selected a number of the worst, most corrupt cops and we've executed them.

"In total, there are almost two hundred cops with IA files that the public should know about. Some will call what we have done cold-blooded murder. We call it justice, our way. We did not take this position lightly. Going to war with the police is not a wise move at any time. We do not have a problem with the police per se; honest cops doing honest police work should not fear. Those not on IA's list, have nothing to worry about. We respect the honest police and the work they do. But desperate people do desperate things. We're not looking for forgiveness or absolution in what we've done. From myself and my associates, the war, as it's been called by the media, is over. The associates used for this operation are gone. Only I remain in town, for now. Thank you."

"Wow," Debra Patton said touching her earpiece. "That, ladies and gentlemen, was the alleged cop killer Ford, in an exclusive statement to Channel Twenty-One. We have reporters dispatched to police headquarters in hopes of speaking with Police Chief Von Pleth and other members of Metro Police about this earth-shattering revelation about members of the Police Department. We, at Channel

Twenty-One, wish to publicly convey our deepest sympathies to the families of the slain police members, and our thoughts and prayers go out to all members of law enforcement who have lost colleagues and associates in these brutal attacks. This is Debra Patton. We now return you to the local news."

The room was stunned into silence. Every detective in the room looked at everyone else and said nothing then eyes shifted to Lamp.

Lamp too was silent. He walked around the room, touching the shoulders of those he passed, then he stopped. "Everyone, back to work. Let's find this son-of-a-bitch before he blows town." He looked directly at Weeks and Mills. "If this bastard lives in New Westminster, then perhaps you should be out there, and not in here. Get. You can work out of New West Metro until we catch this bastard," Lamp said, waving his hand.

CHAPTER

53

FORD SLEPT WELL in the luxury suite at the Rampart. His wake up call at nine-thirty a.m. came way too early, or he'd gone to bed way too late. He recalled being asked to leave the bar at closing time…alone. Ford wasn't happy that all the hotel rooms were non-smoking, so in order to feed his habit, he had to smoke in the bathroom with the fan on. He had a quick shower and shaved both his face and head, then donned his long-haired hippy disguise and left the room just before the eleven a.m. check-out time.

Ford ate a light breakfast in the restaurant then hopped into the loaner car and headed for Langley to pick up his freshly painted Mustang. Twenty minutes later, he pulled into the fenced compound and parked the loaner. Ford walked briskly into the office and placed the keys on the counter. "Hi, I'm here to pick up my car," he said to the woman working the desk.

"What's the last name sir?" She inquired.

"Ford, but I don't think there's a work order."

"If there's no work order, I have to call Marty. One moment."

Marty came out of his office. "Ah, Mr. Ford, your car is all ready. My guys worked late into the night to have it ready for you. Come, let's take a look at her." Marty led the way into the showroom area, where a gleaming white Mustang sat. Ford smiled as he walked around it. "Beautiful. Nice job, Marty, nice job."

Marty ushered Ford back into the office while one of his workers backed Ford's car outside. In the office, Ford pulled an envelope out of his inner jacket pocket and passed it over to Marty. "I think this will cover it," he said. Ford watched the young kid bring the keys in and give them to Marty, who handed them to Ford. Marty looked at Ford curiously then asked, "That wasn't you on TV last night, was it?"

Ford laughed. "Are you kidding me? Nah, that guy's a stone-cold killer. Me, I'm a lover, not a fighter. We just share the same last name." Ford shook hands with Marty then left the office. It would feel good to be driving his car again. The first thing he did was check his compartments to see if they had been tampered with. He was pleased they hadn't been. He transferred his gear back into his car, backed out of the compound and onto Park Avenue then lit up the tires.

It was twelve-thirty p.m. when Ford pulled into the self-storage yard in Queensborough, where he quickly emptied out his rental unit. He backed the car inside while he loaded all of his backup weapons into their storage places. Ford left his sniper rifle disassembled in its case in the trunk. When he was done, he pulled the car out, closed the overhead door and drove away.

Ford drove into New Westminster. All the road blocks were down, but he noticed a heavy police presence along Columbia Avenue. He pulled into an Esso station to fill up and respond to Seven's text about a meeting in Burnaby. Ford said he'd meet him at Everett Crowley Park around four p.m., and told him to look for a white Mustang. It was a sunny day, so Ford went for a drive to clear his head, arrange his thoughts, and to speculate as to what was on Seven's mind. Ford figured that choosing the meeting place himself would eliminate a trap that Seven was capable of setting if he wanted him dead.

Ford found a Starbucks on Columbia, ordered his usual drink, and sat in the sunshine sipping his coffee and enjoying a smoke to the displeasure of others. He grinned.

The afternoon slipped by uneventfully and Ford soon zipped along Marine Drive toward Everett Crowley Park. Ford drove along Kerr Street to the park entrance. He figured the logical place to look for Seven would be in the parking lot. Ford pulled into the parking lot and parked. He was unsure what Seven was driving these days, since they'd parked their rolling billboards. Ford checked his weapon; it was ready. Then he got out of the vehicle. He scanned the lone car in the lot. It was only a young couple necking, no Seven.

Ford walked the length of the small parking lot and peered down the trails leading into the park, nothing. He spotted a picnic table off to one side and decided to wait there. Ford parked his two-hundred pound frame on the table and lit a cigarette. He looked at his watch; it was four-ten p.m. Ford pulled out his phone and sent a text to Seven. *I'm here, you're not?* He waited for a response. Minutes passed. He didn't like the idea of being a sitting duck, so he went back to his car.

Ford sensed something wasn't right, so he backed his car out of the spot and turned it around so he was facing the entrance. Five minutes later, Ford noticed three vehicles turning into the park. Was this Seven's idea of a meeting, or were they just people visiting the park? Alverez had taught him that it's better to be safe than sorry, so Ford readied his main weapon and unlocked his back-up and readied it. The three cars parked strategically in the parking lot, two were next to the entrance while the third parked across from Ford. It was Seven sitting across from him in a blue Acura TLX that appeared to be brand new.

Ford slowly got out of his car ensuring that his weapon was in place, closed the door, and stepped towards the front of his car. He kept an eye on the two cars at the entrance; the occupants remained inside.

Felix Seven opened his door and hopped out as if he was going to see grandma. "Ford, my man, caught your act on TV last night. You made us sound so righteous, so upstanding," Seven laughed as he swaggered towards Ford.

Ford walked slowly towards the middle of the parking lot. "So, you were impressed, were you?" He knew Seven wasn't. "What's with the muscle?"

Seven held out his hands. "You're a scary dude. You're the cold-blooded killer. I'm just being cautious, that's all."

Ford stopped a couple of yards from Seven, and from the corner of his eye he saw two guys get out of the first car. "If you were smart, Seven, you'd tell your muscle to get back into the car before someone makes a mistake." Ford waited, then barked, "NOW!"

Seven jumped back a bit then waved the first two back into their vehicle. "There, how's that?"

Ford shot a quick glance at the second vehicle; it was empty. "And the guys from the other car as well, Seven, unless you plan on taking me out yourself, here and now."

Seven held up his hand. "You see, Ford this is really simple. Give me the right answer and we all go away happy. Give me the wrong answer…well, let's just say you go away, period."

Ford slowly backed up until he was at the front of his car. "Geez, Seven, if I knew there was going to be a test I would have studied. So, what's on your feeble mind?"

Felix Seven took a few steps towards Ford. "Quite simple, *Dustin*. Oscar and I want to know if you want to join our little gang. 'Cause you see, you're a dangerous dude. You know things about us that could hurt us if the cops catch you and make you talk. So you see, it's quite simple join us or not. See, no studying needed."

Ford lit another smoke and inhaled deeply before exhaling. "So let me get this straight, join your group of losers, or what? Die? Is that it, Seven? Is that what the muscle is for, because you don't have the balls or the skill to take me out yourself, you fucking coward?"

Felix Seven was becoming incensed. Ford knew that he was pissing him off. Ford didn't let him answer. "You know you're a pussy. You'd put your bitch in the line of fire just to save your scrawny ass. Like you did coming out of the club on Granville; you made her walk on the curbside so if someone started shooting at you, they'd hit her first. Real manly of you Seven. Real manly. Just like now. I'm not exactly sure where your two goons are, but I can guaran-fucking-tee you that before I die by their hands, you will die by mine. Wanna take that chance, or do you want to drive away right now? What's it going to be, you badass gangsta man?"

Seven began to laugh. "Ford, you are such a prick, you

know that? A real fucking prick. My guys could pop you off any second. All I have to do is give the signal. You want me to do that?"

Ford flicked his cigarette away and lit another. "Ain't gonna happen little man. You know why? Because big brother Oscar would rather have me as an asset than take the chance that you fuck this up and I live, then I hunt all you fucks down and kill you all, one by one. Bam, bullet to the head." Ford walked over to Seven and stood about two feet from him. "So, Fuckhead, either shoot me dead or get the fuck out of my face."

He stared into Seven's eyes. Ford could tell he was scared.

Felix Seven backed down. "Let's get the fuck out of here," he shouted to his muscle. "This guy's poison. Anyone near him is now a dead man." He shuffled backwards to his car. Ford did likewise. As he neared his car door, one hand opened it, while the other found his weapon in the back of his pants. He clicked the safety off and as he got into his car pulled the weapon out and placed it on his lap, all the while his eyes darted between Seven's car and the two cars at the gate. Ford watched as Seven's car pulled away and left the park, then the first of the support cars left. As the last car pulled away, the second car fired three shots at Ford, hitting the passenger side window and front windshield. The Lexan security film on the inside prevented the rounds from entering the car.

Ford was pissed off. He started up his car and dropped it into first gear and tromped on the gas, spewing rocks from the rear tires. He fishtailed out of the park and slid sideways onto Kerr Street, nearly getting hit by oncoming traffic. Ford spotted them ahead and ran through the gears as the car sped up, sixty, seventy, eighty miles an hour, weaving in and out of traffic to keep them in sight.

Ford gained on the third car that was bringing up the rear, shots were being fired at him from that vehicle's passenger. Ford moved up beside the car in the left lane and rolled down his passenger window, then raised his Glock and fired two shots into the driver's window, hitting the driver. The car careened off to the right and smashed into a lamp standard. Ford never looked back, but locked his gaze on the second car.

Ford knew that this car was Seven's protection, so Seven should be just ahead of it. Ford slowed somewhat as traffic came to a stop at the corner of Kerr and Marine Way. He wasn't sure if they would stop or run the light. Seconds later, he had his answer.

Both cars screamed through the red lamp, causing a chain reaction of accidents. Ford slowed down and wove his way through the mayhem, then stood on the gas to catch up to his prey. The trio of cars headed east on Marine Way, all doing in excess of ninety miles an hour, slashing in and out of traffic in a deadly game of cat and mouse.

Ford could see the second car a few yards ahead of him. He checked his rearview. There were no cops yet, but he knew the good citizens of Vancouver would have already called 9-1-1. Ford reached down to get his backup weapon and took off the safety. He looked at his speedometer; he was doing a hundred and ten. Vehicles sped past him, and he hoped that he wouldn't crash before he evened the score with Seven.

All three cars blew through the intersection at Boundary and Marine Way. Out of the corner of his eye Ford caught sight of a cop car, which meant they would soon be joining the parade.

Weeks was driving toward Vancouver on Marine Way when her radio alerted her about two vehicles travelling east toward New Westminster at high speed. Vehicle one, a newer blue Japanese import was being chased by vehicle two, an older white Mustang. Reports of shots fired between the two vehicles had not been confirmed. The report of a white Mustang intrigued Weeks. Could this be the cop killer? She was alone because Mills had unexpectedly come down with a bad case of 'blue flu' and called in sick.

Weeks saw the blue Acura and the white Mustang scream past her in the oncoming lane. She saw the driver of the white Mustang fire at the blue Japanese import. She instantly turned on lights and sirens to pull a police turn in the busy highway. Weeks executed the turn perfectly, and as soon as the car stopped swerving, she pegged the gas pedal and took off after the two vehicles that were causing the mayhem.

"This is Detective Weeks in pursuit of a blue Japanese import and a white Mustang, heading east on Marine Way. Shots are being fired. I repeat shots are being fired between the two vehicles."

Ford was just behind the Seven's protection car, he didn't have a clear shot at the driver or passenger, but he did have a shot at the rear tires and gas tank. He readied his weapon and fired four shots. Two shots hit the tire, sending the car into a panicky fishtail. The other two shots hit the gas tank area, causing fuel to begin leaking onto the roadway. The rear tire shredded and came off the rim. Sparks flew from the rim causing the gas to burst into flames. The car swerved to the shoulder and ended up in the ditch.

Ford's focus shifted to Seven in the blue Acura, several car lengths ahead. Ford checked his rearview mirror. He could see lights from the pursuing cop car; they didn't stop at the burning wreck.

Weeks radioed in about the second car in the ditch, reporting that it was on fire. She continued to speed toward New Westminster. She could easily see the white Mustang ahead of her a few hundred yards. Weeks pushed her car harder and began to gain on the Mustang.

Ford looked in his mirror. He could see the police car gaining on him. He took a quick glance at Seven's Acura; it was ahead of him by a few yards. He rolled down his window and with his left hand fired two shots at the police car, which immediately swerved into the other lane out of the line of fire.

Weeks radioed in that she was taking fire and was still chasing the suspect vehicle. She was able to catch up to the Mustang in the right lane and was sitting just off its right side rear. Weeks strained her eyes to get a look at the driver. He was Caucasian with long hair. Then she saw a familiar mark on his right jaw, a quarter-sized strawberry. She instantly knew this was the guy. This was Dustin Ford. She saw that she was approaching a slower vehicle in the right lane and swerved violently back into the left lane behind the Mustang. "Dispatch this is Detective Weeks. Inform Sergeant Lamp that the suspect driving the white Mustang is our perp, Dustin Ford, and that I'm in pursuit."

Ford saw the police cruiser right behind him so he again fired off two shots with his left hand. He could see that the two shots hit the front windshield.

Weeks hammered on the brakes, immediately slowing

her car down. The front windshield near the centre had two bullet holes in it. Glass had sprayed everywhere including on her. She slowed to a more manageable speed and kept the Mustang in sight.

Ford saw that the police car had slowed and was a short distance behind him, he returned his focus to Seven's Acura. Before long he was right on the Acura's rear bumper in the right lane; he fired two rounds into the back window, blowing out the glass. Seven fired several shots in Ford's direction then swerved into the left lane to get out of the line of fire. Ford copied the move to stay on Seven's rear bumper. "Got you now, you fucking asshole," Ford yelled.

Weeks continued the pursuit of the two vehicles that were shooting at each other. She radioed for back up to seal off New Westminster and to allow the two vehicles to continue. She told dispatch to immediately set up a rolling blockade, forcing the two vehicles into a controllable area.

The two combatants stayed on Marine Way, entering New Westminster via Stewardson Way; Ford had fired a total of six rounds into the Acura. He figured that he had wounded Seven, because his driving had become more erratic and uncontrolled. Seven stayed two or three car lengths ahead of Ford. Stewardson Way was blocked off by police, so Seven had to turn onto Royal Avenue. Ford followed, executing a four wheel drift onto Royal Avenue and gained on Seven. Cops were bringing up the rear, but had fired no shots yet.

Seven sped up Royal Avenue through the 8th Street intersection, which was now blocked off. Ford gained on him and rammed the Acura's rear bumper, causing Seven to nearly lose control. Both cars roared towards 6th Street, but Ford could see that it was blocked, which meant Seven would have to turn…but which way, Ford didn't know.

As they approached the intersection, a police car blocked off the west side of the road, forcing Seven to turn south down 6th Street. Seven's Acura slid around the corner, almost going sideways down the hill. Ford's Mustang handled the corner better, taking it without sliding. Ford dropped a gear and brought his car right up beside Seven's. He fired three shots into the car, and the Acura lurched to the left onto Carnarvon Street. Ford braked suddenly, dropped a gear, and followed suit. Both cars flew up Carnarvon Street, with Ford's front bumper touching Seven's rear bumper and Ford firing into the Acura.

Weeks was a half a block behind the two speeding vehicles, she knew where the blockade was being set up. Blackwood Street was the designated rolling roadblock terminus. She just hoped that it was in place before they got there.

Ford was sure that Seven was hit and hit badly, but he wasn't taking any chances. As they approached the corner of Carnarvon and Blackwood, Ford saw his chance and he rammed his Mustang into the passenger side of Seven's Acura, causing the car to go sideways around the corner and slide down Blackwood Street. Seven's car had a severely damaged the right front suspension, which caused it to grind on the cobblestone sending sparks flying every which way. The Acura's suspension dug into the road surface, causing the car to flip over and slide on its roof down the hill. Ford stayed right up with the Acura.

Weeks gasped when she saw the blue car flip over. She saw the white Mustang do a hard braking stop. She watched as Ford flung open his door and darted toward the blue car. She could see he was armed. Weeks braked hard at the corner, opened her car door and drew her weapon. She could see that the bottom of Blackwood Street was blocked off by three police cruisers.

Ford reached the Acura, gun at the ready. He glanced back up the hill and saw the police car was blocking that escape route. He grinned when he saw Detective Weeks' head poke out from behind the door, he didn't see her gun. Ford quickly kneeled down to see if Seven was alive. He was dead; the right side of his face was missing.

Ford crouched briefly and assessed his situation. He knew he was hemmed in both top and bottom. He laughed, "Looks like the fight is on." He quickly made his way back to his car; he opened the passenger side door and dove into the front seat as the bullets bounced off the vehicle. He squirmed his way into the driver's seat and slouched down.

Weeks continued to fire on the white Mustang, but could see that the bullets were just bouncing off the body and doing little damage to the glass. She grabbed her radio, "This is Weeks, the suspect's car has been armoured; bullets are having little or no effect. Suggest bringing out heavier arms to engage suspect."

Bullets were pelting the car from what seemed like all directions. Ford's Mustang had stopped sideways on the road, and he was looking down the hill at the three cop cars blocking the street. He felt his tires being shot out, and the film on the glass was beginning to shatter, allowing bullet fragments into the car.

Ford looked around. He didn't see snipers on the roofs, which only meant they hadn't been deployed yet. He glanced down the hill and noticed that Metro had deployed "the beast," a battle hardened vehicle that resembled an armoured car on steroids. It blocked his way too. *Just great, Ford. How the fuck are you going to get out of this mess?* He checked his ammo, reached into the under-seat compartment and brought out extra clips for the Glock.

Ford rammed a new clip into the weapon and returned fire up the hill. He wasn't aiming at anyone, but it made Weeks dive for cover, allowing him time to consider his next move. He could hear bullets hitting the car, but the light armouring inside the doors and other panels blocked them. Ford knew that before long they would bring out the big stuff, which would overpower the Kevlar fabric and steel plating. "You should have specified level-one armour plating, you fucking idiot," he said out loud to himself.

Ford put the car in reverse and began to straighten it out so he could go down the hill. He felt a burning sensation in his left shoulder; he had been hit by a heavy round. He slumped down in the seat to get out of the line of fire, his car now facing down the hill. Ford took a quick glance and saw there was a slim opening between one of the cop cars and the building, but it meant jumping a curb and taking out a hydrant…he liked those odds.

He paused for a moment, fumbled for a smoke, lit it, and inhaled deeply, knowing this could be his last smoke. He dropped into first gear and gunned the engine. The car bolted forward. He peeked over the dash as best he could to line up the car to the opening then closed his eyes.

Seconds later he felt a thud from contacting the curb, then he was airborne, and in a blink of an eye he felt the car bounce off the building and slam onto the roadway on the other side of the barricade. Ford shot a glance out the window, and what he saw wasn't good. He had ended up right in the staging area that was crawling with cops. He panicked. His only way out was through the buildings that lined Columbia Street. Ford aimed the vehicle at a Greek restaurant and gunned it. Some shots got through the body armour, but his adrenaline numbed the pain. In seconds, the car bounced off the other curb and launched into the doorway of the restaurant, smashing it to bits.

Weeks moved hastily down the street toward the Blue Acura and looked inside to see if anyone was alive. She quickly determined that the occupant was dead and returned her gaze to the commotion at the bottom of the hill. She saw Ford's bullet riddled vehicle crash through the front of a restaurant. Weeks was shocked. She turned and bolted toward her car at the top of the hill. She needed to get down onto Front Street because she knew that the car was likely to drive right through the restaurant and off the balcony down a steep embankment ending up on Front Street.

Glass and wood flew everywhere as Ford's car ploughed through tables and chairs. He caught glimpses of people diving out of the way. He'd eaten here once a while back, and remembered it was a nice place. Ford kept his foot on the gas as his mind began to wander; he barely remembered the car going through the patio door out onto the balcony and through the glass panel railing.

He was on the verge of passing out as the car plunged off the fifty foot balcony onto a steep hillside below. The car pounded into the ground with its front end, but stayed right side up. In a blur, Ford saw that he was at the foot of the hill atop the construction material that was left there when the parkade had been torn down. His car sailed over the construction debris, landing hard on Front Street, which had been closed for the demolition.

The battered car came to a stop at the edge of the road; smoke billowed from the engine. Ford, in a daze, could hear bullets hitting the car. They were being fired from what was left of the balcony above. He looked around the car; it was wrecked beyond belief, but it still protected him. Ford tried to move, but he was hurting, it took him several seconds to reach his knapsack in the back seat. He grabbed it and his backup weapon and crawled through the missing front windshield, ending up in front of his badly damaged car.

Weeks came down Begbie Street, Code Three, lights flashing and siren wailing. She blew through the lights on Quayside Drive and squealed around the corner into the parking lot. She sped up through the parking lot and put the car into a four wheel lock-up as she neared the boundary of the park. Once the car came to a stop, she flung open the door and bolted toward the park. She could see Ford far off on the other end of the narrow park; he was staggering towards the pier and the river. She pulled out her weapon and began firing; hoping to hit Ford on the run from close to fifty yards away.

Ford saw a helicopter circling overhead, so he fired a couple of shots at it; it moved away instantly. Media bastards, he thought. Ford then saw Weeks running across the park; he fired his weapon in her direction. He remembered little of his plan. In fact, he wasn't sure if he even had a plan. He knew he was alive, just barely he figured, and he knew this wasn't going to end well for him. He was beginning to weaken, and his vision was playing tricks on him. Ford mustered some strength to fire his weapon at the balcony, but the recoil from his weapon caused him to drop it. He gasped as a sharp pain erupted on his right shoulder; he guessed another round had hit him.

Ford struggled to his feet and hobbled across the park to the edge overlooking the Fraser River. He was unsure what he wanted to do. He figured he was going to die, but he had a choice, bullets or water, water or bullets…not much of a choice. Ford looked at his hands; they were covered in blood. He wished he had smoke. A voice inside his head was telling him to get into the river now. Ford looked down at the muddy water six feet below him.

As he was about to jump into the water, he felt two sharp pangs in his back, the vest couldn't stop the rounds and they tore through his upper back. Ford toppled face first into the water still grasping his knapsack. The cold muddy water was a shock to his system, causing him to gasp. The Fraser River, famous for its heavy undercurrents, sucked Ford in, and he disappeared into the murky water.

Weeks arrived at the edge of the pier mere seconds after Ford fell in. She desperately searched the edge to see if she could see him hanging onto one of the pier supports. Nothing. She scanned the water flooding downstream for Ford's body, but again, nothing. Weeks pulled out her radio and keyed the mic. "Dispatch, this is Detective Weeks, has the marine unit been dispatched to the New Westminster Quay yet? We've got a body in the water…somewhere," she said, disappointedly.

CPSIA information can be obtained
at www.ICGtesting.com
Printed in the USA
LVOW12s1148120117
520550LV00001B/3/P

9 781460 295434